# THE HALDANES

Daddy was on his feet. He caught Pauline as she stepped back, pulled her to him, shoulders against his chest, as if he was abducting her at pistol point. One arm about her waist, he extended his right hand and stabbed a forefinger accusingly, not at Mummy but at Grandpapa Haldane.

"You knew she was pregnant all along, didn't you, you conniving old bastard?" Daddy shouted. Pauline could feel his chest heave against her shoulder-blades. His face was so close to her cheek that his glasses scraped her skin. She was almost deafened by his infuriated roar. "You hadn't even the guts to tell me, man to man."

Neither anger nor contrition touched Donald Haldane's benign features. They were soft with age now, pink and passive under the halo of silver hair. He seemed less restrained than indifferent. Even his eyes showed no change in response to Harry's outburst. He remained as bland as cream in coffee.

## About the Author

Caroline Crosby is the pseudonym of Jessica Stirling. Born in Glasgow, she has enjoyed a highly successful career as a writer. Her novels include *The Spoiled Earth*, *The Deep Well at Noon*, *Treasures on Earth* and a recent sequence set in late-Victorian Glasgow: *The Good Provider*, *The Asking Price*, *The Wise Child* and *The Welcome Light*. Her most recent novels, set in eighteenth-century Scotland, are *Lantern for the Dark* and *Shadows on the Shore*.

# The Haldanes

Jessica Stirling

writing as Caroline Crosby

CORONET BOOKS
Hodder and Stoughton

Copyright © Caroline Crosby 1992

First published in Great Britain in 1992
by Hodder and Stoughton Ltd.

First published in paperback in 1993 by Hodder and Stoughton
A division of Hodder Headline PLC

A Coronet paperback

The right of Caroline Crosby to be identified as the Author of
the Work has been asserted by her in accordance with the
Copyright, Designs and Patents Act 1988.

10 9 8 7 6 5 4

All rights reserved. No part of this publication may be
reproduced, stored in a retrieval system, or transmitted,
in any form or by any means without the prior written
permission of the publisher, nor be otherwise circulated
in any form of binding or cover other than that in which
it is published and without a similar condition being
imposed on the subsequent purchaser.

All characters in this publication are fictitious
and any resemblance to real persons, living or dead,
is purely coincidental.

ISBN 0 340 58628 1

Printed and bound in Great Britain by
Mackays of Chatham PLC, Chatham, Kent

Hodder and Stoughton
A division of Hodder Headline PLC
338 Euston Road
London NW1 3BH

# Contents

# ❦ PART I ❦
## Family Matters

# One

*F*or a full generation it had been the fashion in the Haldane family to send the girls to school in Scotland. Grandpa Haldane would have it no other way. It was the done thing and old Donald Haldane was, and always had been, a great one for doing the right thing. Besides, he owned shares in the school company and, while giving his girls a sound education in manners and deportment, he reaped a little profit on the transaction and got to consort with gentlemen whose style and breeding he had always admired.

Pauline's Aunt Bea seemed to have enjoyed her years at St Austin's. But Barbara, Pauline's mother, had not been at all enchanted. She looked back upon her schooldays with uncharacteristic bitterness. She had no good word to say for Miss Aitken or Miss Gaylord or any of the other little tin gods who had been empowered to smother her youthful exuberance and stamp out her wilful tendencies by every conceivable sort of punishment, short of beating and expulsion.

Amid the piles of junk in the glory hole in the Veritys' London flat were precious few remains of Mother's girlhood and none at all, save an empty wicker trunk, to commemorate her eight years at St Austin's. In vain Pauline rummaged in boxes, suitcases and hampers for a letter or postcard, a faded photograph, an inky primer or battered hockey stick, something to indicate that schooldays had left Mummy with even one fond memory.

The little that Pauline had learned of St Austin's derived from a few half-remembered stories told to her at bedtime long ago – before Mummy went off with Captain Tiverton, even before the war – and from the photographs in a blue morocco album that Aunt Bea had produced during Pauline's one and only visit to Flask Hall, in Derbyshire, in the summer of 1915.

Pauline had been eight at the time and quite old enough to realise that something unpleasant was happening at home. She'd had a sense of disharmony in the household long before the day when her mother, without a word of farewell, had finally gone away for good. The following morning Pauline had been packed off to stay with Aunt Bea and Uncle Lewis Jackson in their big house near Matlock. Mrs Dobbs, the Veritys' housekeeper, had taken her up by train but had returned at once to London to look after Daddy.

Pauline retained only fragmented impressions of her two-week exile. High cliffs, steep brambly trails, caves she was supposed to wonder at, iron bridges over a river in a gorge. And Uncle Lewis's dogs, black Labradors that had the run not just of the gardens and stable yards but also of the hall's echoing corridors and gloomy public rooms. She only vaguely recalled her first encounter with cousin Stella who, advantaged by home territory and two months seniority, lorded it over Pauline and patronised her dreadfully.

The one episode that stood out clearly took place in Aunt Bea's private sewing room at the top of the house. Stella had not been present. The boisterous Labradors had been left to scratch and whine at the door. Aunt Bea and she had been alone, seated together on an old chintz-covered sofa. Aunt Bea had put a plump arm about Pauline's shoulders, had untied the album's silk tapes and opened the precious book across their laps. "Now tell me, dear, do you know who this is?"

"Mummy."

"She hasn't changed much, has she? And the girl lolling on the grass?"

"You." Steely summer rain had pattered on the lead-paned window. Aunt Bea had exuded a strange odour of babies and green soap and her gown, too heavy for a humid afternoon, had felt like sealskin against Pauline's bare arm.

"Goodness, wasn't I a proper little porker in those days? Who's this hanging up holly?"

"Mummy again."

"Well done, Pauline. Have you seen these photographs before?"

"No."

Aunt Bea had sighed. She'd squeezed Pauline's waist

4

consolingly and had gazed out of the window at the gritstone sky for several seconds before turning the brown-card pages again. "Ah! The infamous tennis team. Did you know that your Mama had played tennis for school?"

"No."

"She was very agile, even in that ridiculous skirt. It's all uniforms now, of course. We must blame the war for that. Or the grammar schools. In my day tunics were not obligatory, except for games. Blouses and tight belts made us seem quite grown up, don't you think?"

"Yes."

"What age was I when that was taken? Let me see. Look, I'm wearing my monitor's armband, so I must have been seventeen. Seventeen! Where do the years go to?"

"There's Mummy."

"In her straw hat. What a spring we had that year, so dry and hot. Even the well failed. There was talk of water having to be carted from the dam and boiled for consumption. Baths were prohibited and we were obliged to share wash-basins. Your Mama was furious, I remember. She wrote a stern letter to Papa and was all for leading a march on Kingsford House to protest to the Harveys. As if the drought was their fault."

Aunt Bea had chuckled and given herself a shake, the way Mrs Dobbs did when a joke went against her. She had hugged Pauline close, as if to impart a measure of St Austin's mettle or to explain, without having to frame it in words, that Mama had always been impulsive and must be forgiven for it.

"Is that where Mummy's gone to?" Pauline had said.

"What?"

"Has she gone to stay at St Austin's?"

"No, no. Mama's just gone away – for a rest."

"Is she coming back?"

"Of course. She'll come to visit you. She'll take you out to tea. And to the zoo, I expect."

"Has Daddy gone for a rest with her?"

"Oh, my heavens! No, Pauline, Daddy will be here to collect you just as soon as he can. You'll still be living in Weymouth Street. Daddy and Mrs Dobbs will look after you."

"Where's my Mummy?"

"Pauline, I told you. She's had to go away."

"To stay with Jesus?"

"Whatever gave you that idea?"

"When Pamela's mummy went away, she went to stay with Jesus. And she didn't come back. Not ever."

"No, no, dear, your Mama isn't dead. She's just – gone."

"To another school?"

"Really! I should not be obliged to do this," Aunt Bea had said in the sort of voice that had reminded Pauline very much of her mother. "Papa – your daddy – will explain it to you. And when you're older you'll understand. Now. Look. Here's the school in winter. Did ever you see so much snow? Papa, our Papa, used to tell us that Scotland was next door to the North Pole."

"Will I have to go to school there too?"

"That's certainly your Grandpapa's intention. You'll go up with Stella in three years time, when you're eleven."

"Will I be allowed to play tennis?"

"If you wish."

"Will I play tennis with Mummy?"

At that point Aunt Bea had put a hand to her brow and had wept. It had taken Pauline by surprise. She had been so embarrassed and so filled with guilt that she had wept too, let her tears fall, crinkling, upon the photograph of snowbound St Austin's and the high wooded hills beyond.

Pauline did not go off to boarding school at the age of eleven. Instead she continued to live in Weymouth Street with Daddy and Mrs Dobbs and to attend Glades Road Day School for Girls. Tucked away in a cul-de-sac off Marylebone High Street, Glades Road catered for the daughters of prosperous tradesmen and ambitious artisans and offered a polite ladylike education, without frills, at affordable rates.

Harry Verity seemed quite happy with his daughter's progress from junior to secondary school. He was not in the slightest concerned that she had not been blessed with a more exclusive education. He studiously ignored Grandpapa Haldane's threats and Aunt Bea Jackson's predictions that Pauline would be ruined without a taste of St Austin's *esprit de corps* to steer her through life. Pauline saw little of the Haldanes. She saw even less of her mother who, she gathered, had spent the best part of the war years in Truro with Captain Tiverton's sister until Captain Tiverton was killed. After that Mama had moved away to stay in a house near Chichester with someone else.

Life with Daddy was orderly and secure and not at all dull. He took her out to the great public parades that celebrated the end of the war and led her gradually into the joys that London had to offer once the capital slipped back into mufti. And he had brought her the cats, two half-Persian females, mother and daughter. Portia and Dorothea – Pots and Dots – had accomplished more by way of healing than all Dad's assurances that he was not going off to fight the Germans and that there was nobody in the wide world that he preferred to his little Pauline.

At that stage, soon after Pots and Dots had arrived, Pauline had been rapturously in love with them. They would rub against her legs when she got home from school, would sit on the table and dab at her pen while she did her homework and, when Mrs Dobbs wasn't looking, would slither into bed and lick her nose and ears and purr philosophically.

Mummy did not like cats. The very idea of cats running loose about a house that, curiously, she still considered to be her property, had filled her with dismay.

"Who bought you these creatures?"

"Daddy."

"He would! They're tabbies, I suppose?"

"Yes."

"Dirty beasts," Mummy had said. "I do hope you don't let them near the beds?"

"Oh, no." Pauline had already learned guile. "They sleep in a basket in the kitchen."

"What does Mrs Dobbs have to say to it?"

"She doesn't seem to mind," Pauline had said. "She pets them when she thinks I'm not looking."

That particular conversation had taken place on the fourth or fifth occasion that Mummy had called to take Pauline out to tea. Intelligent communication had been impossible during the first three visits. Pauline had clung to her mother and wept, had promised to be good, had begged her to come home. And, because they'd been sitting in the window of the Parisian Tearooms in Oxford Street, Mummy had found Pauline's behaviour frightfully embarrassing.

There had been a long gap between that visit and the next. Crocuses were on display in the parks before Barbara Verity called upon her daughter again. By that time Pauline was reconciled, and had begun to learn some of the rules of the game. She must not talk about Daddy, must not complain about anything, must not touch Mummy, except for a goodbye kiss, and must try to be as polite and distant as Mummy wanted her to be. It did not take Pauline long to become quite good at it.

"One's called Portia, and the other's Dorothea."

"Oh?"

"They're Persians."

Barbara Verity had had enough of cats.

She'd blown a plume of smoke from her cigarette, had cradled her glass in both slender hands. "I really don't know why Harry bothered when you'll soon have to leave them."

"Why?" Pauline had been puzzled.

"When you go off to school."

"I go to school already."

"To a proper school, I mean."

"I don't want to go to St Austin's."

"Nonsense!"

"I thought it was a horrid place?"

"Who on earth told you that?"

"You did."

Babs Verity had inhaled more tobacco smoke, had imbibed more lemon tea. She'd worn a real fur set over a day dress. The fox head and paws were too realistic for Pauline. The fox's sharp little teeth and black nose reminded her disconcertingly of Portia. But the face that rested against her mother's powdered cheek had been quite tame and lifeless.

"Well, you will have to go, Pauline," Mummy had told her. "Your cousin goes up next September, so I expect you should do the same. I'll speak to Grandpapa about it."

Pauline had opened her mouth to protest but had thought better of it. She had felt the gulf between her and her mother

8

grow wide as a lake. She would have to depend upon Daddy who, in all things, was on her side. "If you like," Pauline had said.

It was two years before she saw her mother again.

By which time Captain Tiverton was dead, the war was over, and Pauline had gone on to senior school at Glades Road and fondly imagined that she was old enough to take care of herself.

# Two

*H*arry Verity had always regarded himself as a sort of *boulevardier manqué*, a man who, when the war was over, would strut with the smart set and have a whale of a time with the ladies now that he was shot of Barbara Haldane. In fact, he had not been shot of Babs at all for, beneath his arrogance, he had been badly hurt by her desertion and had refused outright to concede to her demands for a divorce. He had been furious at Babs for taking off with Tiverton and leaving him stuck with a girl child. It wasn't that he didn't love his little Pauline – of course he did – but rather that he saw in Babs' flight from domestic responsibility a wilfulness that he knew in his heart he could never emulate.

The differences between Harry Verity and Barbara Haldane were that he had always had to work for his money and had no family name to live up to. He had been born and raised in Islington, second and final son of a small-time solicitor so dry and diffident of manner that neither Harry nor his brother George were tempted to follow into the suburban partnership by reading for the law. An education at Deanswood, a modest academy in Cornwall, had hardly equipped the Verity boys with much by way of ambition and neither of them had gone on to university. In fact George had packed his valise and had headed out for the United States of America about ten minutes after he had reached his majority. He was settled now, with a wife and family of his own, in Rhode Island where he owned a chain of drygoods stores and, last Harry had heard, was doing quite nicely, thank you.

Death came unexpectedly early to the upright terraced house in Islington. It took Harry's mother and, less than a year later, tugged away his father too. Harry had been twenty-four years old at the time, clerking for the old boy for a pittance while he studied the noble art of accountancy at nights and boned up for examinations. Old Harry Verity's legacy was divided equally between his sons, home and abroad. Sensible George put his share into the purchase of his first little store on the North American seaboard, while Harry, striving to become a grasshopper, sold up the Islington property and took off for a summer on the Cornish Riviera and his first adult encounter with the leisured classes.

It had been a wonderful summer. He had put up at a cottage near Stratton and had spent several weekends as a guest at Nick Goodchild's father's house. There he had met up with all the little sisters who, it seemed, had grown in stature and worldly wisdom since Harry's last term at Deanswood. He'd had a fast and furious flirtation with middle sister Sarah, who was so notoriously wild that she had three broken engagements behind her. Harry had not lost his virginity. He had almost lost an eye instead.

Cycling was all the craze. Wheelers and Flyers and Peddlers and impromptu all-day treks were quite the rage and Harry was not about to be left behind. He had hired an Ajax from a tiny store in Stratton and had flung himself into showing-off with the best of them. He had an aptitude for it and was soon proficient enough to attempt certain acrobatic tricks which, egged on by Sarah, resulted in Harry falling head-first into the Ajax's front wheel and sustaining permanent damage to the retinal muscles of his right eye.

It was all terribly dramatic. And Harry was terribly brave about the whole thing and, before the injury required him to return to London, he cracked all sorts of jokes and was definitely the hero of the hour. The eye, thank God, was saved. Damaged, defective in function, painful as hell, but saved. Harry even managed to convince himself that the puckered scar at the corner of the lid and the gradually-increasing opacity of the old brown orb gave his saturnine good looks a final sinister twist. It bothered him enough, though, to make the winter's final cram for accountancy examinations doubly difficult. He was living like a monk in a rooming house in Holborn to preserve what remained of his cash for another fling in Cornwall in the summer of 1906, the year he first met the Haldanes and fell for little Babs like a ton of bricks.

If Sarah Goodchild had been wild she had never been

reckless. That could not be said for elfin-faced Barbara Haldane. Babs had just been released from penal servitude in some awful boarding school in Scotland and was busy making up for lost time. In a matter of weeks Babs had used the Goodchilds to infiltrate the county set and had embarked on a passionate pursuit of a thirty-three-year-old bloodstock owner named Fletcher who, it seemed, had neither the scruples nor the sense to turn down what was so patently and temptingly on offer.

From the wreckage of that disastrous affair Harry Verity patiently picked up the pieces. He was in no position to be snooty about damaged goods. He was crazy about the girl. He was too relieved to be given a reluctant nod from Donald Haldane to enquire too deeply into just what he was taking on and what would be expected of him as a member of the Haldane family. He had Haldane's influence to thank for his post with Ostermann's Fire & Accident Insurance Company, and for the flat in Weymouth Street. But Harry's gratitude was swiftly tempered by the realisation that there was no satisfying little Barbara. Being loved devotedly by one man, in and out of the bedroom, was not enough for the child-woman who was now, under law, his wife. As Babs had turned against Harry so he had turned against the Haldanes who, in Harry's opinion, had spoiled her and allowed her to grow up twisted. By 1919, however, he was free of Babs and free of his obligations to the Haldanes, or so he thought.

The damaged eye – a blessing in disguise – had kept him out of uniform. Though Harry was as patriotic as the next man he saw no reason not to continue in his chosen profession, particularly as Ostermann's, a Dutch-owned, non-tariff company, were going through hard times. The company had lost its European base and with it the capital necessary to underwrite the industrial machinery that had been its speciality. Extensive offices in the Baberton building in Holborn had been reduced to a single small suite on the fifth floor, and the staff to a handful of decrepit old men and skittish girls. Harry's team of six eager young men-in-the-field had vanished in a puff of military fervour. Harry was spending more time on the road than ever before, travelling to industrial towns in the north and Midlands, away for three or four days at a stretch.

He was, however, still alive, which was more than could be said for many of his former colleagues.

Harry had been celibate since Babs had walked out on him. He was far too sensible to associate with street women and far too wary to begin an affair with some little office bunny. He would give Babs and the Haldanes no opportunity to force him into a divorce that might wrest Pauline from his keeping. It was his one true piece of power over Barbara Haldane and he exercised it patiently.

"No divorce, dear heart," he'd told her. "If I live to be a thousand, no divorce."

For Pauline, however, the post-war years were one long treat. Not for her an annual outing to a pantomime or the ballet. Just as soon as she was old enough to exchange ankle socks for stockings Daddy whisked her on to a roundabout of plays and musicals and visits to the cinema. Daddy was a splendid companion. He cared not a hoot for the snooty looks and disapproving stares that the presence of a child at some of the heavier dramas brought him. Now and then Mrs Dobbs would accompany them to a matinée, particularly if it was a John Barrymore film, but Pauline preferred it when Daddy and she were alone. She had grown tall for her age. She was not petite like her mother. Her impersonation of an adult was aided by the fact that every fashionable female in London was striving to appear like a schoolgirl. By the summer of 1921 Pauline did not seem out of place in the dress circle of the Adelphi or at a table in a Corner House.

It was not Harry Verity's intention to furnish his one and only with a precocious education. He did not regard himself as eccentric in taking her out and about with him. He would admit that it wasn't usual but he saw no harm in it. And Pauline showed no signs of moral or physical degeneration. She was quite capable of separating fantasy from everyday reality, safe in the rooms in Weymouth Street with Daddy, Mrs Dobbs and the cats, with cocoa and buttered toast and fleecy cotton knickers drying on the rack before the kitchen stove.

When postcards arrived from her mother in Deauville or Montreux Pauline scanned them without anguish and just a

13

tiny flicker of envy, as if they came from an older and more sophisticated sister. Daddy did not take her abroad. Holidays were not for him. He was frightfully busy with the insurance business. He was frequently out of town for two or three days at a time, trekking off to Glasgow or Derby or Belfast. Pauline fell into a kind of limbo when he was away and had to content herself with magazines and novels, walks in the park and having her special chums, Andrea and Katy, round for tea.

Perhaps it was the increasing frequency of his absences but now and then Pauline felt that there was something transient about her father, something that could not be marked like the milestones in her mother's life, stuck like postcards round the edges of the mirror or propped against the costume dolls on the dressing table.

Daddy remained adamant in refusing to grant Mummy a divorce. For that reason, perhaps, it had been simply ages since Mummy had called at Weymouth Street. Cards and gifts arrived from time to time but there were no real letters and no telephone calls and this lack of contact transformed Barbara Haldane Verity into a free spirit and, in Pauline's eyes, added romantic lustre to her mother's wanderings.

Daddy had given no hint that trouble was brewing. True, he had been grumbling of late about the speed with which Pauline grew out of her clothes and at the voraciousness of her appetite. There had been fewer theatre evenings and a tendency not to be able to acquire tickets for the circle but to wind up in the gods. Pauline thought nothing of it. Schoolyard conversations led her to believe that all fathers went through fits of economy now and then and that, as Andrea loftily put it, stinginess was endemic to the species.

Certainly Daddy's invitation to take dinner with him in the regal splendour of the Savoy Hotel did not augur impending disaster. It was to be a very special evening and Mrs Dobbs helped Pauline dress for the occasion. Summer taffeta, hair licked into something resembling a bob, a tight little hat and a powder blue coat; Mrs Dobbs, on her knees, made final adjustments to seams and hems and then, rising, gave the excited young girl a hug.

"You're a picture, dear," the woman said, in a queer,

choked voice. "Just remember how growed up you are. An' how good your father's been to you all them years."

"Yes, Mrs Dobbs," said Pauline airily. She was trying to be suave about the treat in store but was not quite up to it. "Do hurry. Mr Williams will be here at any moment and I don't want to keep Daddy waiting."

Pots and Dots were lurking in the long hallway to chase Pauline's shoe-laces and receive a parting tickle but the girl rushed past them with just a flutter of the hand and a cry of "Goodbye, all."

Mr Williams, who was her friend Katy's blacksheep uncle and ran a motor-taxi business, had come up in the lift to collect Pauline and escort her down to the street where his vehicle was parked at the kerb. The inside of the cab smelled of leather, sweet petrol and the fumes of a cigar which a previous passenger had discarded. The aroma was not yet stale and seemed suitably rich to Pauline as she sat back, crossed her legs and sighed with happiness.

She loved riding in taxi-cabs. She loved the London summer evenings, buildings sharp as chrome against a lilac sky and the streets, even at that early hour, changing from workaday to glamorous. She did not notice the inconveniences of scaffolding and deep ditches dug across roads, the scars of bombing and redevelopment. To Pauline these were passing signs of progress and rejuvenation, as fructifying as Nature. So, too, were the motorcars and taxis that swarmed round Oxford Circus, Piccadilly, Haymarket, pouring out cosmopolitan crowds, in fading July sunshine, on to the famous thoroughfare of the Strand.

The cab swung into the courtyard entrance, under the arch on which stood the gilded figure of Peter, Count of Savoy, and glided to a halt before the hotel's bustling doorway. Spendidly arrayed in dinner jacket and black tie – he had changed in the office – Daddy awaited his princess by the step. Pauline restrained herself. She did not rush from the cab. Mr Williams opened the door for her and she advanced with an affected little swagger towards her father who, playing his part to perfection, graciously kissed her hand. With a wave to Mr Williams, who had already been paid his fare, Pauline was led through the swing doors into the glittering hall.

Ushered on by undermanagers, who were all as handsome as matinée idols, Mr Verity and his daughter descended through the vestibule to the Babylonian foyer and thence into the restaurant which was the most enormous room that Pauline had ever seen. It was like an opulent cathedral, or an ocean liner brought to berth by the bank of the Thames. She was courteously relieved of her coat and hat and assisted to sit at the table for two that Harry had reserved in advance. It was the quiet hour, quiet for the Savoy that is. Later, about eleven, restaurant and grill would be packed with celebrities. Harry would have preferred to bring her here then, but not even he had enough nerve, or gall, to crash that fast and frivolous society with a young girl in tow.

Pauline seemed to grow taller. She sat up straight in her gilded chair. Harry had deliberately placed her with her back to the window so that she could gaze into the room itself. He was no habitué of the Savoy and had no idea who might be nibbling on a little something at that early hour. In any case, he had no stomach for star-gazing tonight. He had eyes only for his daughter, for this was her show, sugar-icing on a bitter pill.

"Daddy, don't look round," Pauline confided in a stage whisper. "But I'll swear that's Somerset Maugham."

"Wouldn't be surprised," said Harry. "Is he alone?"

"No, there's a woman with him. I don't recognise her, though."

"And what's young Somerset doing?"

"Eating soup," Pauline, round-eyed, reported. "Oh, look! That's Evelyn Laye, I'll swear it is."

Harry glanced with exquisite casualness towards the palms by the main entrance and caught a glimpse of the lady in question just before she vanished. He was not at all sure that his daughter's guess was correct but said, nevertheless, "So it is. Isn't she a peach?"

"I just knew you'd say that. You are fickle, Daddy. I thought Winifred Barnes was your one and only."

"Winifred Barnes?"

"You know," Pauline sang softly, " 'Bells in my heart are ringing, Out of the sky above, Voices of dreams are singing—' "

"Ah, yes," said Harry. "'Love, love, love.'"

"Why didn't you marry an actress, Dad?"

"Never met one who'd have me," Harry said. "Besides, I met your mother."

"And fell instantly in love with her?"

"Oh, yes."

Pauline hesitated. She so rarely mentioned her mother that Harry wondered if she had deduced the point of the dinner.

"Are you still in love with her?"

In view of what he would have to tell her in the course of the next hour or so he had to be careful how he answered. With an apologetic shrug, he said, "I honestly don't know. I think of her rather a lot, and wish that she hadn't decided to leave us."

"Don't you wish she'd come back?"

"No, sweetheart. I don't think I'd want her back."

"Because of the other men?"

"Because of a lot of things."

With a gesture too hasty to be suave Harry summoned a waiter with the menus.

Nothing was too good for young Miss Verity. The Savoy's kitchen would not let her down. What did she fancy, snails, frogs' legs, caviare? Plovers' eggs, cygnet pie, braised *foie gras*? A whole bullock, lightly browned? Pauline sensibly chose melon, sole, chicken, and meringue. Each dish was perfectly prepared and presented in crystal or on silver. Harry ordered a bottle of Hock to wash it all down and gave Pauline a little in a glass, well mixed with iced water.

During the course of the meal the restaurant gradually filled with sportsmen, financiers, politicians, brash American entrepreneurs, their sweethearts and wives. Outside, stealthily, the Thames grew dark and lamps came on along the span of the Waterloo Bridge. Harry ordered strong coffee, declined brandy, lit a cigarette. His eye ached. He felt almost queasy with apprehension. He dabbed his brow with the back of his wrist.

Filled with food and sated with excitement, Pauline was relaxed almost to the point of drowsiness. Her posture was no longer ladylike but had regressed into an adolescent slouch, her arms hanging loosely by her sides.

17

"Phew!" she said, in stage Cockney. "Whatter buster, eh?"

Harry was taken aback by her resemblance to her mother. He had fooled himself into thinking of Pauline as his child, uncontaminated by Haldané blood. Slumped and sleepy, Pauline bore an uncanny resemblance to Babs when he'd first met her as a knowing child of seventeen. Babs' precocity had been of a quite different order, though; self-dedicated, fiery and without much humour. Babs did not so much attract attention as demand it as her right.

"Pauline, I've something to tell you."

She frowned. "Something unpleasant?"

"I'm afraid so, sweetheart."

She gripped the base of the gilded chair and hoisted herself into an upright position. She placed her hands flat upon the tablecloth and, as girls do, gave her hair a little toss.

"What is it?"

"I – I have to go away for a while." Harry cleared his throat. "There's no help for it. Ostermann's has been losing money on the British market and the directors are closing up the London office. They've offered me a managership in Africa instead."

"Africa!" Her lip trembled and she thrust her forefinger against it to hold back tears. "How long will you be gone?"

"Two years, possibly three."

She knew the truth but tried anyway. She forced a smile, said brightly, "Oh, I shall enjoy Africa. All that sunshine. And lions. Not sure about Mrs Dobbs, though."

"Pauline—"

"Yes, yes, I know." She fumbled in her pocket, brought out a little lace handkerchief, pathetically crumpled, and held it to her nose. "It's all right. I'm not going to cry."

"If I had any choice, any feasible alternative—"

"Couldn't you sell the house? Couldn't we all go to live somewhere less expensive like – like Lambeth or Canning Town?"

Harry shook his head. "I should have told you this before, Pauline, but I didn't think it mattered. I don't own the rooms in Weymouth Street. I rent them from Donald Haldane."

"Grandpapa?"

"Yes, your grandfather's our landlord. Always has been. He's the owner of the building, you see, and when your mother and I were married, he offered us apartments there."

"Free?"

"God, no!" Harry said. "I pay the same as everybody else in our building. Somewhat more, in fact, because of the facilities."

"Have you talked to Grandpapa Haldane? I'm sure he'd lend you—"

"No." He hadn't intended to be sharp and reached across the table between the cups and wine glasses and took her hand. The little handkerchief was damp. "Pauline, I'm broke. That's the long and the short of it. Broke, skint, down on my uppers."

"But how?"

"I wanted to be independent, you see, so I rejected the help and advice that Grandpapa Haldane offered me when I got married. He's not the sort of chap to forget that. I put what money I had into Ostermann's instead of into a company that your grandfather owned. Now, because of the war, things are going badly."

"How will things be better in Africa?" Pauline asked, indignantly but without sarcasm. "What on earth is there to insure in the middle of the jungle?"

"Lots of things. Anyway, it isn't the jungle. I'll be safe and sound in Durban."

"Isn't that in Natal?"

"Well done!" said Harry. "Sub-tropical climate, fanned by sea breezes, never too hot and steamy. So I'm told. I'll be in the offices in the city with just occasional trips up country. Not a cannibal in sight."

"Why can't I come with you?"

"Because you must go to school."

"Aren't there schools in Durban?"

"Well, yes, I expect there are," said Harry. "But they won't be up to much. Education's important, you know. You'll be matriculating in a year or two and then, with luck, you'll be off to college."

"Or married," said Pauline.

19

"It's a bit early to contemplate anything as drastic as marriage, don't you think?" Harry said.

"Please take me with you."

"I can't. Truth is, I'm not allowed to."

"Not allowed to travel with your own daughter! Who says you're not?"

"All right," Harry said. "If you must have the truth, Pauline, I simply can't afford the passage."

"Are you that strapped?"

"Yes, I am."

"In that case I suppose I'll just have to stay put with Mrs Dobbs. Hold the fort. Grin and bear it and all that," said Pauline bravely. "I shall miss you dreadfully though."

"Pauline, sweetheart, there's more." He stubbed his cigarette into a silver ashtray, lit another immediately. He could not bear to look at her white, mournful face. "You can't stay with Mrs Dobbs in Weymouth Street because Grandpapa Haldane will be subleasing the flat while I'm away."

"Where will I stay? And Mrs Dobbs?"

"Well, Mrs Dobbs will go to Dorset to live with her sister."

"So Mrs Dobbs knows all about this?"

"Well, yes. Obviously I had to discuss—"

"So it's all cut and dried," said Pauline. "Except for me. I'm the little inconvenience, am I? What'll you do with me? Put me into a box and store me away with the ornaments?"

"You're going to school."

"I already do."

"To – " Harry picked a fleck of tobacco from his tongue, let out a smoky breath, " – to St Austin's. Boarding. It won't be so bad."

"Yes, it will. My friends are here. Andrea, Katy."

"You'll soon make new friends."

"I don't want new friends."

"Besides, your cousin Stella's at St Austin's. Has been for years. She'll show you the ropes."

"I hate Stella."

"Now, Pauline—"

"What about the cats? What will happen to Pots and Dots?"

20

Harry forced a smile, winked. "Thought of that. They'll go to Dorset with Mrs Dobbs. Not a problem."

"Daddy, they'll hate it there. They're London cats. They'll hate the country. They'll pine and die without me to look after them. You'd be just as well having them put down."

"You don't mean that, surely?" Harry said.

He watched her struggle, inhale three or four breaths that made her bosom heave as if the rich air of the Savoy had become suffocating. Her fingers curled petulantly into her palms. But the initial shock of his news was wearing off, the first flash of panic and despair diminishing.

"No, I don't mean it," Pauline told him. " 'Course I don't." She dabbed her nose with the balled-up handkerchief and firmed her lips. "May I have a little coffee, please?"

As a rule he did not permit her to drink coffee but tonight he did not hesitate. "Of course. Shall I order fresh?"

"From the pot will do."

He poured, hand trembling slightly, allowed her to doctor the cupful as she wished, with sugar and a little cream. She tasted it and drank the liquid quickly, as if it was medicine.

"More?" Harry offered.

"No, thank you." She looked out over the restaurant with what seemed like indifference. "Will they accept me at St Austin's?"

"Yes," Harry said. "Your grandfather wrote on my behalf and explained the situation. Your headmistress, Mrs McAlpine, sent details of your academic achievements."

"She didn't tell me."

"I asked her not to."

"Why?"

"I wanted to tell you myself," Harry said. "You'll have to take some sort of test or examination when you get to St Austin's, so that they can put you into the best form. That shouldn't be a problem, though, not for my clever girl."

She was cleverer than he supposed.

She said, "What exactly does Grandpapa have to do with all this?"

Harry said, "He's meeting your school fees."

"Yet he won't pay for my passage to Natal?"

"He — we didn't feel that Durban was the best place

for you. By the way, he wants to see you before you leave."

"Why?" said Pauline. "To make sure that my nose isn't running and that I don't have lice in my hair?"

"Unfair," said Harry. "I admit that Grandpapa Haldane's a snobbish old devil but this time he's seeing me out of a jam."

"She wants me back, doesn't she?"

"Pardon?"

"Mummy wants me back. And this is Grandpapa Haldane's way of doing it. I'm being bought, aren't I?"

"Don't get carried away, Pauline," said Harry. "I doubt if your mother knows anything about this."

"I'll bet she does," said Pauline.

"Sweetheart, I hope you don't think—"

"I don't think anything," Pauline said. "Tell me, when do you leave for Africa?"

"Middle of September," Harry said. "That's one good thing. You won't have to stand on the dock in a shawl and clogs and wave bye-bye in the rain."

"When does the Scottish school term begin?"

"Saturday, the second. But as a new girl you're requested to arrive on the first, to give you time to settle in."

"St Austin's," Pauline said. "Why does it have to be St Austin's?"

Harry shrugged, guiltily. "Tradition."

"Haldane tradition, not ours," Pauline said. "I take it that Grandpapa insisted on it?"

"I'm sorry, Pauline. I'm really, truly sorry."

"Well, I suppose there will be compensations," Pauline said. "Christmas in Davos and summer holidays in Antibes."

"I wouldn't count on it," Harry said.

"Who's to look after me, then, if not Mummy?"

"Aunt Bea."

"Oh!" Pauline bit her lip, gently put her napkin down upon the tablecloth. "I think you should pay the bill now, Daddy. I really would rather like to go home."

"Darling—"

"If you don't mind."

As Pauline preceded her father between the tables heading

22

towards the exit, she passed close to a group of five men and a woman who were just beginning dinner. She recognised the woman at once; Lady Dianne Chadwick, no chicken now but still beautiful in a shimmering gown and dripping with jewels. The men were obviously foreigners, one at least was an American.

Lady Dianne was not the centre of attention. The prince of the party was a youthful Italian-looking man, so handsome that it almost hurt to look at him. Pauline had a feeling that she had seen him on the screen, that he was becoming famous, but she could not quite recall his name. He glanced up as Pauline approached. His bold, olive-black eyes seemed to caress her insolently as she passed. He gave her a wicked smile and, not caring who saw, opened his hand as if to catch her.

Uncaring, unimpressed, Pauline slipped past him as if he did not exist. She wanted only to be in the taxi-cab with Daddy; then home, safe home, alone in her bedroom where she might cry like a child to her heart's content with only the cats to hear her and offer, with their broad, moist noses and pink tongues, something as honest as sympathy.

# Three

Crises of identity were common enough in Lowland Scots who had crossed the Border with England in search of fame and fortune. The Haldanes were no exception to the general rule although, to give him his due, Donald Haldane had done his best to adopt protective coloration. By tacit understanding he suggested that the 'Half-Danes', in whom the family originated, had somehow gravitated voluntarily from the fenlands of Beowulf's England to the miserable tenement in Glasgow where he had first seen the light of day.

The Haldanes' ancestral records were studded with earls, viscounts and other men of consequence. But the name of the dark horse who had leapt the gate of privilege to sire the common line that eventually fathered young Donald Haldane remained a mystery. Lots of other things about Grandpapa Haldane were equally mysterious; how he had made his first small fortune, and why the child born to him by his first wife, who had died tragically at the age of twenty-six, had been cut off so completely from his favour.

Very little of the family background was known to Pauline. She had visited Grandpapa and Grandmama three or four times a year when Mummy still resided in Weymouth Street. In those days Hampstead had seemed a long, long way off, a strange, quaint place compared with what Pauline thought of as London. After Mummy went away, however, she saw no more of Grandpapa and Grandmama and heard not a word from the house in Ostler's Walk.

It was a hot, humid Thursday afternoon in August before Harry Verity finally got around to taking Pauline out to Hampstead. Drought had already parched the harvest in southern counties and London had been dunned by a brassy sun for weeks on end. The top of the omnibus sizzled in the heat and the 'bus panted and wheezed like an old horse as it carried the Veritys north up Haverstock Hill. Harry tried to make conversation, pointing out that Durban couldn't be any hotter than this and telling Pauline that in Scotland there was always a breeze to blow up the kilts of the natives.

Pauline did not respond. Her cotton dress clung to her and perspiration prickled on the nape of her neck where yesterday the hairdresser had cropped a line with a razor. She realised that her father was also suffering but she offered him no sympathy. The dry air had irritated his sore eye and he had purchased a pair of spectacles with dark brown lenses which made him seem sallow and indrawn, as if he had already become somebody other than the man she had loved for so long.

Pauline had, in fact, fretted herself into such a state of melancholy that at another time Mrs Dobbs would surely have dosed her with sulphur-and-treacle or dollops of Scott's Emulsion. School had closed. Teachers had bidden Pauline farewell and wished her success for the future. Andrea, Katy and her other chums had gone off on holiday and there was nothing left for Pauline to do but to wait for summer to pass and the inevitable to happen.

Pauline knew perfectly well that her father had no wish to leave England. Daddy's jolly prattle about Durban's colonial hotels, modern boulevards and proposed electrical railway system consoled her not one whit. She would waken, hot and uncomfortable, in the wee small hours, convinced that Africa would swallow up her father as it had the missionaries and explorers she'd read about in books. A sense of foreboding cast a gloomy shadow over the glaring summer days. The one and only redeeming feature in the whole horrid mess was that she would surely see more of Mummy. And now that she was almost grown up, Mummy would not find her silly and boring and they would become firm friends.

The omnibus dropped them in Hampstead High Street opposite the Bird in Hand. Pauline recalled the place as through a haze. Usually it had been winter when Mummy had brought her here. In those days Grandpapa and Grandmama had spent their summers in Devon. She did not take Daddy's hand – she was too big for that now – nor did she accept his arm when he offered it. She scuffed sulkily along a half step behind him, hating herself for being so unkind but unable to prevent it. Harry waited patiently while Pauline dithered in front of a confectioners' and then at a bookshop window. Only when she was ready did he guide her across the High Street into Church Row, the hub of old Hampstead.

Mansions and dull, red-brick, Queen Anne houses, two centuries old, led up to the church of St John, brick too with a little tower and a spire. Surgeons, artists and peers of the realm lived here but the Haldanes did not consort with their neighbours. They kept themselves to themselves in a huge old house hidden away behind sycamores on the corner of Ostler's Walk, a house whose upper rooms gave views down the elegant old street with its gas-lamps and delta of trees and whose servants' garrets looked out to remnants of countryside beyond Childs Hill.

Fashionable motorcars shimmered metallically in the sun. Harry spared them not a glance. He wanted very badly to take Pauline's hand, to pretend that she was a little girl again, to believe that his presence would protect her against the Haldanes' pernicious ability to hurt.

No motorcars were parked at the gate of the Haldane residence. The house beyond the laurel hedges had a rustic sort of look, sun-baked yet musty, as if nothing had been changed and not much had happened here in the forty years since Grandpapa Haldane had bought it. It did not remind Pauline of her mother. She could not associate her mother with such a stuffy place.

Harry opened the gate and allowed Pauline to go through. A gravel walk, in need of weeding, curved beneath the sycamores to a pillared doorway. He touched her arm. When she stopped he put his hands on her shoulders and inspected her gravely. The light cotton frock made her seem younger than her years; a far cry from the girl he had taken to dinner at the Savoy. He could not get used to this betwixt-and-between stage. By the time he returned from Durban, though, she would be a confident, self-assured young woman and he would look back with longing on this uncertain phase. He tidied a lock of her hair, what was left of it. He straightened the collar of her dress.

"Now—" he began.

Pauline said wearily, "Speak only when spoken to. Call him Grandpapa, not Grandpa. And don't take two pieces of cake, even if offered, at tea-table."

"You've got it," Harry said. "One last thing, sweetheart, I know it'll be difficult but when the subject of school's mentioned try not to appear as if you'd been sentenced to ten years on Dartmoor."

"Women aren't sent to Dartmoor."

"Don't be smart, Pauline. You know what I mean."

"Don't worry, I won't let you down."

He peered at her through smoke-brown lenses. Sunlight and humidity had made his eyes water. He wiped the rim of his spectacles with the back of his hand. He kissed her on the brow. "All right," he said, "let's get it over with."

The servants that had survived were soundless ghosts, discreet to the point of invisibility. The aged butler who opened the door to Harry's ring was no exception. There was nothing comical in his bearing, though, and his whispering tone seemed sinister. Side by side, Harry and Pauline followed him up a broad uncarpeted staircase that turned back upon itself at a half landing speckled with reflections from a stained-glass window. They climbed another flight of broad stairs, crossed a half acre of varnished floorboards and were finally ushered into a first-floor drawing-room.

The room had once been magnificent. Done in the French style and centred on a marble fireplace carved with fruit and leaves and little cherubim, its ornate furnishings and painted panels had become ingrained not so much with dirt as with a still and pallorless neglect. Grandpapa had suited himself to the room. He had contrived at elegance in a rich quilted smoking jacket and cravat, green velvet slippers upon his feet. His hair was wispy as a halo in the light from the long window. He was seated upright in a high-backed wooden armchair, directly facing the doorway. Grandmama Haldane, who seemed even older than Donald, though he gave her ten years, was appropriately placed behind her husband and off to one side as if she sought, or had been ordered to seek, a corner to hide in. Her chair was quilted in a granular brocade. She crouched down upon it and leaned into a thin ebony stick. She was clad in an ancient black dress with gigot sleeves and voluminous skirts. Her pug face was set in a ferocious scowl. Pauline remembered the room and the couple, unchanged it seemed, from her last long-ago visit.

She hardly glanced at the elderly couple, however, and gave them no audible greeting. Her attention had been immediately drawn to the window, to the woman who stood by it. The woman wore a summery one-piece day dress, light as froth, and a picture hat in matching fuchsia. One hand was raised to the heavy velvet drape as if she had not noticed the Veritys' arrival and watched and waited for them still.

Pauline felt her mouth go dry, her heart thump against her breastbone. "Mummy?"

The woman glanced over her shoulder and, smiling, said, "Yes, darling, it's me."

She looked wonderful. Her eyes were luminous, her elfin face just a little fatter, her skin dusted with a fine, fine tan that she had not bothered to disguise with make-up. She turned from the window, both hands extended and, waddling slightly, came forward to embrace her daughter, the day dress hanging outward from her swollen stomach.

Pauline felt her father's fingers tighten painfully upon her arm and then a sudden break in contact as he staggered backward.

"Oh, Christ!" Harry Verity groaned.

He groped behind him for a chair and, head in hands, sank down upon it.

Tentative exchanges of information in the cloakrooms of Glades Road School and during those ambling and apparently aimless peregrinations that girls of a certain age undertake had provided Pauline with all she needed to know about the rude mechanics of conception and birth. She had been able to add her groatsworth, of course, from interpretation of certain amorous scenes in theatrical and moving picture plays. Andrea, Katy and she were agreed, however, that all of 'that' was really rather nasty and, while necessary for survival of the species, could not have much to do with 'love', as they understood it. Now, in the French-style, mausoleum-like drawing-room of Grandpapa Haldane's house in Hampstead, Pauline was abruptly confronted with the truth. Gossip, fable and fact merged into the ugly bump that her mother carried before her, the bulge that came between them when Pauline was scooped into an awkward maternal embrace. She backed away instantly.

Daddy was on his feet. He caught Pauline as she stepped back, pulled her to him, shoulders against his chest, as if he was abducting her at pistol point. One arm about her waist, he extended his right hand and stabbed a forefinger accusingly, not at Mummy but at Grandpapa Haldane.

"You knew she was pregnant all along, didn't you, you conniving old bastard?" Daddy shouted. Pauline could feel his chest heave against her shoulder-blades. His face was so close to her cheek that his glasses scraped her skin. She was almost deafened by his infuriated roar. "You hadn't even the guts to tell me, man to man."

Neither anger nor contrition touched Donald Haldane's benign features. They were soft with age now, pink and passive under the halo of silver hair. He seemed less restrained than indifferent. Even his eyes showed no change in response to Harry's outburst. He remained as bland as cream in coffee. Pauline felt her father's chest swell. She flinched when he roared again. "Well, who the hell is it? What poor sod's going to carry the can this time?"

"That's no concern of yours," Grandpapa Haldane said.

"Oh, is it not?" Daddy said. "I suppose you'll tell me the ghost of poor Johnny Tiverton put it there?"

"It's no one you know, Harry," Pauline's mother said.

She had eased her weight on to a small sofa. One slender hand was placed on top of her stomach as if to reassure the occupant that no harm would come to it in spite of all the shouting. In the back of Pauline's mind was the faint fond hope that her mother's pregnancy might change everything: Daddy might not go to Durban: she might not have to go to school in Scotland.

"Is it Vernon?" Daddy said.

Mummy laughed. "Good heavens, no."

"Charlie Stanhope then?"

"I haven't seen Charles in years. Honestly, Harry, you don't know the man. Thing is, I am rather in love with him."

"Therefore you require a divorce?"

"Obviously."

Pauline shifted her gaze to her grandfather and grandmother, both mute and motionless as carved statues. Harry reached behind him, found the chair's edge and seated himself upon it. He brought Pauline beside him and continued to hold on to her arm. "I'll bet it's some pipsqueak country squire like Jackson, who lives off an allowance and has nothing better to do with himself than stick every little tart who comes his way," Harry said. "Is he married too?"

"Too?" Babs said. "Come now, Harry. We haven't been married, properly married, for years. I can't understand why you won't face the fact that it's all over and give me a divorce."

"Do you mean, bring an action against you?"

"No, Verity, that's not what she means," Donald Haldane said.

Harry ignored the interruption.

"Let me divorce you, Harry. Please," Babs said. "It'll be quick and simple. And it won't cost you a bean."

Harry circled Pauline's waist with his arm. He shook his head. "Not on, Babs. Sorry and all that."

"Harry, you can't keep her," Babs said. "In three or four years she'll spread her wings and be gone."

"No, I won't," Pauline heard herself say.

Babs flashed her daughter a dimpled smile. "Why, of course you will, dearest. Look at you already, all grown up. Come over and sit by me."

"No."

"Do as your mother tells you, child," Grandmama Haldane growled, speaking for the first time.

"No," Pauline repeated.

"There's nothing to be afraid of." Babs patted the cushion by her side. "Come on, there's plenty of room. Come, give me a cuddle."

"Stop it, Babs," Daddy said.

"You can't possibly keep the child, Verity," Grandpapa Haldane said. "You can't even afford to keep yourself, can you?"

"Why didn't you tell me that Babs was expecting?"

30

"You can't have it both ways," the old man said. "Do you or do you not want me to finance your daughter's education and pay off your debts—"

"Such as they are."

"—while you pursue your career in Durban? Oh, I know all about the trouble at Ostermann's. It's Africa or bust for you, sir."

"I'm sorry you're on the rocks, Harry," Babs said. "Truly I am. However, what Papa says is absolutely right. You can't have it both ways. Look at me, Harry. I'm not your wife any more. What will it cost to give me grounds to divorce you? The lawyers will fix it. You'll be in Africa. You won't even have to appear."

"And if I still refuse, what then?" Daddy said.

Pauline understood exactly what was at stake. She had enough sense however, not to bridle and not to whine. Inside her mother nestled a real child, a child whom her mother would love as she had never loved her. She felt sorry for her father and her pity was somehow strengthening.

"Good God, Verity, this is not an ultimatum. It's a request," Grandpapa Haldane said. "I'm giving you an opportunity to do the decent thing in the circumstances."

"When are you due, Babs?" Harry said.

"In seven weeks."

"Left it rather late, haven't you? The baby won't wait for a divorce and the issuing of a special licence," Harry said. "Will its father?"

"Absolutely," Mummy said.

"How long have you known him?"

"Two years, give or take."

"Is he rich?"

"Not short."

"What does he do?"

"He's a member of the Baltic Exchange."

"Where will you live?"

"London, I expect. At least in the season."

Pauline sensed the moment of defeat. She alone could detect the rim of fluid that leaked from Daddy's irritated eye and gathered against the spectacle lens.

Barbara leaned forward, both hands upon her stomach. "Harry, what difference can it make to you now?"

Daddy slapped a hand on his thigh and got to his feet. He said, "None, I suppose."

"Well?" said Grandpapa Haldane.

"All right," Daddy said. "I agree to your terms."

Grandpapa Haldane said, "You'll have to give grounds, you know."

"I know. I will."

"Soon, Harry, please," Babs said.

"Let the lawyers arrange it," Harry said. "I won't stand in your way."

Babs laughed, a fat, breathless sound. "I'm glad that's settled. Now, do come and sit with me, Pauline darling." She patted the cushion once more. "Tell me all your news." Pauline glanced at her father. Sallowness had spread all over his face and neck. His skin was a faint purplish red, like the complexion of old men who drink too much.

Pauline said, "I think we might be leaving now."

"Oh, don't be so silly, dear. Sit down. Talk to me. There's no reason for us not to be friends."

"Daddy, I want to go."

She offered Daddy her hand. She didn't in the least care if it seemed childish. His grip was moist with perspiration but reassuring.

"Good luck, Babs," Harry said.

"Pauline—"

"Goodbye, Mummy," said Pauline, politely.

It was breathlessly hot and sultry outside. To the south, over London, the sky had taken on a strange unsummery tint, grey as lead. The air smelled rancid, reeking of coal smoke and petrol fumes. As they walked down the drive into Ostler's Walk Pauline felt perspiration start out on her brow and cheeks and down her spine and thighs. The cotton dress clung to her like wet paper. They had been in Grandpapa's house for less than a quarter of an hour yet a whole season seemed to have slid away in that short space of time.

Outside the gate, protected from view by sycamores and laurel hedges, Harry stopped. He leaned, exhausted, against the wall. He took out a large blue silk handkerchief, carefully dried his hands upon it then removed his spectacles. His right eye was livid and shed a clear fluid like tears, but his pallor had returned to normal. He dabbed the damaged eye for a moment or two then returned the handkerchief to his pocket. He brought out his cigarette case and a box of pin-headed cocktail matches and, fingers trembling, extracted a cigarette from the case and lit it. He inhaled deeply and, still leaning against the wall, contemplated the heavy leaden-grey sky.

"Thunder about," he said conversationally. "Rain too, I shouldn't be surprised. Farmers'll be glad. Are you all right, sweetheart?"

"I'm awfully hot," said Pauline.

"Yes, the mean old devil didn't even offer us tea."

"There's a tea-shop by the bus-stop in town," Pauline told him.

"Is there indeed. Do you fancy a cuppa, sweetheart? It might cool us down."

Pauline nodded.

Harry sucked on the cigarette again. He let out smoke with a little throaty woof then grinned. "Quite a turn-up, eh? Your mother being – that way. What do you make of it, Pauline?"

"I shan't see her again if I can help it."

"Perhaps you won't be able to help it." Harry pushed himself away from the wall. "Listen, Pauline, say the word and I'll cancel the whole shooting-match. I mean it. I'll find some sort of job. Take an insurance book if the worst comes to the worst. Say the word and we'll muddle along somehow."

"How much do you owe to Grandpapa Haldane?"

"I'm not really in debt, just – stretched."

"Daddy, how much?"

"Five hundred pounds."

"It's for Mrs Dobbs, isn't it?"

"I can't just send her off with nothing," Harry said.

"What's best for you, Daddy?"

Pauline was grateful to him for not prevaricating. He did not shut her out or patronise her.

He said, "Africa."

33

"Will two years put us on our feet again?"

"Three at most."

"I'll be eighteen by then," Pauline heard herself say.

"My, my! So you will." He smiled then playfully framed her face between spread hands. "Act the Second. The curtain rises on a twilit patio. A beautiful young woman gazes out over a balustrade. She starts back as an old man laboriously climbs the marble steps."

"An old man in a solar topee and khaki rags." Pauline took up the story easily. They had played this game of make-believe before. "He has a bundle on his back and a rusty firearm slung over his shoulder. The young woman recoils in horror."

Harry went on, "'Is it . . . can it really be you?' she cries."

"'Yes, yes, Lobelia. I have returned,' the old man croaks. He lowers the bundle, opens it and brings out a handful of jewels."

"'You found them. You found them, Father,' Lobelia cries. 'King Solomon's mines. We are rich, rich beyond the dreams of avarice. But wait! Who is this? Your faithful servant?'"

"'No, my dear Lobelia, this is . . . ah, the Queen of the Zulus. My wife. Your new mother.'"

"'Not—'"

"'Yes.'" Together, in unison, Harry Verity and his daughter shouted out, "Mrs Umslopogass!"

They laughed in mutual silliness then Harry said, "It's not the second act that concerns me, sweetheart. It's what'll become of us in the interval. Candidly, I don't want to lose you to the Haldanes. I don't want you to become like them."

"I shan't."

"The school, does it worry you going there?"

"It isn't a prison," Pauline said. "It won't be so bad."

"I'm not sending you away just to be rid of you."

"I know that, Daddy."

"Well, on or off? Last chance, sweetheart."

"On," Pauline said. "But promise me – no Mrs Umslopogass."

"On that," said Harry Verity, "you have my word."

"Now can we go and have some tea?"

34

"By all means," Daddy said and linking her arm with his led her downhill towards the High Street just as the first plump spots of rain patterned the pavement and spattered the dusty laurel leaves.

The days – and nights – of her last weeks at home were almost unendurable. Harry did his best to provide diversion. He took her to the pictures, to *What's Your Hurry*, *The Dancin' Fool* and to *The Kid*, which had them both in tears at the end. He gave Pauline as many hours as he could spare from his own hectic schedule. But he had so much to do closing down the London office, arranging for furniture to be stored, as well as legal and financial matters to attend to, that he became thin and nervy and too harried to be sentimental. Mrs Dobbs was deeply affected by the imminent parting from the young girl she had raised from infancy and by the Veritys' great upheaval which, of course, meant radical change in her life too. She bore it all with apparent stoicism until Pauline's last evening at home. Out it came then in a flood of tears which soon had Pauline weeping too so that when Harry came home for supper he found the pair of them red-eyed, pink-nosed and quite washed out with emotion.

Breakfast the following morning was an anticlimax. Pauline felt as if she was surrounded by glass, like a goldfish in a jar. Her trunk waited in the hallway, the same 'ark' of wickerwork and painted canvas that had accompanied her mother to school all those years ago. A telegram message from Aunt Bea wished Pauline well. But there was no greeting from Hampstead or from her mother. Early post brought letters of cheer and condolence from Andrea, who was still in Eastbourne with her parents, and a box of chocolate babies from Katy in Yarmouth. Welcome little diversions while Pauline ate her eggs and toast and Harry hopped about and gulped coffee and tried not to glance at his watch.

The cats were grouchy at being roused so early. Pauline loved them all the more for being their natural selves but came very, very close to bursting into tears when Dots deigned to give her nose a lick before curling up with paws over ears to sleep again. "Don't fret on their account, dearest," Mrs Dobbs told her. "I'll take best care o' them."

Mr Williams and Daddy carried the trunk down to the taxi and left the ladies to final embraces and parting words which, now that the time had come, were strangely calm and resigned.

Mr Williams chatted as he steered the taxi-cab through the early morning traffic. He asked if Pauline was excited at going away to school. She answered him – Yes – politely. Then Daddy and Mr Williams fell to discussing England's gallant performance against Australia on the cricket field, whether Carpentier would get a rematch against Jack Dempsey, and how much money he – and Daddy too it seemed – had lost by not backing Humorist in the Epsom Derby.

King's Cross railway station at five past eight on a drizzly autumn morning was not the best place to say goodbye. Pauline had insisted, absolutely insisted, on making the long journey to Perth unaccompanied. Time and money would be saved as a result. Daddy finally had to admit that her logic was sound. Perhaps he'd guessed that there was a more subtle reason why Pauline did not want him, or Mrs Dobbs, escorting her to St Austin's. She would have enough to cope with in that strange new place without the heartbreak of parting and the humiliation of all-too-public tears.

The sight of her mother's pregnancy had added a kind of fortitude to Pauline's character. She told herself that if she was old enough to comprehend such things she was certainly old enough to stand on her own two feet.

Fruit carts were clopping back from market driven by greengrocers in straw hats and long aprons. A fishmonger and his assistant were laying cod and whiting on a fern-decorated slab. Little shops, restaurants and tea-rooms were being swept out. On Euston Road were buses and trams, shoals of taxi-cabs, horses, and hoardings advertising Scotch Whisky, Bovril, *The Gondoliers*. From the stations poured regiments of artisans and clerks, and in a passing motorcar, the hood swept back, two very young women sprawled in a flutter of tipsy chiffon and showed their silken legs to all the passers-by. All of this, all of London, would still be here tomorrow. But she would not. She would be gone.

The taxi rolled into the shadow of the railway station and drew neatly to a halt by the arches. Mr Williams wished her luck and drove away, whistling. Daddy found a porter to wheel the trunk to the Aberdeen train. He detoured to the bookstall, bought Pauline *Eve*, *Play Pictorial* and, almost as an afterthought, *The School Friend*, and, at an adjacent machine, a platform ticket.

They walked side by side, not touching, up the long platform to the First Class coach next to the guard's van. Daddy explained the situation to the guard and tipped the man a half crown to keep an eye on his daughter and make sure she did not get off at the wrong station. He had arranged with St Austin's by letter and telephone that Pauline would be met at Perth railway station by a school steward who would provide transport for the last leg of her journey.

Settled in a window seat in an empty compartment, her travelling bag safe beside her, Pauline listened to the clamour of preparations for departure. She was frightened, terribly frightened, not just for herself but also for Daddy. She went to the window at the coach's end, let it down by the strap and leaned out. Daddy's hands were in his pockets. His hat was tugged down on his brow. He rocked back and forth on the balls of his feet, not jauntily. When the guard's whistle shrilled he flinched.

"Daddy?" Pauline said. "Oh, Daddy!"

His resolve was broken. He darted forward, reached up and kissed her. Their hats made the kiss awkward and unsatisfactory but Pauline felt his hand against her cheek, stroking, soothing. Then the carriage lurched, doors slammed, and Daddy was forced back.

The train shuddered, moved forward, paused and then quite slowly drew away from the platform, trailing wreaths of smoke and steam. Pauline was not used to trains and had read accounts of dreadful accidents to children. She did not dare lean from the window. She pressed her shoulder against the woodwork and squinted back through the smoke. Daddy raised his hand, waved, and was gone.

Pauline returned to the empty compartment, took off her new hat, wiped her nose with a new handkerchief. Everything was new, from her stockings to the two metal clips that kept her hair in place. She felt stiff with newness. For ten or fifteen minutes she sat still, doing nothing. She was aware only of the rocking motion of the coach, terraces and warehouses and ugly bungalows sweeping past, the unfamiliar bad-egg smell that wafted in through the open window. The guard, a small, square-shaped man with a bulbous nose and a gruff Scottish accent, popped in and asked in kindly fashion if she was comfortable.

"Perfectly. Thank you very much," Pauline answered.

The guard went away again. After a while she glanced through the magazines Daddy had bought for her and, a while after that, opened the lunch-box that Mrs Dobbs had prepared; the last egg-and-cress sandwiches that Mrs Dobbs would ever make for her. Pauline ate them.

Feeling a little better, she scoffed the ripe apple that Mrs Dobbs had tucked into a corner of the box while, with quickening interest, she watched the rural landscapes dip and change as the train rushed north towards Scotland.

# PART II
## The New Girl

# Four

They were waiting for her by the iron gates at the end of the platform, two of them, both tall. They wore the bottle green blazers and unpleated skirts of St Austin's pupils. Straw boaters and white soft-collared shirts indicated that it was still considered summer here in the Highlands, though the late evening breeze that whistled along the railway lines and moaned under the station's glazed roof made Pauline shiver and think of snow.

Unfortunately, she had fallen asleep after the train had left Edinburgh and had wakened, in a panic, only ten minutes before it pulled into Perth. Outside, in gathering dusk, a westering sun had carved great poignant shadows out of the valleys and turned the sprawling forests black while on broad plains sheep and cattle, tiny as toys, had grazed untended on the banks of rivers and streams. She'd had no idea where she was. Pin-prick lights of farms and cottages had seemed utterly desolate in enormous expanses of nothingness and Pauline had felt as if she had been cast adrift on a sea of wilderness. No saying what she might not have done if, at that moment, the little guard had not tugged open the door of the compartment and assured her that Perth was the next stop and that he had her trunk all ready for unloading.

Seeing her white face, her haunted expression, the guard, not quite chuckling, had told her, "Och, you'll like it fine here, lass – when you get used to it."

She'd had time only to rush to the water closet, to wipe off crumbs and stickiness and frantically scratch at her hair with a comb before the lights of Perth winked in at the window. The train braked and stole demurely into the canopied station and Pauline had stepped out on to Scottish soil with a mixture of relief and apprehension. She seemed to be the only early arrival for St Austin's. The guard had shouted for a porter

41

who heaved Pauline's trunk on to a handcart, and a young boy in railway uniform wheeled it away, leaving Pauline to follow as best she could.

Pauline handed over her ticket and hesitantly advanced towards the two tall seventeen-year-olds whose yellow arm-bands marked them as St Austin's prefects and emissaries. Neither of them took so much as a pace towards her and they gave no sign at all that they had been sent to meet her until Pauline stood directly before them and stuttered like a fool, "S-Saint-Au-Austin's, p-please?"

"Verity?"

"Yes."

"Train's late."

"Oh, I—"

"We've been here for ages."

"Not your fault, I suppose." The speaker had long flaxen hair plaited into a heavy pigtail that hung across her shoulder like a pet mink. The ribbon that retained it was, like her armband, bright yellow. Her cheekbones were prominent and her long jaw set and she looked much more mature, even in schoolgirls' uniform, than seventeen.

"Better push along. Driving in the dark's no fun for old MacAdam," she said. "He'll be mad enough at missing his dram."

The blonde's companion was marginally less daunting. Softer, almost chubby, her brown hair was cut short and clipped back with a plain enamelled pin. Though Pauline had no idea what the prefects were talking about she'd had sufficient experience of sixth formers to realise that she could expect no coddling and no warmth to the welcome.

The autocratic blonde said, "Here, I hope he hasn't buzzed off into the refreshment bar."

"No," said the chubby brunette. "I've had my eye on him. He's been skulking over by the ticket office, having a 'crack' with one of his cronies."

Pauline scanned the platforms for sight of the man, Mac-Adam. He was not, as the girls' talk had led her to believe, some scrofulous tinker but a well-set-up chap of about sixty dressed in the sort of brown tweeds that colonels usually wore in country-house farces.

42

"So you're here at last, are ye?" he said, cheerily enough. "Man, but I thought the Indians had attacked the train again."

"Pardon?"

"Take no notice," the blonde advised; and to MacAdam, "Do you want a hand with her trunk?"

"Certainly not."

MacAdam brushed the youthful porter aside, lifted Pauline's trunk by its straps and hoisted it in a swift, smooth motion on to his shoulder. "Well, your ladyships, are we for the road then?"

"Lay on, Macduff," the brunette said, rather to the consternation of her colleague, Pauline thought.

She trailed out of the station behind the girls, the man and her mother's wicker trunk, no longer quite so cold or so desolate as she had been five minutes ago, in spite of the austere welcome.

The bus was an old Halley, a chain driven, solid tyred boneshaker that had been purchased from the Edinburgh Motor Company at bargain price soon after the armistice had released it from war service in France. Two years of transporting hordes of schoolgirls to and fro along the Perthshire back roads had inflicted more damage on the chassis and fittings than ever Jerry had managed to do with bombs and bullets. The leather seats were scuffed through to the horsehair and the windows rattled demonically in their frames as Mr MacAdam in a separate, open-sided compartment at the front, fisted the little steering wheel and navigated the long vehicle out of the station yard.

Darkness had fallen now and the cobbled streets of Perth were quiet. The lights of public houses and a few gas-lamps showed deserted lanes and vennels. Only along the main road did Pauline detect any sign of human life; a horse and cart, a harvest waggon and two small motorcars kept the handful of pedestrians on their mettle. She was seated at the rear of the bus. As of right, the prefects occupied the long back bench and Pauline sat, rocking, on the slippery seat to their left. She had to hang on as best she could when the bus bumped round bends and, leaving the town behind, thrashed off into the darkness of open countryside.

The hills made monstrous black shapes. Hedges and trees poured out of the windy dark and sheeps' eyes glared glassily over the stone dykes in the passing flicker of light. Pauline's wicker trunk slid and scraped on the floor where Mr Mac-Adam had put it.

The prefects had their heads together and were laughing. Pauline waited for a lull then, leaning towards them, shouted, "How far is it to St Austin's?"

The blonde steadied herself with an arm about her companion's waist.

"Pauline Verity – what sort of name is that?" she said.

"I – I don't know. Just a name."

"Sounds frightfully biblical to me," said the blonde.

"New Testament," the brunette added. "You're not RC, by any chance?"

"Pardon?"

"How can she be, chump?" said the blonde. "We may not know what she is but we certainly know what she isn't. She isn't a Jew or a Hindu, or a Roman Catholic." To Pauline, intimidatingly: "What are you?"

Pauline thought quickly. Daddy'd had no time for established churches and her experience of matters religious was confined to services at Glades Road School which was, she supposed, vaguely Anglican. She recalled reading in St Austin's brochure that the school was non-denominational and that the forms of service would be according to the Church of Scotland.

"Well?" the blonde insisted.

"Church of England." That sounded bland enough not to incur their scorn.

"You're not a psalm-singer, are you? Not into tambourines and cosy chats with the vicar?"

"I don't think I am," said Pauline.

There was something about the blonde that reminded her of Andrea, or the way Andrea would be when she grew older.

"Not a swot, I hope?" the blonde went on.

"No," said Pauline emphatically.

44

"What d'you play?"

"Pardon?"

"You've been to some sort of educational establishment, so I assume you play something."

"I've had a few piano lessons."

"Cricket, hockey, croquet."

"Oh!" Pauline, who was not particularly sporty, hesitated. "Tennis."

"Too bad. The season's almost over. We could do with a sturdy full-back on the hockey field, though."

"My mother," Pauline said, "used to play for the school team. Years ago."

"Your mother?" said the blonde.

"Barbara Haldane."

"Good lord! You're the one. You're Stella Jackson's cousin," said the blonde.

"Yes, I suppose I am."

Sighing, the chubby girl said, "Another Haldane sprig. As if one wasn't enough. I hope you're not two of a kind, your cousin and you?"

"I hardly know her," said Pauline. "Besides, I'm not a Haldane. I'm a Verity."

"Not here," said the blonde. "At St Austin's you'll be a Haldane no matter what your father's name might be."

Pauline steadied herself, fists pressed into the leather, shoulders thrust forward. "I am not a Haldane."

"Suit yourself," said the blonde and, pulling a face, drew her companion back against the seat, out of harm's way.

Pauline was not cowed by the girls' attitude. She had enough knowledge of school systems to realise that, at fifteen, she was, in their view, a mere child and not worthy of serious attention. She pursed her lips, clung on to the seat, and looked about her curiously. Eventually the bus nosed up a driveway between oaks and rhododendron bushes, and pulled up in front of a great grey-stone façade on which, thank heaven, there were lighted windows and an open door. Mr MacAdam played a rude fanfare on the bus's rubber horn and braked the Halley to a halt at a half circle of shallow stone steps that led to the school's main doorway.

"Out," said the blonde.

The brunette waited for Pauline on the gravel by the bus's passenger door, wreathed in smiles now. "This way, Pauline." Her voice had a warm and unctuous quality that had been absent until that moment. "Do mind the step. Mr MacAdam will see to your luggage."

The blonde girl had nipped off round the back of the bus. She reappeared, all brisk and proper, just as a small woman came from the lighted doorway at the top of the steps to greet them. Pauline heard the blonde say, "Awfully sorry for the delay, Miss Fergusson. Train was forty-seven minutes late. Pauline's here now, however, all present and correct."

The woman nodded. "Thank you, Bettina. You too, Rosemary. I'm very grateful for your assistance. You may pop off to the kitchen where I think you'll find a hot supper waiting. Oh, by the way, do you know what trains you're meeting tomorrow?"

"Yes, Miss Fergusson," said the prefects in unison, while from somewhere towards the front of the bus a male voice mocked them like an echo, "Yesss, Misss Fergussson."

"Trunk and baggage into the hall, Tom MacAdam, then you may put the bus away," Miss Fergusson called. "And try not to lose it this time."

To Pauline's astonishment Bettina and Rosemary paused to give her a pat on the shoulder before they went off along the driveway towards the rear of the house. Mr MacAdam, burdened by her trunk, trudged silently past and went upstairs into the hall and Pauline and the Head were, for a moment, left alone. The woman smiled and offered her hand which Pauline shook nervously.

"I'm Miss Fergusson, headmistress of St Austin's. You may call me Miss Fergusson or Headmistress. I prefer not to be called Gussie to my face, and not to be called the Dragon even behind my back. Are you scared, Pauline? Not of me – I don't mean that – of everything?"

"Yes, Miss Fergusson, a little."

"You've never been away from home before, have you?"

"No, Miss Fergusson."

"Well, you'll very soon adjust to us, as we will to you." She took Pauline's arm, gave it a squeeze, and escorted the girl up the steps and into the hall, talking all the while. "Think how dreadful it is for the poor wee mites of eleven and how much worse it used to be when they were dumped on the doorstep, trembling like leaves, at the age of eight or nine."

The hallway was deep and angular. Panelled in oak, its doors and diagonally-set staircases had the heavy, uncarved simplicity of a hunting lodge. The brochure's potted history had told Pauline that the main building had once been the residence of the Harvey family until, in the 1870s, a fall in fortunes had caused them to sacrifice the house to the St Austin School Company, whose sons and grandsons, as well as her grandfather, still owned and governed the place. A log fire, blazing in the hearth, formed an island of warmth. It glowed on chintz-covered sofas, deep armchairs and on a faded Indian carpet that defined the limits of comfort. A shaggy black dog, big as a bear, lay fast asleep before the fire, his coat steaming slightly.

"Otto," Miss Fergusson explained. "A Newfoundland. Quite rare, I believe. He's not mine, I hasten to add. I'm not much of a one for dogs. He belonged to my predecessor, Miss Aitken. She hadn't the heart to take him to live in a flat in Edinburgh when she retired. He's been here longer than I have. In fact longer than most of my staff. You needn't be afraid of him in spite of his size, but I wouldn't let him lick your face, if I were you. He does tend to slobber, rather. Do you have pets at home, Pauline?"

"Yes, Miss Fergusson. Two Persian cats."

"Ah, now cats are different," the woman said. "You'll miss them, I expect."

"Yes, Miss Fergusson," said Pauline.

"Now, dear, if you go through that little corridor there beneath the staircase you'll find a cloakroom and a lavatory. You may make yourself comfortable and then come back here. As you're almost the first of our arrivals I've asked cook to make us a special hot-pot which we'll eat here by the fire. I expect you're famished?"

"Yes, Miss Fergusson."

A single tiny gaslight illuminated the corridor. Pauline found a cloakroom and lavatory behind a door marked Staff Only. She used it with trepidation, washed face and hands, combed her hair then followed an appetising aroma of cooked food back into the main hall.

Pauline was puzzled by the headmistress's informality. She had expected an Olympian figure, remote and austere. Janis Fergusson seemed to be none of these things. She could not have been much more than forty years old and emanated a fizzy sort of energy. She had small, pointed features and her hair, cut remarkably short, was licked into wings above her ears so that her face seemed to fly eagerly out at you. Her colouring was sandy and a bridge of freckles crossed her nose and spilled on to her cheeks as if she found enough time in her busy schedule to spend quite lengthy periods out of doors. She wore a loose knitted sports coat in cashmere, with a knitted sash about her middle, and a pleated grey skirt over what looked to Pauline like Cossack boots of soft scarlet leather. No beads, bangles or brooches adorned her person except for a gentleman's wristlet watch of oxidised steel on an old black leather strap.

A card table had mysteriously appeared in front of the fire, the legs carefully placed over the slumbering dog. Two chairs had been placed on either side of it and two bowls of soup steamed on cork mats between steel cutlery. In the hearth was a dumpy iron pot and a covered ashet. As if sensing Pauline's 'spookiness' Miss Fergusson laughed. "No," she said. "We're not being served by ghosts. It's just that school has been closed for eight weeks and it always takes a little time to work up steam again. The domestics will be back in force tomorrow and the girls will begin arriving tomorrow afternoon and, in a deluge, the day after. This may be our one and only chance for a little quiet conversation, Pauline, and I do like to get to know all my girls personally, if I possibly can. Sit."

Pauline sat.

"Do you wish me to say Grace?" the woman asked.

"I . . . I . . ."

"We do in hall, before breakfast." Miss Fergusson passed a basket of soft brown breadrolls. "Otherwise, it's up to you. Eat."

Pauline tucked a napkin into a button of her blouse and

hungrily set to work on the soup, a thick and delicious mutton broth.

"Tomorrow at ten o'clock, you'll report to Miss Gaylord, my deputy. She will present you with a series of written and oral tests. Oh, nothing for you to worry about, I'm sure. Have you done Latin?"

"Just for one year."

"No Greek?"

"No, Miss Fergusson."

"I'll send one of the prefects to fetch you and show you the lie of the land. Or, perhaps, if she's in the mood and does not find your 'aura' hostile, Colleen O'Neal will do the honours. Colleen is our Irish pupil. She arrived yesterday. I'm not absolutely certain how she travelled." Miss Fergusson leaned over the empty soup bowl and confided, "On the wings of swans, perhaps."

"I'm sorry?"

Still speaking in muted tones, Miss Fergusson explained, "Now, you mustn't let Colleen worry you. She's rather a strange girl but harmless. Some of the girls avoid her like a plague. Among other things she has the habit of playing the harp at odd hours and the even more disconcerting habit of breaking into song whenever she feels the impulse. She believes she is not of the world and, candidly, some of my staff members would thoroughly agree with her."

Pauline looked round. "Is she here, now?"

"No, I thought it best if I put her in the San. I've accommodated you in our one and only guest bedroom, here in the main building, where there's some company about. Tomorrow you'll be moved into your house."

"Are there no other new girls, Miss Fergusson?"

"Of course, thirteen of them. But they are all much younger than you and none of them will arrive before tomorrow. We have no Junior School at St Austin's now. I'm glad of it, really. I must confess that I do not approve of children being separated from their parents much before the age of eleven. Do you?"

"I don't know, Miss Fergusson. I never really thought about it."

"Your mother and your aunt came early, if I recall. Have they not foisted an opinion upon you?"

Pauline felt blood rush to her cheeks and she was glad of a diversion below the table as the huge, hairy dog, snorting, rolled over and almost upended her chair.

"Be still, Otto," said Miss Fergusson. "Well, Pauline, have they?"

"My aunt liked it here."

"And your mother?"

"No, I don't think she was happy at school." Pauline looked directly across the table. "Miss Fergusson, my mother does not live with us. My father and she are separated and will shortly be divorced."

"Yes," Miss Fergusson said. "Yes, dear, I know. I wanted you to tell me, however. And it was brave of you to do so. It's not your fault and you have no reason to be ashamed of your circumstances. Do you understand what I'm saying, Pauline?"

"It's not a dark secret?"

"No, it's not. So don't make it into one."

"I understand," Pauline said. "Did you attend St Austin's as a girl, Miss Fergusson?"

"Five years. I remember your grandfather very well. He used to attend prize-givings."

"I'm not really a Haldane, Miss Fergusson," Pauline said.

The woman smiled and rose. "Of course you're not. You're Pauline Verity, an individual in your own right. You shouldn't have to carry family names about with you like albatrosses. That's another snobbish foible of which I do not quite approve." She stooped and, using her napkin as a glove, lifted the tubby pot to the table, and then the ashet. "Hot-pot?"

"Yes, please," said Pauline.

The room was very small but, to Pauline's relief, it was on the first floor and not far from the main staircase, so that she did not feel isolated. When she padded along to the lavatory in her brand-new dressing gown and slippers, she could see firelight from the hall prettily reflected on the memorial boards that graced the landing. It gave her, already, a feeling of belonging, though she would be glad to have company, glad too to have her tests over and to be settled once and for all.

A hot water bottle had been put into the bed and the sheets turned down for her. Everything smelled clean, though the linen, she noticed, was patched and the rug on the floor had a hole in it. There was a little bedside table lamp and a single bow window which looked out over the roof of the kitchens to dark wooded slopes and a hillside that seemed to fall almost vertically out of a clear starry sky. On her return from the lavatory, Pauline lingered by the window and gazed out at a scene without a single light visible upon it. She could not recall ever having seen such a thing before. The vastness of the sky and the looming landscape made her shiver and hop quickly into the warm bed. She left the bedside lamp on for a moment, turned on to her back and put her arms behind her head.

It was now about half past ten o'clock. London's streets would be lively with traffic. In theatres along the Strand and Shaftesbury Avenue last acts would be underway. She wondered where Daddy was and what he was doing. And if Mrs Dobbs had given Pots and Dots a special supper. And if they missed her. It was all very strange. She could hardly believe that fifteen or sixteen hours ago she'd been eating breakfast at home. Weymouth Street already seemed like another world, far away in space and time. Her eyelids drooped. She yawned and rolled on to her elbow to switch out the lamp. Then she froze.

Somebody was turning the door handle.

Pauline shot up, just as a voice said, "Are you there, Pauline Verity, are you there?"

"Who is it?"

Taking the question as invitation a strikingly beautiful girl of about Pauline's age pushed open the door and entered. She was barefoot and bare-legged and wore only an immodest nightdress of lawn so fine that it was almost transparent. Long black wavy hair cascaded over her shoulders. She had jet black eyes and severe brows, a high-bridged nose and a small mouth with a curved upper lip that made her seem almost regal. In the crook of her arm, cradled like a baby, she carried a little harp of plain, thumb-polished wood.

Closing the door with a graceful sweep of her foot, she said, "I shall play for you."

"No, I really don't think so," Pauline said. "How do you know my name?"

"Ahhh," the girl said, breathily. "Ahhh."

Pauline was not used to having strangers in her bedroom. She sat bolt upright and snatched the sheet to her throat, covering her bosom.

"Sure and I will sing you a lullaby."

"I don't want to be sung to, thank you," Pauline said. "Are you Colleen O'Neal, by any chance? I thought you were in the sanatorium."

"A cold place. Smells of death." The girl seated herself upon the foot of the bed, slung the harp into her lap and struck from it a swift silvery chord. "Stella told us you were comin'. I'm a Dublin Protestant myself. We have cottages in Connemara too. I sleep on the boat, myself. If you'll not be wishin' a lullaby, I shall sing 'Poor Johnny's Dead'."

"What did my cousin tell you?"

"Ahhh, ahhh!"

"Has Stella been spreading stories about me?"

"My gran'mother once sang for Oscar Wilde."

"I don't care if your grandmother takes tea with Bernard Shaw," said Pauline, "I do not want to be serenaded at this hour of the night."

The girl's head lolled on to her shoulder. She slanted her eyes so that they looked upward into a corner of the room and with a limp sweeping motion of her wrist she brushed back a wisp of wavy black hair from her brow. "He came and stood beneath my window once, and sang as if his heart would break, and the moonlight on his tragic face—"

"Who?" Pauline said. "Oscar Wilde?"

"No, Michael O'Hara from Galway, my own true love."

"Buzz off," said Pauline scornfully.

She could smell affectation a half mile off and Colleen O'Neal was soaked in it. She was not so anxious to make new friends that she would seize on the first girl to come along, particularly a show-off like this one who was also, perhaps, a chum of Stella Jackson's.

Colleen slipped from the bed. Everything she did, every

movement and gesture was a sort of performance. Insults and rejections were absorbed into it with a fey and languid self-regard that her musical accent and undoubted beauty could not disguise. There were those who would find her fascinating and charming. But Pauline was not taken in.

Cradling the harp to her breast, the Irish girl regarded Pauline slyly. "She told you about me, did she not now? I saw you breakin' bread with her while I was consigned to sup alone in the San."

"If you mean Miss Fergusson, yes, I did have supper with her downstairs in the hall. And I thought she was very nice."

"Ay, that's her way. It's not enough for that owd sow to rule with a rod of iron. She wants you to adore her. She tries it on with all the girls, the teachers too. She's got the half of them dazzled into thinkin' she's a saint," said Colleen O'Neal. "She's no saint, that one. She has this school grasped in her fist and she never lets it slack. Watch out for her, that's all I'm sayin' to you. Do not be taken in."

"Thank you for your advice," Pauline said, drily.

"Give me an orange for it."

"I don't have an orange."

"An apple then."

"Sorry."

She contemplated Pauline for a split second longer, the small, curved upper lip lifted in what might have been a sneer, and then she was gone, the door closing behind her with a soft little snap.

"Well! Well!" said Pauline aloud. Stretching, she quickly switched off the lamp before some other unwelcome apparition could drift in from the San to threaten her rest with an oboe or a solo on the bass trombone.

# Five

*I*f breakfast was anything to go by, St Austin's girls were not liable to die of starvation. Porridge, a grilled haddock and a profusion of moist and leathery toast made palatable with marmalade, set Pauline up for the rigours of examination.

There were eight other people in the dining hall, four pupils and four mistresses, all keeping themselves to themselves in separate divisions. The staff occupied a table raised on a low platform at the far end of the room. To Pauline's disappointment there was no sign of Miss Fergusson.

Clad in a long jade-green velvet gown that was entirely unsuitable for scuffing about in, Colleen was pointedly aloof and did not even bid Pauline a good morning. It was left to Rosemary, the chubby prefect, to show the new girl the ropes. Now that she was away from her blonde chum Rosemary was quite friendly and exceedingly thorough. She gave Pauline the tour-de-luxe, pointing out the halls and filling in local colour in the form of anecdotes. Finally she made sure that Pauline had sharp pencils, a pen of her own and a decent ruler, and that her uniform was all straight and her hair neat, before she delivered her to the deputy headmistress for testing.

Miss Gaylord was not as sprightly as her name suggested. She was short and squat and, when she sat at her desk, her rather stumpy legs did not quite reach the floor. A string of tiny curls, dyed black, added to her calf-like appearance. She wore a long hand-crocheted jumper, so stretched that the sleeves were for ever drooping over her broad hands and had to be shoved up with great frequency. From a schoolgirl's distorted perspective, Miss Gaylord was definitely an antique. She was also a martinet who did not encourage familiarity.

She put her initial questions to Pauline curtly and without preamble. The written tests were short and comparatively easy. Four papers of ten questions, to be completed in thirty minutes each paper. Pauline coped well enough, even with the algebraic equations, and concentrated on making her handwriting legible. The oral examinations were more difficult, particularly French conversation. Miss Gaylord was no Mam'selle. Her grammar might be nonpareil but her accent – in Pauline's opinion – was execrable and Pauline, cowed by lack of comprehension, felt that she had fared badly. Fortunately she was not tested in Latin for by eleven o'clock she was distracted by the activity outside.

Set on a gable, the ground-floor room had two wide bow windows through which Pauline glimpsed the arrivals and departures of the big school bus, in addition to several motorcars. She was further disturbed by shrieks and yells, by laughter and clatter in the corridors and, at the last, by a sound that resembled a one-legged giant dragging himself upstairs.

Miss Gaylord seemed impervious to the racket, to glimpses of girls dashing past on the gravel, even to one small face that dared to scowl in at the window and then, uttering a cry of dismay, vanished again.

While Pauline completed one test paper, Miss Gaylord marked its predecessor. And at last, at ten minutes to one o'clock, it was over.

Miss Gaylord gave no clue as to how she had fared. The deputy continued to make little chicken-scratches into a notebook with a fountain pen and, without even looking up, said, in her dry Scottish brogue, "You may go now, Miss Verity. Wash before luncheon, if you please. Report to me here punctually at half past two. I will put you into a house and allocate you a form at that time."

It was on the tip of Pauline's tongue to enquire if ninety minutes was sufficient to reach such momentous decisions but she prudently kept her mouth shut.

She dropped a somewhat stagey curtsey, muttered, "Yes, Miss Gaylord," and let herself out into the corridor to be swept willy-nilly into the bedlam of first arrivals.

When Pauline entered the dining hall she noticed that Miss Fergusson was already ensconced at the raised table. She had surrounded herself not with her staff but with a batch of new arrivals, all of whom looked incredibly young. Form and house mistresses had spread themselves among the tables. The room was more than half full of girls, some in uniform, most in their own choice of dress. At the far end of the long, solemn room were two tables at which visiting parents were being served.

The noise was terrific. Gabble of voices was punctuated with the clack of plates, the clatter of cutlery. The waitresses were all young girls, some hardly older than Pauline; plain country lassies, she supposed, brought in from Pattullo and its surrounding farms. The excitement that Pauline had felt when she'd escaped Miss Gaylord's study vanished like a puff of smoke. She felt icy and isolated, more afraid than she'd done since she'd left Weymouth Street. Enquiring glances were directed at her. Whispered comments were exchanged between girls of about her own age. But no hand was raised to welcome her, nobody signalled her to come sit with them. She looked for Stella. She had vowed to herself that she would not suck up to her cousin but at that particular moment she would have accepted a kind word from the devil himself and seated herself by him without a qualm. She had no strong impression as to what Stella would look like now that she was no longer a child. She was dependent upon instinct to draw her to her cousin.

At a table under the window Colleen O'Neal was surrounded by five or six other girls. They did not chatter but conversed with murmurous, side-of-the-mouth maturity, as if they were already plotting mischief.

Pauline was still standing helplessly half way up one of the aisles when a handbell rang, rang again, and Miss Fergusson's voice cut sharply through the din. "Girls. Girls." Pause – the handbell – the voice: "Girls, be silent."

Miss Fergusson advanced to the edge of the dais. In her hand was a brass bell on a wooden handle with which she stroked the air expertly and loudly until a cloud of silence descended upon the hall and there was stillness, save for a few last minute movements of soup spoons and bowls. Pauline felt as tall, awkward and conspicuous as a giraffe but, even as Miss Fergusson began the first of several informal speeches of welcome to parents and new pupils, a hand plucked at Pauline's skirt. She glanced down, saw a bare brown arm downed with fair hair, and a frank brown face, ducked low.

"Here, sit here with us," the girl hissed.

Pauline slid thankfully on to the empty chair. She smiled thanks to her rescuer and, with spine as straight as a ramrod, looked expectantly towards the headmistress who, easy and charming, was delivering herself of a few witty platitudes at the expense of the parents present.

Though she laughed when the others laughed, smiled rigidly, and clapped enthusiastically when the speech was over, Pauline heard hardly a word of it. She was too conscious of the girls around her, three of them, who, she knew, were cautiously weighing her up too. As soon as Miss Fergusson had returned to her flock of little darlings at the head table, the babble started up again and waitresses re-emerged from behind the wooden screens that shut off sight of the kitchens.

"Soup, miss?"

"What sort is it, Anna?" said a tiny girl from her chair opposite Pauline.

"Leek and potato, miss."

"Four, please, Anna," said the weather-brown girl by Pauline's side, politely.

"Do we have a choice of menu?" Pauline tried to sound intelligent.

"Uh-huh." The third member of the trio, a pleasant-looking girl with bright blue eyes enlarged by horn-rimmed spectacles. "Take it – or leave it."

"At least you can leave it," said the tiny girl.

"Not that you ever do," said the brownie.

"Better than my brother's school," said the tiny girl. "There they stuff it down you whether you like it or not. You sit at table until the plate's clean, even if it takes a week. And they serve up some disgustin' muck too, so Bobby says. I'm Elfreda. What's your name?"

"Pauline." Unable to hide her desire for companionship she said, rather too gushingly, "Thanks so much for asking me to sit with you."

"Well, you did look a bit like a maypole standing there."

The brownie offered a broad hand with bitten fingernails. "I'm Gossamer Johnstone. Goss, for short. The little 'un's known as Elf, which is absolutely appropriate, though we hope to fatten her up this term."

"And I'm Elizabeth Frognall," said the girl with glasses. "No prizes for guessing my moniker."

"Frog, of course," said Goss Johnstone.

"Don't your parents disapprove of that nickname?" Pauline asked.

"They pretend to hate it," Frog said, grinning. "But they haven't a leg to stand on. Papa constantly refers to me as his 'wee tadpole', so what can he expect?"

All three were Scottish but Pauline could not yet separate the regional accents.

"Are you from London?" Frog asked, as the waitress brought four bowls of soup on a tray and distributed them.

Pauline said that she was and, in the course of breaking bread and consuming soup, explained a little of her background and the circumstances that had brought her to St Austin's. Tactfully she did not mention that she was a Haldane and related to Stella Jackson. She had already received an impression that kinship to Stella implied allegiances that she did not yet understand.

"Hard cheese, that," said Goss. "Your father having to cut off to Durban. I expect your mother won't be too pleased, or is she going with him?"

Bearing in mind Miss Fergusson's advice, Pauline came straight out with it. "My mother and father are separated."

Elf's face fell. She reached swiftly across the table and patted Pauline's hand in spontaneous sympathy. "Oh, I am sorry. It must be terrible for you."

"Mummy left a long time ago," said Pauline. "I'm quite used to it, really."

"Do you see much of her?" said Goss, who could be direct without being offensive.

"Not much. I think she's going to marry again."

"To somebody you know?" said Frog.

"No, nobody. Some stockbroker."

"Isn't it odd," said Elf, "having a mother who's yours but not yours, if you see what I mean?"

Pauline was brought up short by the question. "I suppose it is," she said, frowning. "I never thought of it like that before."

"Well," said Elf, matter-of-factly, "at least when my father died I knew he was gone for good. And he was still sort of mine, if you see what I mean."

"Oh, how long since—?"

"Four years. In the war. At the Marne. I still miss him terribly." Elf mopped away at the dregs of her soup with a pinch of bread and popped it into her mouth.

"All right, ladies, let's not get too morbid first day back," said Goss, busily stacking the bowls. "What form will you be in? Has the Gaiety Girl told you yet?"

"After lunch," said Pauline.

"If it's our form, it might be our house," Frog said. "Three cheers for good old Teal. There's a bed in our dorm. Wouldn't mind taking in a foreigner. Would you, girls?"

"Could put up with it, I guess," said Goss Johnstone, grinning. "Just pray that they don't stick you in with Stella Jackson's crowd."

Pauline opened her mouth to ask what was wrong with Stella Jackson, thought better of it and said, "I think I should warn you that Stella Jackson's my cousin."

"Oh-oh!" Goss said. "Small foot in big cowpat."

"So you're the famous cousin Stella was rattling on about?" Frog said. "We expected something on a broomstick with a wart on her nose, actually."

"Frog, really!" Elf made a prissy face and shook her head.

Pauline said, "I've only met Stella once in my life and, if it's any consolation, I couldn't stand the sight of her. She may be a relative but she certainly isn't a friend."

"Really?" said Elf.

"Really," Pauline answered.

"Stella may have other ideas about that," Goss said.

Pauline sensed in the broad-shouldered girl a certain suspicion, a faint cooling. She said, "Tell me, is the Irish girl one of Stella's 'crowd'?"

"Oh, yes, I might have known our lovely Colleen would be on to you like a leech. When did you meet her? Last night?" said Frog.

"She barged into my bedroom offering to sing to me," said Pauline. "Not offering – insisting."

"What did you do?" said Elf.

"Told her to Buzz Off."

Goss laughed. It was a soft, throaty sound, jolly without being exhibitionistic. "Good for you, old son."

"What did she do?" asked Elf.

"Performed a sort of dying swan impersonation and then swept out," said Pauline. "Is she always like that?"

"Worse," said Frog. "She's a pain in the knickers, frankly, and madly passionate about your cousin."

Pauline blinked. "What?"

Goss said, "She's your cousin's permanent 'crush'. There are others too, of course, dozens of them. A whole army of love-lorn souls who would just die for a kind word from Stella Jackson. If you take my advice you'll avoid all of them."

"They are very strange," said Frog.

"Of course," Goss Johnstone said, carefully, "we don't want to prejudice you, Pauline. Perhaps you'll like them."

"I'm not a spy for Stella, you know," Pauline heard herself say.

Elf chirped an ineffectual protest. Elizabeth Frognall was embarrassed and looked away towards the kitchen screens in the hope of interruption by a waitress. But Goss Johnstone was not a lawyer's daughter for nothing.

She shrugged. "Unfair, I know, but I'm afraid you may have to prove yourself, Pauline."

"How do I do that?" asked Pauline.

"Time will tell," said Goss, not at all mysteriously.

Pauline nodded towards the table by the window. "Is that Stella's crowd over there?"

"Yes, most of the inner clique," said Elf.

"Where's Stella?"

"She won't arrive until the last possible moment. Her father travels with her as a rule," Frog explained. "Your uncle."

"He puts up at one of the posh hotels, Gleneagles or the Hydro, and wheedles Gussie's permission to take four or five of Stella's chums out for a slap-up before he departs in his motorcar in a cloud of dust," Goss Johnstone said. "Perhaps you'll be invited, Pauline."

"I don't really know him from Adam. Why should I be invited?"

"Blood's thicker than water," Goss said.

"Talking of water," Elf put in, "here comes the gravy jug."

"Good," said Pauline. "I'm starved."

Empty soup bowls were exchanged for plates of slightly overdone roast beef, accompanied by potatoes, carrots and peas.

Elf lifted her knife and fork. "How fast can you eat roast beef?"

"Very fast," said Pauline.

"Bet I finish first," said Elf.

"Bet you don't," said Pauline.


The Head and her deputy met in the latter's study at twenty minutes to two o'clock. Miss Janis Fergusson had no liking at all for Phoebe Gaylord, though she respected, to a degree, her efficiency. There was no love for education, for girls or for St Austin's left in Phoebe Gaylord. She functioned like a piece of clockwork, stiffly and automatically. Her aims and objectives were not those of the twentieth century and certainly not those that Miss Fergusson had set for herself and her school.

Miss Gaylord was one of the ancient guardians of childish innocence, a moralist whose lack of experience of the world had so narrowed her perspectives that she could not see that the very nature of innocence had changed. She had been cloistered too long in boarding schools. Twenty-six years out of her thirty-four in the profession had been spent here in the hills above Pattullo, watching – without curiosity – the young girls come and go. Even the war, that Great Upheaval, had almost if not quite escaped her attention. She had been in cahoots with the previous Head, Miss Aitken, and they had made a formidable pairing, so girdled about with righteousness that even the Harveys had not been able to stand up to them at governors' meetings and foist much-needed change upon the school's attitudes and curriculum.

Being a fair-minded rationalist, however, Janis Fergusson

had to admit that it was only the presence of Phoebe Gaylord that calmed and controlled her desire for sweeping and radical changes and kept intact the structure of rule and tradition that might easily have collapsed under her own enthusiastic onslaught on the bastions of privilege and cultivated ignorance. She would die before she would admit it but she had learned a lot from Phoebe Gaylord.

China teacups with painted roses, a delicate blend of teas infusing in the pot, slices of lemon in a painted dish, a 'loaf' of sugar from which fragments were broken with the back of a spoon so daintily, so delicately that the action reminded Janis Fergusson of certain surgical procedures upon the iris of the eye. She detested the formal ritual that accompanied the drinking of tea. It had been like this in 'the old days', under Miss Aitken, when the Head, her deputy and other august old warhorses of the teaching staff would closet themselves away and make everyone – parents as well as pupils – await their pleasure. There was a kind of power in the ability to be discourteous without fear of criticism, to be unpunctual without shame.

"No tea for me, thank you, Miss Gaylord," Janis said. "I can spare only five minutes and then I must be off to show the new girls and their parents the gymnasium."

Miss Gaylord put down the teapot.

Miss Fergusson said, "Please, by all means enjoy your refreshment while we talk."

"I'll wait." Miss Gaylord pushed the little tea-trolley away from the side of her desk to make way for a brown card folder. "Do you wish to see Pauline Verity's test papers?"

"No, I'll accept your assessment."

Miss Gaylord's faded gaze rested on the document in the folder on the desk. She did not challenge the Head, even with a glance. "Intelligent child. Articulate and well-informed. Rather too precocious, perhaps, in her reading. Her Latin is very weak, but that will hardly matter, I suppose," Miss Gaylord went on.

"Why will it not?"

"She's Donald Haldane's granddaughter."

"Yes, I know that, Miss Gaylord," said Miss Fergusson, frowning. "What difference does that make?"

"The Haldane girls – the two I've known – have never been destined to be scholars."

"Scholars are made not born," said Janis Fergusson.

"She will, I expect, marry well enough without Pindar or Horace to support her."

"What if the girl does not wish to marry? What if she wishes to embark upon a career, to earn her own living and make her own way in the world?" Janis Fergusson consulted her wrist-watch, felt the anxious pressure of a woman who has too much to do and not enough time to do it. She pulled out a chair, seated herself upon it and held out an open hand. "Let me see her papers, please."

Marking was strict, results higher than average. Whatever its social failings, Glades Road School had provided Pauline Verity with something more than a rudimentary education. She scanned Miss Gaylord's commentary on the oral portion of the examination – an upright, unhurried hand, unlike her own scribble – and returned the card folder to the older woman.

"Miss Milligan's form is right for Pauline I think," she said.

"Really? I would have placed her with Miss Shadbrook. She is, after all, younger than her cousin."

"Stella lacks application. Let's see if Pauline can be extended. I have a feeling that she might rise best to a challenge."

"And her Latin?"

"Extra tuition, extra prep. She doesn't appear to be musical, certainly not an instrumentalist, so she will have a little time to spare."

"And the house?" Miss Gaylord gave not the slightest hint that she was annoyed at being over-ridden. "Teal?"

"Yes, Teal. Admirable."

"With her cousin?"

"No, not with her cousin."

"There's room, Miss Fergusson."

"Be that as it may, put Pauline in with Johnstone and Edgar."

"May I ask why?"

It was out now. Phoebe Gaylord, like several of the staff,

was drawn to Stella Jackson and favoured her. They were flattered by her attentiveness, taken in by what they regarded as 'leadership quality'. Janis Fergusson was not deceived. She saw Stella Jackson more for what she was, a schemer, a manipulator, rather sly and cunning. The only 'steadiness' in her character was a desire to have her own way in all things and the cleverness, often, to get it.

It was now three minutes to two o'clock. Parents would be loitering in the garden awaiting her. The new girls would be massing nervously in the hall to be allocated houses and rooms, to meet the mistresses who would dominate their school years and, possibly, influence the rest of their lives.

Miss Gaylord awaited an answer.

Janis Fergusson hedged. "Putting her in the same house is quite enough. I would prefer the girl to make her own friends and not rely on her cousin. For all we know, Stella may not wish to be burdened with the responsibility."

Miss Gaylord gave a quick nod, as if to say that she had expected no more candour than she had been granted.

"Teal House, Room No. 11?" said the deputy, uncapping her fountain pen and making a note upon the top of Pauline's scant file. "Fourth Form, under Miss Milligan."

"That's it," said Janis Fergusson, and made for the door just as a timid knock sounded upon it.

Pauline Verity stood nervously in the corridor, hands clasped together as if in prayer. She had managed, already, to anoint her dress with gravy and – Miss Fergusson peered critically at the budding bosom – with chocolate mould pudding too. It seemed that young Miss Verity had already been talked into an eating contest with Elfreda Edgar who was, without doubt, the uncrowned champion of that particularly messy sport. Last night, in isolation, the London girl had seemed quite mature for her age. Now, though, she was nothing but a child, a typically tense, eager, ingenuous, untidy schoolgirl, almost indistinguishable from all the others.

"Miss Fergusson! Oh! Oh, I'm sorry! I thought – Miss Gaylord said . . ." Pauline stammered.

"Did you enjoy your lunch, Pauline?"

"Yes, Miss Fergusson. It was lovely."

"Is that why you're saving some for later?"

"What?"

Miss Fergusson pointed. Pauline tucked in her chin and looked down her nose at her bosom. "Oh, no!"

"Spit, a hanky and elbow-grease," the headmistress advised, "then go straight in."

"Yes, Miss Fergusson."

Three girls were loitering in the corridor not far away, trying to appear nonchalant, which was something that young girls could somehow never manage to do. Janis Fergusson recognised them and, though she was late on her schedule, paused long enough to enquire, "Are you waiting for the new girl?"

"Yes, Miss Fergusson," Goss Johnstone answered.

"Would you like to have her in your room, Gossamer?"

"Wouldn't mind, Miss Fergusson."

Janis Fergusson resisted the temptation to administer a reassuring wink. For some reason she felt confirmed in her opinion that little Pauline Verity would be safer billeted with Johnstone, Elfreda and the Frog than with the crowd that hung on Stella Jackson's every word, like maids round a queen.

"Well, you never know your luck, girls," Miss Fergusson said and, peering at her watch again, hurried off to find the parents and show them quickly round the grounds before, with envy, she watched them drive off in their powerful motorcars.

Although she had been in charge of St Austin's for a mere thirty months Janis Fergusson's influence had already permeated deep into the school's everyday life. The piecemeal removal of fifteen or twenty irksome minor rules had slackened the grip of the Victorian regime without, it seemed, bringing down the pillars of the Temple and laying discipline to ruin. Gone was the Lavatory Book, that demeaning record of daily bowel movements which demonstrated on the part of the mistress who had originally inaugurated it a morbid interest in 'production' and self-control which, in Janis Fergusson's opinion, went beyond decency let alone reason. Gone too were long hauls up and down the staircases in the house by Tom MacAdam and his forty-year-old lad. Four healthy girls working as a team could manage four trunks, one at a time, more efficiently than two men. The value of labour and self-help was thus inculcated and MacAdam was left free to drive the bus to and from the railway station.

Gone was the long formal harangue that filled the hours between tea and bedtime on Arrival Day, with every girl, young and older, expected to turn up in Best School Dress and sit still and silent while staff members read a role of achievements in their own departments and the housemistresses – one after another, ye gods! – repeated the endless rules that governed communal living. Gone too were the standard dressing gowns that Messrs Williams & Gloag, Outfitters, had supplied in branches from Wick to Wicklow, heavy brown sackcloth things with cords like hangman's rope and no more warmth in them than tissue paper. Girls were now permitted a touch of individuality – here and there and tread with care – and Miss Fergusson's belief that none of them were silly enough to turn up with slinky silk things slit to the thigh had been so far proved correct.

"Jolly, what!" Frog emerged from her partitioned cubicle and executed a pirouette that twirled the skirts of the floral-patterned dressing gown around her like a bell. With a towel bound round her newly-washed hair and heavy socks protruding from under a flannel nightdress, Goss turned from the room's washbasin into whose drain, with the aid of a crochet hook, she had been poking away telltale hairs, to be rid of the evidence of her illicit shampoo.

"What on earth is that?" she demanded, shielding her eyes.

"Birthday gift," said Frog. "From Mum. Don't you like it? I like it. It's jolly."

"It's alarming, that's what it is," said Elfreda. "Miss Milligan will never let you keep it."

"*Fait accompli*." Frog admired herself in the thin strip of fly-blown mirror to the left of the basin. "Anyway, it obeys all the rules. It's modest, has pockets, and it's very becoming."

"Hoh-hoh," said Goss. "What's it becoming, that's the question." She came closer, rubbed an enquiring finger on the gown's broad lapel. "Quilted, indeed! Very posh."

"It's big enough," said Elf. "We can all crawl inside it and have midnight feasts when the wind blows cold."

"What do you think, Pauline?" Frog asked.

Until a half hour ago Pauline had been on the same plane of exuberance as her room-mates. She had been delighted to be allocated a bed in Room No. 11 in Teal House and, keen to prove her allegiance to the three friends, had thrown herself into lugging trunks and unpacking, hooting with laughter like the rest of them. There had been so much to do, so much to learn, so many things to see, and, in spite of Goss's warning, she had felt not in the least left out of things.

Tea had been followed by a carefully-planned Impromptu Concert in the Harvey Assembly Hall, with piano pieces and solos and a violin duet by two prefects and finally a rowdy community sing-song which ended with a hymn and a lusty rendering of the school song. Tomorrow would be time enough for official introductions to staff members, the establishment of pecking orders, the laying down of inflexible laws governing behaviour and a listing of punishments for dis-obedience; a dreary hour and a half of it, first thing, followed by House Meetings, room inspections and then compulsory games. Classes would begin in earnest on Wednesday, and the Autumn Term would be off and running.

In the last half hour, however, Pauline had begun to feel strange and to regard the girls with whom she would share this four-bed dormitory as strangers which, in fact, they still were. She wished that she could return from the day's novelties and adventures to her own room in her own home, to tell Mrs Dobbs and Daddy all the tales.

The peculiar smells of polished linoleum, of other folks' clothing, of scented soap and the sickly-sweet effluvia that came from beneath the wash-basin added to her melancholy. She had friendly faces about her, no doubt of that, but what she longed for was a familiar face, an old friend not a new one: Daddy, even Mummy, to check for a moment the spiral of time passing and tuck her in and kiss her and let her imagine that she was still a child, too young to have to prove herself.

Pauline seated herself disconsolately on the side of the bed while Frog paraded her new dressing gown.

"Pauline?"

"It's . . . it's very nice."

"Are you all right?"

"Yes, I'm fine."

Goss appeared. She was rubbing away at her towelled head and in the turban seemed even taller and more majestic.

"Feeling a trifle bleak, are we?" she asked.

"'Fraid so, yes."

"You'll get used to it," Goss said.

She seated herself upon the side of the bed and patted Pauline's shoulder. "Miss Milligan will be along soon. She's all right, is old Milly. She won't mind at all if you have a bit of a snivel on her shoulder."

"I usually do," Elf said. "In fact, I can't think what's wrong with me this year. I'm actually fairly glad to be back."

In night attire Elfreda Edgar seemed incredibly frail. Her arms, though liberally downed with dark hair, were thin as pipestems and her sharp-pointed face, in the wan light from the electric globe, appeared at once childlike and wizened. She had a strange bony stoop to her shoulders and when she seated herself upon the bed she seemed to make no impression at all upon the quilt. Frog leaned upon the bedrail, the new dressing-gown forgotten. Without her spectacles she looked much, much younger, with the defenceless, slightly startled manner of all shortsighted folk.

"Can we get you something?" Frog offered.

"I've a chocolate bar, if you'd like that," said Elf.

"I think I might even be able to unearth a slightly squashed banana," said Goss Johnstone.

"I'm – I'm not hungry."

"Oh, dear!" said Frog. "Dear, dear, dear!"

"I—" Pauline began to cry. "—I want my Daddy."

In another room, with other girls, she might have been mocked for such sentiment, told to stop being a baby, to shape up to the inevitable. But the girls in Room No. 11 had fashioned their own code of behaviour and it did not include bullying.

It was both shaming, and at the same time a relief, to let the sudden tears flow. She tried not to lean into Goss

Johnstone, to seek a contact, a warmth that the girl might not wish to share.

"I'm no good at this." Goss patted Pauline again. "Froggy's better. Here, Frog, shift in and lend us your bosom for a couple of minutes. I'll be back in a jiff."

With a final vigorous scrub at the towel, Goss stripped it off and tossed it expertly out of sight under a bed. She tugged up the hood of her long brown dressing-gown and, still wearing her gamekeeper's stockings, whisked away out of the dormitory and left Elf and young Miss Frognall to act as comforters.

"I'm sorry, I'm sorry. I don't know what's come over me," Pauline sobbed. "I just – I can't help it. I want my Daddy so badly."

"It's not us, is it?" Frog said.

"No, oh no," said Pauline, shocked by the suggestion that she might have insulted her room-mates. "It's – it's—"

"You'll have me off in a minute," Elf said, sniffing.

"Don't you start," said Frog. "When you start there's no stopping you."

Even as she clung to Frog, sobbing, Pauline realised how soft and woolly and comforting the alien accents sounded, lacking the high, edgy ring of London voices.

Three or four minutes passed, then the door opened and Goss hurried in. In robe and hood, like an engraving of Retribution, she stretched out her hand. "Come on."

"What?" said Pauline.

"Come on, come on. Quickly."

"Where?"

"Trust me."

It was a relief to be moving, to have this unexpected event intrude upon her hollowness. She took Goss's hand and was led out of Room No. 11 and along the corridor. She could hear muttered conversations from other dormitories, peals of laughter, the torrential flush of a lavatory from the water closets at the corridor's nether end. Two dim unshaded bulbs marked the west staircases, up and down, but the little half-landing between the floors was dark, made darker too by an enormous castor-oil plant flourishing in an emerald pot.

"Where are you taking me?"

"Surprise." Goss pushed Pauline ahead of her up the narrow staircase, and said again, "Trust me."

Sliver of light; a door opening; Miss Milligan, Teal House's resident mistress, willowy and youthful in an evening dress of pink chiffon studded with tiny crystal beads; a small comfortable study cum living-room; bookcases, more potted plants, a fire in the grate, a Turkey carpet, two armchairs and a miniature divan.

"This way, Pauline." Miss Milligan beckoned and pointed. "There, on the table by the window. Be quick."

It was an upright telephone, with an earphone shaped like a large black harebell and the mouthpiece on a stalk. The earphone lay on the table on a coiled cord, separated from the horned springs. Out of it came peculiar sounds, indistinct yet vaguely familiar.

Pauline glanced round. Miss Milligan smiled and nodded encouragingly. "Take it up, girl. It's for you."

Pauline lifted the earphone, stepped close to the table, stooped to the mouthpiece and said, "Daddy?"

"Sweetheart? Is that you? How are you?"

"I'm fine."

"How's everything?"

"Everything's fine, absolutely fine," Pauline said and to her complete surprise realised that she meant it.

Miss Milligan's evening dress was not worn for the benefit of the girls but, when her duty was done and responsibility for the security of the house handed over to the prefects, she was obliged – no hardship, really – to attend the headmistress's supper party in the dining hall. She had not been at all put out by Gossamer Johnstone's unusual request. The telephone, only one of four in the school, had been allocated to her because of an ailing mother who, as mothers will, needed an ear to bend and the consolation of having a loved one on call if required.

Miss Milligan was gratified at the pleasure that the brief telephone call gave to the new girl from London, though she made it very clear that she had no intention of turning her rooms into a public box and that other homesick waifs and strays would have to be comforted by more orthodox methods. She did not even have the gall, under the circumstances, to chide Johnstone for washing her hair at the dormitory sink and not in the bathroom at the corridor's end. She would raise the subject at a more appropriate time, tomorrow.

Thoroughly settled by the unexpected conversation with her father, Pauline Verity had gone back to her room smiling, the brave face put away for use on another occasion.

Goss had pretended to be very offhand about it all, as if bearding old Milly – who was twenty-eight – in her den was something that she did often. It had been a shrewd manoeuvre, though, and perfectly fair, and Goss was a sound judge of character when it came to teachers.

The housemistress had made her rounds just before and just after the Lights Out bell had sent its echoes along the corridors and had spent only seconds in Room No. 11 but much longer with the youngsters in the rooms on the floor below, mopping up tears and listening to their stories. By a quarter to ten, however, all was quiet in the corridors of Teal House, and the noise from the dining hall in the main building did not impinge upon the sleepers or the sleepless in their iron cots but blew away like dust across Big Field to be lost in the birches of Pennant's Hill and amid the pines of Crow Wood.

Pauline was tucked up warm and private between the partitions. She could hear the other girls breathing and Elf snoring already. She had been so surprised, so pleased to hear Daddy, to have a word with Mrs Dobbs. Somehow the telephone call had connected St Austin's closely to London, the new life to the old, had reduced space and time to elements that she could cope with and not feel lost.

The bed was hard but comfortable. The pillow smelled clean and slightly soapy. She felt languorous and dreamy as if she had come through an illness and was on the mend now. She slipped the tip of her thumb into her mouth. She wondered if her mother had felt this way on her first night at school, wondered if she would have a half-brother or half-sister and, if the latter, if she would come to St Austin's too and where she herself would be then, in ten or twelve years time.

71

Pauline was almost asleep when the roar of a motorcar engine and the harsh growl of tyres on gravel startled her awake. Yellow beams of light roved across the dormitory ceiling, angled across the edge of the partition and flitted away. She lifted her head from the pillow.

From the far side of the partition, Goss drowsily answered Pauline's unspoken question.

"Stella."

"At this hour?"

"At any hour. Go to sleep."

Pauline nodded, let her head sink heavily down on to the pillow again and, thumb against her lips, was soon too deeply asleep to be disturbed by her cousin's welcome into the room next door.

# Six

"*B*last your eyes, Ronnie! Open this blessed door or I'll peach to the Kaiser."

Goss rattled the worn brass handle of the bathroom while the other occupants of No. 11, Pauline included, shivered in the corridor behind her, towels and sponge-bags clutched to their chests.

"You wouldn't dare, Goosey."

"Wouldn't I? Just try me."

"Use next door."

"Next door is full." Goss pounded on the varnished oak panel with fist and knee. "Anyway, I'm damned if I'm sharing with kids. Open up."

The snap of a bolt, the door swung open an inch or two and a very thin, red-haired girl peered at the intruders.

"Lang-guage, lang-guage, Goosey! Most un-ladylike."

"Out of my way, Ronnie." Goss pushed forcefully past the thin girl, Rhona Somerville, and led her little band into the communal bathroom.

The bathroom was large and moist. Six sinks stood over wooden draining boards perched on a tiled floor. To the left were three footbaths, something Pauline had never seen before, and four doors behind which were baths. A large oblong window of thick corrugated glass let in brilliant morning light while two fanlights, both wide open, let out steam and smoke.

Cold water ablutions were a thing of the past, apparently. At this hour of the morning the boilers in the basements of both residential wings burbled and gurgled, chugging out hot water for the mandatory strip wash or morning bath. Since the day would include a Matron's examination, hygiene could not be ignored even by the laziest of pupils. Though modesty was one of the maidenly virtues extolled by school rules, heartily

73

endorsed by the girls' natural inclinations, a certain amount of showing off was inevitable in the early morning scurry.

Pauline, however, had not been prepared for the sight that met her eyes. The girls who had taken possession of the bathroom seemed to have no sense of propriety at all. They wore nothing but knickers or, in one case, only thin white cotton liners. Towels were draped about their necks and fastened, crosswise, over their breasts like native women in blurred photographs of Polynesia that Pauline had once stumbled on in one of Daddy's travel magazines. The display of flesh did not seem to bother them and they had just as much arrogance in that state as a normal girl would have in her best party frock. Not only that, none of them were washing. They had done with water and were lolling against the sinks' rims under the window – smoking cigarettes.

Involuntarily Pauline covered her eyes with her hand and felt blood rise to her cheeks until, almost instantly, they burned scarlet. She kept close to Goss as, in a huddle, the new arrivals advanced on the sinks.

The thin girl, Ronnie, shot the bolt on the door behind them.

"You've started early." Goss peeled down the collar of her bathing robe but carefully kept her body covered. "I can smell that muck half way along the corridor."

Elfreda and Frog, flanking the Goss, began to wash too, carefully and with much use of the cloths from their bags. Pauline had a sudden horror of exposing any part of herself. She ran water into the basin, opened her soap box and began an ineffectual dabbing at neck and ears, bent over, her tummy against the sink's rim. Acrid smoke floated across her vision and made her cough.

And then a voice said, "Aren't you even going to say hello, Pauline Verity?"

Pauline glanced up and turned towards the window. She had been afraid from the first that one of the girls in the steamy, smoke-wreathed room would be Stella but she had not recognised her cousin and had not dared to scrutinise the half-naked strangers closely.

Stella had changed. She looked nothing like the child that Pauline remembered from photographs and, of course, bore

74

no resemblance to the little eight-year-old who had bossed and bullied her on that long-ago holiday at Flask. Even so, Pauline should have identified her cousin immediately for Stella had become more not less familiar. Petite, with legs that seemed too long and too shapely for her slender childish body, she was an exact replica of a girl in school photographs taken twenty years ago, not Beatrice but Barbara Haldane.

Stella was perched on the window ledge. Legs crossed at the knee, shoulders lifted forward, a cigarette, in a fine ivory holder, was angled between thumb and forefinger with an air of expert insouciance. Everything – posture, the cap of short hair, the dark eyes and heart-shaped face – reminded Pauline of her mother. Shocked by the resemblance she stepped back a pace, bumping into Frog who, with water dripping from her hands and her glasses off, observed the confrontation blearily.

"Don't you know me, Pauline?"

"Stella?"

"Sorry I missed you yesterday. Didn't arrive until all hours," Stella Jackson said. "I see you've got yourself into bad company already."

"No, Goss has been very—"

"We'll put you up in our room. I'll have a quiet word with the old Mill as soon as she's had her fruit salts and got rid of her hangover."

Stella's flat Derbyshire accent seemed strange for already Pauline's ear had become used to Scottish voices.

"I – I don't think I want to be in your room, Stella."

"Rubbish!" The girl slid from her perch, put the mouthpiece of the cigarette holder between her lips and inhaled deeply. She blew out pale smoke. "You don't know what you want yet, Polly. Leave it to me. I'll fix up a transfer."

"I'm perfectly happy to stay where I am, thank you."

"A crush on the Goose," said somebody else. "I don't believe it."

"Shut your mouth, Daphne," Elf said.

"Oh, and what will you do if I don't?"

"Stuff my sponge-bag down your throat."

"You and what army!"

There was a little unfeminine scuffle behind Pauline but she did not turn around to observe it. Stella minced towards her. The towel ends had parted company from the waistband of her knickers, showing small, formed breasts with prominent nipples.

"You'll soon change your mind, Polly, dear," Stella said, "when you find out how much fun . . ."

"Cheese it." Red-haired Ronnie dived from the door towards the window, flapping her arms like a gull.

There was sudden, well-rehearsed activity all around, haste but no panic. The cigarettes were gone, stubbed out in one sink, the ashes washed away by water driven hard from the hot tap. Steam swirled about and poured away through the window as towels were whirled like bolases about the girls' heads. To Pauline's amazement, Goss, Elf and the Frog joined in while the remains of the cigarettes, and the holder, were put away into an oilskin pouch which vanished into Stella's undergarments. Seconds of fleeting nakedness, vests pulled on, water splashed about, and, astonishingly, voices raised in song. The school song was bellowed out in cheerful unison a moment before the door handle rattled and a voice shouted, "I SAY, WHAT'S GOING ON IN THERE?"

Goss pulled Pauline down to share a sink as Ronnie, still darting like a gull, skipped past the door, snapped the bolt and was back at a sink before the door opened and the blonde prefect, Bettina, strode, hands on hips, into the bathroom.

"Good morning, Bettina. How were the hols?" Stella shouted as she turned from the sink, towelling her shoulders.

The school song continued, wet and lusty, as the prefect stepped cautiously over the draining boards, sniffing.

"Drains," Stella suggested.

"You've been smoking."

"What?"

"I smell tobacco."

"Bettina, really!" Stella appealed to her companions, friends and enemies alike. "Has anyone been smoking here?"

"Too busy, Bettina," Goss said, shrugging, as Stella's quartet let the song lapse and splashed like mermaids. "Almost bell time."

"Well," the blonde girl scowled, "get a move on."

76

"Shake a leg, girls," Stella Jackson said and, under the Kaiser's hard, blonde, pressing stare, finished her toilet and led the others out at a scamper, back to their separate rooms.

"Vulgar, she's unbearably vulgar, your cousin." Goss's indignation was muffled by the gym tunic that she was tugging over her head. "Sorry to say it, Pauline, but it's plain fact."

Busily polishing her glasses with the end of a brand new school tie which fitted, untidily, under the collar of a crisp new shirt, Frog disagreed. "No, 'vulgar' isn't quite the word, Goss. And it isn't just Stella. The others are almost as bad."

"She's the ringleader, though."

"Absolutely," said Frog.

"I hate her," Elfreda remarked.

"She can be very charming when she sets her mind to it," Frog said.

"Do you find her charming? I don't find her charming," Goss said. "Neither does the Kaiser. The Kaiser has her mark."

"The Kaiser has everybody's mark," said Elf. "The Kaiser won't be happy until after the election."

"Election?" said Pauline.

"Bettina wants to be Head Girl," Frog explained.

"It's a staff decision, and not at all democratic, by all accounts. If Miss Fergusson likes you then you're off to a flying start," Goss said.

"When will the winner be chosen?" Pauline asked.

"Over the weekend. Announcement, with due pomp and ceremony, Monday afternoon, before prep," said Goss. "The sixth formers get all excited about it."

"One can hardly blame them," said Elf. "I wouldn't mind being Head Girl someday, or even a prefect."

"You'll have to grow taller," said Frog.

"I'm doing my best," said Elf.

"Two plates of porridge," Frog suggested.

"Three, if you like," said Elf cheerfully, just as the bell in the corridor rang to summon the girls to breakfast.

The morning was calm with long lathes of auburn cloud across the mountains on the horizon and just a milky wisp or two

77

of mist lingering on the high hills that enclosed the valley of the river Eggar to north and west. From over the trees that screened St Austin's playing fields and gardens rose smoke from the village of Pattullo, snug in the vale by the head of Loch Teal. It was up the long walk from the village, by Burnham's Brae, that most of the school's domestic staff trudged morning and evening, except for Tom MacAdam's brood who lived on a smallholding on a strip of good ground near the Powfray Home Farm on land rented out from the Harveys.

From the fringe of Big Field, from the driveway, from the summit of Champion's Crown or the south flank of Pennant's Hill, the old school looked as picturesque as any building in Perthshire. From almost everywhere else, however, the 'new' wings and 'modern' attachments spoiled the aesthetic appeal. Miss Gaylord called the house blocks 'excrescences' and detested them. In fact they were faced with the same grey stone as the old Hall and tiled with the same black slate. It was, perhaps, the umbilical connections to the original that made them seem rather ugly, square flat-roofed shoebox constructions that kept the girls dry on their frequent trips to and from the dormitories and common-rooms.

Pauline thought it odd to have so much space and serenity on display outside and so much crowdedness and clamour within. She had no means of knowing that the first day of a new term was always marked by restlessness and that the staff, even the Head, had to battle to settle the assembly and to stitch together collective attention.

The unexpectedly intimate meeting with Stella had disconcerted Pauline tremendously. She was both drawn to and repelled at one and the same time by her cousin's forwardness. She could not deny, though, that Stella was attractive in a way that other girls were not. She possessed an intangible magnetism to go with her good looks with, for Pauline, the troubling resemblance to Mother to complicate things still further. If she had not already chummed up with Goss and the others, Pauline would surely have surrendered to her cousin's sharp charm and would have slipped into the circle of mischief and temptation that gathered around Stella. She did not, however, want to betray Goss. Already she had a strong sense of loyalty to the girls of Room No. 11 and a stubborn reluctance to let them down. They had accepted her, taken her on trust, and she felt obliged to prove herself. An opportunity to do so arose much more quickly than Pauline had supposed it would.

In the quarter hour break between the first of the morning's meetings and dispersal into forms, Pauline was sent for by Miss Fergusson and escorted by a prefect to a small, over-furnished room next door to the Head's study. Here her Uncle Lewis Jackson awaited her.

She had only the haziest recollection of the man. He had never visited her in London with Aunt Bea and she had not clapped eyes on him since she was eight years old. The image she'd held of an elderly bull-like chap in riding breeches and hacking jacket had been a childish exaggeration of the truth. Uncle Lewis Jackson was quite small in stature and rather rotund, his cheerful, crinkled features were dominated by a bulbous nose from which was suspended a bristling little badger's-brush moustache, and a heavy black briar pipe that poured out a stream of thick acrid smoke. He wore an expensive three-piece suit of brown loden cloth, a chequered shirt, and a tie whose design proclaimed an interest in fox-hunting. His hair was slicked down with brilliantine and he gave off a strong male odour of tobacco, alcohol and perfumed shaving soap that Pauline, for some reason, found more appealing than disgusting.

"Ha! Pauline."

He offered her his hand and when she took it, he removed the pipe from his mouth and pulled her to him, gave her a hug that was as sincere as it was indecorous. The sprig of heather that he had fixed in his buttonhole was crushed by her breasts and his moustache tickled when he kissed her forehead.

"Bit at sea, old gal, are we?" he asked, pushing her away from him but continuing to hold her hand while he surveyed her. "I say, you are my little niece, aren't you?"

"Yes. Yes, I am."

She noticed that the door to the Head's study had been left discreetly ajar, affording privacy but not too much of it. Miss Fergusson, or possibly Miss Gaylord, would be right next door, not quite listening to the conversation.

"Met Stella yet?"

"Yes, Uncle Lewis. We met this morning before breakfast."

"Got on famously, I hope?"

"Yes."

"Ain't she a cracker?"

"Sir?"

"Shouldn't play favourites, I know, but when it comes to children she's the one who can twist her Papa round her little finger. Now," he said, drawing Pauline to a leather armchair as if he was about to take her on his knee. "Now, about this luncheon, you will come along, won't you?" He seated himself with a grunt, dropped the reeking pipe into a convenient ashtray and coaxed Pauline down on to the chair's arm, his hand about her waist. "Didn't Stella tell you?" he asked.

"No, she – we were rather rushed."

"Bells, bells, bells. Yes, I remember how it was. If they caught you standing still you got scragged good and proper. Anyhow, I've got permission – usually do – to stand Stella and her chums a slap-up before I speed away by loch and mountain track. Up at Crieff Hydro. Temperance place, alas, but they make up for it with the table." He smiled at her and interspersed his harangue with tiny winks and shakes of the head, as if he was an arch-conspirator in some boyish jape. "Keep a bottle in the motorcar, case of emergencies, and a flask for the old nightcap. What about it? Game?"

A friend of Andrea's older brother had behaved like this, trying, patronisingly, to bring himself down to the level of a chum, so hearty and unsophisticated that he had drawn scorn from the girls he had sought to impress.

Pauline said, "I have a games meeting to attend, Uncle Lewis, thank you all the same."

"Oh, no, that's all off. I've fixed that with the," he lowered his voice and grinned, "the Dragon. You're free from half-past twelve until six. Verbal permission from On High. Got to look after you, Polly-Wolly. Orders from your Auntie. What'say?"

Pauline was embarrassed at her hesitation. She sensed that in spite of his clowning her uncle was trying hard to be friendly. She wondered, in passing, what Stella's friends made of him, how much their cynicism was blunted by his generosity and indulgence. She felt mean but, nonetheless, said, "I'd rather not, if you don't mind."

"Oh!" He was clearly taken aback. He slid his hand from her waist. "Oh! Mind if I ask why?"

"I've promised to play tennis with – with friends."

"Friends already? That's good, that's good. Can't quibble at that, Poll." He was disappointed but put up a good show of understanding. "Wouldn't be fair, would it? Lure you away from new chums. Stella will be down in the mouth about it, I'm sure. Still – if that's the way of it."

"I'm sorry, Uncle Lewis. I'm grateful to you for inviting me," said Pauline, politely.

He reached around her, plucked up his pipe and put it in his mouth, rose, puffing on the blackened stem. He did not seem to be angry or slighted. Perhaps he realised that she was not yet prepared to become one of Stella's set or simply misinterpreted her caution as shyness.

Just outside the visitors' parlour one of the school's umpteen electrical bells jangled noisily. Pauline glanced towards the door of the Head's study but there was no movement there, no shadows or sounds. The bell went on for thirty deafening seconds. When it stopped at last the silence between Pauline and her uncle seemed doubly awkward and uncomfortable.

"Well, shan't see you again this trip, Pauline." Uncle Lewis buttoned his jacket over his waistcoat and titivated the sprig of fresh heather in the lapel buttonhole. "I'm starting back this evening, put in some miles before gloamin', sort of thing. Look, anything you need – you write to me. With your pater abroad – well—" He hesitated, thrust a hand into his trouser pocket, fished about and brought out a banknote, offered it to her. "This'll keep you in buns for a bit. No need to hand it in to the Dragon. If you're anything like Stella you'll make good use of a little extra chink. Go on, Polly-Wolly. Take it."

Flushing, Pauline accepted the generous gift, folded the note and put it into her pocket.

"Thank you very much, Uncle," she said.

Outside the stampede had gathered force, heels and voices in a swamping rush of noise along the corridor.

81

She heard Miss Gaylord's cry, "Stop that cavorting. This is not a zoo, miss. Walk properly, walk properly. No running in the corridor."

Uncle Lewis raised his brows, grinned, and before Pauline could retreat clasped her to his chest again and gave her a hug and a pat on the back. Pauline felt guilty at refusing his invitation to luncheon, less because of the gift of money than because of his friendliness. He felt sorry for her, she realised, and she was distressed at her inability to warm towards him. If he had not been Stella's father, if her cousin had been of a different stamp, how welcome his support would have been.

"Please give my regards – my love – to Aunt Beatrice," Pauline said.

"Of course, of course," Uncle Lewis said. He winked. "We'll see you at Christmas. Looking forward to it. Do a good Christmas at Flask, so we do. Do you ride, by the way?"

"I – No."

"Time you learned." He had advanced beyond her and had opened the door to the corridor a little. The sound of the herd had diminished. "Anyway, I mustn't keep you late. The Dragon might give me detention, if I do."

Pauline hesitated. "Christmas? Am I coming to you for Christmas?"

"Of course you are," Uncle Lewis said. "Where else would you go? Trot along now." He patted her lightly, winked. "Enjoy your tennis match."

"Yes, I will," Pauline said. "And thank you again."

"Pleasure's mine," her uncle said.


Games were taken seriously at St Austin's. Healthy minds in healthy bodies; Miss Fergusson had brought the motto with her. She had also seen to it that during the period of recruitment which followed her appointment as headmistress the women who applied for posts on her staff were sufficiently like-minded to support her modern approach to the education of the female child.

In addition to one gym mistress and one games mistress, several of the younger teachers had colours in sport at school and college level and were expected to pitch in with coaching and in general to set examples for the girls to follow. If impressionable young things were doomed to conceive 'pashs' on teachers and sixth-formers, which of course was inevitable, then Miss Fergusson wished to make sure that benefits accrued both to the 'pashed' and to the 'pasher'; that the inculcation of an indefatigable sense of honour went along with learning to bowl a Yorker at cricket, walk the gymnasium beam with a glass of water in each hand or play a Bach three-part invention on the piano in the hall while an impromptu game of badminton was going on over your head.

September was not the best month to take your first lesson in tennis. The competitive season was squeezed into a short eight or ten weeks from the beginning of May until school broke up in July. The coarse red blaes courts were kept in immaculate condition by MacAdam Junior, aided and abetted on the heavy roller by his sister Mary, and there were those to whom that particular summer game held a fascination beyond the merely decorative. While the sun shone, they delayed the onset of hockey fever and rejected the school's general obsession with left-hand lungers, right-hand cuts, mastery of the latest hit-and-rush manoeuvre, and the oiling of dry sticks.

Dry sticks had no place in Miss Fergusson's energetic curriculum. Malingerers were scoured out of cupboards and from under beds in dormitories by the Dragon and Old Flo, the Matron, each games' afternoon. Only bona fide musicians and, later in the year, rehearsing members of the Dramatic Society were excused the horrors of running up and down one hundred calf-wrenching yards of muddy grass while your pigtails froze to your scalp; or – even worse – spending the so-called voluntary games period clawing your way up hairy ropes or barking your shins on the big leather vaulting horse in the new gymnasium.

"What are you doing?" Old Flo had shouted at Pauline, as she returned from lunch a step or two behind her companions.

"Tennis, Miss Florence."

"Keen player, are you?"

"Oh, yes, Miss Florence."

"Miss Milligan will see to you then, down at the courts."

Pauline had never struck a tennis ball in her life. It had not been a sport on offer at Glades Road. She had watched elegant ladies and dashing gentlemen play on grass at the private club in Landers Avenue, though, and had pressed her nose inquisitively against the wire netting of the public courts in Regent's Park. But she had never quite got herself away from the vast and disorganised games of rounders that grew in the playground of her old school and had not thought to ask Daddy to book her lessons in tennis. She had, however, had the foresight to acquire the necessary costume, but no racquet and so turned up, nervous and shy, at the four stone steps that led to the beautifully lined and netted upper courts where a half dozen young women, and one tiny, dynamic junior, were already bashing balls about.

When she had left the dorm after changing, Pauline had felt no end of a toff in her new cream gaberdine tennis skirt and voile jumper, white stockings and shoes. But the bunch on the courts, even the junior, put her to shame immediately. They had 'style' in all sorts of ways that somehow eluded her. She would have turned away quickly if Miss Milligan had not spotted her and, smiling, stopped her game to make Pauline welcome.

The Kaiser had been playing in the doubles foursome with Miss Milligan and did not seem well pleased at the interruption. She looked intimidatingly Amazonian in her blouse and embroidered skirt, hair wisping out from a broad ribbon worn around her forehead. She was pink from exertion and stood by the net-post impatiently twirling her racquet while Miss Milligan, very graceful in a single-piece dress, escorted Pauline on to the court.

Three sides of the upper courts were protected by giant privet hedges above which towered chestnut trees and elms and Pauline had a feeling of being confined on a stage from which she could not escape.

"Have you played before, Pauline?" Miss Milligan asked.

"No, miss."

"Do you have a racquet of your own?"

Pauline shook her head and was duly found a racquet from

a small collection that Miss Milligan had thoughtfully brought down from the Equipment Repository.

"I'm in the middle of a set, but I'll show you a stroke or two later. Meanwhile, perhaps you would like to knock up with Anne and Hilary."

Anne was the junior. She came forward at Miss Milligan's signal, swaggering. Her dress was a mite shorter than Pauline considered quite decent, even for such a young girl. It came up almost to her knees. Though she was almost a head shorter than Pauline she managed, somehow, to look down her nose at the novice and did not seem particularly well pleased to be asked to play with her.

As they walked back to the vacant court, the little girl said, "I'm Anne Knight. My Daddy played at Wimbledon, you know."

"Yes, but he never got past the first round," said the other girl, offering Pauline her hand. "Hilary Marshall. Unfortunately I know this morsel. We're from Bearsden. The way she's going on you'd never guess she'd only arrived yesterday. She's just as bad at home. Other side of the net, kid."

As the little girl, not at all put out, skipped off to take her position on the far-away baseline, Hilary said, "Are you in Milly's house?"

"Yes."

"We're in Ossian. I think, come summer, we'll give your lot a run for your money."

"I – I've never played before, you know."

"Nothing to it," said Hilary, grinning. "Twenty hours' practice against the gymnasium wall, hail, rain or snow, and you'll be fit for the team come May. Teal are strong on top but always have to dig for a fourth couple."

"What do I do?"

Hilary was brown-haired, with the flat, hard cheeks of a girl who spent much time out of doors. She had a brisk voice and manner. She paused on the enormous expanse of red shale just long enough to fit Pauline's right hand around the racquet handle.

"Sweep, don't snatch. And don't run towards the ball. Let it come to you," she said then called out, "All right, kid. Whale away."

For the first twenty minutes Pauline felt like a complete ass. The racquet seemed to have a life of its own, dragging her arm this way and that like a recalcitrant dog on a leash, while the ball bobbed and swooped and shot past her, untouched by gut or wooden frame.

Hilary was patient but the tiny girl, who was obviously a skilled player in spite of her age, was mocking and gleeful. In due course, however, and with occasional advice from Hilary, the ball's trajectory became more predictable and now and then Pauline found herself making connection with some degree of control. So absorbed did she become in her efforts to improve that she was unaware that the match on the adjacent court had finished and that Miss Milligan was leaning on the net-post watching them.

"Anne." The girl had been conscious of the mistress's scrutiny and had been whipping away backhand shots and thumping her forehands in good style. "Anne, I think you may take my place with the older girls and play a match. You have obviously played a great deal of tennis."

"My Daddy played at Wimbledon."

"Yes, I think we've all become aware of that."

"Put out in the first round," said Hilary. "Slaughtered."

Pauline was glowing. Every pore on her skin seemed to be exuding a pleasant heat and she felt, almost with amazement, the drip of perspiration on her brow. Printed in her mind was the image of her mother in a long hobbling skirt, standing up on the grassy bank by the netting; her mother caught in action by the camera lens, stretching for an invisible ball in that far corner where the high, protective hedges met.

The older girls were mopping themselves with towels and drinking lime juice while the sun strolled over the lawns and tinted the blaes maroon and made every tiny leaf on the privet hedges sharp as an etching. In the tower the clock struck gently, almost wearily, the chimes drifting over the trees. From Big Field came the shouts of the hockey players, Goss and Frog among them. Pauline felt herself expanding, filling with invisible air like a yacht sail or a soap bubble. She felt herself billowing, trembling with the novelty of her experiences, and wondered why she had ever feared this friendly place.

"Now that you've tried it do you think you would like to play the game?" Miss Milligan asked.

"Oh, yes, miss," Pauline answered eagerly.

"Come then," Milly said, touching her arm. "Come, and I'll show you how."

Janis Fergusson's attraction was not so much to the man as to the machine. Her passion for the internal combustion engine in virtually any of its manifestations had been bred in the bone. It had sparked into existence on that day, almost thirty years ago, when her father Laurence and her Uncle Sorley had come puttering through the gates of Charlescroft, near the Lothian town of Haddington, in a brand-new Knight petrol-engined four-wheeler. She had been on holiday from school, had just returned from spending a month with her grandmother in Dunblane and had seen almost nothing of her father and uncle who had been off for much of the summer plotting some mischief or another. The mischief had turned out to be the purchase of the motor-machine, the automobile, a ridiculous piece of machinery which was still preserved in the barn at Charlescroft and which her uncle, now that her father was dead, still now and then filled up and took out just for the fun of it, upon the quiet farm roads.

How ridiculous the Knight seemed now, like a cross between a buggy and a bathchair. In fact it was only Janis Fergusson's bi-annual ministrations to its primitive engine and steering cables that kept it going at all. But she loved the old veteran, for it had provided her with her first taste of power, her first set of spanners, her first sniff of petrol and the black grease that coated the cranks and exposed rear springs. She had driven a lot of motorcars since then and repaired them too. She had spent a portion of the Great War behind the wheel of various lorries and transporters on the Glasgow docks, dressed unbecomingly in canvas overalls and a big leather coat – and had never been happier.

The passion was not exactly a secret but she was careful to keep it in proportion. She did not wish to be thought of as one of those eccentric headmistresses whose sorrows were sublimated in an obsession with breeding terriers or the hybridisation of roses. She had a trim new four-cylinder

Hillman 10 hidden away in the Harveys' stables. She did not, however, drive it much except during the holidays.

It was not, then, the character of Lewis Jackson that Miss Fergusson found attractive so much as the man's taste in wheeled vehicles. She had very little respect for the fellow, really. She knew the type only too well; a slightly pompous provincial English squire who had sold off his estates for building, most like. He would live without responsibility on income from the proceeds, would ride to hounds, and shoot anything that moved. She suspected that he might even have a fondness for women and a mistress or two on the side, though she had absolutely no justification for that slander.

What Lewis Jackson had, apart from a daughter at St Austin's, was a twenty-four-horsepower, four-cylinder Alfa that he had brought into the country directly from Italy back in 1913 and had preserved with a great deal of tender care ever since. Preserved was perhaps not the right word; Lewis Jackson was not like Fergusson père or Uncle Sorley. The Alfa was no toy. It had been bought to be driven, and driven it was.

Lewis Jackson thought nothing of hopping into the open double-landau, buckling on his leather helmet and goggles and driving up from Derbyshire two or three times in the school year. He never failed to deliver Stella at the start of term or to collect her when term ended. He was more attentive, more visible, than half the fathers who lived only forty or fifty miles away. Miss Fergusson could readily understand why it was that Stella was spoiled. She experienced not dismay or disapproval but, perhaps, a thin kind of envy for the girl's opportunities. She was lenient with Stella Jackson not for the sake of her father so much as for the sake of the Alfa, which she coveted.

Whistles had shrilled over playing fields and courts and the shadows of the school buildings had gone out, like long soft arms, to draw the girls back indoors. Though she had a great deal to do in the office, and Miss Gaylord's record of accounts to check through and initial, Janis Fergusson loitered like some moon-struck junior on the steps of the main building, not to watch her brood straggle in, all hot and weary from their games, but to catch a glimpse of Jackson's Alfa as it roared up the driveway.

Stella and her chums would be wind-blown and excited, ducked down in the deep leather cavities and Lewis, with pipe in mouth and helmet flapping, would wave like a hero as he weaved up to the steps and braked. As usual he was packed and ready for the long drive south. He would drive and drive, averaging twenty or twenty-two miles in an hour, and he would be home, she supposed, all grubby and exhausted but triumphant in time for a bath before dinner tomorrow evening. And her heart, as it always did, would go with him, at least until he stepped out of the automobile.

The girls climbed out of the Alfa without any dignity, showing their legs and frilly undergarments, giggling, too excited to be intimidated or even cautious in the presence of the Dragon. They had Uncle Lewis to protect them and were aware that old Gussie had a 'thing' for Stella's papa, and giggled slyly and furtively at that thought.

"Girls," said Janis Fergusson, out of obligation. "Less noise, please, and a bit more decorum. Colleen, straighten your skirt."

"Sure and I will, Miss Fergusson."

Janis Fergusson did not approve, but she understood. She was too rational for her own good, too forgiving.

Stragglers from the playing field, lumpy in their tunics, trailing leaden hockey sticks, paused to watch. Stella Jackson's father was too far removed from their own parental experiences to wring their hearts with homesickness. They were simply agog. He brought with him a kind of outrageousness that seemed glamorous, a magic that distilled itself in Stella and added to her charisma.

Smiling indulgently, Janis Fergusson watched the girls thank Mr Jackson for the treat he had given them, watched them simper and drop silly curtseys, intentionally making mock of formality, while Lewis Jackson laughed and revelled in it all, like some stout schoolboy.

He kissed Stella upon the mouth, once and then again. Janis Fergusson felt within her a ridiculous worm of envy at that too. She stepped brusquely down from her perch on to the gravel to chase the girls to their rooms to change for tea and, with her arms folded over her breast, squared up to Lewis Jackson.

"That's it then," the man said. "Duty done. Time to hit the trail, what!"

"Will you drive all night?"

"Of course," Lewis Jackson lied.

"Thank you again on behalf of the girls for your generosity."

"Nice girls, all. I like 'em. You certainly treat them well, Headmistress."

He had his hands on his hips, the thigh-length skirts of his quilted coat thrown back, the big painted steel buckle of the belt showing prominently. The moustache, Janis Fergusson decided, suited him. She offered her hand. "I will not detain you, Mr Jackson."

He shook her hand and, just for an instant, it seemed as if he might forget himself completely and kiss her too on the mouth. Miss Fergusson stepped back, her arms folded firmly over her breast. She knew what he would do now. He would pretend that he was twenty again, spry and nimble, and would vault the Alfa's half door. She half-hoped that he would come a cropper, but he never did. On this occasion, however, Lewis Jackson hesitated.

"Ah," he said, "just a word before I whizz off. The other one, my niece Pauline; I don't know quite how much her father told you."

"I know that he is going abroad soon. Africa?"

"Yes, and not out of choice either. My father-in-law's meetin' the fees."

"Paid already, I believe."

"Fine, but – well – if the girl needs anything extra, see that she gets it and plunk the cost on to my bill. Will you do that, Headmistress?"

"I'll make a note to that effect immediately."

"I don't want her to go short."

"I understand," Janis Fergusson said. "Is that all?"

Frowning, Lewis Jackson said, "She might have some – how do I put it? – some emotional problems. Is that right? Emotional?"

"We're used to dealing with homesickness. We don't lock

them in dark cupboards just for shedding a few tears, you know."

"No, I realise, but her mother—"

"Barbara Verity?"

"Did he – did Harry Verity tell you?" Lewis Jackson fumbled for his pipe, thrust it unlit into his mouth. "She's – ah, she's expecting."

Janis Fergusson's brows shot up.

"No, no, no," Lewis Jackson hastily explained. "Not Pauline. Her mother. She ain't quite married yet to the new father, alas. I have a suspicion it might hit Pauline very hard when it happens. So if it does—" He raised his hands. "You'll know what's at the back of any blubbing that goes on. Hope I'm not being indiscreet."

"Not at all. When is the birth expected?"

"Couple of weeks, I think."

"Oh, dear!" Miss Fergusson said. "Pauline does have a lot to cope with, doesn't she?"

"Indeed she does. But I'm sure you'll look after her."

"You may depend upon it, Mr Jackson," Janis Fergusson said and stepped back as the man readied himself and sprung over the half door straight into the driver's seat.

From the windows of Ossian and Teal houses there came muffled cheers from the crowds of girls gathered there to watch Stella's Dad make his usual flamboyant exit or, as must surely happen some day, disembowel himself on the steering wheel.

Janis Fergusson did not, however, quit her post at the steps of the main door until the clanging of tea-bells finally blotted out the distant, diminishing roar of the Alfa's powerful engine. She experienced a certain regret that she could not be out there too, roaring across the broad landscapes with the evening's hard cold wind on her face. But she also felt a certain relief that the last parent had departed and that the term might begin properly at last. As for Lewis Jackson's request, she would definitely keep an eye on Pauline Verity, screen arriving mail and ensure that Housemistress Irené Milligan was made aware of the girl's domestic situation. Milligan was a kindly soul, a sincere comforter. Unless Miss Fergusson missed her guess, the young housemistress would soon win Pauline Verity's confidence and, just possibly, her undying devotion too.

Janis Fergusson took a last sniff of the exhaust fumes that lingered in the sharp autumnal air and then, without further hesitation, went indoors and closed St Austin's big main door against the encroaching night.

"What is it?" Pauline asked, leaning over the dish that the maid had just put down.

"Egg puddin'," said Goss.

"It looks awful."

"And smells worse," said Frog.

"Cat's pee-pee, I think that's what it smells like," Pauline said.

"Well, I'm starved," Goss pushed back the sleeves of her clean, starched supper dress and reached for the serving spoon. "Hold your nose and dig in, is my advice."

Pauline watched the spoon scoop out the thick, clotted yellow substance, noted that beneath the crinkling rather blackened skin the texture seemed more attractive and realised that the afternoon's activity on the tennis court had sharpened her appetite too.

"Don't be so miserly, Goss," she heard herself say. "I'll get rid of another dollop, if you like."

From down the long table came cries of protest. Another clique of Middle School pupils were waiting for the ashet and their share.

Miss Milligan, who presided over each table in turn, glanced round. She had attached herself to the juniors tonight but was attentive to what was going on elsewhere. She caught Pauline's eye and gave a smile, even as she shook a warning finger. Pauline felt herself blush and, embarrassed by her display of greed, peered at her plate and dutifully passed the serving dish on. The pudding tasted much better than it looked and she ate her portion quickly.

At a table to her left Stella and her friends were making a mock of Cook's efforts. Holding their noses, they ate each forkful in unison, with a harmonized groan after it, until Miss Milligan, sounding surprisingly sharp, called out, "That's quite enough," after which they settled to whispering and laughing over neglected plates.

"Look at them," said Elf, sighing. "Stuffed to the gills. Lucky pigs."

"Yes, and I'll bet they've got all sorts of goodies hidden away too," said Frog.

"How do they get away with it?" Pauline said.

"Better ask your cousin," Goss said.

"I doubt if she'd tell me."

"Why didn't you go with them today?" Goss asked.

"I didn't want to. I wanted to play tennis instead."

"Is that the only reason?" Goss said.

"Look," said Pauline, "I don't know what you think I am but I'm not a spy or anything like it. I don't know Stella, even although she is my cousin. From what I've seen I don't want to know her either. She isn't my type at all, nor are her chums."

"Don't be so sure," Goss said. "There are lots of advantages to being 'in' with Stella."

"I can't imagine any," said Pauline.

"That's because you're an innocent," said Goss.

"I am not."

"Compared with Stella, you are," Goss said.

"We all are – compared with Stella," Elizabeth Frognall, who had not appeared to be listening, put in.

For a moment, there in the crowded dining hall, Pauline had a flashing recollection of the half-naked girls in the washroom that morning, of their flaunting casualness amid the haze of cigarette smoke. She wished that she might somehow acquire a similar freedom from the shame and embarrassment that, for no real reason, tormented her from time to time, acquire it, though, without paying the price, whatever that price might be. Pauline glanced furtively at her cousin.

Arm draped around the back of Ronnie Somerville's chair, Stella was smirking and batting her lashes like a copybook vamp at one of the new girls who, face aflame, sat rigid and trembling with humiliation, until, heads together, the girls of Stella's set sniggered and then exploded into laughter.

Spinning round, Miss Milligan gave them a hard stare but by that time there was nothing harmful to be seen and Stella was politely dispensing the last of the egg pudding to a favoured group at Table Four.

"*Tu comprends?*" said Goss.

"Not exactly," Pauline said.

"You will, alas," said Goss.

# Seven

*I*rené Milligan was nervous. She had been to Kingsford House before, of course, for the Harveys were nothing if not hospitable. They put themselves out to entertain the school staff, quite royally, two or three times each year. But to be a guest at one of the more exclusive dinner parties was a new experience for the young housemistress and she was not at all sure of herself or, for that matter, of the suitability of the dress she had chosen to wear. It had cost her 29/6d in Jenners in Edinburgh. Her mother had told her that it made her look like a trollop which was part of the reason she'd bought it. Now, however, she was having second thoughts.

She turned this way and that in front of the mirror and wondered if the skirt was too short, if the artificial silk was too clinging. She had taken in the waist, for she was very narrow and rather elongated, and had tried to do something about the bosom with a sort of scalloped flounce, an experiment that had proved unsuccessful and which had had to be unpicked. She did not know why she was so apprehensive. Perhaps because Miss Gaylord and Miss Fergusson would be dressed frumpily, the former in the residue of Victorian fashion, the latter in something heavy that would seem to have been thrown at her from half way across the room. She did not wish to embarrass her superiors or to dismay the members of the Harvey family who, she suspected, would take no account of the fact that, housemistress or not, she was only twenty-eight years old.

Tonight Teal would be in the charge of Aileen McIntyre, the games mistress. Aileen would make the bedtime round with hockey stick in hand, scowling and shouting. The girls – even the old hands – could never be quite sure just how much worse was Miss McIntyre's bark from her bite and not even the Jackson crew had ever had the temerity to try to find out.

95

Irené wondered what the girls would say if they could see her now, uncertain, timid and tense. How naive of them to suppose that she was a model of aplomb. She glanced at the clock. Seven minutes. She had seven minutes to dither and fret. Seven minutes until Miss Fergusson, punctual as the one o'clock gun, would come rolling up to the door in her motorcar; and Miss Gaylord, tight grey hair covered with something that resembled a beekeeper's net, would cautiously emerge from the old porter's room, descend the steps and ascend, disapprovingly, into the back seat of the motorcar; and then it would be her own turn to climb gracefully into the front seat beside Miss Fergusson. There would be girls at the windows – there were always girls at the windows – and one or two of the seniors who had finished prep would be casually hanging about the lawn to criticise what she was wearing; and – no sense in not admitting it – two or three of her devoted little slaves mooning and sighing soulfully as they caught a whiff of her toilet water in the hall.

She was desperate, absolutely desperate, for a cigarette. She had acquired the habit at Glasgow University and had never managed to shake her craving for the weed. She smoked often, furtively, in her room and felt so guilty about it afterwards that she wondered if it was worth it. She had a box of Du Maurier Virginias hidden away beneath her underthings in a locked drawer and was just on the point of fishing it out for a quick puff when there was a tentative knock upon the door. She assumed that it would be Aileen and, glad of the diversion, opened the door hastily. It was not, however, her colleague but Stella Jackson. The girl had insinuated herself into the room before Irené could think to step out on to the landing.

"What do you want, Stella? I'm going out this evening. Miss McIntyre will be in charge."

"Oh, Miss Milligan, you look so beautiful. What a pretty frock. So becoming on you. Where did you have it made?"

"Thank you, Stella. I—" Irené caught herself in time. "What do you want?"

"To give you this, Miss Milligan."

The girl's eyes had been everywhere about the room, quick, acquisitive magpie glances, assessing and adjudicating, searching out secrets. Now, though, she fastened her gaze upon the mistress and, on the palm of her hand, held out a dainty pink velvet box.

"What is it?"

"Take it, please."

"Stella, I can't possibly—"

"It's perfume. Real perfume. It's for you."

"Look, you know it's against the rules."

"I asked my aunt to bring it over from Paris. Especially for you. It is you, miss. It isn't from me, though. It's from all of us in Room Thirteen. Especially from Colleen. Please take it, Miss Milligan."

The girl's dark blue eyes were pleading and the little elfin face radiated a sincerity that temporarily dispersed Irené's dislike. Irené heard herself say, "Why didn't Colleen bring it?"

Stella answered, "I drew the long straw." She thrust out her hand, the box upon it. "Please, at least smell it."

Irené could not resist. She knew just how well off the Jacksons were, not to mention Daphne Gore's father, and she was curious to see what scent the girls had chosen for her, what perfume they considered her to be. She lifted the box and opened it. The bottle was bedded in silk, like a jewel.

Stella said, "Renaud's Moonflower."

"Really!"

"It's you to a tee, Miss Milligan."

The bottle was tiny, heavy, with a beautiful little embossed label.

"Try it," Stella said.

Irené sighed. Resistance weakening, she removed the stopper, dabbed a droplet of perfume on to her fingertip, spread it on to the back of her wrist and sniffed. It was delicious, subtle and sensuous. She wondered if the girls saw her as some glamorous cosmopolitan? In spite of herself, she was flattered. She stoppered the bottle, pressed it back into the silk and tried to return it to the girl. "It is lovely, Stella. And I'm grateful to you all. But I can't possibly accept. I'd be in hot water if Miss Fergusson found out. Oh, it's all very well exchanging little gifts at Christmas, but not perfume. And not in September."

Stella Jackson put her hands behind her back. "We'll be so

insulted, you can't imagine. Colleen in particular," she said. "I think you should accept it in the spirit in which it's given. We'll not say a word to anyone. Not anyone. Wear it tonight."

Irené laughed. "Oh, I suppose the whole school knows that we're off to dinner at Kingsford House?"

"We're all thrilled that it's your turn, Miss Milligan. Honestly, we are," Stella said. "A Paris perfume will be the perfect finishing touch. Don't you like it?"

"Oh, yes, I love – I think it's very nice."

"Well, then." Stella was at the door before the young housemistress could think quite what to do. "Wear it for us, Miss Milligan."

"Stella, really! I can't."

Too late; the girl had scooted away, leaving the door to the corridor landing ajar.

Irené hesitated. She sniffed her wrist again. The perfume was heady but not, after all, heavy. She tried to imagine its effect upon the Harveys. Would they think her brash and forward to wear such expensive scent or would they regard it as a sign of the times and be graciously pleased? What, too, would Miss Fergusson have to say about it? Would the Head recognise the difference between common toilet water and this expensive essence? Miss Gaylord, of course, would not approve.

Thinking of the deputy Head's grim countenance, Irené suddenly made up her mind. She ran to the mirror of her dressing table and applied a delicate touch of Moonflower to the sides of her neck, beneath her ears and another at the base of her throat. The perfume, warming, gave her a certain confidence and made her feel stronger and less nervous. She lifted herself on tip-toe, did a little pirouette, smoothed her dress over her hips, hastily hid the gift away beside the box of Du Maurier and locked the door with its little key. Seconds later, exactly on time, she hastened down the staircase and across the hall. She was grateful to the girls in No. 13, though she still nurtured guilt at having accepted such an intimate gift from Stella Jackson's crew.

Jeannie Lawrence, the newly-appointed Head Girl, had come out to open the doors of the Hillman for Miss Gaylord and Irené. She closed them with a firm hand as soon as the teachers were safe inside the motorcar. Jeannie waved, smiled, waved again and, vigilant as always, made sure that none of the kiddies were prancing about the driveway, just dying to become St Austin's first victims of a traffic accident. Seemingly in good spirits, Miss Fergusson pumped the horn and received responsive cheers from sundry groups lurking in doorways, at windows and under the doleful boughs of the big, sad oak.

In the back seat Miss Gaylord sniffed audibly. "What on earth is that smell?"

"Perfume," said Irené. "Renaud's Moonflower, to be exact."

Miss Fergusson glanced at her and raised an eyebrow. "Really?"

"Yes, I – I treated myself to it this summer."

"Expensive, was it?"

"Fairly expensive, yes," said Irené, trying to sound casual. "Do you like it?"

"No, I do not," said Phoebe Gaylord stiffly.

"Well, I rather like it," said Irené. "I think it's much – well, me."

"Of course it is, dear," said Janis Fergusson.

Taking one hand from the steering wheel Miss Fergusson patted the innocent young housemistress on the knee and kept to herself the suspicion that the so-called Renaud's Moonflower was no more French than she was.

"Did she fall for it?" Daphne Gore asked.

"Of course she did," Stella answered. "Didn't I tell you she wouldn't be able to spot the difference between the real stuff and those cheap dregs we concocted? She has no breeding, our Milly."

"But she is rather nice," Colleen sighed. "I thought she looked ravishing in her evening dress."

"You would!" said Stella.

"Hand-me-downs," said Ronnie Somerville. "God, you could practically smell the mildew."

"No, not hand-me-downs," said Stella. "Ready-made."

"Even worse," said Ronnie.

They were gathered in the little cubby hole where Teal

House girls stored their cloaks and outdoor shoes. The evening's recreations were well underway and, now that the term was three weeks old, a certain uninhibited quality had entered the playing of games and pianos. While the cat was away the younger girls were engaged in a dangerous sort of leapfrog on the staircase, to the accompaniment of squeals, monstrous thumps and an occasional sharp cry of pain.

"Obviously our Milly is the sort who judges a bottle by its label," said Daphne. "What did you put in it, by the way?"

Ronnie guffawed while Stella made an airy little gesture. "Oh, this and that."

"What?" said Daphne, who had been party to the fraud but not to its details. "What! Not that?"

"Just a drop, a single drop."

"You filthy beast, Stella." Daphne gave her chum a little shove with the flat of her hand, and giggled. "And she didn't have a clue?"

"Well, there was enough of the original to cover the scent of toilet water and all the other ingredients. I had the devil of a job filling the bottle."

"Oooo, I would like to have seen you do it," said Daphne Gore.

It was Stella's turn to administer an affectionate punch. "Not that way, you idiot. I borrowed Colleen's eye-dropper."

"Which is now rendered useless, and stinks to the high heavens," said Colleen, dolefully.

"There were gallons of the stuff left," said Ronnie.

"I hope you got rid of it?" said Daphne.

"Poured it all over your bed."

"Beast!"

"What did you do with it, Stella?" Ronnie asked.

Stella seated herself on the bench under the line of cloaks, crossed one knee over the other and smiled enigmatically. "Three guesses?"

Colleen O'Neal gave a little grunt. "I know what you did with it, darlin'. You sprinkled it all over our neighbours' floor, sure an' you did?"

"Sure an' I did, right enough," said Stella.

*

The summons came out of the blue. The girls were frightened that it had to do with their squabble with Miss McIntyre, who had picked up the sickly pong of homemade perfume as soon as she'd stepped into the corridor and had quickly traced it to Room No. 11. Denials and protestations of innocence had quickly degenerated into heated argument. The peculiar scene of one mistress and four girls all stalking about, sniffing at empty air, had ended with a turn-out of lockers, a situation which Goss declared to be "a diabolical liberty". The debate had ended unsatisfactorily, with the girls in Room No. 11 admitting that the smell existed but with Miss McIntyre unable to find a shred of evidence that they had been operating a perfume factory.

The first class after breakfast was History, a subject that Pauline adored and in which she tended to shine. No shine that morning, however, for she, together with Frog and Elf, was screwed up tight with anxiety over the fact that Goss had been 'sent for' by Miss Fergusson and had been gone for the best part of a half hour.

When Goss returned to class, her brown cheeks glowed scarlet and her lips were pursed but there were no signs that she had been weeping. By glances and little shakes of the head, she managed to indicate to her friends that they were not involved. She sat very rigidly, however, and when Miss Shadbrook asked her a question about the Old Pretender, James Stuart, she answered in a most un-Goss-like whisper and had to be told to speak up.

It was mid-morning break before the girls found an opportunity to corner their friend and, clutching mugs of hot tea and Abernethy biscuits, allay their fears about a general punishment.

"Not you lot, just me," Goss told them.

In spite of drifting rain, the four had gone out on to a corner of the terrace and cowered in the shelter of the gable.

"Nothing about the pong?" said Elf, shivering a little.

"Not a blessed word. If you ask me old McIntyre didn't even report it," said Goss, gloomily.

"What was it then?" said Frog. "Come on, Goosey. Out with it. A burden shared, and all that."

"I had words with Mr Guy Harvey at the stables last Saturday afternoon, just before riding. Apparently he shopped me to the Dragon."

"Did you sauce him?" said Frog.

"Not exactly. He said that the French ate horses and that Alphonso, the hunter I was booked to ride, would go down nicely with some boiled spuds and garden peas."

"He would be making a joke," said Elf.

Goss hesitated, sipped milky tea from the beaker, nibbled the thick, dry biscuit. "I took it the wrong way and informed him that there were thousands of poor folk in Britain who would be glad of a meat meal, horse or otherwise."

"What did he say to that?" asked Pauline, who had no clear idea who Guy Harvey was or what power he wielded.

"Oh, one thing led to another. He accused me of being a Socialist," Goss explained. "And, I'm afraid, I raised my voice and demanded to know what was wrong with being a Socialist."

"What is wrong with being a Socialist?" asked Pauline.

"Russia," said Frog.

"Russia?" Pauline repeated.

"Revolution," said Frog. "Some people who should know better think that if you even mention the poor then you're next best thing to a Bolshevik. Don't you read anything, Polly?"

"I know about the Peasants' Revolt, of course," said Pauline, whose concept of Russian history was based largely on images of Cossack dancers from a cinema picture whose name she could not recall, and a hasty excursion into and out of a novel by Dostoevsky.

"Was the Dragon breathing fire about it?" said Elf, still shivering as rain drifted in thickening grey veils over the trees.

"Fire and smoke," said Goss. "No riding lessons for a month and an essay on 'Manners' by Sunday tea."

"Not 'Manners' again!" said Frog.

Within the building a bell rang. The girls swallowed what was left of the tea and hurried through the haze of rain to the common-room doors.

As they went, Pauline said, "Are you a Socialist, Goss?"

"No, not really."

"I don't see why you shouldn't be a Socialist if that's what you want to be," said Pauline.

Goss paused, shoulders hunched against the wetting rain. She shook her head ruefully and said, "Ah, Polly, what a lot you have to learn," then darted indoors before she could collect another black mark to add to her catalogue of crimes.

It was not class work but the school's incessant communal bustle that distressed Pauline as September wore on. She thought with longing not of Glades Road and the friendly roar of London's West End but of quiet nights in the kitchen with just the cats and Mrs Dobbs for company and an enjoyable novel upon which to focus her mind. Lack of privacy was not however the root cause of the melancholy that enveloped her towards the month's end.

Miss Fergusson – naturally – had done away with the vetting of girls' personal mail. Letters home were no longer placed unsealed in the long basket on the table in the hallway. Letters from the world at large were dispensed unopened at the door of the dining hall just before lunch. There was, of course, a residue of official caution. Post-holiday letters with foreign stamps upon them or strange eager handwriting would lead to a discreet enquiry from the recipient's housemistress and out-going missives reeking of scent and addressed to an unknown male would be held back from posting until the destination had been satisfactorily explained.

Pauline received a letter every two or three days. Harry Verity was shrewd enough in the ways of educational establishments to print his name and address upon the back of the long cream inlaid envelopes so that there was no mystery about them. Two letters had also arrived from Dorset, cheap blue envelopes addressed in pencil; Mrs Dobbs, departed from Weymouth Street along with the cats, who were thriving in the country, sent Pauline her love. Each letter she received deepened Pauline's depression. She could not delude herself that she would soon be back where she belonged, with Daddy in Weymouth Street, and that twenty-five days of Christmas treats and jolly surprises awaited her. All that was over. Now that the novelty of being a new girl at St Austin's had worn off she was left with a bedrock of loneliness that even her chums in Room No. 11 could not chip away.

The dates were marked on the flyleaf of the notebook that Pauline used as a diary: Daddy Sails. September 30th. And the other suffixed by a question mark, on the 10th October: Mummy Due.

The flat in Weymouth Street was already occupied by strangers. Daddy had spent his last weeks in London as a resident of a small hotel in High Holborn. He waxed amusing about his temporary quarters but there was a strained quality to his wit. Pauline knew him well enough to read between the lines.

"Finally closed the offices. Glad to be rid of that chore," Daddy would write. "Celebrated by going to the Gaiety but didn't feel very gay since there was nobody with me to nudge me in the ribs and tell me when to laugh." Another letter: "Saw *The Return of Tarzan* at a matinée yesterday. I do not think I would suit a tiger skin so I had better not get lost in the jungle. It's been very wet and cold in London. I just wish I could be on my way as I feel rather like a ghost myself, just fading away. My boxes have gone to the shippers. It will be my turn next, thank goodness."

There was no word about the proceedings for divorce, about Pauline's mother or the Haldanes. Pauline did not have the temerity to put questions that might seem impertinent or, in Daddy's present circumstances, immaterial. She filled her long letters with accounts of her friends, lessons, teachers and rather matronly reminders to her father to take care of his eyes and to protect them against the sun.

Then it was the last day of the month and Pauline, silent as stone, felt disjointed and out of sorts all day long. When she lay down in bed that night, closed her eyes and put her fingers in her ears to shut out the night-sounds of St Austin's she thought she could hear the roaring of the sea. Fingers pressed against her nose, she prayed irreverently that there might be a sudden war or general disaster that would turn her Daddy back again and keep him in England, keep him safe for her.

Goss whispered, "Are you all right, Polly?"

Pauline swallowed, took in a little steely breath. "Yes."

"Would you like a cuddle?" Elf asked.

"No."

"A cuddle often helps," said Frog.

"I'm just tired, that's all."

"Hush then," said Goss Johnstone. "Let's all try to get some sleep."

The dream was worse than any Pauline had ever had before. It possessed her utterly, tangled her reason like weed in a pond so that she could not break free of it, pull herself into consciousness, try as she might.

She was immersed in a plane of unruffled black water that seemed to stretch to infinity. Her body hung beneath the oily water and only her eyes were above the surface, on a level with it. She opened her mouth and cried out for rescue. But she did not know whether she cried to Daddy or to Mummy or to somebody else, for the dark water, like a sheet of cork, absorbed all sounds, except for the loud pulsing of her heart, a throbbing machine-like beat that changed into the rhythm of a dance band and, at the same time, the rotation of a ship's propellors. She scooped at the unresisting water and raised herself and saw, far, far away on the horizon, an ocean liner, cut out in silhouette, green against black. The music came from the orchestra on its deck and propellors unfurled a white wake upon which the lights of the cabins were glassily reflected.

Pauline watched helplessly as the white wake grew into two forked white arms out of which the ship's hull loomed, sudden and huge above her. She tried to scream. Felt her mouth fill with brine. Thrashed the water to draw attention to herself. She screamed and screamed. And no sound came. No one came to rescue her. The liner's hull grew larger and larger and through a window in the side she saw Daddy and Mummy dancing together, her head upon his shoulder. She cried out once more and stretched to reach them and then, in an instant, they were gone and the liner was nothing but a shape cut out of paper against the moonless sky.

Polly polly polly polly polly: bobbing in the water beside her was a strange creature who called her name in a trembling, plaintive little voice. She did not know at first whether it was man or woman for the features were wizened, the eyes large and bright as those of a fish. The head was small and round, with fine sparse hair plastered to it. The creature seemed to be smiling at her, beckoning, and waved its stubby little hands as it bobbed in the wash from the liner. With a shock, Pauline realised that the creature was a child, a girl child, and the calling of her name was a cry for rescue, as hers had been to Daddy. Even as she reached out to draw the merbabe to her, it vanished beneath the sea. And there was nothing but the guddle of water and faint romantic music from the paper ship, far, far, far away. And she began to weep, to weep as if her heart would break.

"Polly, wake up."

Drenched in perspiration, Pauline snapped open her eyes and shouted, "WHAT?"

They were gathered round her bed, Elf, Frog and Goss, anxious faces underlit by a battery torch, all staring at her. "What?"

"Are you ill, Pauline?" Goss asked.

"Bad dreams," said Frog. "Was it a bad dream, Pauline?"

"Yes, yes." She was still weeping. She had carried the sorrow out of sleep and into reality. "Dreams."

"Is it your time?" Goss climbed on to the bed and knelt beside her.

"No, not just yet," Pauline answered. It did not seem like her voice. She heard the words come out as if from a stranger's lips. She felt as if she had to get back to that blind ocean, to slide down into it, as if she had never left it. She heard herself crying.

"Perhaps we should fetch Milly," Frog suggested.

"It's just a bad dream, isn't it, old son?" Goss said. "We needn't disturb Milly's beauty sleep for that." She eased herself down on top of the quilt, put an arm about Pauline's shoulders and drew Pauline's head to her chest. There was something so comfortable about Goss Johnstone's size, her warm smell, the strength of her arm, something so unimpeachably real about Goss that Pauline felt the dream recede, ship and sea and merbabe all slide back, become memory. She could not stop shaking, though. She was glad when Frog brought a blanket and tucked it round her shoulders.

"There," Goss said. "There, hang on to me."

"Th-thanks, Goss," said Pauline, shakily.

"Think nothing of it."

"It'll be all gone and forgotten come morning," Elizabeth Frognall said.

In fact, on that count the Frog was wrong.


Miss Milligan's brow had a tiny crease of concern upon it as she took her seat beside Pauline at the breakfast table. It was not Milly's turn to grace that particular table and the girls from No. 11 exchanged puzzled and slightly apprehensive glances through the steam from the porridge bowls and the almost visible aroma of grilled pork sausages.

"You look a bit pale this morning, Pauline," Miss Milligan said. "Are you quite well?"

"I didn't sleep very well."

"No, I expect the reason isn't hard to guess," said Miss Milligan. "You must be dwelling on your father's departure."

"I expect that's it," said Pauline.

Miss Milligan ignored the bowl that Frog placed before her. From the pocket of her skirt she produced a small yellow-paper envelope and handed it to Pauline, saying, "Well, this arrived for you very first thing this morning. For obvious reasons we – the staff – feel it's best to open telegrams immediately. I hope you don't mind."

Pauline shook her head. "Is it from my father?"

"Yes. Perhaps you'd prefer to read it in private?"

"Is he . . . all right?"

"It isn't bad news, Pauline."

Miss Milligan patted her hand reassuringly, then deliberately busied herself with her porridge while Pauline unfolded the telegram form and read its cryptic message:

"SAILING WITH THE TIDE STOP MISS YOU STOP LOVE QUATERMAIN STOP."

Pauline put her tongue against her teeth and pressed very hard. She did not know whether she wanted to laugh or cry. Tears were not far beneath the surface and the image of the bevelled expanse of jet-black ocean still haunted her. But Daddy had taken the sentimentality out of it by reminding her that sailing to Africa was an adventure of sorts, one that should not be grudged. Pauline laughed. She folded the form and put it into her pocket. She felt very weak and shaky still but she knew that she would not break down now and that she would get herself through the day without tears.

Miss Milligan, who had been carefully monitoring Pauline's reaction, glanced at Goss and gave the sort of secret little nod of understanding that the girls usually reserved for themselves. Goss raised one thick brown eyebrow in acknowledgement and Elf, who had been eating steadily, paused long enough to enquire, "Salt or sugar, Pauline?"

"Sugar, please, Elfreda."

The canister was passed down the table and placed in front of Pauline who shook it generously over the substance on her plate. She added fresh milk and, without coaxing, began to eat.

Miss Milligan cleared her throat and then, as if the question was entirely casual, asked Pauline if she had read *The Ancient Allan*, Rider Haggard's latest. Pauline said that she had not read that particular one, though she had read the reviews which were very favourable. Elf met Frog's eye and shrugged while the housemistress and the young Londoner fell into enthusiastic discussion of Haggard's novels which, to Pauline's great surprise, old Milly seemed to know inside out.

"I'll lend you *Ancient Allan*, if you like," Miss Milligan said, munching sausage.

"Oh, yes please. When?"

"I'll bring it to class at eleven. It's in my bookcase and I've finished with it, temporarily."

"Oh, thank you, Miss Milligan," said Pauline.

"I've the newest Sabatini too, if you're interested?"

"*The Sea-Hawk?*" said Pauline.

"*Scaramouche.*"

"Is it good?"

"Brilliant!" said Miss Milligan.

Goss made the tall eyebrow again, to her chums this time, and Elf, cheeks bulging, hid her grin with a napkin while old Milly and young Polly continued to discuss romance.

# Eight

*T*he first frosts came early that year. Much to Pauline's regret, Tom MacAdam was out first thing to uproot the tennis nets, sweep the leaves from the courts and padlock the gates. The shale had been turning soft anyway and the players' pumps had gouged out troughs here and there along the baseline and MacAdam, who was very proud of his work as a groundsman, was delighted to see the fine stiff white rime of frost which was his signal to put the courts to bed until spring. The same hard morning frosts stiffened up the turf on the hockey field, however, and Tom's 'boy' was out with the long roller. The heavy iron contraption, like a medieval instrument of war, was drawn back and forth across the field by two magnificent Clydesdale stallions steered by the young MacAdam from a high, rattling metal seat.

From her desk in French class Pauline would look out at the scene and become so rapt in contemplation of the seasonal rituals that Mademoiselle would have to bark at her, and other little dreamers too, to bring them back from their wanderings.

The crisp clear October weather galled Gossamer Johnstone. Good hunting weather, she called it. Every Wednesday and Saturday she would glower and grumble, sulk and curse herself for being fool enough to have sauced a Harvey and be banned from riding for the whole of the best month in the year. Goss consoled herself with hockey, of course. She charged up and down the field with such speed and energy that Frog's prediction that she would be picked for the school first team seemed, to Pauline at least, like a very safe bet.

Pauline had no taste for the rough and tumble of field games. Instead she opted for Gymnastic Dancing. She expected some airy-fairy class with hoops and trailing ribbons and graceful Grecian movements and was absolutely astonished

109

to discover herself embroiled in two hours of sweaty Highland reels, led by Miss Heather Jamieson, mistress of Eggar House, to music tunefully tickled from a large, glittering accordion by none other than Mademoiselle Jalabert.

It was soon obvious to Pauline how Mad Jamie had come by her nickname. She was a small, muscular woman in her fifties with ginger hair and a nose with a kink in it. She wore thick, rimless spectacles which, for the duration of the dancing class, she affixed firmly to her face with a red rubber band. She wore an old tartan skirt, frilled blouse and a sort of black leather bolero that did nothing to constrain the rhythmical bouncing of her formidable chest which seemed to have a life independent of its owner and, like a snake in a bag, to be responsive to every chord extracted from the French teacher's ornate squeezebox.

In class, Mademoiselle Jalabert was a model of neatness and moral rectitude. But for two hours every Wednesday afternoon, and again on Saturday, she would accoutre herself in a long scarlet gown with an alarming *décolletage*, thrust out one long thigh and strap herself on to the accordion like, Pauline imagined, some midnight denizen of a Montmartre café. She could play anything, apparently. All the old Scots tunes poured from her fingertips and from under her elbows with effortless ease while the Mademoiselle grinned and, now and then, threw back her mane of loose black hair and laughed, wickedly.

There was nothing wild or undisciplined about the instruction, however. It was Mad Jamie's conviction that every young girl should be able to meet with every eventuality upon the dancing floor and that men were there to be captivated not just by good manners but by dainty steps and flowing lines, whether you were to be 'brought out' in a baronial hall in Inveraray or a hotel on the Oban seafront. Goss patiently explained the terminology, Frog translated the more esoteric Scottish phrases, and Elf, who also attended Jamie's class, discoursed off-handedly on the advantages of cutting a pretty figure for the gentlemen who could be so easily deceived into mistaking gracefulness for breeding, lightness for submissiveness and so forget that behind every piece of thistledown lies a nettle.

110

Highland Dancing swiftly became part of the fabric of the week for Pauline. It brought her into closer social contact with girls from other houses. She might even have encroached on the Saturday Session, which took the form of a country dance proper, if she had not been drawn to another pastime, one more intimately connected to the mood of the countryside and its pervasive spell.

"Riding?" said Goss. "Have you ever been on a horse?"

"I've been on a pony," said Pauline.

"Where? Blackpool sands?"

"Regent's Park, actually."

"Riding costs extra, you know, Polly," said Elf. "And you don't learn in a fortnight."

"How much?"

"I think the charge for beginners is a half crown the hour," Goss answered. "Ponies in the paddock, sort of thing. When you graduate to a horse it's three and sixpence, and advanced instruction from Mr Roddy costs five."

"Expensive," said Pauline. "I can afford it, though. I have money that my uncle gave me."

"What about tuck?" said Elf.

"My father deposited pocket money to cover treats," said Pauline. "I think I'd like to learn to ride. I can see myself hunting foxes."

"No jumps," said Goss. "Miss Fergusson put the kibosh on jumping. She's frightened of horses, I think. And of accidents. Daft rule, if you ask me."

"Only because you were born in the saddle," Frog pointed out.

"Hardly," said Goss. "I do admit that I wasn't very old when I was dragged screaming to Liberton and stuck up on some windy old pony's back." She grinned. "After that first time I had to be dragged screaming away from the stables."

"Does your father ride?" Pauline asked.

"Not him. It's too undignified," Goss said. "Look here, if you're serious about taking lessons at Fourstones go to Milly and tell her so. She'll clear it with the Dragon and let you know when Roddy can take you on."

"Roddy?"

"Roderick Harvey. He runs the stables."

"Is he related to—"

"He's Charles's son," said Frog.

"Oh, really?" said Pauline.

"If you imagine that a half crown will buy you the thrill of his strong hands and fluttering eyelashes, think again, old son," said Goss.

"Why? Isn't Roderick Harvey handsome?"

"*Très beau, je suppose*," said Goss, with a shrug. "It's just that—"

"Just what?" said Pauline, intrigued.

"Nobody thinks of him in that way," said Goss.

"Oh, no! I'll bet they do," said Pauline.

"But they don't, Polly," Elf put in. "Honestly."

"Why ever not?"

"There's just something about him. Something odd," Goss said. "Can't quite suss out what it is. He appears to have absolutely no interest in girls."

"He prefers horses," said Frog.

"Well, I can't blame him for that," said Goss.

Pauline giggled. "Who knows, perhaps I'll be the first fair damsel to catch his attention."

"I greatly doubt it," said Goss Johnstone and, bored with the subject, pointedly returned to her book.

For much of the humid Indian summer that had covered Devon and the West Country in a perspiring, dusty haze Barbara Verity had been hidden away like a prisoner in Mark Straker's cottage in a flowery fold in the ridge below King's Barley. She had stayed there many times before. In the early days of their affair the cottage had been their hideaway, their love-nest. Now, however, with stomach swollen and pain her nightly companion Babs found the beetle-browed thatch and half acre of wild garden as stifling as a lime kiln and had grown to hate the place.

She had no means of escape, no diversions or excursions to distract her from the heavy, fluid discomforts of her pregnancy. Mark was gone for most of the week and Babs was left to the tender mercies of Kendall, a local woman, who, in spite of a soft accent and simpering manner, was as dictatorial as a school mistress; and seemed hellbent on denying Babs not only the essential comforts – gin and cigarettes – that might make life bearable but also sympathy for her present predicament. Kendall had been Mark's choice of a housekeeper and, on paper, she had seemed ideal. She had had some experience as a nurse, could cook, and did not shirk the niggling chores that residence in the primitive old cottage demanded of her. At first Babs and she had rubbed along well enough. But after a month in the woman's company Barbara Verity could have cheerfully strangled her – if she'd had the strength.

Fatigue, exhaustion at the slightest effort and a sort of permanent biliousness had blighted Barbara's existence, made her weepy and cross. She realised that she was being beastly to Mark and that the poor chap was doing his best yet she nagged him constantly to do something about her pain. Old Doctor Worsham from the cottage hospital at Nettleton had examined her from top to toe. He had probed and pried and mumbled and muttered, and declared that he could find nothing wrong with her or the position of the baby. He had given her a dark green liquid which, he said, would ease the trapped gas that was responsible for much of her discomfort.

It was the first time that Barbara Verity had lost control of her body. Bearing Pauline had been a piece of cake, really. Once she had got over her dismay at having to share herself with an alien creature, the months of that first pregnancy had hardly impeded her enjoyment at all and – small mercies – had kept Harry away from her for the best part of a year. Labour had been short. She had recovered quickly. Therefore, she had assumed, quite wrongly, that bearing Mark's child would be no worse, and probably better since Mark's child had been conceived in love.

How wrong, how utterly wrong, she had been. She could not have predicted the tortures that the various phases of her confinement would put her through, the innumerable shades of physical discomfort that the thing swelling inside her had discovered with which to torment her. Walking, sitting, lying down, it made no difference to the little demon within her. It had knees like hockey sticks, elbows like croquet mallets and a head like a football. It had the fiendish knack of making her

113

feel seasick, though King's Barley was a dozen miles inland from the coast. It heaved and writhed and roiled against her organs like water-logged flotsam, nudging and knocking endlessly, until her body felt like a barrel filled to bursting with briny debris. She wanted to be sick. But could not. She wanted to pass water. But could not. She wanted to lie flat on her back. But could not. She wanted to smoke a cigarette, but dared not, to sip a cocktail without retching, eat a lobster salad without feeling as if she had swallowed the claws. But the inhabitant of her womb would have none of it.

As she crouched, sweating, in the shade of the laburnums at the bottom of the wild garden where Kendall couldn't see her, stealthily supping Dr Worsham's green glop straight from the bottle, Barbara wondered if all babies conceived in sin were mortal enemies to their mothers; if this was not some hideous disciplinary device, some mortification inflicted to steel the character and purify the soul. God knows, if she'd been a Roman Catholic she might even have prayed for atonement. As it was she prayed only for Mark to return from London, for the throb of the Rolls-Royce engine and a glimpse of the Silver Ghost as it threaded its way down the track from King's Barley, to feel his kiss upon her cheek and hear his calm, cool voice, and to be reassured. But before the weekend was half over, she would be praying that Mark would go away again, for he had given her nothing, no release, no respite from the interminable discomforts of pregnancy.

He was cool, Mark, and too cautious by half. He did not seem to want to touch her. It was as if pregnancy made her contaminated. He would wash his hands fastidiously before supper. He would eat the pie or the cutlets that Kendall had prepared for him and would hold out a piece, steaming on his fork, and say, "Will you not try some, Barbara? It really is delicious, I assure you."

"No, Mark. I – I can't face it."

"Go on. Do." The fork would be pushed closer to her face. She would catch a whiff of the dripping meat and would feel physically revolted and would have to excuse herself and rush to the closet under the staircase and kneel by the bowl.

Mark was discreet. He would not disturb her. She would creep upstairs to her bedroom and lie there, curled up, her left elbow stuck into her side to still the gurgling ache and wait for him to come to her.

He was very solicitous. But he would not touch her. He would tell what he had done in the City that week, how much money he had made, how he had taken time to call upon her father in Hampstead and report on her health. "Donald appreciates it, you know. Being kept informed. He is exceedingly fond of you, Babs, in spite of everything."

"What do you mean – everything?"

"The merry dance you've led him."

"What merry dance?"

"Still." Mark would fold one long leg over another, sit back in the wicker chair, bridge his fingers before his face, peep at her critically through the arch. "Still, it will be all right soon. Once we're married."

"Have you heard from the solicitor?"

"Not yet. These things cannot be hurried, you know."

He had a beautiful face, chiselled and tranquil with cool, steady grey eyes in which she had never seen a spark of anger, no matter how she tried his patience.

"Mark, sit by me please."

"Oh, there isn't room, Babby."

"Please."

He would unfold himself from the painted wicker chair and come towards her. Her heart would compress itself against her breastbone the way it had done in their first passionate days when she had not known what he would do to her, what to expect, and then it would deflate again as he leaned over and kissed the top of her head, as if she was a child. She would try to reach out to him but he would evade her, wag his finger, say, "Now, now, Babby. None of that," and would blow her another kiss from the attic doorway before he slipped away downstairs again to eat his pudding and drink his wine.

Barbara would lie motionless, calmed not so much by Mark's presence in the cottage as by the realisation that she was being unreasonable. She had no option but to bear the anguish alone. She would crush her elbow into her swollen side and, in the few moments of ease allowed her, would dream of other days, other men. Of Harry.

She wondered exactly where Harry was, at what spot

on the ocean. And what he was doing. Was he dancing clumsily with some elegant lady or playing a few rubbers with some wealthy businessmen at a sovereign a point? She wondered too, listlessly, just what he had done with the hired co-respondent in that seedy Brighton hotel, if he had taken advantage of the situation. And, if the woman had been low enough to allow it, had she asked for more, had put it on the bill.

She had no right to be critical of Harry. She was at fault. She had never loved him, had never been excited by him. She supposed she had sold him a false bill of goods. She rather wished he were here now. She might even apologise to him, in exchange, of course, for one of his comforting bearhugs. Strange how she had once been so irked by those holdings and huggings, by his arm about her, his hand upon her breast. How she had hated it when he had put his ear to her abdomen when she was carrying Pauline and had laughed and said, "I can hear it singing. I really can."

"What, for God's sake, are you prattling about, Harry?"

"Tap-dancing too. And listen, is that a tambourine?"

"You fool. Leave me alone."

And thinking of Harry she would think, with wistful longing, of Pauline, who had given her hardly any trouble as a baby or even as a child, apart from being rather too clinging. She knew where Pauline was. She remembered enough of St Austin's to be able to conjure up a picture of her daughter seated at one of the upright desks in the gaslit common-room where prep was done. She hoped that Pauline was happier there than she had been, more conscientious, less agitated and rebellious. She doubted, though, if Pauline would ever earn the admiring soubriquet 'An Expert on Boys'.

Lying in the humid half light of the Devon evening, Barbara was moved to write to her daughter, to offer advice, to – what? – apologise to Pauline too. But when the letter composed in her head grew too long, too hazy to be held there and she leaned out to open the drawer for paper and a pencil, to transform thought into deed, the thing in her belly stabbed her jealously and she was flung back, gasping, to lie exhausted on the bed again.

"Mark?" She could smell cinnamon from the apple dumplings, smoke from his Cuban cigar, coffee and brandy too. "Mark, Mark?"

From the bottom of the narrow staircase in the narrow hall, he called out patiently. "What is it, Barbara?"

"Will you please come?"

"Are you unwell?"

"No, I . . ."

"In a little while. I'll come up in a little while."

"Mark?"

"I'm finishing my supper, Babby," he would say, and Barbara would bite her lip, tell herself not to be selfish and roll, unaided, on to her left side again.

She must not think of Harry or of Pauline. She must dwell on the rain and cool air that Mark said would make her feel better. And the day, not too far hence, when she would be relieved of this burden, this insufferable burden, and might once more call her body her own.

"Is that him?" Pauline asked.

"The one and only," Frog answered.

"I didn't realise he was quite so lame."

"They say he was lucky not to lose the leg," Frog told her. "Apparently the kneecap is only held together with wire and he has no calf muscle at all. Shot away by shrapnel, or something."

"Can he still ride?"

"After a fashion," said Frog. "But Goss tells me he's no good at all now. He used to be a wonderful rider, so they say. Won half the point-to-point races in Scotland and rode with the Pennant hunt too when he was young."

"He doesn't look all that old now," said Pauline.

"I dunno," said Frog. "Thirty?"

"Quite old," said Pauline.

It was a lowering day with still dark grey cloud pasted all over the sky. The hills had no definition, black against it, as far as the eye could see. A keen, unclear little wind seemed to hug the contour of the braes, cutting close to the ground so that the pine tops were without motion but all the leaves that had fallen from the oak and beech and

117

sycamore around Fourstones had scurried and danced and whirled hither and thither and sprang up in restless spirals in corners of the yard.

Frog wore an enormous tweed overcoat, topped by a knitted muffler. Her second best felt hat was tugged down over her ears. She was doing Pauline a favour by accompanying her to the riding lesson, for she had no particular fondness for any outdoor exercise except swimming which, of course, was a summer sport. In the autumn term Frog tended to do as little as possible on Saturday afternoons.

Dress rules and regulations were, by convention, relaxed for girls who took riding lessons. Those who trekked down to the Toffee Shop at the head of Burnham's Brae or managed to jaw their way on to one or other of the prefect's parties for a trail round the fleshpots of Pattullo and an afternoon tea in The Hut were bound to wear St Austin's walking-out uniform. But those who took to the hills, on a guided Nature Ramble, or just mooched about the touchlines of the hockey fields were granted, within limits, carte blanche.

There was nothing carte blanche about Bettina, however. Strutting about the yard, waiting for her hunter to be drawn by one of the stable lads, she was resplendently arrayed in full riding habit of jacket, waistcoat and apron skirt. A silk topper was tapped raffishly on to her blonde braid. Olive Moore, Head Girl of Ossian House, was similarly attired, similarly haughty and impatient. Perhaps they had a right to be so. Pauline had seen them on the bridle path that wove through the forest on the slopes above the school, galloping flat out, crouched down low to the manes. Pauline had thought how romantic it looked, how exciting. That glimpse of Bettina – though the prefect was unaware of it – had been partly responsible for luring her to Fourstones in the first place, more so in fact than Uncle Lewis Jackson's parting injunction.

By comparison with the young women, Roderick Harvey seemed shabby and impoverished. He wore old corduroy breeches with leather strappings, a stained cable-knit pullover and a frayed shirt open at the throat. Only his boots were expensive, odd shaped items of shiny brown leather and coarse canvas which came up, like waders, almost to mid-thigh. He was bare-headed, his dark hair long, curled untidily over his collar. He was very brown, very lean and probably tall too, though it was too difficult to gauge his height for he had a deferential stoop to his shoulders that reduced him considerably. He walked with a dragging motion of the left leg, hauling the foot behind him as if it was in constant danger of being left behind.

Pauline and Frog paused at the gatepost that marked the opening to the yard. Fourstones was a half mile north of the school buildings, on a broad path that had once connected the carriage houses to the Harveys' mansion. A public road, unmetalled, ran east and west, linking the home farm of Powfray and smallholdings about the base of Champion's Crown to both school and village. On the far side of the road were paddocks where elementary lessons were given and beyond them pastures where ponies were grazed and horses exercised. Fourstones was no mere recreational establishment devoted to serving schoolgirls, however. Roddy was responsible for all Kingsford's draft animals, the huge Shires and Clydesdales that were used in forestry work and timber haulage. Horsemen, grooms and stable lads formed an exclusive community in which, to Pauline, the little girls seemed anomalous, priggish and intrusive. She had never been more conscious of being a 'townie'. Her London accent seemed embarrassingly out of place in this rough, manly world of corduroy, leather and straw. "What do we do now?" she whispered.

"Wait. Mr Roddy'll be with us when he's ready," Frog answered. "It's not half past two yet. You pay for an hour, an hour is what you get. He may not say much but he runs this place like clockwork."

Pauline felt conspicuous and foolish, an obvious impostor buttoned and strapped into clothes and boots borrowed from Goss. Her toes curled against the newspaper balls that filled the boots' vacant spaces and, although she had on baggy breeches below it, she had the shameful feeling that the wind was about to blow her apron skirt right up over her head.

Bettina and Olive Moore ignored the younger girls. Pauline watched in amazement as Bettina pointed her riding crop at Mr Harvey and snapped, "Well, Roddy, where's my Talisman? I don't like to be kept waiting."

Roderick Harvey gave no answer. He stared down sheepishly at the flat cobbles. Bettina took a stride towards him. In her topper, she seemed much taller than the man and towered over his hunched frame. The wind flicked and billowed at the fine silk scarf at her throat. Imperiously she tapped Mr Roddy's shoulder with the butt of the crop.

"Don't tell me Talisman's been coughing again?"

Mr Roddy shook his head.

"He isn't one of your farmyard hacks, you know," the young woman said. "He cost my father a great deal of money. I admit he's always been a delicate feeder but that has nothing to do with it. He should be ready when I want him. My time is very limited, very precious, I'll have you know."

Bettina seemed to be talking to the air above Mr Roddy's head. She was at full height and imposing, breasts thrust out and chin pointed. The crop hung loose in her gloved hand now, twisting, twisting against the immaculately cut skirt. The man paid her not the slightest attention, though he did not move away. He seemed browbeaten and Pauline's dislike of Bettina switched to anger. The Kaiser had no right, no right at all to treat the man so, especially as he was a Harvey, and crippled.

Frog placed a hand on Pauline's shoulder just as a stable lad led a magnificent chestnut stallion, already saddled, from the back of the stable buildings. Pauline knew nothing about horses but she would have been willing to stake her life that Bettina Grant's mount was in perfect health and superb condition.

The prefect offered no apology. She smiled, showing her even white teeth, stepped instantly around the stable owner and advanced, not too rapidly, to greet the horse. She took the rein from the lad's hand and, cooing and crooning, rubbed her cheek against the stallion's neck and stroked his muzzle. The horse reared and neighed in pleasure, beat his head down against Bettina's face, knocking her hat askew. She laughed, beautifully, and without waiting for her fellow steward, swung herself up lithely into the saddle and walked the stallion forward past Roderick Harvey, saying not a word as she went.

Pauline tore her gaze from the young woman just in time to catch the lift of Mr Roddy's head. His eyes were liquid with a kind of withering disdain. He gave a silent little grunt before he picked up the water bucket and came on, limping horribly, towards Frog and Pauline, while another horse, smaller but no less smart, was led out for Olive Moore to ride.

Pauline tried vainly to hold herself in, to make Goss's clothes mould to her body like a skin. She felt like some fat pudding shrunk and unappetising inside a cloth.

Roderick Harvey looked down at the cobbles.

"First time?" he said.

"Yes, Mr Harvey."

Pauline's cheeks were scarlet with embarrassment. She heartily regretted having witnessed the scene with Bettina, having caught that final darting glance. She did not know whether to pity him or hate him too now.

Frog said, "It's just Pauline. I'm not going out today, Mr Harvey. But I'll watch, if you don't mind."

Roderick Harvey said, "That's fine."

He extended the empty bucket in his left hand and the stable lad, no more than ten years old, who had led out Bettina's mount, whisked the bucket away in passing while another boy, a year or two older, brought out a saddle and bridle, transferred them to Roderick Harvey's left arm and shoulder and then, with a swift up-and-down glance at the girls, went off whistling towards the tackroom.

Roderick Harvey gave the saddle a hunch against his hip, secured it under his elbow and then, without a word, headed off through the gate and down the narrow roadway towards the pastures, leaving the girls to follow on behind.

"Where's the horse?" Pauline whispered.

"In the field," said Frog. "Not a horse, a pony."

"Oh!" said Pauline. "Is that better than a horse?"

"Idiot!" said Frog chummily and took Pauline's arm just in case her London friend made a dash for it before they reached the pasture where the amiable little ponies waited, patiently nibbling grass.

Stella and her crowd had long ago given up on Fourstones. There were no gains to be made there, no opportunities to be found. Stella and Daphne were both excellent riders so supervised trots through dripping pine woods yielded no thrill to girls who had lifted prizes at gymkhanas and, in Christmas vacation, still rode out with the local hunt. Mainly though, Stella's gang found the boys at Fourstones either too young or too insufferably ignorant to be worth the sacrifice of Saturday afternoons and the opportunity, however remote, of meeting the males of Pattullo.

In Miss Aitken's day informal exchanges between 'her girls' and the citizens of Pattullo would have been unthinkable. Class divisions as well as maidenly virtue had to be protected at all cost and the girls were forbidden to leave the school grounds unless accompanied by a teacher. Miss Fergusson, however, believed that the school was part of the community and that the girls were entitled, within limits, to share in the life of the little town, particularly as the good folk of Pattullo were on the whole conservative and greatly respectful towards the Harveys and St Austin's. Policed by prefects, the girls were allowed to visit the town on Saturday afternoon if they so wished, and also to participate in church activities at other times in the week.

Saturday classes finished prompt at noon. Lunch was served at a quarter past. At one o'clock the House Banks were opened in the old hall and the housemistresses, armed with registers and cashboxes, dispensed the weekly allowances according to each girl's needs. Next stop for the little scholars was the Toffee Shop, a commercial enterprise managed by two stout sisters named McFall. The shop had been converted from the old smithy at the top of Burnham's Brae only yards from the school's main gate. Prefects and monitors manned the pavement, barking like sheepdogs in an attempt to keep order as the St Austin's flock caught wind of homemade candy and, heedless of traffic, weather and the fact that they were supposed to be well-bred young ladies, rushed out of the driveway and across the road towards the coconut snails and almond toffee as if they hadn't seen food for a fortnight.

Only six girls were permitted to enter the shop at one time. The rest milled about on the pavement, giggling, chattering and clutching the lists of goodies which they had been instructed to buy for friends and housemates who were engaged elsewhere.

The stout sisters had mob management down to a fine art and three plump nieces were employed to help cope with the Saturday stampede. Crisp paper bags of popular items were weighed and measured in advance, ready to be handed over the long counter. More expensive delicacies, like chocolates and marzipans, were dispensed at a separate counter, while mineral waters were doled out from crates by the door. The cardinal sin was not greed but indecision and ditherers were poked and jostled and howled at. The McFalls were placid creatures, kept even of temper by the jingle of the till and the rattle of coins tumbling into their coffers.

Pauline, Frog and Goss left Saturday shopping to Elf who was much under the spell of the Toffee Shop's sickly ambience and, with pockets crammed and purse empty, could be in and out again in three minutes flat.

Stella, Daphne and Colleen O'Neal would not have missed the afternoon's excursion at any price and would later persuade a prefect to take them down into the town for an afternoon tea. The attraction, for Stella at least, was not the candy but the boys who congregated on the wall of the kirkyard some fifty yards west of the Toffee Shop.

Even the most naive schoolgirl knew why the boys were there. It was not fascination with the ancient monuments and stones that lured them but the intriguing sight of so many maidens gathered en masse, and all of them untouchable. If brought face to face with any one of the girls the freckled, speckled, uncouth farm lads and apprentices would have been drained instantly of cocksureness. They would have wilted like oxeyes in the sun. They would have blushed, mumbled and would have slouched away, feigning indifference to pretty things in gymslips and lisle stockings. In a pack of eight or ten, however, the boys felt secure and manly. They could snicker, spit, mutter, brag, and speculate on what went on in the St Austin's dormitories after Lights Out, oblivious to the fact that their rampant male passions were not universal and did not leap the fences of gender and class like a bullock loose at a country fair.

To certain members of St Austin's staff the boys were a

source of consternation. Miss Gaylord, acting on her own initiative, had even tried to have them removed by law. But Constable Jeavons, the local bobby, could find no reason for moving the lads along. They certainly added nothing to the beauty of the old kirkyard but they were breaking no law by sitting on the wall and, in his opinion, did not constitute a threat to public safety. So the farm boys gathered, and pretended to ignore the schoolgirls. And the schoolgirls, with less difficulty, pretended to ignore the boys, all except one or two who had early learned the art of allure and could show themselves off without seeming to, and flirt just by a movement of the hip, the hand, the head.

"He likes you," Daphne Gore hissed.

"Oh, I know he does," said Stella. "Is he looking at me?"

"Goggle-eyed," said Colleen O'Neal. "Sure, his lips are wet with desire and he's so much of atremble he's near fallin' into the gutter."

"Oh, you're so romantic sometimes, Colleen," said Stella, lifting her head and turning it and, at the same time, modestly tucking the waist of her shirt more tightly into the band of her skirt. An almost audible groan drifted from the kirkyard wall and Stella laughed, head thrown back, hat well off her brow. "I do believe he would have me if he could."

"Have you?" said Daphne. "Have you what?"

Colleen chuckled at her aristocratic friend's innocence and the faint rose tint that Stella's outrageousness invariably brought to the Gore cheek.

"Take her like a bride," Colleen purred.

"Oh, but you couldn't possibly marry somebody like that, even if he is good-looking and quite mad about you."

"Of course not," said Stella. "I've no intention of marrying anyone until I'm good and ready. And only then if he's fabulously wealthy and willing to be my devoted slave. Meanwhile, I can't help it if men find me fatally attractive."

"Absolutely," said Daphne. "But they aren't men, my dear, only silly boys. Is it worth the bother, I ask myself?"

"It isn't the least bothersome." said Stella. "Besides, I don't think that Charlie is a boy at all. In fact, I know he isn't. He's exceedingly manly."

"Stella!" Daphne glanced to left and right and drew her

friend a step out from the tail of the queue. "Surely, you don't mean to say that—"

"He's in love with her, poor devil," said Colleen.

The object under discussion was Charlie MacAdam, very youngest of Tom MacAdam's brood. He had reached his eighteenth year unscathed by drink, and had been two years a forester in Guy Harvey's employ. He was not especially tall but had a stocky muscularity and an almost animal-like gait, quiet and soft and not gawky, that set him apart from the other lumpkins. He was fair as a wheatsheaf and had gentle, brilliant blue eyes.

Sightings of Charlie MacAdam had sent many a little heart into secret flutters, though he was too remote and distant from St Austin's as a rule to become an idol. He had not been seen upon the wall with the other, younger boys until recently. Besides, Charlie was a Christian and, it was thus assumed, had been trained to know his place in God's scheme of things and wouldn't dare give offence by harbouring an impure thought let alone address himself informally to anyone so far above him on the social scale.

"Fiddlesticks!" said Daphne. "He hardly knows her."

"Oh, Daphne, how wrong you are," said Stella, with an expressively gay gesture of her hands. "Charlie knows me very well. Very well."

"Just look how he's staring at her," Colleen put in.

"Sabbath School?" said Daphne.

Stella laughed and nodded.

"How long has this been going on?" said Daphne in mock outrage.

"Since we got back," said Stella.

"Why haven't I been kept informed?"

"Well, a girl's got to have some secrets," said Stella, "even from her very bestest friends."

Daphne whirled on Colleen. "Did you know?"

"Ah," said Colleen darkly. "Sure an' I knew without havin' to be told."

"So that's why you volunteered to teach the village brats on Sunday forenoons," said Daphne. "Come along now, Stella, out with it. What has been going on?"

"Lots," said Stella and then, with infuriating enthusiasm

125

added, "Oh, see, it's our turn at last. What's it to be, girls? Chocolates or marzipans? My treat."

"I'll buy my own sweets, thank you, Stella," said Daphne Gore and brushed haughtily past her friends to be first at the box counter.

Colleen pulled a wry face. "Huffy, I'm sure."

"Jealous," said Stella and, hugging herself at her latest small triumph, followed Colleen into the shop.

Colleen had no liking for chocolate or marzipan or even the sticky, brittle toffee that came, hammered, from the trays. She preferred hard candy, the shiny big-button-shaped peppermint Imperials one of which would lie in her mouth for hours, exuding its vivid flavour, until she felt like cracking it with her strong teeth.

Sometimes, when she did that she had a clear memory of Finn, the wolfhound on her grandmother's ground in Connemara.

She had loved Finn but had hated her grandmother; a woman made of iron, with rusty red hair and hard hands that had too many slaps in them for Colleen's liking. It had been lonely on the headlands of Connemara. She had seen very little of her father and mother who were too busy enjoying themselves with artists and poets in Dublin to have time for small children. Her four brothers had been put out to school almost as soon as they could walk. She hardly knew them at all. They, at least, had each other. All she had was her grandmother, the wolfhound, and the harp.

It was to attract the attention of her parents that Colleen had begged to be allowed to take music lessons. She had learned first the piano and then, because the harp was the passion of her old teacher, she had taken to strings. The teacher, Miss Flannigan, had a house only a quarter of a mile beyond the day school that Colleen went to, and it had become for a while her second home and the teacher a second mother to her.

She had learned the arts of fingering and stroking and plucking and had quickly memorised the sad old songs that Miss Flannigan had crooned to her. She had picked up from the woman too a belief that she was somehow sanctified

126

by her talent, made special, no matter how indifferent her parents might be to it and to her. She still went gladly back to Connemara, though Finn and Miss Flannigan were dead, and her Gran old beyond belief.

She had taken prizes with the harp in festivals in Dublin and in Cork. Thereafter, she had been invited to her parents' grand house up in Broad Street three or four times in the year to perform at one of their Musicals. She had met the finest singers in the land there, had been patted on the head by them and called 'precocious', and 'a natural talent'. Dada had been inclined to send Colleen to study music in London but – though nobody had thought to tell her so – she had been marked for St Austin's, her mother's old school, from birth. At twelve, she was uprooted from the sod and sent away across the sea, quite alone and, in a sense, uncaring. She knew that she was endowed with special gifts and, because of that, would always be a stranger and an outcast wherever she roamed.

It had not taken Colleen long though, to realise that she was not so special after all. She'd had to work hard at cultivating a reputation for mystery and eccentricity to protect herself from being absorbed into the ruck. To be special she had to be different. An ability to pluck a harp was not enough. She told herself that she did not care what the other girls thought of her but the truth was that she cared too much. What she could not do was release herself from the beliefs that Miss Flannigan had given her for, having nobody much else to love, Colleen O'Neal had learned to love herself.

Falling under Stella Jackson's spell, however, had not been part of Colleen's plan.

It was to appease Stella, to keep Stella in sight, that Colleen sacrificed her Saturday afternoons to the boredom of trailing the one-horse town of Pattullo and taking tea in The Hut by the river, guarded over by prefects and surrounded by other bored schoolgirls to whom the Saturday expeditions were the least of several evils.

Colleen found the little town not only tedious but suffocating. The Hut, in fair weather or foul, was shabby; worn oilcloth on the tables instead of cloths, hideously patterned cups, knives that would not cut butter let alone the raisin scones and rock cakes that came with each pot of stewed tea. Weary, unwatered pot plants stuck between soiled floral curtains hid the view of the Teal's brown pool and Saturday traffic on the Wade's Road bridge. In spite of its lack of style, The Hut was invariably packed in autumn and spring terms. The prefects themselves were half the attraction, for each of the sixth formers had a gaggle of younger admirers who, though largely ignored, thought it no end exciting just to be in the proximity of their graceless heroines.

"Fools!" Stella would say scathingly, though she understood only too well the interplay of power and emotional gratification that could be gained from fostering such attractions and was, just a little, jealous of the ease with which the prefects accepted adulation as their due.

To observe the younger girls bickering and blushing over some prim, tea-sipping lump was, to say the least of it, unedifying. The games that Stella Jackson played were more subtle and more dangerous. Unlike Daphne and Ronnie, the Irish girl was not entirely unaware that Stella traded ruthlessly on her friendships. Ruthlessness was part of Stella's magnetism, the envied, unemulable part, together with her expertise in matters relating to boys.

There could be no question that Stella knew a great deal about sexual matters. How this knowledge had been gained and to what use it was put were enigmas, however. Increasing amounts of boasting went on in the wake of vacations, of course, with many dark hints about this boy or that. But these were, at best, trivial incidents blown up to serve vanity. What set Stella apart was her daring. For almost two years now she had been cultivating her allure, flirting with men as well as boys.

As she'd matured, Stella's skill in putting out signals had increased. Dark hints in gossip sessions were given veracity by disturbing but fascinating detail. What was more, it could not be denied that she was attractive and put out – as Ronnie once expressed it – a sort of pollen that seemed irresistible. The occupants of Room No. 13 in Teal House were held together by Stella, not in commonplace chumminess, not in deep but innocent affection but by warm and secretive intimacies that had, as yet, no overt physical manifestation.

With each new term, each passing month, however, the nature of Stella's hold grew more intense as she played her three companions one against the other in competition for her favours, and her secrets.

Colleen was dimly aware of what Stella was up to. Perceptiveness made her less resentful than Daphne, less ingratiating than Ronnie. Nevertheless, she wanted Stella all to herself and, like the others, was jealous of everything and everybody that threatened the fulfilment of her desire, including Stella's latest conquest, young Charles MacAdam.

In fact, Colleen would rather have been at Saturday dancing class than stuck in The Hut in Pattullo. Curiosity gave her patience, together with the fear that Stella would be offended if she showed a will of her own. Besides, she too had peeped at Charlie MacAdam out of the sides of her eyes and had discovered in herself a weak but wistful longing to know him better. Sensing disloyalty to Stella, who was, after all, their elected surrogate and champion, Colleen put this longing hastily aside.

Ronnie, Stella and she strolled down Burnham's Brae arm in arm, following and followed by prefects. It was hardly a formal crocodile of schoolgirls but rather an aimless queue strung out along the town's narrow pavement. There were few shops; a linen draper, a tobacconist, a newsagent, provision merchants' smelling of cheese and tea, fish and hung meat. The afternoon was grey and lowering, the sort of sky that, in a month's time, would presage snow.

There was no sign of Charlie. Colleen assumed that he had gone skulking off to do whatever young men did on their afternoon of freedom, to lounge about until the public house opened. No sign either of Daphne who had probably gone back to the house to throw herself on her bed and weep hysterically at imagined slights. Stella was gay and jubilant. She pointed out this and that in the shops' dull windows, remarked on the passers-by and, admiringly, on the heavy-horse traffic that hauled drays and long carts along the buckled little Main Street towards the bridge. The prefects were conscientious but, for the most part, not bossy or bullying. It was a simple matter for Ronnie to slip into the tobacconist's shop and purchase a tin of Navy Capstan cigarettes, the week's supply, from the old man behind the counter, paying him, at Stella's suggestion, a shilling more than the price for his uncritical cooperation in supplying a St Austin's pupil with forbidden fruit.

Thirty minutes of aimless drifting brought them, under Carol-Anne's command, to the 'second shift' in The Hut. It was a little after three o'clock. Early dusk had begun to settle into the river valley so that the lights in the tearoom seemed, from a distance, almost welcoming. Same wilted plants, though. Same rock cakes and stewed Co-op tea. Same scowling, disapproving waitress.

The three friends commandeered a little table by the window, far enough from the rabble and prefects to converse as they willed, and to look out at the still, black pool and the bridge arch. Leaning on her elbows, cup in both hands, Ronnie was saying, "I think it's awfully clever of you to have joined the Teachers' Class at Pattullo Parish, Stella. How did you know that Charlie would be there?"

Stella smiled and sipped tea. "Ways and means, my buttercup, ways and means."

"He obviously adores you," Ronnie said.

"Oh, totally," said Stella. "He's my slave. I could make him do anything I want."

"What sort of things?" said Ronnie.

"I could make him come to our room, late, after dark."

"You wouldn't dare, Stella."

"I'm not saying I will. I'm saying I could."

"If he — if we were caught, though, we'd be instantly expelled."

"Not at all," said Stella. "We'd just deny that we'd invited him and kick up a tremendous fuss. Who'd dare take his word against ours?"

"What would we do with him there?" said Ronnie.

Colleen stirred sugar into her tea. She was bored by the conversation. She found no stimulation in idle conjecture. She could be drawn into it easily enough when they were closeted in the room of a night, when forbidden subjects were discussed in breathless whispers, when they gathered all four on Stella's bed, touching, brushing, warm under the tented quilts. But not here in the tedious grey light of a Saturday afternoon.

"That remains to be seen," said Stella. "Wouldn't you like to have Charlie MacAdam for a plaything, Ronnie?"

"I – I don't know."

"He's a labourer," Colleen put in. "He wouldn't know what to do with us. Sure, an' it's not us he's mad about, Stella. It's only you."

"Don't bring him to the school, Stella," said Ronnie, frowning. "It's far too risky."

Stella glanced at her watch and put down her teacup. She said, "Shall I ask him if he wants to come?"

"What?" said Ronnie. "When?"

"Now," said Stella.

Colleen said, "Don't tell me you have an assignation?"

"All arranged," Stella said. "Settled it last Sunday. He may appear to be shy, our dear Charlie, but he's a lion at heart. He wants to meet me – alone."

"Where?"

"Out there, just under the bridge. He'll be there now, pacing up and down, working himself into a lather."

"Oh, golly!" said Ronnie as Stella, without further explanation, got to her feet, slipped between the tables and spoke quietly with Carol-Anne for a moment. "What's she doing. Colleen? What's this all about?"

The prefect hardly glanced at Stella. She nodded dismissively, and Stella went out of the side door of the tearoom to where the little row of lavatories clung to the back wall, brick-built and more solid than the wooden-walled hut. Conveniences for Ladies. Facilities for gentlemen were parish-owned, a good hundred yards away, nestled discreetly below the iron gate that led down from the pavement to the riverbank.

"Oh, God!" Ronnie groaned. "What if she's caught? What if she's expelled?"

"For talkin' to a fellow Sunday School teacher," said Colleen, "even if he does hail from the lower orders? No."

"She'll persuade him to kiss her. I know she will." Ronnie cupped a hand over the side of her face. "Can you see them, Colly? I can't bear to look."

131

Colleen lifted herself slightly and peeped from the window. "No can do. Sorry."

"We'll be assembled to leave in five minutes," Ronnie went on. "What if she's still outside, kissing and – and things? What if Carol-Anne goes to look for her?"

"Stella won't get caught," said Colleen. "If, by bad luck, she does, she'll charm her way out of trouble."

"But what if she—"

Ronnie's fretful speculations were interrupted by the chime of the tearoom's front door bell. A split second's silence while a newcomer was perused was followed by a collective shrug as the schoolgirls returned to their chatter.

"Daphne!" Ronnie said. "We thought you'd gone back to the house."

Self-consciously Daphne Gore seated herself at the table. Upon the oilcloth she set down one of the Toffee Shop's chocolate boxes, neatly wrapped in green paper and fastened with a thin pink ribbon tied in a butterfly bow. Cheeks scarlet with embarrassment, Daphne said, "I came to apologise to Stella for being so awfully rude. I've brought her a peace offering. Rose creams. Where is she? I thought she'd be here with you, Colleen, since she seems to be so inexplicably attached to you these days."

"More attached to Charlie MacAdam, alas," said Colleen. "She's outside, under the bridge with him, right now."

"What!" Daphne exclaimed. "She's gone off with a boy?"

"What if she's caught?" Ronnie touched her friend's arm. "She'll be sent away. And then what will we do?"

"You encouraged her, didn't you?"

"'Course I didn't," said Colleen. "When it comes to boys Stella doesn't need encouragement."

"You egged her on. You're a bad influence, Colleen O'Neal. I've always said so."

Like Ronnie, Daphne Gore was near to tears. She clasped her gloved hands and stared down at the chocolate box in its gift wrapping and when the waitress brought her a teacup and a plate of dainties, she did not even snap at the woman but remained bleakly oblivious to the service.

Used to insults, Colleen sighed. "What's got under your skin, Daphne?"

"I'm afraid for her, out there, with a boy."

"I think you're jealous," said Colleen. "Question is whether you're jealous of him or of Stella."

It took Daphne a moment to understand the implication, then she leaned forward and hissed, furiously, "How dare you suggest—"

"It's all right." Ronnie interrupted the quarrel. "Here she comes."

Stella re-entered the tearoom by the side door. She slipped quickly between the tables and seated herself with her friends. The buttons of Stella's topcoat were undone. She held one arm folded tightly over her breasts. She was white-faced. Her blue eyes were round and she did not, Colleen noticed, pay the slightest attention to any of them. She appeared to be in a state of shock.

Daphne reached for her hand and whispered, "My dear, what happened? What did he do to you?"

"Nothing. He did nothing," said Stella.

Colleen too reached for Stella's hand but it was jerked violently away.

Startled and hurt, Colleen said, "Didn't he turn up? Is that it, Stell? Did he jilt you?"

"He was there."

"What happened?" Ronnie demanded. "Did he try to kiss you? To touch you?"

Stella shook her head then she snapped, "He did nothing. And he will do nothing, not to me. Charlie MacAdam is a clod. I have no wish to discuss him further, not at this moment or ever again." She snatched her hand from Daphne's and got to her feet. She paused, frowning, and peered down at the gift-wrapped box. "What's this?"

"A present," said Daphne. "Peace offering, dearest. From me to you, with my profuse apologies for flying off the handle." Daphne gave a little simper as if the confections represented something naughty. "Rose creams. Your favourites."

For an instant it seemed as if Stella might strike the box, sweep it to the floor, stamp it into the boards. She was trembling slightly, underlip pinched between her teeth. She sucked in two or three deep breaths and, just as the prefects rose to gather the flock and leave, seemed suddenly to find an inner strength that transformed her into her old, gay, brittle self. She lifted the box by its bow and held it out admiringly. "Why, thank you, Daphne," she said. "It's entirely unnecessary but very thoughtful of you. We'll share the contents together, you and I. Make greedy pigs of ourselves, shall we?"

"Tonight?"

"Yes, tonight." To the girls' astonishment Stella blessed Daphne with a beaming smile and kissed her fleetingly upon the cheek. "Now, be sweet, Daphne. Pay my bill for me while I have just one word with Colleen."

Daphne opened her mouth to question the order and then, still flushed by Stella's kiss, thought better of it and, with Ronnie, joined the queue at the little bow-fronted desk to the left of the door. Colleen remained seated.

From inside the breast of her topcoat Stella extracted a box identical to the one that Daphne had given her, except that the ribbon was gold not pink. Screening the box with her body, Stella put it down carefully amid the crumbs and cups directly in front of Colleen.

Colleen raised her dark brows enquiringly. "What's this?"

"Fruit creams, I think."

"From you?"

"No, not from me. From Charlie MacAdam," said Stella, grimly. "It isn't me he's fallen for. It's you."

"Huh!" Colleen placed one finger gently on the box. "Are you sure?"

"I've been used, dearest, used by that lummox to get to you." Stella inclined herself from the waist and whispered into Colleen's ear. "I don't like being used, Colleen. In fact, I hate it. As far as I'm concerned we're finished, you and I. Finished."

"My! My!" said Colleen softly, as Stella turned and flounced away. "My! My! My!"

"How was the lesson?" Goss Johnstone asked.

"Not bad," said Pauline.

Goss had expended her energy on the hockey field and, after her bath, had a wonderfully shiny glow. She was seated before the dressing table in No. 11, tugging at her tangled brown hair with a hairbrush. She wore a voluminous brown dressing gown over cotton underwear and her best Saturday frock was laid out upon the bed, together with an underslip and a pair of silk stockings.

Tonight, after supper, the girls of Pennant House were playing hostess to the girls of Teal. Hostessing was one remnant of a genteel tradition that the Dragon had let stand. Interhouse entertainments were, however, no longer stiff with drawing-room ceremonies and good manners. They began decorously enough but tended to degenerate into rowdiness. Elaborate parlour games and community singing had replaced polite conversation as the coinage of social intercourse and housemistresses had been instructed to permit the girls, within reason, to let off a little steam. Naturally, the houses vied with each other to provide the best entertainment possible and House Nights were anticipated with an enthusiasm that the departed Miss Aitken would, in itself, have considered un-ladylike.

Unaccustomed quantities of fresh air and exercise had made Pauline sleepy, though. She would have preferred to nap on her bed for a half hour before the supper bell rather than wash and dress and struggle with pearl buttons and garter straps.

Frog and Elf had shot off to fight for places at the warm-water sinks. Pauline knew that she too must soon begin her toilette. For a blissful moment, though, she lay back against the pillows, arms behind her head. She stretched out her legs, wiggled her sore toes and said, "I brought your boots back, Goss. I cleaned them as best I could. They're in your locker in the boot cupboard."

"Did they fit?"

"Sort of."

To Pauline's surprise Goss appeared at the partition and, still brushing her hair vigorously, seated herself at the foot of Pauline's bed. "You're not stiff, surely?" Goss said.

"No, just a little bit tired."

"Did you enjoy it, that's the rub?"

Pauline rolled on to her side and propped her head on her hand. "It wasn't what I expected."

"Hoh! I suppose you thought you'd swing into the saddle and be off like the wind?"

135

"I was only on board the pony for about a quarter of an hour. The rest of the time was spent in learning how to fit on the saddle. Mr Roddy made me do it myself."

"What do you think of him?"

"He doesn't say much, does he?"

"Never does. Did he touch you?"

"My hands, yes. He put them in position on the reins."

"He isn't being nasty, you know. He's a very decent instructor, even if he doesn't talk."

"I know. It didn't even seem like touching." Pauline drew up her knees and inched herself closer to Goss who was looking at her quizzically. "What's actually wrong with Roderick Harvey?"

Goss hunched her shoulders as if the long practice on Big Field had left her tired too. "The war, I suppose. I've heard that he used to be the life and soul of the party. 'Course, it must go hard on him not being able to ride the way he used to."

"Is he in pain, do you think?"

"Shouldn't be surprised. You liked him, didn't you?"

"Yes," said Pauline, hesitantly. "I think I did."

"Some of the girls – Stella, for instance – hate him," Goss said. "They call him the Crip."

"The what?"

"Cripple."

"That's cruel."

"Isn't it, though," Goss said. "I don't think they ever stop to think what it must be like to be a man."

"Quite awful," said Pauline.

"Oh, I dunno," said Goss. "Sometimes I think I'd like to have been born a man. I'd like to have fought in the war for one thing."

"Surely not."

"My father did. Army Intelligence. Apparently he was some sort of liaison officer and spent a great deal of the war fighting with the Italians against the Austrians. All along the Alps. I don't know how that came about," Goss said. "He talks about it a very great deal but he never makes it clear what he was actually doing there in the first place. I reckon he enjoyed it enormously."

136

"Did he kill people?"

"Oh, I expect so."

"I couldn't. I couldn't kill anything, not even a wasp. Could you kill someone, Goss?"

"If I was a man I could," Goss said.

"I can just see you as a gallant cavalry officer, charging against the foe with sabre flashing."

Goss grunted. "Don't get carried away."

Pauline rolled on to her back and wiggled her toes again. "I'd love to learn to ride like the Kaiser."

"Don't build up your hopes, old son. The Kaiser's been riding since she was two years old," Goss said.

"Do you think Mr Harvey likes her?"

"I don't know who Roddy Harvey likes," Goss said.

"I hope he likes me," said Pauline.

"Oh, so riding's the thing this term, is it?"

"I have to learn something useful, apart from maths and French," said Pauline.

Goss nodded. She tugged at her hair for a while and then got to her feet. "Tell you what, you keep my riding gear in good order, and it's all yours. Permanent loan."

Pauline sat up. "What are you saying, Goosey? Aren't you planning on riding again when the ban's lifted?"

"Truth to tell, I've rather lost the notion."

"But why?"

"I think I'll concentrate on hockey instead."

"School team?"

Goss grinned, winked. "All too easy."

"Play for England?"

"Scotland," Goss said indignantly then, tapping Pauline's shins lightly with her hairbrush, advised her to shake a leg or risk missing the perennial Saturday supper of piping hot toad-in-the-hole.

The dainty little dishes of sugared almonds, homemade petit fours and washed hazel nuts that were strategically placed around the Pennant House common-room were emptied within minutes of the guests' arrival. The two deep enamel bowls of non-alcoholic fruit punch were drained dry in a quarter of an hour. Plates of egg-and-cress sandwiches and two rich fruit cakes cut into sixty-four neat slices remained veiled under muslin on the room's sideboard in promise of another gorge before thanks and farewells at ten o'clock.

Meanwhile accumulated energies, mental and physical, were expended in an elaborate treasure hunt that carried the girls from Teal all through the lower floors of Pennant House and into the corridors and halls of School where – to everyone's dismay – the girls from Ossian were similarly engaged in finding and solving clues hidden by a separate committee from their host house, Eggar. Even the most solemn competitive instincts were waived by this piece of gross mismanagement. Great hilarity ensued as clues were exchanged and deliberately misinterpreted and girls spilled shrieking and giggling on to the terraces and back by various doors and groundfloor windows to report to the Great All Wise – the housemistresses – who were seated on piano tops in appropriate common-rooms struggling to concoct a fair result.

By a quarter to nine high-jinks were over. The presence in the corridors of Miss Gaylord and the Dragon sobered the girls enough to enable the prefects to round them up and pen them again in the common-rooms. Results of the treasure hunt were announced to cheers and countercheers. Then the performers for the evening were nervously brought forth to sing and recite mainly Scottish airs and comic poems, while the girls made themselves comfortable on sofas and chairs and on the carpet of Ossian's packed common-room and, mellowed by community spirit, generously shared sweets and apples with friends old and new.

The four from No. 11 claimed an armchair. Like gibbons on a rock, they piled themselves on to it, Elf on Frog's lap and Goss and Pauline balanced on the broad arms, their cheeks bulging with the afternoon's haul from the Toffee Shop. Pauline felt sad and happy, lonely and gregarious all at once. She had smiles from Goss, a pat on the thigh from Frog, a lavender drop from Elf, a little wave, at one point, from Miss Milligan who was still seated on the top of the piano and, in the warm light, looked hardly more than a girl herself. Pauline did not understand half the words of half the old Scots songs but the emotions they conveyed were stirring and sympathetic and needed no interpretation. They made her think of her father soon to arrive in Africa, of her mother, of the half-sister or little brother new born or soon to be born; and, most oddly, of poor Mr Roderick Harvey, smelling of straw and horses, as he limped about the paddocks like a hare.

Miss Gaylord had slipped into the room. She was seated on an upright chair, hands folded in her lap, head cocked to one side as if the evening roused in her, too, emotions too complex to define. Her eyes were faded, wistful, sad, and she was oblivious to the girls who sat on cushions on the floor a little to her left, screened by the wings of a deep armchair; to the Irish girl who stood all alone in the doorway corner smiling secretively to herself and, now and then, pursing her lips as if in practice for a parting kiss.

Stella had no ear for music, no eye for whirling leaves or crackling sparks. She balanced herself on the cushion, Ronnie leaning into her on one side, Daphne on the other, calves and ankles touching with little rasping caresses of silk in an intimacy that was not so much affectionate as conspiratorial.

"And what will you do then, dearest?" Daphne whispered.

Stella traced a fingernail down the back of Daphne's hand and rubbed her hip against Ronnie's thigh. "Spoil him," she said.

"But it isn't you he wants, is it?" Ronnie said.

"No," said Stella, "but it's me that our dear Charlie will get."

"When?" said Ronnie.

"Three weeks from tonight."

"How on earth will you manage it?" said Daphne.

"Leave that to me," said Stella and, digging her nail more deeply into tender flesh, made Daphne shiver, and wince.

# Nine

*D*addy had warned Pauline that there would be a lapse in correspondence. He had promised to send a cable the moment he arrived in Durban and to write at length just as soon as he unpacked. It was not so much the absence of communication from her father that worried Pauline as the complete lack of news from and concerning her mother. Days grew into weeks. A cable from Daddy arrived eventually and was conveyed to Pauline by Miss Milligan – a relief, of course – but Pauline's enquiries, growing ever more anxious, for word of her mother met with blank silence.

Since first meetings in September Pauline had not cultivated her cousin's friendship. She did not like Stella or Stella's crowd and steered well clear of them. Between the cousins there was a cool recognition of kinship, a nod of greeting in a corridor, an occasional guarded exchange in class. Pauline had elected to go her own way at St Austin's, however, and it was not in Stella's nature to forgive that sort of disloyalty. Out of class and out of house the girls saw little of each other.

By the week of the October gales which stripped the last of the leaves from the trees and drowned Perthshire moors and mountains in lashing rain, Pauline's anxiety was beginning to affect her schoolwork, her pastimes and her friendships.

"For heaven's sake," Frog would say, "why don't you write to your mother and just ask her outright."

"I told you, I don't know where she is exactly."

"Write to your father? He's bound to have heard something," Goss would suggest.

"It'll take weeks for a reply to reach me."

"Write to your aunt then."

"I did," Pauline moaned.

"Didn't she answer?" asked Elf.

"Yes. She scribbled away about how glad she was that I

140

was settling into St Austin's and that I had taken up riding. And she sent me a ten shilling postal order."

"Not a word about your mother?"

"Not a scratch."

"Ask Stella," Goss suggested.

"And seem like a fool."

"Oh, for heaven's sake!" Goss exclaimed in exasperation. "It can't be that much of a secret, Pauline. If anyone knows what's happened, it'll be Stella."

"Why haven't I been informed?"

"Delicate sensibilities," said Elf.

"What does that mean?" Pauline demanded.

"Perhaps your mother isn't sure how you'll take it," Frog explained. "Having a baby brother or sister at this late stage in your career, I mean."

"Ask Stella," said Goss again.

"Are you sure you lot don't mind?"

"Of course we don't mind," said Frog.

"Stella may be a horrible cow," said Goss, "but she's still your cousin."

"Blood's thicker than water, after all," Elf added.

"Ask her," said Goss emphatically.

Back in the bad old days Miss Aitken had seen to it that culture was thrust upon her girls with all the subtlety of a cavalry charge. Self-improvement was the motto by which Miss Aitken lived and governed. No opportunity was lost to force-feed the principles of industry and learning, along with guilt, meekness and subjugation, to the school as a whole. The annual Haydock Lecture was a relic from those grim and joyless times but one into which Janis Fergusson had managed to inject a little colour and vivacity.

Until his death in harness in 1920 the Reverend Matthew Haydock had been minister of Pattullo Old Parish Kirk for as long as anyone could remember and had founded the annual lecture. The fact that he visited the school two or three times every week and was never off the platform in the Harvey Hall did not seem to matter. The Haydock Lecture was delivered year after year by the great man himself; a whole Saturday evening devoted to such inspiring topics as Why Ye Are Dead and What Wilt Thou Do on Judgement Day?, thundered out at one hundred and twenty girls all dressed in Best Uniform, who shuffled and rustled, stretched their spines and discreetly wriggled their bottoms and wondered why, if there was a God, He did not answer their heartfelt prayers and strike the daft wee mannie dead which, in the fullness of time, He did.

On paper the 1921 Haydock promised no improvement in entertainment value. Announcement of its subject brought groans from the girls and a pleased smile to the face of Miss Gaylord: The History of Education by former HM Inspector of Schools for Clackmannan, James Henry Knott. James Henry Knott might be retired from his professional position but he still carried with him the ineffable air of glowering disapproval that was the mark of such men. The wife whom he brought with him was even less promising; a dour Victorian biddy with grey buns and beady little eyeglasses and never a smile for anyone at the guest table in the dining-room during Saturday supper.

Surprisingly, none of St Austin's eagle-eyed observers had noticed that Tom MacAdam and the school bus had been gone for half the afternoon and that, under cover of gloaming, had returned to the rear of School where a great deal of unpacking had taken place.

Assembly began about twenty-five past seven. Ant-like columns of girls emerged from house corridors and converged upon the open doors of the Harvey with its shiny maplewood floor, imposing platform and rows of punishingly hard benches. There was very little chatter, no sense of anticipation at all. The wearing of uniforms on a Saturday evening was imposition enough and the dry, dusty appearance of the Knotts, linked to an unappealing subject, gave no hope of relief from creaking tedium for the next hour and a half. Goss was gloomy, Elf resentful, Frog resigned. Pauline, however, was protected by her preoccupation with matters happening far from St Austin's. While pony riding under Mr Harvey's watchful eye, she had decided to broach Stella sometime in the course of the evening in the hope that her cousin would be generous enough to throw light upon the mystery. She moved with the mass towards the Harvey

142

isolated by nervous self-concern. Of course she could have knocked upon the door of Room No. 13 at any time and sought an interview with her relative. But this way was better, less pointed and, oddly, more private.

She glimpsed Stella arm in arm with Daphne Gore as the pair descended the staircase from the dormitory floor. She glimpsed Stella again, as she paused before Miss Milligan for a once-over, and then lost sight of her completely. Curiously she did not notice Stella again until the lecture was over. What was curious about it was that Daphne Gore and Rhona Somerville were seated directly in front of Pauline. And when she leaned forward and asked, politely, "Where's Stella?" shot her such startled glances that she retreated at once without an answer and settled – unexpectedly – to enjoy the show.

Dido and Aeneas, let alone Jessica and Lorenzo, would have been hard put to it to find a dry corner for love-making if they had been condemned to rendezvous on such a night as had settled down over Perthshire on that late October Saturday. It had been dry enough throughout the afternoon but cloud had scudded in on the blustery remnants of the gales and filled the glens with misty rain that thickened with the night and drove now, pattering, against the wooden walls of the little tennis pavilion and slashed down from its fretted eaves.

Charlie had been waiting for the best part of an hour. Smoking one cigarette after another, stubbing out the butts and, collar turned up, burying them in the sodden grasses of the hillside that rose steeply above the tiny building, his romantic ardour had been replaced by fear; fear of discovery, fear of what the beautiful dark-haired Irish girl might expect of him, fear of her loveliness, her voice, her money and her education, fear of the humiliations that she might heap upon him if he did not match up to her ideal, fear, most of all, of the fact that he did not know what he wanted of her and why he had allowed himself to be talked into this dangerous situation at all.

The trouble with Charlie MacAdam was that he never had much going on in his head. He had mooched through school in the knowledge that if he was still breathing by the time he reached fourteen then a job with Mr Guy Harvey's timber business would be ready and waiting for him. Ambition not being a strong suit among MacAdams, he had gone along willingly with that easy option. He had no vision of his future and, unlike many of the gangers and fellers with whom he came into contact, no brawling animal appetites to keep him going from one Saturday to the next. Even his Christian faith, about which Mr Haydock had made so much fuss, was hardly faith at all but just the church-going habit for Pattullo Parish kirk had provided Charlie with a refuge and a little sphere of importance without which not even a lad as dull as he could survive.

To say that Charlie had been putty in Stella Jackson's hands would have been an understatement. As a youngster he had been frightened of the girls from the school. In fact when the girls from the school had been invited to participate in the 'organisations' – that is to become teachers in Sunday School, members of the Youths' Bible Study Group and to attend midweek meetings of Fellowship – he thought of resigning from the church completely. Irresolution and his father had prevailed upon Charlie to stand his ground and, he had to admit, he had found St Austin's pupils a bit different from what he had expected and not at all like he had been led to believe by his father and brothers. The girls from St Austin's treated Charlie and the other young teachers from the town, male and female, with kindly disdain. They were charitable, patient, almost regal, but they lost no opportunity to show off their superior knowledge and command obedience from the kiddies who were under their charge for an hour every Sunday morning.

It had been fine, really, until Miss Jackson had shown up. She was not quite like the others. She did not hold herself apart. She was free and friendly and eager to talk to him and to Bobby Stewart and Crawford Littlejohn and was for ever having quiet 'sincere' conversations with Mr Prentice when she could get him off into a corner on his own.

Charlie had raised Miss Jackson's name one evening at the supper table, just to see what his father might know of her, for his father knew everything about everyone up at St Austin's.

144

"The Jackson lass?" Charlie's father had seemed startled. "She's comin' to the kirk, is she? Well, son, steer clear o' that one."

"She seems quite nice," Charlie had said. "Mr Prentice thinks she's nice."

"Aye, well, Mr Prentice had better mind himself," Tom MacAdam had said. "And you too, son. Give Miss Jackson a fine wide berth."

Charlie had nodded obediently but somehow, in the warning, had discovered the seeds of intrigue. He had not heeded his father's advice. He had stumbled and mumbled and blushed his way into a friendship of sorts with Stella Jackson, more out of vanity than either liking or desire.

It was not until the Irish girl had strayed across his path that Charlie had fallen headlong from vacant contemplation of nothing very much and into a sticky morass of love-sickness which sucked away his common sense and clogged his senses and gave him something to moon over during his long stints tushing fallen trees or winching logs on to the pole wagon or trudging down behind the Shires from the forest to the sawmill.

She – the Irish girl – had come to sing at a Sunday School concert in the park at the end of the summer term. She had sat up in the bandstand on a chair all alone with just the wee harp on her lap, and had charmed the whole audience with her sweet clear voice and the sad, sad look in her jet black eyes. Charlie had near fallen off his chair. He had been to talk to Stella like a shot the following Sunday, the last of the season, and had found out that the singer's name was Colleen O'Neal.

If Charlie had had time to gather his wits he might have made it clear to Stella where his heart, as the song put it, had flown. But it was right on the edge of the summer vacation and Charlie had had the best part of six weeks to come to terms with rapture and, by tuning in to the frank talk of the men with whom he took his dinners in the woods, to misinterpret love as natural, manly lust.

Desperately ashamed of his confused emotions, Charlie learned to hide them behind a dour and implacable mask. He learned this trick so well that when his Dad fuelled the school bus and drove off to Perth to pick up the first of St Austin's arrivals, he even managed a snarl of derision. When he first encountered Stella Jackson at Sunday School the following weekend, he gave her no hint of the thoughts that had burned away all summer long or of how much he had been changed by them. Stella Jackson held no serious attraction for him. She was too skinny, too sharp, far too aware of herself to change the direction of the needle of his compass. He played up to her, though, in the hope that she might introduce him to Colleen.

He hated himself for taking to the wall with the younger lads but it was the only way he could get to cast eyes on his beloved. He hated himself even more for trailing her into town, for loitering like a clown about The Hut. And it was to relieve himself of this burden of limitless stupidity that he plucked up his courage and did the bit with the chocolate box. And when she turned and waved to him and smiled, and did a wee pirouette, Charlie nearly swooned away and fell like a gaffed salmon into the Teal forty feet below.

Next day, Sunday, he could hardly wait for the first half hour of the long morning service to be over and done with and for the children, ages five to ten, to be led out of the kirk and into the side hall. There they gathered round their little tables and were instructed and kept amused for an hour or so by a dozen youthful volunteers including four from the school. He'd sidled up to Stella and, without preliminary, had asked her what Miss O'Neal had said in response to his gift.

"She was awfully flattered, of course."

"Did she – ah, gi'e you anythin' for me?"

"What did you expect, Charlie?"

"I dunno. A letter, maybe."

"Colleen wouldn't dare write to you. What if the letter was discovered? She'd be in dreadful hot water at school."

"Can you – can you tak' her a message? No' written, just spoken."

"Verbal. Why certainly, Charlie."

"Tell her—"

"Tell her what, Charlie?"

"Uh – nothin'."

146

The following Saturday he was on the bridge again. He had made no arrangement to rendezvous with Stella and had not dared suggest that Colleen put herself in peril of reprimand by slipping away from the stewards to meet with him. But he was there on the bridge. And he got his wave and a little dance to keep him going. And next morning Stella told him that Colleen wanted to meet with him.

"Under the brig on Saturday?"

"No, that's impossibly risky."

"You managed it."

"Yes, but Colleen's not as daring as I am."

"When then? Where then?"

"I'll let you know."

Saturday afternoon it rained cats and dogs. Charlie wore his big crackling fisherman's oilskin and an old cap but got soaked nonetheless. Not one of the girls from St Austin's ventured further into Pattullo than the Toffee Shop. He was the only boy out on the wall. His reward was a bold wave from Colleen and a smile that warmed him through and through, before she scampered off under a prefect's umbrella into the sanctity of the grounds.

"Hail, rain or shine," Stella told him the following morning, "next Saturday you star-crossed lovers will meet."

"Lovers?"

"A figure of speech, Charlie. Don't you want to speak to Colleen alone?"

"Aye, aye, 'course I do."

"What are you going to say to her?"

"I – uh – I dunno."

"Are you going to tell her you're madly in love with her?" When Charlie gave no answer, Stella went on. "It's the night of the Haydock Lecture on Saturday. Can you be at the little tennis pavilion behind the courts at about half-past seven?"

"In the grounds?"

"Come now, surely you don't expect Colleen to break bounds?"

"Aye, I'll be there then. Will she come, though?"

"If she can," Stella said. "If she possibly can."

That afternoon there was an Irish wave at the Toffee Shop

and another Irish wave and a bit of a jig on the gravel outside The Hut and Charlie went away full of high expectations, and fear.

He came in by the back track that wended round Mac-Adam's garden, which was easy enough, though finding an excuse for going out at all had been more difficult.

"I hope you're no' goin' to the pub?" his mother had shouted after him.

"I'm just goin' for a walk."

"In this weather? You're daft."

Now, five cigarettes later, Charlie was beginning to think that his mother had been right. What did he expect to come of this meeting? What could come of it? Nothing – except trouble.

"Charlie?" said the voice, and he nearly jumped out of his skin. "Where are you?"

She came around the corner, bustling and not at all furtive. She wore a sort of jade-green cloak over her uniform but even before she pulled down the hood Charlie knew that it wasn't Colleen but Stella.

After a first surge of guilt and excitement he felt less disappointed than relieved. Stella was very quick, very darting. She took his hand and drew him around the side of the pavilion on to the little platform that looked out to the hillside. It was pitch dark. Charlie could not see her at all. He could feel her though, her tiny, delicate hand in his, the cloak brushing against him, he could smell the perfume from her, not musky but flowery and sharp.

"Where's Colleen?" he growled.

"Colleen couldn't come. She wanted to but she couldn't slip away. It isn't all that simple, you know. It's all very well for you – you're a man and can do what you like. But we're young ladies, guarded day and night."

She was prattling. He liked it. He was nervous still and had this fancy that her clear bell-like English voice would carry over the shoulder of the woods to the school and that some teacher or other would hear it, or that the wet wind would transport it over the rump of the hill to the farm and his mother's ears.

"Wheesh, Stella," he told her. "Somebody'll hear."

"They're all at the lecture, silly. Nobody can hear us. Do you have a cigarette to spare?"

"What?"

"A fag, a gasper."

The cheap paper packet was damp. He had only two Woodbines left in it and, anyway, he felt a strange sort of moral repugnance at granting Stella's request. He did not think it proper for St Austin's girls to smoke. He fished the pair of cigarettes out of the packet, though, and offered her one. In the darkness, the pitch darkness, she did not see it.

"Where?" she said, then, "Light it for me, there's a good boy."

He put the cigarettes into his mouth, fished for the matches and lit one. When flame flared up and gave light he was too taken aback to bother with the cigarettes which stuck out of his mouth like fangs.

Stella giggled. "What's wrong, Charlie?"

"It's – you."

She giggled again. "Of course it's me. What is it? What's wrong?"

How could he tell her that he had never seen anyone, not even his dear Colleen, quite so strikingly pretty. The folds of the hood, the soft matchlight did it. Her features were framed softly. Her hair, released from its ribbons, was the colour of old gold, her eyes brilliant and mischievous.

"Stop looking at me like that, Charlie MacAdam," Stella said, delightedly, and, stretching up on toe tip, blew out the burning match. "There, that's better."

Charlie swallowed. "I – I thought y' wanted a gasper?"

"In a moment," Stella said. "And only if you promise not to look at me like that."

"Like – like what?"

"As if you wanted to kiss me."

"That – that's daft."

"Promise you'll behave."

"Aye, all right."

"Well, go on. Light my cigarette. If you're going to give me one, that is."

He shook the box in his closed fist. He had eight or ten matches left, eight or ten pieces of light. He wanted to look at her again; the cigarettes were inconsequential. He could not understand why he had never noticed how pretty she was and, in spite of her size, grown up. No, she wasn't like Colleen, strong and musky and mysterious. But Stella was here and Colleen was not. He felt more confident with Stella because he had at least spoken to her and because they had something in common, even if it was just Sunday School, never mind the business with the chocolates and the messages.

Charlie struck a second match. He held it steady long enough to light both cigarettes and gave one to Stella. Even after the flame went out the tiny firefly glow of tobacco coals provided focus. He heard Stella inhale and saw the drift of smoke from her nostrils.

Stella said, "What's wrong, Charlie? Are you sorry it's me and not Colleen?"

"Naw, it's just—"

"What," said Stella, "would you do if it was Colleen?"

Charlie paused. "Talk."

"Would you ask her to kiss you?"

"Naw, I couldn't do that."

"Why ever not?"

"It wouldnae be proper."

"Oh, and do you think it's proper to meet a girl alone in the woods on a dark night?"

Charlie said, "Would she no' come, was that it? Does she no' like me?"

"Colleen likes you very much, Charlie, though she hardly knows you, of course. The truth is that she hadn't the guts to come. Perhaps she was frightened of what you would try to do to her."

"Didn't you tell her?"

"Tell her what, Charlie?"

"That I'm no' like that."

"I don't know what you're like, Charlie. I'm taking a fearful risk meeting you alone, like this."

"I'm no' goin' to do anythin'," said Charlie, with more regret than nobility.

Stella chuckled. "Have you ever done anything? With a girl, I mean?"

150

"Naw, I mean – aye, sure."

"Really? What?"

"None – none o' your business."

"Have you, for instance, kissed a girl before?"

"Aye, dozens o' times."

"In that case why don't you kiss me?" Stella said.

Charlie hesitated. He was sweating now inside the twill shirt and heavy tweed jacket. He felt thick and stupid and sticky. He felt as if he smelled too. He was a clown, her clown, and he hated her for laughing at him.

"B . . . b'cause," he told her, gruffly.

"That's a conjunction, not a reason."

"You're different."

"No, I'm not. I'm just the same as those dozens of other girls you've kissed. Two arms, two legs, a head in the right place," said Stella. "If I was Colleen and I invited you to kiss me, what would you do, Charlie?"

"I dunno."

"Oh, you do so know. You'd take her in your arms, wouldn't you, you would press your lips to hers?"

"I might."

He watched the coal of Stella's cigarette arc out into the weedy darkness and extinguish itself in the rain. He smoked on, furiously and resolutely until there was nothing left of his cigarette and he was forced to drop it and stamp on the grains.

"Of course you would," Stella said. "Imagine, just for a moment, that I'm Colleen. Show me what you'd do, Charlie."

He made no move towards where he thought she would be. He might have slunk away from her if he had been less thick-witted. When she touched him, though, groped for his hand, guided his hand to her waist, he did not shrink away.

"See," Stella whispered. "Like this."

She pressed herself against him. She lifted herself on toe tip once more and touched his lips with hers, both her arms about his waist. Her lips were the lightest, softest things that Charlie had ever felt. It was like kissing milk.

Stella whispered, "Hold me, hold me tightly."

He had thought that she – any of them – would feel as

151

soft as they looked. But she was hard, hard and lithe as a fresh-caught grayling. He kissed her, this time without being coaxed. She leaned into him, all the length of her body, rubbing her knees against his knees and her stomach against his thighs.

The force between them was so great that Charlie staggered. He caught at her. He drew her with him until his back was to the wall of the pavilion. Pale light from the town's street sheened the water that fell from the eaves. He could see Stella's face. Eyelids fluttering, she nuzzled and groped for his mouth again, for all the world like a suckling calf greedy for the teat. It was not what he had thought it would be. There was no tenderness in it. Even so, another ten or fifteen seconds and he would have succumbed. He sensed that he could win control over her just by slipping his hands down lower, by thrusting that part of him against her. Even through the sliding weight of the school skirt and whatever garments were beneath it he could feel her body. He wanted to explore it – but not enough to yield. Daft though he was, thick and uneducated, he had sufficient intelligence to control himself. He pushed her, quite roughly, away.

She was making strange little panting sounds, sounds that both fascinated and disgusted him. Her lids were fluttering like a moth's wings. Suddenly he felt quite commanding.

He said, "I'll have t'be goin' now."

"No," she said. "No."

"Aye, Stella," he said.

She tried to catch hold of him. She tried to make him hold her closely once more. Charlie stepped to one side. He was afraid, even now, of what she might make him do. She hung her head, not looking at him in the faint, faint light that pervaded the sky through the pine trees and slicked the wet surfaces of the little building.

Charlie said, "I'll see you tomorrow. At the kirk."

"Charlie?"

He put his trembling hand into his jacket pocket and found only the empty paper packet which, in his frustration, he crumpled in his fingers into a tiny hard ball.

"Aye?"

"Will you meet me again?" Stella said.

152

"Aye, t'morrow."

"I mean like this. Alone, the two of us."

"What about Colleen?" Charlie MacAdam said.

"What about her?"

"I thought I was meetin' her."

"Isn't it better with me?" said Stella. "Wouldn't you rather have me?"

And Charlie, to his credit, said, "No."

Within minutes of entering the Harvey the girls' collective gloom was replaced by curiosity. Almost as soon as the curtain rose on the little velvet-draped stage that had been erected on the platform, they knew they were in for a treat.

Certainly Mr Knott's lecture contained a certain amount of instruction on the history and development of educational principles but, by and large, form far outstripped content. Glove puppets and string puppets popped up and down, into and out of the lighted oblong of the little stage. Each one was a perfect caricature of a teacher or type of pupil from time past to time present. The lecture was conducted by a hatchet-faced female puppet in a funereal black cloak and mortar board who wagged her cane at the audience and harangued it in a shrill voice, enhanced by the use of a swabble. Years of suppressed good humour had gone into the planning and preparation of Mr James Henry Knott's seventy-minute show. The puppets were beautifully modelled and, Pauline guessed, somewhere behind the scenes Mr Knott and his wife were working very hard indeed.

Pupils through the years did not escape the inspector's wit; the Swot, the Dodger, the Sport were all represented. The Dunce had a head moulded from an empty ginger beer bottle which the teacher rapped now and then with a cry of "Empty, empty, empty." There was, in fact, a good deal of whacking and yelping in each of the little playlets and Pauline found herself laughing uproariously and shouting out in participation, along with all the rest of the school, her melancholy mood temporarily dispelled and her worries put aside.

At the end of the performance Mr Knott and his 'able assistant', Mrs Knott, received a standing ovation. In return they offered to show the workings of the puppets to any interested parties before they departed. Quite a rush ensued. It was all the prefects could do to keep order at the steps of the platform while housemistresses, teachers and the Dragon – a sign of the new democracy – served cocoa and cut cake in the front hall.

Spirits were high. Goss, in particular, had been rendered speechless with mirth and went back over the performance with Frog, reviving choice bits of dialogue. Cocoa mug in hand, Elf did a fair impersonation of the Dominie and, not alone in the throng, cried out "Empty, empty, empty" while knocking on the side of her head.

Pauline would have joined in the general merriment if she had not at that moment caught sight of her cousin. Stella was tucked in a shadowy corner by the dining-room doors. Daphne and Ronnie were with her but not the Irish girl who, it appeared, was not currently in favour with her room-mates. Pauline hesitated. Hall and corridors were filled with girls and the din was terrific. She sipped cocoa, swallowed the last of her ration of cut cake and, with sudden determination, weaved through groups of girls towards Stella.

The three were oblivious to Pauline's approach. They were engaged in an intense conversation and none of them smiling. Stella had a slightly dishevelled appearance and her complexion was even paler than usual. Again Pauline hesitated. She might not have dared intrude if, at that moment, Miss Fergusson had not appeared from the Harvey leading Mr and Mrs Knott towards the parlour where a substantial supper would be laid out, together with alcoholic refreshment of some sort.

Miss Fergusson was beaming. She had also enjoyed the puppet show and had not been in the least put out by its irreverence towards the teaching profession. "Well, girls," she enquired in passing, "did you enjoy yourselves tonight?"

"Yes, Miss Fergusson," the three answered in chorus but, as soon as the Dragon and her guests had passed, doubled over with laughter as if Miss Fergusson had said something hilarious.

Glancing up, Stella met Pauline's eye. "What do you want?" she demanded.

"Might I have a word with you, Stella?"

Daphne frowned. Ronnie clutched at Stella's arm as if Pauline had uttered a threat. Stella shook her head slightly then smiled at Pauline. "Concerning what, cousin dear?"

"A private matter. It'll only take a moment."

Stella sighed but left her chums and steered Pauline towards the long corridor that led to the darkened classrooms. She stopped somewhere along its length, leaned her back against the wall and sipped from the cocoa mug that she held in both hands.

"I looked for you in the hall, earlier," Pauline said.

"So?"

"I didn't see you there."

"Who put you up to this? Goss?"

"No, nobody put me up to it."

"I suppose Johnstone thinks she has something on me now. Well, tell her from me that it won't wash, Pauline. I've a dozen friends prepared to swear I was with them throughout the silly lecture."

"What on earth are you talking about, Stella?"

"What are you talking about?"

"My mother."

"Your mother! What does she have to do with—" Stella uttered a little grunt of wry amusement and relief. "Oh, I understand. Do you mean she hasn't told you yet?"

"Told me?"

"Strange, I thought you would have been the first to be told. On the other hand, perhaps not. Yes, perhaps she felt it would be better not to distress you."

"Stella, what news have you had from home?"

The blonde girl's attitude softened a little. She glanced up the passageway towards the lighted, noisy hall and then, not meeting Pauline's eye, stooped and put down the cocoa mug. "I shouldn't have to do this. It shouldn't be up to me," Stella said. "I heard by letter only this morning. I just assumed, somehow, that you'd been informed."

"Informed of what?" said Pauline, trying not to shout. "Has my mother had her baby?"

"Yes, two or three weeks ago, I gather."

"Two or three weeks—!" Pauline stiffened. Pain ate into

her stomach and she felt her loins cramp with fear. "What was it, Stella – a girl or boy?"

"I – I'm afraid I really couldn't say."

"Stella—"

"It was born dead, you see."

Pauline shed no tears. She gave no outward sign that anything was wrong. Confused by this lack of visible emotion, Stella did not accompany her cousin as she walked back into the front hall and through it and on towards the house. In twenty minutes time the bedtime bell would ring. A quarter hour after that, Lights Out. Pauline did not want to have to explain to Goss or the others what the loss of the half-brother or sister meant to her. At the back of her friends' platitudes would be an unspoken acknowledgment that, under the circumstances, it was perhaps best that the love-child had not survived. She did not doubt that Stella had told the truth. If Stella had sought her out, had made a thing of it, then she would have suspected her cousin of malice, of taking some nasty satisfaction in the infant's death. But Stella had behaved as Stella would always behave in the face of another's misfortune. Casually.

What did it matter, after all? She had seen so little of her mother in recent years, and had never even met the baby's father. She remembered the swollen, ugly stomach, the waddling gait that had spoiled her mother's daintiness but she could not associate it with the child she had dreamed about, the sister she had created in her imagination and, in her imagination, had loved.

Pauline crossed the darkened common-room of Teal House and tried the handle of the French door that led to the terrace. It opened before her. She stepped out into the slough of rain that bent itself about the great stone corner of the building and ruffled the shallow puddles on the flagstones. A half hour ago she had been laughing and carefree. Now she was burdened by a leaden sorrow. She leaned against the wall in a sheltered niche by the door and rubbed her eyes with the heel of her hand. No tears, no tears at all. She tried to weep but could only manage a shuddering sigh.

"I like it here in the rain," a voice said. "They say it's the tears of angels. I feel their sadness, don't you?"

156

"Colleen? What are you doing here?"

"I might ask you the same sort of thing."

"I just – just wanted a breath of air before bedtime."

The Irish girl's hair glistened damply. Pauline guessed that she had been walking on the lawns, face upturned to the winding rain.

Colleen said, "You've had bad news, haven't you?"

"How did you know that?"

"Ah!"

"Stella told you, didn't she?"

"She said something; not much, to be sure, but enough of a hint," Colleen said. "There, I've let the cat out o' the bag, have I not?"

They were together, side by side, leaning on the wall in the protected angle, with the rain at their feet and the puddles ruffled like little seas. Colleen said, "Is it an illness, a death?"

"My half-brother or sister."

"At birth?"

"Yes."

"Are you disappointed?"

"What an odd word," said Pauline. "Disappointed? Yes, perhaps that's what it is. I've no other brothers or sisters, you see."

"And a half would have been better than none?" said Colleen. "But none there is. Is your mother ill?"

"I haven't been told, I haven't even been told that the baby – I had to ask Stella for news."

"It wouldn't matter to her."

"No, it didn't," said Pauline.

"Aren't you goin' to cry?" said Colleen.

"I don't believe I am."

Colleen nodded. She put an arm across Pauline's shoulder in a manner that was more fraternal than sisterly. "You can cry if you like. It's only me here an' I know what cryin's all about."

"Have you got sisters and brothers?"

"Brothers. I never see them, hardly. Do you love your Mama or your Dada best?"

"My Father. Oh, yes, my Father."

157

"She left, didn't she? Your Mama, I mean."

"Yes, a long time ago."

"That's why you love your Dada so much. Because you don't have to share him. I don't have either, really. God, I hardly know them."

"I'm sorry," said Pauline.

Colleen settled her arm more firmly about Pauline's. She said, "I wonder where they go?"

"What? Your parents?"

"Tiddlers, babies. When they die before they breathe, I wonder where they go."

"To heaven," said Pauline uncertainly.

"Up there?" Colleen nodded towards the swirl of rain that shrouded lawns and trees and, beyond, the looming moor and far dark mountainsides. "Nah, that's not for them."

"Because they're unbaptised?"

"Catholic talk, that," said Colleen mildly. "My Gran told me they went back to the sea an' swam, like little fishes, to the Isles of the Blessed. When I would ask her where that was, she would say it was west of Killarney, where the sun went down. She would say that if I looked along the sunset path into the setting I would see them, all the little heads, dark and fair, scudding back to rest eternal."

"Did you believe her?"

"I'd like to."

Without warning, Pauline began to cry. It was soft within her, like something melting. She felt tears trickle rather than start upon her cheeks. At first she had been annoyed by the presence of the Irish girl but now she was glad of the arm about her shoulder.

Pauline cried for two or three minutes during which time Colleen O'Neal studied the lacy rain in the evergreens. When Pauline's tears had eased to an occasional sob, Colleen produced a large white-linen handkerchief, spotlessly clean, and held it out to her housemate. "Better now?"

Pauline blew her nose. "Much."

The arm abruptly detached itself from about Pauline's shoulder and, with a skipping step, the Irish girl went through the French doors. Pauline started after her into the darkened common-room. "Colleen, your handkerchief."

"Keep it."

"Colleen?"

"What now?"

"Thanks."

"No thanks required," said Colleen O'Neal, and was gone.

# Ten

*I*t was a rare thing now for Donald Haldane to come into London, rarer still for him to lunch with his son-in-law. He resented Lewis's insistence that they meet in the dining room of the Royal Automobile Club's luxurious premises on the site of the old War Office in Pall Mall. Lewis's polite refusal to drive out to Hampstead to pick him up had cost him the price of a motorcar hire, a piece of highway robbery in every sense of the word.

Even with a stick to support him, it was painful for Donald Haldane to walk. He put on the limp a bit as he was ushered to the table that Lewis Jackson had reserved, though he shook off gruffly and without thanks the manager's steadying hand on his arm. Lewis rose to greet him. As always, the younger man smiled affably and pretended to be concerned about Donald's comfort as he was settled into a chair at the table.

The broad room was crowded. There was to the gathering a prattling enthusiasm and lack of discretion that served to confirm Donald Haldane's low opinion of motorists. He had to admit, however, that the room reeked of money not petroleum, and that his rustic son-in-law had somehow managed to disguise himself as a big city gent in a hand-cut three piece suit of fine dark blue pinstripe material. Donald Haldane knew the younger man hardly at all. The problem was that Lewis Jackson had never asked him for anything, except the hand of a daughter in marriage. Lewis seemed quite unaware of or impervious to the fact that he, Donald Clark Haldane, was worth the best part of a quarter of a million pounds in cash and capital assets.

"Would you care for a drink, sir?" Lewis asked, after the scant preliminaries of greetings were over. "Whisky, perhaps?"

Donald Haldane shook his head. His legs throbbed and

he was still sulking at Lewis for dragging him to town. He studied the carded menu without hunger but ordered the most expensive plates he could find upon it just to teach the inconsiderate youngster a lesson. Lewis Jackson was not in the least put out by the extravagance and ordered, without consulting his elder, a bottle of the 1900 Château Latour, and a preliminary Chablis of no great distinction with which to fill his in-law's glass. Beneath the cover of the table Donald Haldane massaged his legs with hands that had no muscular strength at all.

Lewis said, "Sorry about the rush, sir. I'm only in town for the day and have a considerable amount of business to transact. To tell you the truth I really cannot abide London. Too busy, too congested for a simple country fellow like me."

Out of his element and out of his time Donald Haldane had no stomach for small talk. He said, "I suppose you know I'm not going to live for ever?"

"Oh, really!" said Lewis Jackson and then, regretting his flippancy, added, "You're not ill, are you?"

"At my age, Lewis, you're always ill. You die by yards, not inches, every damned day."

"Is it to discuss your demise that you asked to see me?"

"In a manner of speaking," Donald Haldane said. "I'm concerned about what'll happen to the girls after I've gone."

He pronounced it 'gurls', an intonation that gave the word all sorts of implications that were not consciously intended. The voice had faded like old leather but it was tough still, tough in that Scottish manner that Lewis found slightly intimidating.

Lewis said, "Let me assure you that you need have no concern for Beatrix, or Stella for that matter. They will be perfectly well taken care of whether you're here or not."

"It's not them I'm worried about. It's Barbara and her girl."

"Which girl?"

"Pauline."

"Oh, I thought for a moment you meant—"

Donald Haldane ignored the unfinished sentence. He said, "I want this marriage to stick, Lewis."

161

"Barbara's marriage?"

"Aye. You may not think much of Straker but he's a type of man I understand. That weakling Verity was never for her. Straker's a different proposition. He'll keep her in her place and see to it that she doesn't go flyin' off the rails – if he's handled right."

Lewis, though he had serious doubts about the old man's judgment, nodded then said, "What do you mean – handled right?"

"Kept loyal."

"To whom – to you?"

"To Barbara."

"Well, that's not my province, sir. Sorry," Lewis said. "I've more than enough on my plate looking out for my own family. Besides, I don't see what—"

"I've named you as the executor of my estate."

"Oh!"

"Have no fear, my lawyers will have my instructions written down to the last letter and all legally binding."

"In that case why do you need me to act as executor?"

"I don't trust Verity."

"What?"

"Look what he did to Babby."

"As far as I'm aware he didn't do anything to Barbara."

"Aye, well, you're too honest a chap to understand the deviousness of men like Harry Verity. He'll be after a share of my money when I'm gone. He's a wastrel, a no-good. And I don't want him spoiling my grandchild's future or robbing her of what's rightfully hers."

"Harry Verity's not like—"

"Is he not? Look what he did to his child."

"Pardon?"

"Deprived her, deprived her of a decent upbringing just to appease his own pride."

"I think he loved her," said Lewis. "Barbara, I mean. And I don't see how you can doubt that he loves Pauline."

"I could have done a lot for Verity, you know."

"Why didn't you?"

"He refused all my offers, all my help." Donald Haldane squinted at his son-in-law and then, frowning, added. "So did

162

you, of course, but it was different in your case. You didn't need it."

Lewis pursed his lips. He felt a soft seething anger at the old man's arrant snobbery, his refusal to admit that Barbara had been reckless and vain and that he, Donald Haldane, had been too preoccupied to notice where she was heading or, after the event, to lay blame where it was due. And that was not on poor Harry Verity.

Lewis said, cautiously, "And do you regard Mark Straker as a better proposition?"

"He'll not abandon her, that's for sure," Donald Haldane said. He gave a little wry grunt. "Not while she has money."

Lewis sat back in the chair. "So that's why you need an executor in addition to lawyers – to keep Straker from milking Barbara of whatever inheritance you leave to her?"

"Do you blame me for my concern?"

"Certainly not. Anything but."

"The welfare of my daughters and their seed are all that interest me."

"Seed, uh-huh," Lewis murmured, trying to envisage Stella, Lew and Olly in dry biblical terms, and failing utterly. "Do you mean all the seedlings?"

"All that are worth acknowledging."

"I thought the – that matter had been taken care of?"

"It has."

"Do you mean that Straker isn't going to marry Barbara?"

"Of course he is."

"What then is the problem?"

"Pauline's her mother's daughter. Babby will need her more than ever now. There are times when a mother needs a daughter's love as much as the other way around," Donald Haldane said.

"Perhaps Babs will have more children."

"No."

"Do you mean she can't?"

"I mean she daren't."

"What does Straker have to say about that?" said Lewis.

"He's prepared for it. He's a decent enough fellow, you know," Donald Haldane said, "even if one does not entirely

163

approve of his morals. In spite of what's happened he remains devoted to Babby."

"You still haven't told me what you want me to do apart from executing your will – eventually."

"Take Pauline in during the holidays."

"Oh, that's nothing," said Lewis. "I'd intended to bring her down to the Hall for Christmas in any case. Poor kid, where else has she to go?"

"And ask Babby and her husband too."

"Fine," Lewis agreed. He added, "Does Pauline know what's happened? To the child, I mean?"

"Not yet."

"What? But that's unfair. She should have been told. She's not an infant, Donald. She's a young woman now and she's bound to be concerned about her mother."

"Your girl will have told her, I expect."

Lewis Jackson scratched his memory to recall what tale Bea had passed on to Stella. He was as generous to his daughter as he was to his sons, but he was not given to letter-writing. He left all that sort of stuff to his wife.

Donald Haldane leaned forward. "You didn't tell your lass the truth, did you?"

"Of course not."

Nodding, the old man sat back. "It's for the best, you know. Best all round, in fact."

Out of the corner of his eye Lewis glimpsed the waiters assembling themselves with the first course. In a moment it would be soup and wine bottles and servility. He wished he had not ordered the Château Latour. He was in no mood now to enjoy it. What the old man had asked him to do was little enough and seemed simple. But nothing that Donald Haldane did was simple. He was a devious old buzzard and, even in his dotage, well worth the watching. Lewis said, "Is that it? Is that all you require of me?"

"For the time being," said Donald Haldane and with an imperious little gesture signalled to the waiter to pour him his share of the red.

No other teacher in St Austin's, except perhaps the Head herself, taught with such lack of formality. Irené Milligan was a prowler. She meandered up and down the aisles between the desks, paused by the windows, circled round behind her own high and imposing desk, wrote on the blackboard almost on the run and, when the lesson caught up with her, would park herself temporarily on almost any flat surface, long legs carelessly stretched out or folded away under her. She had a Thespian's grasp of the power of movement and linked it, by instinct not training, to the power of the spoken word.

Unlike her predecessors in English class, Irené Milligan was unafraid of the charged and unscrupulous emotions that poetry could rouse in the breast. She read with sincere conviction, wandering, book in hand, about the classroom. She would pause only on key lines or at those silences that gave a word or phrase a resonance and poignancy that could make the fine, frail hair rise on the nape of your neck or a teardrop swell against your lash. Few, if any, of her pupils were unaffected. Some were quite transfixed, quite wrung out by Shelley, Newbolt and Rossetti, by Tennyson and Stevenson and by the braw old tales and ballads that chimed with the landscape of their lives in Perthshire's brooding hills.

> Why does your brand so drop wi' blood,
> > Edward, Edward,
> Why does your brand so drop wi' blood,
> > And why so sad go ye O?
>
> O I have killed my hawk so good,
> > Mother, Mother,
> O I have killed my hawk so good,
> > And I had no more but he O.
>
> Your hawk's blood was never so red,
> > Edward, Edward,
> Your hawk's blood was never so red,
> > My dear son I tell thee O.

And on Miss Milligan would go, not declaiming but confiding, acting out the wheedling voice of the mother and the son's weary confessionals until even pragmatists and those to whom passion was just a word began to tense up with the glimmering of what was to come and what it all meant below the surface. Somehow Miss Milligan always reached the tall desk just in time for that final chilling verse. She would stand straight and dignified and arrogant and say:

> And what will ye leave to your own mother dear,
> Edward, Edward?
> And what will ye leave to your own mother dear?
> My dear son, now tell me O.

And the sweet Miss Milligan would change. Her eyes would crinkle and her voice roughen and she would hook one hand over the desk's edge and crane out, hunched towards the class, and stun them with her sudden vehemence.

> The curse of hell from me shall ye bear,
> Mother, Mother,
> The curse of hell from me shall ye bear,
> Such counsels ye gave to me O.

There would be no murmur of approval from the desks, no stirring for several seconds, not until Miss Milligan had dismantled her pose and, laying the book aside, leaned back against the blackboard and asked, rhetorically, "Now, girls, what do you think is the reason for Edward's bitterness?" Then there would be an uncomfortable shifting and shuffling as if the putting into words of Edward's tragedy went all against the grain of proper little girls and the inhibitions of genteel drawing-room society.

Though she had used the ballad a dozen times or more in teaching practice Irené Milligan was never blasé about its effect and was, in a sense, prepared for almost anything by way of class response. She was not, however, prepared for Colleen O'Neal's cackle of laughter. "Colleen, what do you find so funny in this poem?"

Still chuckling, Colleen had answered, "The curse of hell, Mother, Mother. The curse of hell, Mother dear," in a tone that had so flustered Miss Milligan that she had moved on at once to Masefield and safer ground.

It was not, though, the ballad of Edward's betrayal that

166

Irené Milligan had chosen to read that cold November afternoon when, it seemed, dusk had loitered all day long just beyond the Grampians. She had picked another favourite poem of hers, one of less complex rhythms and emotions but almost as sinister and mysterious. Strangely subdued by the oppressive wintry half-light, the class had been waiting quietly for her to find position, waiting with a kind of resignation as if they expected her to spring upon them some brittle ultra-modern piece to prick them from collective torpor and were all ready to resist her efforts. She began with her back to the big window that glared out over the garden. Early-lit electric light already sheened the glass and the classroom was caught and suspended like a spectral stage in the cold air above the river and the town. The girls looked at her but also at themselves, bloodless and insubstantial in receding, reflected images and tried to think of suppertime and cocoa, buttery toast and the hot red fire in the common-room.

Soft, cautious and unhurried, Miss Milligan commenced her reading:

> It was many and many a year ago,
>   In a kingdom by the sea,
> That a maiden there lived whom you may know
>   By the name of Annabel Lee . . .

Even as she read, and she hardly had need even to glance at the page, Miss Milligan began her slow traverse of the window bay. They were listening, not yet perked up, but at least listening. Some rested brows on wrists, others curled their fingers listlessly in their hair, some followed her movement with their eyes as if they suspected her of a trick and would not be caught out by it.

> I was a child and she was a child,
>   In this kingdom by the sea;
> But we loved with a love that was more than love –
>   I and my Annabel Lee . . .

Pauline, who had been wrapped in her own small miseries and

as listless as anyone, heard the poem in her ear as if each word was shiny new and had been minted for her benefit. She had not to her knowledge ever heard the poem before and had no interest in its origins, its constructions or anything else about it. She was one who sat up, who inclined her head and watched intently as the teacher, measuring her pace to the beat of the poem, turned and came down the aisle between the desks. Pauline watched the woman's mouth, her lips, as if she might catch from them a breath that did not belong to Miss Irené Milligan but came from some other source.

> And this was the reason that, long ago,
>   In this kingdom by the sea,
> A wind blew out of a cloud, chilling
>   My beautiful Annabel Lee;
> So that her highborn kinsman came
>   And bore her away from me,
> To shut her up in a sepulchre,
>   In this kingdom by the sea.

Pauline had only seen the sea on one occasion; the long shingle beach at Brighton where her father had taken her for a day trip one blistering summer Thursday when, even for Harry Verity, London had become insufferable. That was the sea for Pauline – flat and rippleless, more brown than blue but, from the rail on the prow of the Palace pier, with a surge to it, a ceaseless hungry sucking motion that had rather frightened her. She remembered the sea's flatness, its limitlessness, the little indistinguishable things upon and within it, far and near, and how she had not felt comfortable until Daddy had taken her away from the esplanade and into the gardens to look at the Royal Pavilion.

Miss Milligan's skirt brushed Pauline's shoulder. She lifted her gaze to the teacher who was intent upon reading and passed without noticing her towards the raised desk where under the scalding light from the electrical bulb, and mirrored again and again in the pane to her right, she impressed the last verses upon her pupils with a restrained intensity.

But our love was stronger by far than the love
  Of those who were older than we,
  Of many far wiser than we;
And neither the angels in heaven above
  Nor the demons under the sea
Can ever dissever my soul from the soul
  Of the beautiful Annabel Lee.

Pauline uttered an audible sob, heard herself do it with surprise. And then the floodgates seemed to open within her and, for no reason at all, she was weeping tears by the bucketful. "Oh!" she said. "Oh! I'm sorry." She rose from her chair and without asking permission rushed from the classroom and along the short corridor that led to the front hall which, at that hour, was deserted.

Behind her – or so she imagined – she heard Ronnie, Stella and Daphne laughing at her sentimental outburst, at the nonsense that had floored her. She threw herself down on the long, spongy couch and, startling Otto, who looked up with an enquiring growl from his spot before the smoking fire, buried her face in the cushions and tried to hide.

Arms wrapped over her head. She did not hear the woman approach and did not move when Otto let out a single fond bark and the woman's hand touched her shoulder.

"Pauline, dear, what's wrong?"

"Noth . . . nothing."

She felt weight upon the couch and pushed her face further into the cushions, pressed her knees down into the upholstery. She was beside herself, almost literally. She knew what a fool she was making of herself. She sensed that the giant Newfoundland dog had hoisted himself into a sitting position and was blinking wetly at her, head cocked.

An arm went about her. Gently but firmly she was lifted into a sitting position.

"Is it a cramp?"

"No, Miss Fergusson."

"You're not in trouble?"

"No, no."

At that moment Miss Milligan appeared in the hall, puzzled and anxious. Seeing the headmistress, however, she checked her running steps and halting, said, "I was reading poetry, Miss Fergusson, and Pauline simply – I mean, there was no incident, no misbehaviour."

"Of course not," the Head said.

"Shall I send for Matron?"

"I doubt if that will be necessary," Miss Fergusson said. "Pauline and I will have a cup of tea, wash our faces, and that, I suspect, will be prescription enough. What do you say, Pauline? Are you ill?"

"I don't know what's wrong, Miss Fergusson."

"Go back to your class, Irené."

"But—"

"And leave Pauline with me."

It had been ages since anyone had washed Pauline's face. She felt rather foolish seated on the edge of a little moquette-covered pouffe in the headmistress's parlour while the woman knelt on the rug at her feet and gently dabbed away her tears with a flannel dipped in a bowl of warm water.

Miss Fergusson sat back on her heels and surveyed her handiwork. "There. That's a bit better. Give your hair a comb and you'll be almost presentable."

Embarrassed, Pauline rose, but the Head tapped her knee and told her to remain seated. "The kettle's on and a good hot cup of tea will complete the job."

Carrying the bowl, towel and flannel Janis Fergusson went off into a little kitchenette that adjoined her first-floor suite and gave Pauline, who had never been in the Head's private quarters before, a chance to look round.

She had expected something much more grand. The parlour was hardly larger than a housemistress's room. It was cluttered, in a cosy sort of way, with far too much furniture and too many ornaments. In spite of the daily ministrations of the housemaid, it had a 'whirly' look to it, with books and papers scattered on the tables and on the top of the little rolltop desk. The fireplace was narrow and high and the mantelshelf was littered with an assortment of framed photographs and other items of memorabilia; a corn-dolly, a Japanese fan, an old dance card, a carved meerschaum pipe in a plush case and, of all things, a rifle bullet balanced upright against the bevel of a tiny carriage clock. Intrigued, Pauline would have loved to poke inquisitively among the stuff but she was far too mindful of her manners and remained glued to the pouffe until Miss Fergusson returned with tea-things on a tray.

The Head made no ceremony out of it. She poured and served Pauline with a cup at once and, holding her own cup in two hands, seated herself upon the rug by the fire, rested her back against the edge of an old armchair and stretched out her short legs under the loose black skirt. It all seemed very friendly and informal; too friendly and informal. It did not seem right for somebody in Miss Fergusson's position to shed her dignity to such a degree. Miss Fergusson was no girl now and her casualness had to it a certain disquieting calculation that served to put Pauline on her guard, which was, perhaps, quite the opposite of the effect intended. Calm and under control, Pauline sipped the hot sweet tea and tried not to stare.

"What was Miss Milligan reciting that upset you?" Janis Fergusson began.

"Edgar Allan Poe."

"'Quoth the Raven, Nevermore'?" Miss Fergusson asked.

"No. 'Annabel Lee'," Pauline answered. "I really don't know why I was so overcome."

"The power of the spoken word," said Miss Fergusson, "can bring nations to their knees or, indeed, inspire cowards to take up arms. Poetry has always been capable of making young ladies cry. I used to weep copiously at almost anything by William Blake. I know not why." The woman took a mouthful of tea, swallowed, sighed, then with a certain slyness glanced at Pauline. "You received two letters today, did you not?"

"Yes, Miss Fergusson."

"One, I suspect, was from your father."

"Yes."

"Could that, perhaps, have upset you?"

"No. Dad – my father seems well and quite excited by the possibilities of his new job. He's disappointed in Durban which he says is a bit like Balham on a hot day. I expect he's exaggerating."

"And the other letter?"

Pauline paused. The principle of privacy which the Dragon

had introduced was not without its loopholes, it seemed. Under the circumstances it would have been impossible to refuse to answer, even to prevaricate. A wave of sadness swelled and swooped through Pauline but passed, fortunately, without breaking.

"From my grandfather," Pauline said.

"Your Grandfather Haldane?"

"I only have one grandfather, alive."

"I hope it didn't bring bad news?"

Carefully Pauline put the teacup down upon a table. The carriage clock told her that the bell for the end of classes would ring in six or seven minutes. She tried to conjure up excuses to leave, to wriggle away from what was rapidly becoming an interrogation.

"I am, you know, entitled to ask," said the Dragon.

"Oh, yes, Miss Fergusson. I know."

"The situation is rendered slightly more awkward by the fact that your grandfather is a partner in the school company and that we are professionally acquainted." Pauline nodded. Janis Fergusson went on, "It's exceedingly indiscreet of me to tell you this, Pauline, but your grandfather did everything he could to baulk my appointment as Head of St Austin's."

"But why?"

"Let's just say that our ideas about education – and practically everything else – are emphatically not in harmony."

"I hardly know Grandfather Haldane. I've only met him once since my mother – since she and Father parted."

"Did the letter from your grandfather concern your mother?"

"Yes."

"Has she had the child?"

Pauline was startled, but only for a moment. She realised that she had not come clean and pristine to St Austin's, and that the Haldanes' long-standing connections with the school were bound to cheat her of anonymity. "It was stillborn," Pauline said.

"Oh, my dear. I am sorry. It's small wonder that you were distressed. You should have told Miss Milligan at once."

"I really did not think there was a need, Miss Fergusson. I already knew, you see."

172

"Did you? May I ask who gave you the news?"

"My cousin, Stella Jackson."

"By word of mouth?"

"Yes."

"Did you believe her?"

"Stella wouldn't lie, not about a thing like that."

"Of course she wouldn't." Miss Fergusson hoisted herself from her position on the rug, found space for her cup among the bric-a-brac on the mantelshelf, then folded her arms. In a moment informality had been replaced not by aloofness but authority. "For all that, Pauline, you did not quite take Stella's word for it, did you?"

"Perhaps not, Miss Fergusson."

"Until your grandfather's letter confirmed the sad truth, the loss had no meaning for you."

"Yes, I expect that's it."

Miss Fergusson brushed at a stray hair on the side of her cheek and then, oddly, reached out and tidied Pauline's fringe with her fingertips. "Are you feeling more composed now, more adjusted?"

"Yes, thank you, Miss Fergusson." Pauline got to her feet in the belief that the interview was over, that the Dragon had done her duty.

Janis Fergusson said, "It doesn't do to keep things bottled up, Pauline. It's very much better to have them out in the open, to talk them over with somebody older and wiser than you are. You should have gone to Miss Milligan with your problem. Housemistresses are always very understanding. Miss Milligan is no exception."

"Miss Milligan has been very kind, already."

Janis Fergusson said, "The letter from your grandfather, do you have it with you?"

As it happened the letter was folded small and hidden in the pocket of Pauline's tunic. It had been there all afternoon under a crumpled handkerchief, an India rubber and four sherbert limes welded into a paper bag.

Miss Fergusson held out her hand. "May I see it, please?"

"Honestly, there's nothing in it that—"

"Show me the letter, Pauline."

Pauline pursed her lips defiantly for a moment and then

173

capitulated. She fished the wad of paper from her tunic pocket and, without unfolding it, placed it into the headmistress's hand. Carefully Miss Fergusson opened it, wiped the sheet flat with her hand and, holding it to the light, read the contents.

The missive was neatly typed on bond, perfectly set out according to the Commercial Handbook, and as impersonal as an order for steel sheets or copper piping. It had obviously been dictated to a shorthand secretary or into the mouthpiece of a Dictograph.

Dear Pauline Verity,

I regret to inform you that the child your mother was scheduled to bear on 20th Ult., suffered the misfortune of stillbirth. Your mother has, however, fully recovered from her ordeal and has sustained no lasting ill effects.

I trust that you are well.

Yours sincerely,
DONALD CLARK HALDANE

Janis Fergusson gave a little grunt and, forgetting herself for an instant, shook the letter fiercely in both fists as if to extract from it one drop of sympathy or affection or, more likely, as if she had her hands round Donald Haldane's throat.

She remembered Haldane from long, long ago. Pompous, self-important and crass. He had seemed like an old man to her even then. The instinct of all well-bred St Austin's girls had been to despise him because of his imperiousness and the fawning of Miss Aitken, Miss Gaylord and most of the other lady teachers. Even to girls used to such qualities, Donald Clark Haldane had exuded an aura of masculine superciliousness, not vigorous but cold. His addresses to school were so riddled with coarse clichés and vaunting self-righteousness that they had become memorable, though he had never been regarded as a laughing-stock like the Reverend Haydock.

Since the day she'd left St Austin's for Girton, back in the year of 1901, Janis Fergusson had not encountered Donald Clark Haldane. She had not forgotten him, however, and, though he had been inactive in school affairs since before the war, he had brought himself north for the selection of the new headmistress. He had been exactly as she had remembered him, not one whit different, except that his vigour had diminished and his coldness had increased. He had been voluble during the interview, hostile, so direct that, once or twice, Charles Harvey had felt it necessary to defend her views. Though none of the Harveys had ever discussed the matter with her, Janis Fergusson had the feeling that she had obtained the post of headmistress not against but because of Donald Haldane's bitter opposition to her appointment.

She folded the letter and offered it to Pauline; then changed her mind. She said, "I think I'd like to show this to Miss Milligan, if you've no objection."

"But why, Miss Fergusson?"

The Dragon hesitated then said, rather lamely, "To explain why you ran out of her class."

"Will I get it back?"

"Of course. You will wish to reply to it, no doubt."

"No, Miss Fergusson, I don't think a reply is called for on this occasion. Do you?"

"Perhaps not. In fact, no. Nonetheless I'll see to it that the letter is returned."

At that moment the bell for the end of afternoon classes rang loudly and, a moment later, the first wave of noise from the corridors below rose cheerfully up to the first floor suite.

"Do you feel better, Pauline?"

"Yes, thank you, Miss Fergusson."

"No more tears?"

"No, Miss Fergusson."

"Good," said the Dragon. "Just remember that it doesn't do to bottle things up."

"I will, Miss Fergusson," said Pauline and escaped, with some relief now, into the corridor that led to the stairs.

In spite of its situation in a narrow side passage off Corinth Street, near Piccadilly, Merlin's was not a truly Bohemian nightclub. You did not dare turn up here in plus fours, looking as if you had just stepped off the golf course, and expect to sail past Selwyn, the cashier, in his little grilled sentrybox.

If you weren't attired in white tie and tails, if you did not shimmer in evening silk and have a touch of mink about you, then it was goodbye and try the Bullfrogs just around the corner where they'd let in any old riff-raff if you slipped them a fiver.

Barbara had been here before, years back, with Johnny Tiverton, before jazz and gin fizz, before the war, when the place had been called the Diplomat and the little red door had been painted blue. Mark reached over her shoulder, pushed the door open and with both hands about her waist steered her remorselessly forward into a haze of smoke and piano music.

The Merlin consisted of three rooms knocked into one. In the centre division you danced. In the adjacent apartments you ate, drank and whispered across the table-lamps, rubbed knees beneath the trailing linen table cloths. To Barbara's immense relief the ingratiating elegance of the Diplomat had been swept away in favour of gaudy intimacy. Johnny Tiverton and happy memories had vanished with the soda siphons and palm-court trio. Now there was only a pianist, a dark-haired, olive-skinned fellow dressed like a Mexican bandit in a medallioned bolero and puffy black silk pantaloons. He was wringing some sort of jazzy rhythm from "Back Home in Tennessee". And a crowded dance floor. And far too many tables. And, on walls and ceilings, more of those whizzing stars and comet trails. The waiters were no longer intimidating. They too were done up like Mexicans, or gypsies, or something vaguely Welsh – coalminers scrubbed clean for the evening, perhaps.

"There's Sydney."

Mark pushed Barbara forward and danced her through into the restaurant at the rear where the smoke was thicker still and the clatter of pans and the cry of cooks from the kitchens added a kind of makeshift urgency to the atmosphere.

Mark had brought her back to the city only two days ago and, after Devon, London seemed raucous and tawdry. She had expected to feel liberated, bubbly, now that it was all behind her and she was back where she really belonged, among the smart set. But it was proving more difficult to adjust than she had expected it to do. She was vibrating with nerves, was so nervous that she felt scalded by the noise and heat in the nightclub. She'd felt shrivelled in Bond Street, swollen in Regent Street and had almost fainted in the Trocadero where Mark had taken her for a celebratory lunch. Now she had to face up to Sydney Ruddock and his little powderpuff plaything, Silvia Howard, who, just because she wore a Chanel gown and diamonds from Cartier, would treat her as if they were somehow equals.

Sydney had never really forgiven Babs for stealing Mark away. Sydney was the jealous type who wanted attention, from males as well as females. Compared to Mark he was ugly, so awfully ugly, and so awfully rich! He rose at once, arms extended, and, ignoring Barbara completely, embraced his friend with great hugs and adoring groans.

"Wonderful to see you. Thought you'd got lost in the fog. Despairing. Wonderful that you made it, Mark, darling. We must celebrate." He snapped his fingers and shouted, "Waiter. I say, waiter, bring us the champers. Magnum. Bollinger. *Vite. Vite.*"

Sydney had grown no more pretty in the months since last Barbara had seen him. His swarthy jowls had grown heavier. His brown moustache looked unclean and his thick horn-rimmed spectacles needed wiping. Sydney, however, was Mark's best friend and she would put on her most winsome smile to greet him, if he ever got around to noticing her.

Sydney might not have been paying her much attention but Barbara was all too aware of Silvia's scrutiny, the hard, quizzical stare that the girl usually reserved for eligible bachelors with pots of money. It was Silvia who spoke to her first. "I think you should sit down, Babs, darling."

"What?" said Sydney. "Why, of course! How remiss of me. Dreadful ordeal, and all that." He jerked out one of the silver painted chairs and fitted it again, with Barbara on it, into the narrow space at the table. "Must say, you don't look too bad. Pale but, as always, interestin'."

The men were still standing when the champagne arrived. The waiter, on instruction, plucked the dripping bottle from the ice-bucket and opened it expertly, making the cork pop. Barbara heard Sydney sniggering, the crunch of the magnum as it was thrust back into the ice-bucket, the strains of the piano playing "The Cauliflower Rag", some ass behind her braying at a lame joke. Silvia patted her hand. Silvia's hand was slender and smooth, almost unformed, with no creases at the knuckles. She wore a little bangle of pure gold and two rings, diamonds and amethysts. She patted away at Barbara's wrist until she got Barbara's attention then whispered, "Was it awful? Was it truly dreadful, your ordeal?"

The question had been lying in wait for so long that Silvia's fear had gathered on it like dust. The girl could not disguise the fact that her interest was selfish. It was perhaps the only experience to which Silvia's body had not been subjected, the one thing that frightened her. She was not Barbara's friend, though, and she had no right to blurt out such a question at all.

Barbara gave her nothing to chew on. She answered, "I was well taken care of."

"He didn't even bring you to London, though, did he? I mean, I wouldn't want some provincial quack grubbing away inside me."

An obscene retort started instantly to Barbara's lips but she stifled it and repeated, "I was very well taken care of, Silvia."

"But if you'd been in London—"

"It was nobody's fault."

"Did Mark tell you that?"

"Did Mark tell her what?" Mark interrupted. He had one hand flat on the table and leaned between the women, his head inclined towards Silvia.

She was almost fifteen years younger than Barbara but had none of the apparent vacuity of somebody in her early twenties. She was slender as a willow but not as pliant and her high cheekbones glowed with embarrassment as Mark leaned closer and delicately kissed her cherry-red lips. "Hullo, Silvia," he said.

"Hullo, Mark."

"I say, that's quite enough of that." Sydney laughed and obstreperously pulled Mark away and into his chair.

Barbara wondered if Mark had slept with Silvia, before, or even after, she had been taken up by Sydney. Wondered what the girl had done to please him, which of the ungentle pleasures that she had indulged in had been passed on as instruction to the girl at her side. She felt no resentment at the thought.

Mark said, "What am I supposed to have told her, Silvia?"

The girl was confused. In pressing the point he was baiting her, probing that soft, secret centre that had no carnal counterpart. And he was enjoying her discomfort.

Barbara said, "It's a woman's thing."

"I say!" Sydney craned forward, pretending to be agog. "Let's hear more of this."

"No," Mark said, the humour gone. "It's done, past, over with. Babs doesn't want to think about it, do you, darling?"

"'Course she doesn't," said Sydney Ruddock. "Why spoil a good party with all that messy stuff." He stabbed a sausage-like finger into Silvia's face. "No more, y' hear?"

"I hear, master, and I obey," Silvia told him with a sarcasm that fell quite flat. "A taste of that Bollinger might help shut me up."

"Expect it would," said Sydney and called to the waiter to bring fluted glasses and do the honours.

When the glasses were filled, Sydney adjusted his spectacles, brushed a hand over his greasy hair and pondered a toast suitable for the awkward occasion.

"To Mark," he said, at length. "Welcome back."

"And Barbara," Silvia added.

"Yes. To Mark and Barbara. Back from the dead."

"Matter of fact," Mark said, "I can do better than that."

"Do away, old chap."

"To Mr and Mrs Mark Straker. How's that?"

"Married, you're married?" said Silvia.

"Not just yet," Mark said.

Sydney's mouth was open and his tongue lay out against his lips like that of a dog. "M . . . m . . . marriage?"

"A venerable institution, Sydney," Mark informed him.

"But I thought – after what – after all that's happened – I thought you'd – I mean – wait a while."

Barbara said, "Why don't you come right out with it, Sydney? What you mean to say is that you cannot see the point in marriage now that our little problem has been taken away."

179

"Well, I say, Babs, that's pretty blunt."

"A new side to my nature, Sydney."

"Not sure I like it," Sydney said.

Silvia said, "Actually, I think it's marvellous of you both. Mark especially. To actually go ahead as if nothing had happened."

"Shut up, Silvia," Mark told her. "Thing is, it's next Friday. Half past eleven Ack-Emma. Chelsea Registry Office. Can you be there?"

"Us?"

"Both of you," said Mark. "We need witnesses."

"Ungodly hour, what!, at which to do the murky deed."

"Will you attend?"

"Formal, is it?" said Sydney.

"Absolutely not," said Mark. "Lounge suits, not even morning dress. Only the four of us present. It's all arranged. I'm counting on you, Sydney."

"In that case, why not? Might be a wheeze, at that."

"Might put you in the mood, darling?" said Silvia.

"Fat chance," said Sydney Ruddock then, pouring more champagne, raised his glass to toast the groom and, as an afterthought, Mark's blushing bride.


Poor Mr Prentiss was the first to succumb to winter's ills. He had been feeling off-colour on Monday. By Wednesday he had slight fever and soreness of the bones and, after ministering to the burial of an old parishioner on Friday afternoon, had staggered home to the manse with a soaring temperature and a quinsy throat. His housekeeper, Mrs Chapman, had put him straight to bed and had sent at once for Dr McNab who, with the back of a teaspoon, had inspected the offending organ, declared that it would be ten days at least before the lad would be fit to resume his pastoral duties and three weeks before he would be ready to deliver a sermon.

"What shall I do about Sunday?" Mr Prentiss croaked.

"Fetch in a locum," Dr McNab advised.

In spite of how it sometimes seemed to miscreants and unbelievers, Church of Scotland ministers did not exactly grow on trees. The presbytery were hard pushed at that time of the year to find a replacement on such short notice which is why the Reverend Doctor Magnus Hare was dug out of his lair in St Andrews' University Library, requested to put aside his research into Old Testament metaphors and, like a saint about to be martyred, was shipped off to Pattullo to do his bit for God and the parish.

Sunday morning service began promptly at eleven and ran smoothly enough until the time appointed for the minister's Address to the Children.

Dr Hare chose The Message of Job as his theme and seven minutes waxed into seventeen, into twenty-seven and finally, at around thirty-five, dwindled away just before open rebellion broke out in the junior pews.

Mr Calum Cameron, Superintendent of the Sunday School, leapt to his feet as if the pew had caught fire and yelled, "Children to the hall, children to the hall, quick," before the visiting preacher could change his mind and start off again about the Grace of Patience and the Virtue of Humility.

It was thanks to Mr Prentiss's quinsy throat and Mr Hare's long-windedness that Stella and Charlie MacAdam were able to steal five or six minutes alone in the little kitchen that stuck out at the back of the Old Parish Hall. Normally, vigilant eyes would have been upon the pair, for there had been some unsubstantiated rumours in that direction, but even the most vigilant eye had been rendered somnolent by metaphor. With thirty restless little bladders bursting, it was all that Mr Cameron and his senior staff could do to prevent disaster in the cloakrooms and havoc in the lavatories.

Hardly had Stella pulled the young man into the kitchen and snapped the bolt behind her than the kissing began. It was not Charlie's doing or his wish. He was as passive in the proceeding as a plank. He did not even put an arm about the girl as she rubbed and wormed against him and dunted his chin and mouth with her lips.

"What's wrong with you, Charlie?"

"We canna do it here."

"Nobody can hear us. Come on, kiss me, please."

"No, Stella. I've had enough o' all this."

"All what? We haven't done anything wrong, really wrong."

"It's all right, maybe, in the woods, but if we're found in the kirk, t'gether—"

"Oh, Charlie MacAdam, you're a cry baby."

"I am not, damn it."

"Language, please!" Stella leaned closer against him, pressing him against the scrubbed wooden top of the draining board. "I thought you liked me. You told me you liked me a great deal."

"Aye, well, only because you asked," said Charlie. "Look, if I'm found in here wi' you I'm for the high jump."

"Don't you want to kiss me all you can?"

"No," said Charlie in his best blunt Sunday accent.

He did not know what was wrong with him. He was not consumed by guilt, other than a vague anxiety that his meetings with the St Austin's girl would be discovered. No more, however, was he consumed by desire. Something was on offer but Charlie was too inexperienced to fathom out what it was, though he did have an inkling that it would not be anything worth risking his security for.

The fact of the matter was that he did not like Stella Jackson. He found her teasing ways repugnant, though he did not know why since the foresters and carriers had told him in no uncertain terms that one woman was as good as another when you had them flat in the grass. Perhaps it was his stiff blue suit, tight braces and starched collar, the effluvia of mothballs that the clothes gave off that not only dampened Charlie's ardour but washed it away completely.

"No?" Stella cried. Charlie glanced at the door, thinking to make a run for it. "Why, what's wrong with me?"

"You're a flirt, Stella."

"I am not a flirt. You're the flirt. I thought you loved me."

"Well, I don't."

"I suppose you'd rather it was Colleen O'Neal here with you now?"

"Aye, I would."

"You'd kiss her quick enough, wouldn't you?"

"Aye, I would."

Stella tossed her head, blue eyes sharp as scissors in the light from the knurled-glass ventilator.

"She wouldn't kiss you, Charlie MacAdam," Stella informed him. "I've told her all about you. And she hates you." Charlie frowned. "If you must know, Colleen thinks you're low, common and vulgar and wants nothing to do with you."

"You're a damned liar."

"Am I?" Stella tossed her head again. "Why do you think she's refused to meet you, even after you gave her" – Stella spat out the word – "chocolates?"

Charlie hesitated. He had thought of Colleen incessantly these past weeks, had wondered why he had landed Stella Jackson and not the beautiful soft Irish girl. He combed his memory for confirming signs that what Stella told him might be true but found sufficient evidence to the contrary to say, "She's never come t'meet me 'cause you never told her about the arrangements."

"Nonsense! Of course I did. I gave her every opportunity. She just hates you, Charlie MacAdam. It's as simple as that."

Outside, along the passageway, the thunder of little hooves was not in the least stilled by Mr Cameron's roar for silence. Charlie cocked his head and listened to Mrs Williamson's anxious birdlike chirping, "Children, children, chil-dren, behave if you please or Reverend Prentiss will be very angry with you."

Charlie said, "You never told her nothin', Stella, an' she never said nothin' against me."

"Aren't you the cocky one?" said Stella. "Think every girl falls for you on sight, do you? I don't know what I ever saw in you. Truly, I don't."

Charlie shrugged. "You're just a flirt, Stella. If it hadn't of been me it'd've been some other man."

"How dare you say that to me. You – you labourer."

"Ach, well. I'm goin' now."

"Charlie, wait."

But the young man had had enough. Disregarding the hazards that might lie in the passageway, he brushed Stella aside, unfastened the little catch and stepped out of the kitchen, leaving, with nothing but relief, the English girl behind.

"Ah, Charles," Stella heard Mrs Williamson say, "have you seen Miss Jackson, from the school?"

"Aye, she's in there, ss."

"Doing what, pray?"

"Search me, miss," said Charlie.

Stella uncurled herself, unclenched her fists, slackened as best she could the twisted knots of anger that had contorted her body at Charlie MacAdam's desertion. She straightened slowly and asserted the self-will that was the legacy of her class and product of her schooling. She adjusted her hat and coat and, just as Mrs Williamson came looking for her, stepped out of the kitchen too and said, as gaily as a child, "Getting myself a drink of water, Mrs Williamson."

"Oh, well. I suppose that's all right," the woman said and, pressing herself deferentially against the wall of the passage, let the nice young lady from St Austin's sweep quickly off into the hall.

# *Eleven*

*I*n each of the three terms there was a time at which
the pressure of education, weather, season or the glands
seemed to catch up with every girl in school and a strange,
almost palpable disposition to hysteria became collectively
apparent.

Janis Fergusson had encountered the phenomenon before.
Indeed, it had manifest itself in one form or another in
every school in which she'd taught and at one, a large
repressive establishment near Harrogate, it had broken out
as a rebellion against the regime and had ended in near riot.
The Harrogate incident had, of course, been extreme. Even
so Janis Fergusson was wary of midterm groundswells and
sensitive to unspecified restlessness. In the autumn term,
however, the Dragon had a trump card in her hand and had
no hesitation in playing it. As a restorative to stability nothing
acted more quickly than a reminder that Christmas was on
its way. The Dragon would wait until instinct told her that
she dare tarry not a day longer then would summon the
housemistresses and stir them into organising the Christmas
Gala Concert, that grand event which would bring the autumn
term to a close.

Musicians and choristers had already been practising for a
month or more for, as representatives of the school at large,
they would be here and there about the county throughout
December, doing St Austin's proud at public festivals. The
Gala Concert, however, was much less formal. It was held
before an audience of parents, school servants and local
personages and there was fierce competition between the
houses to produce star entertainment, an "item" that would
steal the show.

Ossian would confine participation to a handful of seniors and would, in consequence, produce a polished playlet

185

with Classical overtones and no relevance to Christmas whatsoever. Eggar, as a rule, fell back upon a Minstrel act which was jolly and sentimental and involved all the girls in the house hidden behind burnt cork and rattling tambourines. Miss Milligan, however, was more ambitious and more imaginative than her colleagues. Last year she had produced dramatised scenes from *A Christmas Carol*, featuring three of the four ghosts and Elf as a pathetic little Tim Cratchit whose final cry of "God bless us, every one," had quite brought the house down. Miss Milligan, it seemed, was very keen on ghosts for this year she had prepared an even more elaborate play derived from one of *The Ingoldsby Legends*.

It was a terrific night for a house assembly. Winds howled down from the north and brought smatterings of hard icy white granules that bounced like apple pips against the parlour's panes. Pine logs roared in the hearth and the corridors were full of the sounds of slamming doors and trembling slates. The common-room was crowded. Girls lay on the carpet, sprawled like puppies on sofas and made pyramids of legs and arms upon all the old armchairs. Miss Milligan had pride of place by the fire, of course, a thick cardboard folder laid rather ominously across her knees.

"Who's Ingoldsby?" asked one ingenuous junior.

"He wrote legends," another answered her.

"You don't write legends. Legends just sort of grow, don't they, Miss Milligan?"

"Yes, Marion, you're quite right. As a rule legends are traditional stories passed down by word of mouth. But the Ingoldsby Legends aren't authentic. A gentleman named Barham invented them."

"What for?"

"Money, I expect." Colleen was seated by the window, the harp in her lap, forehead pressed against an uncurtained section of the cold pane.

"Well, yes," said Miss Milligan. "Richard Barham was a professional author. His work appeared in *Blackwood's Magazine*."

"He was also a vicar, wasn't he?" Goss was not renowned for her knowledge of literature. "The legends are pure cod."

"Cod?" said the junior.

"Fake." The Kaiser, as befitted her status, had the second best armchair to herself. She was deftly slinging wool on to four long needles in process of knitting socks for her eldest brother.

"Written in verse," Goss went on. "All blood and gore but funny at the same time."

"How can they be horrible and funny?" the junior persisted.

"They just are," said Goss.

"My father adores them," said the Kaiser.

"Mine too," said Goss. "He claims he hears stranger tales in the High Court every day."

Pauline had not read *The Ingoldsby Legends* and could not for the life of her see what they had to do with Teal's entry for the Christmas Gala. She listened with interest, though, resting comfortably against Frog's shoulder.

As if sensing the air of mystification Miss Milligan came to the point. "I have taken the liberty of rewriting one of the Reverend Barham's narrative verses, putting it into a Scottish setting and making it into a play."

"Which one?" said Goss. "If it's *The Jackdaw of Rheims* then Stella could play the jackdaw."

"Ha-ha-ha!" said Stella.

"It's the one called *The Dead Drummer*."

"Oh, yes," said Goss, enthusiastically. "One of my favourites. Very spooky."

"Spooky?" squeaked two juniors in unison.

"What will it require by way of casting?" Rhona asked.

"Eight speaking parts in rhyme, the drummer lad, and ten or so for crowd scenes."

"At the hanging?" said Goss.

"Hanging?" chorused the juniors.

"In the revised Scottish version," said Miss Milligan, tactfully, "the hanging scene is omitted."

"Pity," said Goss. "I'd have made a good hangman."

Frog had certain reservations about parading herself on stage. "Do we all have to appear?"

"No," Miss Milligan answered. "The production will require a dozen hands backstage. And there will be plenty for them to do, I promise. Thundersheets to flap and lightning flashes to operate, that sort of thing."

"Feeding the raven?" Goss suggested.

"Raven?" said the Kaiser. "I don't recall a raven."

"The one that pecks out the corpse's eyeballs."

"Oh, how awful!" shrieked several sensitive souls in horror and delight.

"The raven, like the gibbet, is omitted," said Miss Milligan hastily.

"No part for Stella then," said the Frog.

"Do shut up, you lot," Daphne Gore snapped and gave Stella a hug to compensate her for the insults.

The Kaiser said, "Personally I'm none too sure that Ingoldsby will work in dramatised form. Sorry, Miss Milligan."

Miss Milligan said, "You may be right, Bettina. Perhaps we should do an excerpt from *Twelfth Night* instead."

"No, no," came cries from the majority.

Miss Milligan said. "You're looking very thoughtful, Pauline. What do you think?"

"Doing a ghost story is an excellent idea. Grand Guignol, isn't it?"

"Very close to it, Pauline," said Miss Milligan.

"French, are we doing it in French?" Ronnie cried in genuine horror.

"Fool!" said the Frog.

Miss Milligan opened the card folder on her lap. "Before we make a final decision, perhaps I should read you a little of Milligan's Revised Version. I've made a great many changes as you will see. For example the piece is now entitled *The Drummer of Dundee*."

"Oh, yes, perfect." Goss wriggled deeper into the sofa and rubbed her hands in gleeful anticipation.

"Shall I begin?"

"Please do," said Bettina.


"Settled," Goss said. "Thank heavens. What a corker it'll be. Bags I the part of Whaler Bill."

"If the Dragon approves of the project," said Frog, her sobriety in contrast to Goss's high excitability.

"'Course she will," said Goss. "The Dragon's not stuffy.

188

She'll see the fun in it. Setting it in Dundee instead of on Salisbury Plain is a masterstroke."

Not all the girls had shared Goss Johnstone's enthusiasm. There had been a quarter hour of fierce if friendly argument before a hand ballot had put *The Demon Drummer* firmly into production. The evening had ended with cocoa and sponge cake, a good deal of loud laughter and ham acting and the corridors and dormitories had echoed with howls and strangled screams until the Kaiser and her cohorts had done the rounds and threatened punishment for noise after Lights Out.

Goss had been uncommonly animated. She had insisted on trying on various bits of clothing that might form the basis of a sailor's costume and had even practised a clumsy hornpipe until her room-mates, with some force, advised her to stow it. At last Goss had leapt into bed with a final, "Arrr, me hearties. Nightie-night then, one an' orl," and had pulled the covers over her head.

By then Pauline was too sleepy to be interested in Goss's antics. She had been amused by Miss Milligan's reading and not in the least frightened by the content of the play. She lay warm in bed, the taste of toothpaste and cocoa mingling pleasantly in her mouth. She listened to the moan of the wind around the buildings and the tiny tip-tap-tip of snow grains upon the window, felt pleased at the prospect of the fun that the stage production would surely bring, especially if she was fortunate enough to be given a speaking part.

For a moment or two, as she hung poised on the edge of sleep, she recalled her childish fantasies about becoming a famous actress whose performances would bring the West End to its knees and gather her accolades and honours galore. She wondered, last thing, if Mrs Dobbs would come up from Dorset, and if Daddy would sail back from Durban for opening night.

She frowned into her pillow and clucked her tongue in annoyance at her silliness. Of course her father would not be there. The best she could expect would be jolly Uncle Lewis Jackson who was Stella's daddy, not hers. She sighed wistfully, and then fell asleep.

And dreamed a foul dream in which she foundered in a tar-black sea with the ugly little merbabe wailing inconsolably in her arms.

Stella had been watching the house match with less than desultory interest. She was chilled to the marrow, fed up with the hearty cheers that rang around Big Field as Teal stole a march on Pennant by one goal and then another.

Stella had nothing but contempt for the lumps who clumped and slithered up and down the grass park. Hockey meant nothing to her. She considered it not only a waste of energy but a thoroughly degrading activity for young women to engage in. If she could have found a more secluded spot in which to sulk she would have gone there instead. She was, however, not a favourite of the sporting set and they left her pretty much to herself.

The match finished before the crowd returned from town and Stella followed the rest of the house supporters up the long gravel drive that wound round behind the tennis courts and the little pavilion. It really was bitterly cold and the wind scudded dark dusty clouds across the hillsides, covering and uncovering pools of clear evening sky in which a star or two glittered like diamante.

Stella felt more depressed than sulky now. She had deliberately sent her disciples off to town to spy on the Irish cow and had, as a kind of sacrifice, devoted her afternoon to the game. The sight of Cissy Morrison, Donette Raeside and Goss Johnstone – Teal's leading athletes – being dogged and fêted by doting juniors had done nothing for Stella's morale, however.

She had been in a black, vengeful mood for almost a fortnight and though she had tried to dismiss the boorish Charlie MacAdam from her mind she found that she could not do so at will. Every single one of the stupid, boorish accusations with which he had rejected her still flickered steely hard in her memory. Besides, she could not put Charlie MacAdam out of mind when she was living cheek by jowl with Cow Colleen.

Colleen went about these days with a permanent smile on her coarse Irish face and seemed impervious to every wounding remark directed at her by Daphne and Ronnie and completely indifferent to the fact that she, Stella, had rejected her for ever.

Stella broke away from the straggle of girls that trailed the teams towards the long, primitive shed under the oaks where there would be a lighted iron stove and an urn of scalding hot tea and plates of buttered scones to warm not only the players but the hardy supporters too. She had been in the shed just once, in her first year at St Austin's when she had nurtured a milky crush on a Titian-haired Amazon named Rosamund Ogilvy, who had later gone on to keep goal for the ladies of Scotland in international matches. She had not been at all sure what she had wanted from the flame-haired girl, who was charitable but basically aloof, and had hated the smelly barn in which post-match devotions were paid. She had turned on her heel and walked out, nose in the air, and had never gone in there again.

Quite alone for once Stella entered Teal House by the side entrance. She wiped her shoes on the grid, climbed the back stairs to the first floor and, seconds later, was hauling away the heavy white-painted bedside locker to get at the hoard of illicit goodies that were hidden in a biscuit tin under a floorboard under the plain brown rug.

There was half a bottle of Gordon's gin which Ronnie had filched from her father's cabinet, several boxes of cigarettes and matches and a military lighter that created sparks by the million but nothing resembling a flame. In Stella's treasure box there was also a pretty little palm-sized mirror with a mounting of painted shellac, a twelfth birthday gift from her handsome, dashing cousin Bertie Jackson. Bertie had just become an officer in the Royal Navy when he'd given her the mirror. Weeks later he was blown out of the water on his first voyage when his destroyer had attempted to ram a U-boat amidships. Stella was none too fanciful but sometimes when she looked into the mirror she imagined that she saw Bertie behind her, not dead at all but come to carry her away.

It was a dreary time, fag-end of a tedious winter's afternoon. Stella rinsed a toothglass at the little sink, poured a thimbleful of gin into it and filled the glass half with water. She sipped thoughtfully and still wearing her coat, hat and

191

outdoor shoes seated herself on the bench by the window, lit a cigarette and blew smoke in gentle plumes out of the little aperture which let in the cold sound of the wind.

She saw them coming; Daphne and Ronnie arm-in-arm to the fore, hurrying through the dusk. The other town-trippers straggled behind them, cold-looking. Far to the rear, all on her own and skipping like a kid through shoals of fallen leaves, was Colleen.

Stella lit a second cigarette, refreshed the water in the toothglass with a dash of precious gin, then packed away everything and stowed the tin back under the board. When Daphne and Ronnie burst into the room, Stella was seated calmly on the side of her bed with a cigarette in her mouth, and another in her fingers.

As soon as the girls entered she offered them the glass and a lighted cigarette. "Oh, you are a sweetie," said Daphne Gore, plucking the glass from Stella's hand and, with a shiver, drinking from it. She dabbed her mouth with her wrist, said, "Lord, I needed that," and passed the drink to Ronnie. "It's freezing outside. Freezing."

"Never mind the weather report," said Ronnie. "Tell Stella what happened. Quick, before you-know-who strolls in."

"She met him. Bold as you like," said Daphne from behind a cloud of cigarette smoke. "She dived off and confronted him on the bridge and talked to him for a full ten minutes."

"I really don't know how she could debase herself by consorting with someone so common," said Ronnie.

Stella rose, drifted back to the window, opened it and fanned smoke out into the night air. "Did Bettina see her, do you think?"

"The Kaiser wasn't there today. We went with Carol-Anne and Peggie Orr, from Eggar. Dodging the house matches, I expect," said Ronnie.

"Point is," said Stella, "was Cow Colleen's little assignation remarked upon by anyone?"

"I doubt it," said Daphne.

"She got off with it, I think," said Ronnie.

"How fortunate," said Stella.

"For her?"

"For us," Stella said.

Daphne glanced at the door then sidled closer to her friend, drawing Ronnie with her so that all three were huddled by the little basin near the window. "What's afoot, Stel?"

"She'll have made an arrangement to meet him. She'd never have had the gumption to do it unless I'd shown her how, of course, but she'll have gone into it like a lamb to the slaughter."

"And?" Daphne asked.

"All we have to do is guess when and where and we can make sure she lands in real hot water," said Stella.

"Oh, I say – peach on her, do you mean?" said Ronnie.

"I'm not sure I'd want to do that sort of thing," said Daphne Gore.

"Don't you want to be rid of her?"

"Why, yes, of course I do. But peaching – bit drastic and all that. I wouldn't want to have a chap expelled."

"Cow Colleen is not a chap," said Stella. "She's a plague, a black spot, an embarrassment to the house. I think we'd be doing everybody a favour if we got rid of her."

"Somewhat moot," said Daphne Gore. "She isn't going to confide in us, not now. I mean, how will we discover the time and place of the tryst?"

"Deduce it," said Stella. "Use your grey matter, ladies. Come along now. How would I do it?"

"The pavilion?"

"Probably next Saturday evening," said Ronnie. "When everyone is busy with rehearsals."

"Brilliant people," said Stella.

"Will you really peach on her?" said Daphne.

"No. Put the wind up her, that's all," Stella said.

"Stella, do you have a plan?" Daphne asked.

"Of course I do."

"Do tell us."

"No," Stella said. "Just wait and watch – and be duly amazed." She took the toothglass from Ronnie's hand and, smiling, held it up in a self-congratulatory toast. "What say, old chums?"

193

"Chin-chin," said Ronnie, grinning too, while Daphne smoked the remains of the cigarette and looked just a mite perplexed.

Colleen could hardly contain herself all that long week. Of course, she'd said not a word to her room-mates about her assignation with Charlie MacAdam and she trusted him not to say anything to Stella if he should happen to meet her at Sunday School. On this particular score Colleen need have had no worry. Stella had swept past Charlie like a little iceberg and had already indicated to the Superintendent that, with great regret, she would have to resign from her teaching post at Christmas, due to pressure of schoolwork.

In Room No. 13 an uneasy truce had been declared. Colleen was too wound-up to deduce its significance. She saw nothing sinister in the changed attitude of her former chums. They were not all gushing and forgiving but neither were they mean and sarcastic. They left her pretty much to herself as the days dragged by towards Saturday.

With *The Drummer of Dundee* cast and the script in its final phase of revision much of the free time of the girls of Teal House was taken up with preliminary rehearsals. Colleen had been co-opted to provide a suitable accompaniment on her harp and empowered to experiment with the battery of off-stage drum-sounds that would enhance the atmosphere and embellish the text.

She had been pleased enough with this part in the event and had even bent her attention down from her pink cloud to cope with it. She had made a beginning by experimenting with biscuit tins, bottles and boot-boxes struck with sticks scrounged from a cupboard in the music room, the thud and clatter of timpani interspersed by chords on the Irish harp which, like a mischievous chum, seemed to come up with ideas all of its own making.

Scholars and performers were now at war. Skirmishes and full-scale battles would be waged in each of the houses and in school itself for the remaining four weeks of term. Certain stuffy sixth formers and one or two girls from the fifth were obsessively engaged in study for examinations and had no patience at all with the fripperies of playlet and pantomime that possessed the majority and transformed the November evenings into bedlams of piano chords and warbled choruses, amplified by the frosty air in corridors and bedrooms. Miss Fergusson was well pleased. All was going according to plan. She was used to dealing with minor complaints and arbitrating, when necessary, between warring factions. School had begun to hum like an electrical dynamo and she much preferred energetic activity to the fishy undercurrent of hysteria which, thank goodness, had been swept away by it.

And then it was Saturday again, the weather clear and hard. Teal played a hockey match against Ossian on Little Field, with the ball skidding and slicing off the frozen grass and the spectators all cheering and stamping to keep themselves warm. Dancing class was cancelled in favour of rehearsals. Pauline went to ride on the slippery, frost-crackling track, with Frog as her chaperone in place of Bettina who had found something better to do. And some girls – not Stella – went to town as usual to drink tea and kill the afternoon.

Colleen had been racked by indecision. Should she or should she not risk going to The Hut, risk a meeting with Charlie, risk possible discovery? Should she hide herself away that afternoon, nurse her impatience, allow her imagination to run riot? Would Charlie be on the bridge and if he was not how would she know of it? Perhaps he had taken cold feet about the whole thing. In the end she could not resist and in the afternoon went down to town with the others. She saw Charlie, resolute on Wade's Road Bridge. She gave him a sign, the soldiers' sign, with the tip of her thumb sticking up out of her fist. And got back a nod that said it was on.

That evening the school was alive with activity. Supper seemed like a mere impediment. The school choir, including eight girls from Teal, were off to participate in a concert in Crieff and the bus was being driven by Young Tom, since his father was under the weather. Miss Fergusson and Miss Gaylord had decided to accompany the choir because Young Tom and icy roads were not a happy combination and Miss Fergusson, if it came to the bit, was not above taking the wheel herself for the return journey.

The choristers were in high spirits, shrieking, waving

scarves from the bus window and, in spite of all that the choir-mistress, Miss Graves, could do to hinder it, broke full volume into a chorus of 'Master John', a ditty that could be rendered very risqué indeed by sudden pauses and omissions. The school came out in force to cheer the bus off down the driveway, then assembled gaily in the main hall to be herded and arranged into sundry rehearsal groups by housemistresses and prefects, the Kaiser among them.

"Colleen, where are you going?"

"The music room, Bettina. I've got it all to myself to practise the drums."

"Which music room? Ours?"

"School," said Colleen vaguely, already hurrying away.


"Are you there, Charlie?"

"Aye, I'm over here."

"Where? I can't see you."

"Right here."

"So you are. Oh, I'm glad you came."

"Did you think I wouldn't?"

"I didn't know what to think."

"I'm just glad you're not Stella."

"Are you, Charlie? Are you really?"

"Aye."

"What do we do now?"

"I dunno," said Charlie MacAdam.

"Shall we go for a walk?"

"That wouldna be wise."

"I'm not feeling very wise," said Colleen. "If I was wise I wouldn't be here at all. Shall we sit down for a while?"

"Aye, why not?"

"It's awfully cold for sitting."

"I don't mind that," said Charlie.

"Where shall we sit? Here?"

"That'll be fine."

There was a sheen upon the lawns and tennis courts where the frost held whatever light the sky contained. It was not pitch dark. Even in the corner of the verandah of the little pavilion, on the hard bench, there was light enough for the young man and the girl to peep at each other and recognise awkwardness, a nervous inability to know what to do next.

"Is this where you came with Stella?"

"It's where she met me."

"What did you do when she was here?"

"Wished it was you I was with," said Charlie, the compliment direct and honest and not intended to deceive.

"Sure an' is that the truth?"

"The whole truth," said Charlie.

Colleen nodded. Her toes were cold but every other part of her tingled with a peculiar warmth. She had seen boys before, had thought of boys before; fisher lads on the quays at Port St Moore in Connemara, young singers at the Bray musical festival; a priest once, though she was a Protestant, with such a handsome, gentle face that it would have broke your heart. She had imagined what it would be like to sit with some of them, like this, in the dark, and what she would feel and what she would do and say, and what they would say to her.

"Would y'like a gasper?" Charlie asked.

"Pardon?"

"A ciggie, a Woodbine?"

"No, thanks all the same."

"Mind if I—?"

"No, I like a man to smoke."

The flame of the match seemed incredibly clear in the cold air. Colleen admired the young man's profile by its light. She had never been to a picture show, not even in Dublin and she had no standard of comparison, no relative images to muddy the appeal of his innocent blue eyes, the curl of his fair hair over his forehead. He wore a black flannel jacket and a sort of cravat and his hands, cupping the match, were wonderfully veined and strong. He blew smoke away from her.

"When did you first – I mean, when did you decide to send me chocolates?" Colleen asked.

"When I saw you singin' on the stage in the bandstand in the Montrose Park. Last summer. Remember?"

"I remember."

Charlie looked at the match, blew it out. "I thought – thought you were beautiful."

197

Colleen made a little sound, like a purr. "We all imagined it was Stella you really admired."

"Her!" Charlie snorted. "She's nothin' compared wi' you. You – you're like a – an angel."

"That's a lovely thing to be saying, Charlie MacAdam."

"It's the truth, but," Charlie whispered.

These were the very last words that Colleen would ever hear from young Charlie's lips.

He leaned towards her and placed his hand lightly upon her arm. She was surprised but not startled and, with eyes wide open, prepared herself for his first adoring kiss.

"CHARLIE! DAMN YOU!"

Colleen did not scream. She bit down on her lip and plunged off the bench and to her left as the man rushed at them out of the shrubbery and grabbed Charlie by the neck.

An instant later she was running like the wind itself across the frozen lawns and through the rhododendrons, back towards the lights of school and the window she had left unlatched in the wall of the ground-floor music room. Behind her she left the struggling shapes of father and son and an erratic line of footprints indented on the frosty ground.

Janis Fergusson had been in a hearty mood on rising. The concert in Crieff had gone very well. The choir had sung exceptionally and had quite outshone the boy soloist from Morrison's Academy and even the brass octet from Perth. If it had been a competition Janis was sure that St Austin's girls would have won hands down. She had not had to take the wheel of the school bus on the way home either, for young Tom MacAdam had restrained himself and had steered them along the winding roads cautiously while the girls, tired now, dozed or crooned in groups of three or four and Miss Gaylord and she had chatted amiably enough as they'd watched the dark landmarks roll past. Now, before eight o'clock on a Sunday morning, here was old Tom MacAdam in his Sunday-best clothes, squirming in her study and a whole new situation looming up like conjuror's smoke from the paper he had spread on the desk before her.

Janis Fergusson said, "Did you actually see the girl, Tom? Can you identify her?"

"No, Ma'um."

"Are you sure she was from St Austin's?"

"Certain, Ma'um. She wore the uniform." Tom MacAdam paused. "She ran awa' towards the school building."

"Why didn't you go after her?"

"I had our Charlie t'deal with. Besides, it wasn't my place t'chase one o' the young ladies."

"No, of course it wasn't." Janis Fergusson said. "Am I right in thinking that your son – Charlie – has refused to name her?"

"Won't budge. Won't tell me nothin' though I've thrashed him till my arms ached."

"Perhaps he'll talk to me."

"No, he won't, Ma'um. Charlie's gone."

"Gone?"

"I sent him off first thing this mornin'. He'll work wi' his uncle in the pit at Dare. He went out on the milk train."

"What did your wife have to say about it?"

"It's no concern o' hers. She does what I tell her. Anyway, Charlie can go to the dogs if he wants to but he'll no' do it here on our doorstep."

"All right, Tom. It's your prerogative to deal with your son as you see fit," said Janis thinly. "Now tell me about the letter."

"It's as ye see it," Tom said. "It was fastened to a broom handle an' leaned against the cold side o' the boiler when I got there yesterday mornin'."

Janis Fergusson scrutinised the letter once more. It was composed of single words in different typefaces snipped neatly from newspapers: FOLLOW YOUR SON TONIGHT. The clippings were pasted neatly on to a page from a standard school jotter and the work would have earned praise as an example of enterprising handicraft.

"Why didn't you bring this message to me yesterday?" Janis Fergusson said.

"Didn't know what it meant then, Ma'um. Didn't know if it was genuine or just one o' the young ladies' pranks."

"I see."

With the tip of her forefinger the Head turned the letter towards her. All sorts of silly things were prancing

199

about in her mind, gleanings from the reading of detective novels. Undoubtedly it was from some cheap novel, an Edgar Wallace perhaps, that the author of the malicious letter had cribbed the idea. Any one of fifty girls could have been responsible. She toyed with daft notions of investigations, fingerprinting, searching dustbins for mutilated newspapers but instantly acknowledged the futility of such a course of action. If the perpetrator had been clever enough to devise such a plot then the perpetrator would have been clever enough to hide all traces of its execution.

She said, "How did you know that the letter referred to Charlie and not one of your other sons?"

"Charlie's been actin' funny for months."

"For months?" Janis Fergusson's irritation was suddenly tinged with alarm.

"Aye, Ma'um. Since before the start o' term."

There was no doubt now that she must act quickly to discover the girl who had been associated with Charlie MacAdam, to wring from her exact details of what had been done to her.

She said, "Is Charlie a Sunday School teacher?"

"He was, aye. A good Christian, reared in the faith an' knowledge o' God," said Tom MacAdam. "He knows right from wrong and why he's been punished an' didn't baulk at that. But he still wouldn't tell me who the bi . . . who she was."

"Or how many times they had met in secret?"

"No, Ma'um."

"Could you identify the girl, Tom, if you saw her?"

Kneading the rim of his bowler hat in clumsy fingers Tom MacAdam shook his head. "They all look alike t'me, Miss Fergusson, unless they're prefects."

"Didn't you hear her voice?"

"I couldn't hear her at all. They was talkin' so soft. I waited till I was sure."

"Sure of what?"

"Till he touched her."

In another man Janis might have suspected prurience but not in Tom MacAdam. She could imagine the effort it must have cost him to lie hidden in the shrubs, how violent his out-rage must have been and the bitter sense of disappointment in his son. She was on the point of asking if the touch had been of an intimate nature but she feared that MacAdam, for all his worldly swagger, would not understand a delicate phrase or euphemism and that she would be plunged into an explanation that would embarrass them both still further. Besides she had at her disposal a dozen effective means of discovering exactly what had happened and which girl was involved.

She got to her feet and Tom followed suit. He dropped his bowler in the process and stooped, puffing, to retrieve it. Times in the past she had bridled at his arrogance and insolence. Now, though, she would have had him back to his old assured self, the past ten or twelve hours wiped completely away.

She said, "You were right to inform me of this occurrence, Tom. It's a serious matter and I will make sure that the girl is found and punished."

"It was our Charlie's fault. He's to blame."

"I would not be entirely certain of that," said Janis Fergusson.


Excitement and apprehension in about equal measure caused an electric atmosphere in the Harvey Hall where the whole school had been assembled immediately after breakfast.

Worry on the faces of the housemistresses had commu-nicated itself to prefects and monitors and, through them, down to the rank and file. Buried guilts had been stirred up and minor lapses in behaviour, silly infringements of school rules loomed up suddenly in the echoing grey hall. Small girls were terrified and seasoned hands disconcerted simply by this unexpected disarrangement of the timetable and what it might portend.

Nobody felt right. This was Big Stuff. There was not a mistress in the hall and the prefects were as mystified as everyone else. The long, long wait – about ten minutes – brought doubt and speculation to fever pitch. The density of noise, a groundswell of whispers, rose to a roar that ceased abruptly when Miss Fergusson, in black teaching gown and mortar board and followed by Miss Gaylord, similarly attired, appeared at the main door and swept down the aisle to the platform steps. Housemistresses and teaching staff began to gather like prison guards along the walls of the hall. None of them sought to be seated, as if they anticipated riot or a sudden mass exodus which they were positioned to stop. It was not yet nine o'clock on a quiet, cold Sunday morning.

"Somebody's dead," whispered Elf.

"No, it's worse than that," said Goss from the side of her mouth.

Twisting a handkerchief in her lap, Pauline was convinced that her father had been killed and she was in process of preparing herself to take the public announcement bravely, like a man.

Bettina and Carol-Anne had reached the conclusion that a war had broken out, that Germany had torn up the Agreement of Armistice and had reinvaded France. Both had been here on that November day when Miss Aitken, her voice steady as a rock, had announced that the Great Conflict was over, and both had felt then a sense of awful let-down, as if they had been neglected by history and had lost their chance to shine.

Stella, Daphne, Ronnie, quiet and calm and too clever to smirk, had buried themselves in the centre of the gathering and, with hands between the benches, touched fingers, thrillingly, in a little chain.

Colleen was not in uniform. She was clad in a long emerald green skirt, frilled blouse and high button outdoor shoes. She sat at the end of a row, legs thrust out, eyes fixed on the wax-polished boards a yard in front of her. She was pale but otherwise as calm as anyone except for a telltale finger that now and then worried at a strand of hair above her right ear. Colleen did not even glance up when Miss Fergusson took her stance at the reading desk in the centre of the platform and, with Miss Gaylord hovering just behind her, launched into her announcement.

"It has been brought to my attention that one of our girls has been seen breaking bounds to meet, after dark, with a young man." A gasp like a typhoon passed through the assembled schoolgirls. Miss Fergusson waited without comment until it had dwindled into silence. "Unfortunately the girl in question escaped detention and made her way back to school where, one must assume, she mingled with her fellows and pretended that nothing had happened."

Heads turned, necks were craned, questions were put, frowning answers were received. Pauline had stopped tearing at her handkerchief. She, like Goss, shifted her position and sat bolt upright.

"Perhaps the guilty person imagines she is being – what's the current coinage – being 'smart'. I am here to tell her that she is not in the least 'smart' and that what she did was worse than dishonourable. It was downright dangerous." Miss Gaylord leaned forward, touched the Dragon's sleeve, whispered to her. The Dragon nodded. "Now, I am tempted, very tempted, to conduct a full investigation into this sordid and sorry business and – take my word for it – such an investigation would be quite thorough enough to unearth the name of the culprit. I am not going to do that, however. I am going to take another course of action. I am going to prohibit all excursions – all excursions – beyond the perimeter of the school bounds. Yes, that does include the Toffee Shop, the stables. and – it goes without saying – the town, until the young woman comes forward of her own accord and admits her guilt to me, freely and without excuse."

Protest was voiced in a single howl, a long aaaaaawww, that the headmistress ignored. Muffled murmurs of discontent rippled through the gathering and thin sibilant accusations pierced it like silver arrows.

"Quiet. Quiet," Miss Gaylord barked.

Only when order had been restored did Miss Fergusson continue. "It may seem unfair to impose upon you all a punishment for one girl's crime. But we are a community and, as such, we must all share responsibility for our least sensible member. You will ask how long the ban will last. Until we break for Christmas term and, if I see fit, throughout the spring term too." Another cry of outrage and despair. "Yes, this will mean that you will be prevented from buying Christmas gifts for your loved ones. That cannot be helped."

Pauline thanked her stars that she had been quick off the mark regarding Christmas gifts. She had written to Hatchards weeks ago and requested that they send a copy of the latest Dornford Yates novel to her father in Africa, had forwarded a postal order in payment and a gift card inscribed with her love to be included in the package. She had also purchased, from the drapers in Pattullo, a tartan scarf which she would post to Mrs Dobbs. The rest would have to wait until the last minute.

"I do not expect you to keep the matter to yourselves," Miss Fergusson was saying. "Indeed, I will expect each and every one of you to write to your parents within the course of the next day or two and inform them of what's happening. And the reason for it." Miss Fergusson adjusted her mortar board with a quick little snap of the hand. "What I do not expect you to do is to discuss the affair with domestic staff or with strangers. It is none of their concern and ill-founded gossip will not be beneficial to the good name of the school. I will punish any girl who is caught disobeying my order in this respect."

The girls were impatient for the Dragon to conclude so that they might huddle into cliques and pool tidbits of rumour and observation and, like girl detectives, come up with an answer to the mystery as to what had been done to whom.

"You will go from here directly to your houses where your housemistresses will say a few words to each of you. Those among you who wish to attend religious worship will be permitted to do so, of course. Please assemble in the main hall in one hour's time. You will be accompanied to services by a member of the teaching staff and you will remain with her, or in close proximity to her, until service is over when you will return at once to school." And then Miss Fergusson swept her gown about her and, looking as dragon-like as anyone could remember, positively leapt down the steps and flapped up the aisle and through the doors of the Harvey with Miss Gaylord waddling along behind.

As soon as the Head had gone there was instant pandemonium; no rush at all to leave the Harvey Hall but a furious, monkey-tribe chatter above which the voices of the housemistresses could hardly be heard.

"Well, she's done it now, the cow," Goss declared. "Sorry,

old son, I know she's your cousin and all that, but she really has got us all into hot water this time."

"Stella? Do you think it was Stella?" Frog had to shout to make herself heard.

"'Course it was Stella," Goss said. "It would be that boy from the kirk, the young MacAdam."

"How do you know so much?" said Elf.

"Everybody knows. It's been the talk of the school."

"In that case she'll be found out," said Pauline.

They had edged from between the benches and had begun to drift up the aisle along with the tide. A girl from Ossian tapped Goss on the shoulder and said, "Here, Goose, it wasn't you out there, was it, learning a few wrestling holds from a forester?"

"Teaching him a few holds, more like," put in another hockey fanatic.

"Not funny," Goss said. "Not funny at all."

"I agree," said Frog. "This is a very serious matter. She could have got herself into trouble."

"Trouble?" said Elf.

"Don't be obtuse," said Goss. "What Frog means is that she might have got herself pregnant."

"But how?" said Elfreda.

Goss threw up her hands in despair and it was left to Frog to point out the obvious: "Perhaps she is."

"What?"

"Pregnant."

"Stella, do you mean?"

"Well, why not?" said Frog. "She's only human after all."

"It wasn't Stella," Pauline said.

"Is that family loyalty speaking or do you know something we don't?" said Goss.

"Look behind you," Pauline said.

All four turned and hesitated in the wide space at the rear of the hall, stared back at Stella who, with Daphne and Ronnie and a gaggle of young admirers about her, was laughing fit to burst.

Irené Milligan was no less anxious than her charges about the consequences of the scandal that had darkened that already gloomy Sunday. She had the oddest feeling that it was one of the Teal House girls who had been lured into a rendezvous with Master MacAdam and that she would not have to look further than Room No. 13 to find the guilty party. What really upset her was that identification of the girl would reflect badly upon the housemistress and her ability to exercise discipline. She could imagine the attitude of the other housemistresses, all senior to her, imagine too the capital that Phoebe Gaylord would make out of the affair and how she would use it against Miss Fergusson.

Irené was also inhibited about questioning her girls individually. What worried her most of all, though, was that she would extract truth by accusation, that one of her girls would 'clipe', to use the old Scottish word, on another. She could not bear to have a sneak in the house. Better to harbour a love-struck fool than a tattletale.

"I do not believe that anything very intimate happened," Miss Fergusson had told her housemistresses. "I think it was an emotional entanglement, not a physical one. Nonetheless, the girl must be found, for her own good as well as the good of the school."

Irené Milligan could not but agree. After bracing herself with a cigarette in the depths of a staff lavatory, she marched into the house parlour and, acting out a part, commenced a round of questions. There was nothing cosy about the morning's gathering. The girls were tense. They too suspected that the breaker-of-bounds was one of their own. Nobody sprawled. They sat upright, prim and solemn as councillors, with Stella and her crew in occupation of the window seats.

Irené leaned against the dresser, arms folded.

"Well, you all know why we're here," she said. "So I won't waste time beating about the bush. I require each of you to account for your whereabouts between half-past seven o'clock and, say, nine last evening. I can personally vouch for over half of you. Those who were in Crieff with the choir or in the Harvey at rehearsal will you please stand up."

Twenty-one girls got instantly to their feet, Stella and Pauline among them.

"Orchestra?"

Seven more girls stood.

"Janine, where were you?"

"Sewing a costume in the handiwork room."

"With Marion and me," said another girl. "You sent us there, Miss Milligan. Don't you remember?"

"Were you together all evening?"

"Yes, Miss."

"Except for going to the lavatory."

"How long did that take?"

"Just a minute or two," came the embarrassed reply.

"There were lots of girls from other houses there too, Miss Milligan. You can check with them, if you like."

The housemistress nodded. Three girls remained seated.

"Alison?"

"I went to the San with Morven to visit my sister. You gave us permission, Miss Milligan. We were there for about an hour. Matron saw us, talked to us."

"And you, Colleen?"

A sudden stifled guffaw from the window seat told Irené Milligan all that she needed to know. She moved swiftly away from the dresser to bring the trio from Room 13 into clear view. "Do you find this amusing, Daphne?"

"No, actually."

"Stella?"

"Certainly not, Miss Milligan. I think it's awful."

"Then why are you laughing?"

The girls were silent.

Irené said, "Do you wish to tell us all something, something relevant to the matter in hand?"

"No. No, Miss Milligan."

"In that case I'd be obliged if you'd hold your tongues and let us get through this painful business as quickly as possible." She had brought herself close to the piano stool upon which Colleen was seated. "Now, Colleen, where were you last evening?"

"In the school music room."

No flush on the sallow cheeks, no hesitation in the delivery, no squirming – but Colleen O'Neal did not meet Miss Milligan's eye. The housemistress said, "I thought the orchestra members were practising there?"

"They were in the gymnasium, Miss Milligan," said Colleen promptly. "Bettina knows where I was."

"Yes, that's right. Well, you told me you were going there. I didn't actually see you there."

"Sure, did you not hear me, battering away?"

"Can't honestly say I did, no."

"How long were you there?"

"I don't really know. Most of the evening, maybe."

"Did anyone, in passing, hear Colleen – battering away?" Irené looked round the room, expecting no positive answer.

"Yes, Miss Milligan. I did."

"You, Pauline? I thought you were – in fact I know you were in the Harvey. We went through lines together."

"I heard Colleen when I went to the lavatory. I saw her too, sitting by the stove, hitting a board with her sticks."

"I didn't see you," said Colleen.

"I didn't want to disturb you," Pauline said. "I looked in through the little window in the door. I watched you for a minute or two. You were very busy."

"Pauline, why did you go near the music room?" said Miss Milligan. "The nearest lavatories are—"

"They were engaged. I ran down to use the staff cloakroom, though I know I shouldn't have."

"What time would that be, approximately?"

"Ten past eight," said Pauline. "Exactly."

"Are you sure?"

"Absolutely certain," Pauline Verity lied.


"How on earth did you manage it?" Stella enquired. "I mean, how in heaven's name did you persuade my dear sweet cousin to lie on your behalf?"

"Perhaps she told the truth," said Colleen.

Daphne Gore brayed with scornful laughter. Ronnie and she were sprawled each on their separate beds with a litter of magazines about them. Stella, on the other hand, had only just returned from church in Pattullo – guarded over by Miss McIntyre – and was in the process of taking off her hat and overcoat.

Colleen said, "How do you know it isn't the truth?"

Daphne brayed again and Ronnie giggled.

Titivating her hair with a comb and brush, Stella turned from the mirror. "Do you imagine that you're the only girl in school endowed with 'mystic powers'? How vain you are, Colleen, and how stupid sometimes."

"What's happened to him?"

"To whom? Oh, to your errant lover. How would I know?"

"Was there no talk at the church?" said Colleen, trying desperately not to let her anxiety show.

"Of course there was talk at the church. You could hardly hear the organ for the buzz." Stella settled herself at the foot of Daphne's bed and playfully tickled the soles of Daphne's stockinged feet, which made the aristocratic girl shriek. "Are you asking me what was being said about this shocking affair?"

"I'm asking you if Charlie was there."

More laughter: Colleen stood her ground. She was positioned close to the door, leaning back against the wall, arms hanging by her sides. She watched Stella rest her shoulders against Daphne's bridged knees. It was a favourite position, comfortable and companionable, one that Colleen had shared until recently.

"What say, ladies? Shall I put this poor Irish maiden out of her misery?"

"No, let her roast a while longer," said Daphne.

"After all she's got us all gated, her and her uncontrollable passions," said Ronnie.

Stella, her arm over her eyes, said, "God, I could do with a cigarette."

"Best not to risk it," said Daphne, "not with things as they are."

"True, O wise one," said Stella.

"He wasn't there, was he?" said Colleen.

Stella sighed and peeped out from under her delicate elbow. "No, my flower, Charles is no longer with us. He am goneded. Goneded away."

"Gone where?"

"Far as I know he's been packed off to sea."

"Sea?"

"Well, sent in that general direction. One thing is for absolutely certain – none of us will see him again."

"Did he say—?" Colleen bit off the question.

"Now, now, use your loaf, Colly-bird. How could Charlie have revealed all and us still be here?"

"Charlie kept his mouth shut, his mouth shut, his mouth shut," Daphne chanted softly. "Charlie kept his mouth shut, the brave grenadier."

"Otherwise," said Stella, "you would have been on the boat back to the Owd Sod with just your memories and that ratty box of chocolates. No, Charlie proved to be a gent, a proper little toff, under that uncouth exterior. He kept his mouth shut and took his medicine like a man."

"He could have told on you too, Stella," Colleen reminded her.

"Ah, but I rejected his lustful advances. I wasn't the one who was nearly caught with him, petting furiously round the back of the pavilion. I was here in school, spouting my silly lines in full view of all."

Ronnie sat up. She had acquired already the faint unwholesome scurf that would mark her cheeks and brow throughout the winter season and had greased the areas with a cream that made her skin shine like old porcelain. "Here," she said, "you aren't thinking of confessing, are you, Colly?"

"What difference would it make to you?" said Colleen. "Sure, none of you were involved."

Stella frowned and lowered her arm from her brow.

"Oh, come off it. You know perfectly well that any admission of guilt would cause trouble for all of us. I mean, it would reflect so badly on the house for a start."

"So you're worried about the house, Stella, are you?"

Daphne stirred and sat forward. "I say, Colleen, you aren't actually going to peach, are you?"

"You'll be expelled on the spot," said Ronnie.

"Sent home in disgrace."

"Think of that before you do anything rash."

"Talking of peaching," said Colleen, "I wonder how Mr MacAdam knew where Charlie would be last night?"

No response came from the girls for a moment. At length Stella said, "God, don't tell me you've been taken in by the Dragon's nonsense, all that tosh about honour and integrity? She's just being crafty. She expects somebody to confess."

"She's counting on it," said Ronnie.

"Don't you see," Stella went on, "old Fergusson needs the whole mess cleared up quickly and the guilty party swept out of sight so that she can write to our parents and exonerate herself from blame."

"I'll have to think about this," said Colleen.

Ronnie was on her feet at once. "What!"

"She'll want to know everything," said Daphne. "She'll wheedle it out of you whether you like it or not. Everything that happened between you and that boy."

Colleen gave one of her laughs, less fey than usual. She said, "Charlie wasn't a boy, Daphne. Charlie was a man."

"What?" shouted Ronnie; a question this time.

"Very much a man."

"You cow!" said Stella. "You're trying to pretend that you did something awful with Charlie. But I know you didn't do anything, anything at all."

"Well, that's a matter between me and Miss Fergusson," Colleen said and, just as Stella got to her feet, cupped a hand to her ear and added, "Ah, I think I hear the luncheon bell."

"Colleen, wait."

But Colleen didn't.


Nothing about Mark Straker was quite what it seemed. On close examination his identity, his persona, appeared to be composed of a series of half-truths and outright lies which he put forward with such conviction and lack of shame that Barbara herself was set to wondering if the man she loved was really, clinically abnormal. It was, Mark had explained to her, his foible, part of his mysterious charm and perhaps he did not quite know himself who he was or what he stood for.

The Straker 'family seat' was nothing more grand than a bungalow on a street of pebble-dash bungalows in Torbay. There Mark was welcomed by his stupid mother and pompous old bore of a father as if he was the Redeemer Returned and she, Barbara, on the two or three occasions she'd been taken there, had been treated with a superciliousness which suggested that the Strakers thought of her as an inferior

211

being, a gold-digger or a trollop, who had dragged Mark away from a brilliant future.

The father, Rupert, had been nothing but a grain merchant, though it was through his offices that Mark Straker had found a place for himself and a means to make money. Mark was a perfectly respectable and quite wealthy member of the Baltic Exchange, the great shipping and commodity centre in St Mary Axe, and had bought shrewdly into several companies during the flotation scramble just after the war.

Mark had not escaped his National Duty. He had been conscripted into the Royal Artillery, had earned a commission and had fought for months at the sharp end. He may have lacked commitment to the cause of freedom but he did not lack courage, though this period, curiously, was one he did not talk of at all, not even to dissemble and exaggerate and certainly not to boost his stock with other men or to impress women. Everything Mark did was done and put away without regret, and that included trench warfare. He had, Barbara suspected, no conscience, a lack that had saved him from suffering.

She did have a conscience, though. It had come up out of nowhere like a reef from a calm sea, had ripped the bottom out of her self-esteem and had all but sunk her in the dark days after her daughter's birth. Such a burden of sorrows and sins had been hidden away inside her that the tragedy had seemed inescapable and self-determined, like punishment deserved.

Mark had even lied about the location of his flat. True, it lay in that blue-blooded and reverently regarded canton of privilege known as Mayfair – but only just. In effect the Strakers did not breathe quite the same air as dukes and duchesses but were closer to the cheerful, not quite vulgar thoroughfare of Shepherd Market in a cul-de-sac known as Jenner's Lane. The doorway to the Strakers' residence was cheek-by-jowl with the frontage of an Italian provision merchant and the three small first-floor rooms floated on an atmosphere of cheese, olive oil, salami and sawdust that dainty white-painted furniture and floral rugs could not disguise or eliminate. Mark's Rolls Royce was well billeted, however, in a long dry shed a step or two away. He would spend much time there with the car, tinkering with its engine or polishing its bodywork as if he were no better than a common chauffeur.

Barbara might have found solace in shopping or in taking lunch with friends, if she'd ever bothered to cultivate friends. But Mark was jealous of her time, inquisitive to the point of suspicion and required her to account for every minute of her day when she was out of his sight; a demonstration of possessiveness that did not, it seemed, cut both ways.

Something in Barbara had changed, however. London no longer seemed like the haven it once had been. Out of altered attitudes new habits were growing. Take Sunday, for instance; on Sundays, for no reason that she could discover in herself, Barbara felt the need of spiritual solace and had taken to attending services at All Hallows in Benedict Street. She would do herself up, as Mark mockingly put it, like a rich war widow, in black furs and veiled hats and toddle off to "All Haloes" – Mark again – and come back, not exactly regenerated but at least calm and, for a little while, settled in her mind.

She liked the cold Sunday mornings, the almost empty streets, the distant sound of bells from spires and steeples, the narrowness of Benedict Street, the sight of All Hallows' narrow lighted doorway, cramped into a corner and defended by two listing old iron horseposts. She liked the fact that she was a stranger there, faintly mysterious, perhaps. Most of all she liked the aloof clarity of voices and the sanctified emptiness upon which not even the most devout of Sabbath worshippers could impinge.

"You're not going all religious on me, Babs?" Mark would say.

"Of course not. It just seems the right thing to do now. I don't know why."

"Penance," he would say. "It'll be the confessional next."

"Hardly."

"How interesting that would be for some lucky priest, to hear the details of all your carnal sins."

"Won't you come with me?"

Mark would just laugh, roll over in the broad white-painted bed and with his head buried in the pillow wave her an indulgent farewell.

She was not entirely surprised to find Mark still in bed when she returned from church. He had been up, though. A coffee cup and his cigarette case were on the nightstand and he lay back upon the pillows and bolsters like some Oriental potentate, watching her through the angles of hall and living room.

"Babby?"

"What is it?"

"Come here."

"As soon as I take off—"

"Come now," he said. "Just as you are."

She wore a French seal fur with a high collar and two large buttons. It was lined with dark plum-coloured silk. Her hat was narrow-brimmed, black velvet, her stockings black silk, her black shoes of glacé kid with a height of heel that was dangerously high. She stood by the open door of the bedroom looking at her husband. His eyes were hooded and speculative. His hair was mussed and hung in little coils, like those of a girl, about his ears. He was handsome, muscular, languorous. He had opened the buttons of his Chinese pyjama jacket as if the room was summery and not touched by the morning's frost. Barbara could see the fine hair across his breastbone, thick corded veins on the side of his neck, hair-downed forearms folded behind his head.

"Come closer," he said.

"What do you want, Mark?"

He grinned. Almost casually he lifted back the bedclothes and folded them to one side.

"What do you think I want?" he said.

There was a time when his desire would have stimulated her. She had never before failed to be roused by his whim, by an inappropriate moment or an unexpected place. But no longer. Since the birth of her child she had felt nothing. She tried to turn away from the sight of his nakedness. He was too swift for her. He grabbed at her wrist.

"You can't leave me suffering like this, Babs," he said thickly.

Playing for time, she said, "Let me at least take off my coat."

"If there's any taking off to be done," he said, "I'll do it."

214

He shifted his hold upon her wrist, clasping it tightly while, shifting his hips, he rolled towards her. He began to stroke the sealskin fur with his free hand, spreading his fingers in broad strokes up the front of her body and around her flanks. "Don't you like what you see, Babs? You used to like it very much. It's all this piety. It's spoiling you."

"It's not that." Barbara tugged at her arms and tried to draw away. "I'm – I'm just not ready yet."

"Well, damn you, girl, I am."

She knew precisely what he wanted of her. A year ago she would have been not just pliant but eager to please him. Now the thought of touching him filled her with revulsion. She felt a sudden cold knifing pain in her loins, though there was nothing amiss in that department, no damage, so the doctors had told her.

Mark jerked her forward until her thighs were pressed against the edge of the mattress. He was so close that she could see the rivulets that his breath made on the soft black fur. When he slipped his hand between the coat's front folds and beneath her skirts, she flinched.

"I never could resist black, remember?" Mark said. "Do you know what you look like? You look like a nun. Oh, wouldn't that be fun, Babs, if you were a novice?"

She flinched again as his hand caressed her stockings. She could see the cascade of her skirt over his wrist, hear the faint rasp of silk under his palm. He was very strong now, full and uncomfortably strong.

He said, "Am I going to have to insist, Babs? I think you'd like that."

Beneath her dress she wore a light corset of woven porous elastic. She had no need of the corset to shape and smooth her hips but her tummy had lost its flatness and something about the practical little garment gave her physical consolation. Two straps, set close together by the inside of her thighs, held up her stockings at the front, two more at the back. She felt his finger slip and probe beneath one strap and then the other, probing as if there was some secret spot that she had kept hidden from him until now. He lifted the strap and, with his thumb, deftly unfastened it.

Barbara felt the silky tension slacken. The other rubber

215

knob popped under Mark's fingers. He gave a sigh, a stifled groan. Pulling her clumsily to him, he reached beneath her dress and pulled her stockings down, ripping the buttons at the back, then ground the heel of his hand blindly into her while she lay passive across him, black fur and plum lining pressed against his flesh.

"I think you've forgotten how, Babby. Seems I'll have to teach you all over again what wives are for."

"Mark, I don't feel well."

"You feel fine to me," he said. "Let me see." He eased her weight from him, pushed her upright and unbuttoned her coat. "Lift up your skirt."

"No, Mark, please."

"Do you honestly think I'm going to take No for an answer?"

She lifted up her skirts, furling them in her gloved hands. She could not bring herself to watch him now, to see the greedy pleasure that the sight of her body gave him. She felt foolish, sick with embarrassment, though it was she who had taught him this game, just two or three days after they had met.

Mark was not like Johnny. Dear Johnny Tiverton would have coaxed her into doing his bidding. Mark was not like Harry who was too kind ever to put his needs before her wishes. Mark was not even like the man at Charlotte Harmon's weekend party, that time, who had taken advantage of her tipsiness and had hurt her quite badly. Mark should have respected her – and didn't. She knew what he would do. She did not have the gumption to resist. She was filled with fear that he would impregnate her again, that out of their mating would spring another poor creature like the last.

He was excited by her reluctance. Her long recuperation had made him imagine himself gentle and patient. She would not give him fuel by refusing, by struggling, and when he tugged at her garments again she eased her body downward to make it easier for him.

"Huh!" he murmured. "You can't kid me, Babby. Nothing will ever change you."

He swung himself from the bed, pushed her face down on to the quilt and moved himself against her.

216

Crushed against the man-smelling sheet, hat askew, Barbara inclined her head to look out through the window at the quiet grey day, vaporous and cold.

"This is what you want. Isn't it? This is what you want," Mark hissed in her ear. "Isn't it, Babby?"

"Yes," Barbara answered, through gritted teeth. "Yes, damn you, yes," and promised herself that if his seed took she would kill it – and herself – before she would bear Mark Straker a second imbecile child to be cast off, without compunction, like the first.

"What did he do to you?" Janis Fergusson asked.

"Nothing, Miss Fergusson," Colleen answered. "We were only together for two minutes. Nothing happened."

"Did he not try to touch you?"

"He did nothing. No more did I."

"You must have done something?"

"We just started to talk."

"Talk?"

"We hardly knew each other, Miss Fergusson."

"Had you never met at the pavilion before?"

"Oh, no, no."

"Where did you meet?"

"In town. On the bridge. Once," said Colleen.

"On Wade's Road Bridge?"

Colleen nodded. "Just once."

"Was MacAdam one of those boys who sit on the wall?"

"I think he was there. Sometimes."

"Looking for a silly girl like you?"

"No, Miss Fergusson. Not any silly girl, just me. When he came it was for me only."

"I think you've been deceived, Colleen."

"No. I've done wrong. But I was not deceived."

"I see," said the Dragon. "Why do you think that Charles MacAdam picked you up?"

"He saw me at the Summer Concert in the park. He heard me sing. He – he liked me from the first."

"Did he tell you that?"

"Yes."

"And, of course, you believed him."

217

"It wasn't what you think, Miss Fergusson."

"And, pray, what do I think?"

"That he was just after hanky-panky. He could have had that with—"

"Go on."

"With village girls."

"But MacAdam didn't want village girls. Perhaps he thought he was too good for village girls."

"It wasn't Charlie's fault, Miss Fergusson. I'm here to take the blame."

"Tell me once more what happened."

"I met him on the bridge and we talked for two or three minutes, when I should have been taking tea in The Hut with the other girls. That happened just once. I wanted to see him again so we arranged to meet at the pavilion last night and that's what we did."

"Colleen, what did you expect to gain from last night's excursion? In fact, what did you anticipate would be the outcome of this relationship?"

"I never thought about that."

"It was pointless, Colleen. Charles MacAdam had nothing to offer you. He isn't, and never could be, your – your type of young man. You know that, don't you?"

"Yes, Miss. But he liked me."

"That isn't enough, Colleen. You disobeyed school rules. You imperilled your own safety. Have you any idea what can happen to young girls who consort with men like Charlie MacAdam?"

"They can get babies."

"Well, yes, of course."

"I would never have let him do it, Miss Fergusson. Never. No matter how much I liked him or he liked me."

"I don't think you have any idea what you're talking about, Colleen."

"Yes, but I do."

"How did you acquire this information?"

"I've seen the cattle at it."

Janis Fergusson coughed and cleared her throat. "That's as may be, Colleen. But we are not cattle and we do not behave like beasts of the field."

"I thought it was the same, more or less."

"It isn't the same at all. Cattle do not love each other, do not know mutual respect. They have no natural modesty and are driven only by the need to – to procreate." Janis Fergusson paused. She had a feeling that she was beginning to sound cant-ridden, like the shade of old Miss Aitken. She said, "Simply because you have come forward of your own volition, Colleen, I am not going to let you off lightly. You must be aware of how serious your offences have been?"

"Don't expel me, Miss Fergusson. Don't send me home in disgrace, please, please," Colleen begged with hands clasped as if in prayer.

The Dragon said, "Your father will be bitterly disappointed in you, you know."

"No, he won't. It's about all Dada expects of me. He doesn't think I'm worth anything anyway." She held out her clenched fists in supplication. "If you send me away from St Austin's, I'll have nowhere to go. He'll just send me somewhere else, somewhere worse."

"Colleen, Colleen, what am I to do with you?"

"Anything, miss, any punishment, except don't send me home to my father."

Janis Fergusson pondered for a moment then said, "Do you realise that you have ruined one young man's life by your stupidity and have possibly cost St Austin's the services of a reliable employee?" Colleen nodded miserably. Miss Fergusson went on, "In addition you have brought the school into disrepute and have damaged our good relations with the community."

Colleen said nothing while the Head continued in this vein for several minutes. At the end of the harangue, however, and to Colleen's infinite relief, Miss Fergusson said, "I have decided, though, not to expel you and not to involve your parents. In exchange I want you to give me your solemn word that you will not break bounds again."

"Oh, yes, Miss Fergusson. I promise, I promise."

"And not endeavour to communicate or to meet with Charles MacAdam while you are a pupil at this school."

"I give you my word on that too."

219

"If he, the young man, makes any attempt to contact you, you must tell me at once."

"Of course, of course."

"Your punishment – and it is less than you deserve – is to be barred from leaving school grounds on any pretext at all until the end of the summer term. If you require dental or medical attention then Matron will notify me and I will make arrangements. But otherwise you will not participate in any activity that will take you out of school. If you deceive me, if you infringe upon these rules in the slightest degree, Colleen, I will have no hesitation in sending you home instantly. Do I make myself clear?"

"Yes, Miss Fergusson. Thank you, Miss Fergusson."

"You may go now." Colleen shot to her feet. "No, wait just a moment." Very quietly Janis Fergusson said, "I know why you came here, Colleen. You came here to admit your guilt because you did not want to be in someone's debt." The Head held up her hand to prevent any blurting out of names. "That was the most sensible thing you could have done, far more sensible than the behaviour that preceded it. It occurs to me that you were not entirely alone in fashioning this escapade. I won't ask you to tell me who else was involved or what the extent of their involvement might have been. Just this – would you feel more comfortable if I were to remove you from Room 13, put you perhaps into another house?"

"Yes, Miss Fergusson, I would."

"It will not reflect well upon you, Colleen. You may have to put up with a certain amount of hostility from your new companions. Are you prepared for that?"

"Sure, Miss Fergusson, and I am."

"Very well," Janis Fergusson said. "I will announce to the school that the matter has been settled and that the ban has been lifted. I will not tell them who it was that confessed. I suspect that I won't have to. Keep silent about what happened and what has passed between us and about the whole matter. You have nothing to be proud of, Colleen."

"No, Miss Fergusson." Colleen hesitated. "Miss Fergusson, I think you should take these."

The box had been hidden in the folds of her tunic, tucked into one of its voluminous pockets. Now it was in the Irish girl's hand, held by a grubby gold ribbon between finger and thumb, twirling gently.

"What is it?"

"Chocolates, Miss. Charlie gave them to me."

"Did he, indeed?"

"Don't you think you should take them?"

For an instant Janis Fergusson felt a strange weak pang of pity for the girl and her pathetic gesture. She would have trouble explaining her decision to Miss Gaylord, and Irené Milligan would no doubt feel slighted that the girl was being removed from her charge. But these were matters that she, Janis Fergusson, was trained to cope with and they paled in comparison with the confusions and compulsions that beset children like Colleen O'Neal.

The Dragon shook her head. "Keep them, Colleen."

The girl looked at the little box hung from the ribbon in her fingers. "I think they're probably spoiled by now."

"Then get rid of them," Janis Fergusson said.


There were girls everywhere, girls hanging around with an air of deliberate casualness. They were waiting to spy on her, to observe her distress, her tears, to see her marched out, bag and baggage, and sent away then and there, packed off in shame to the railway station never to darken the doors of saintly St Austin's again.

Colleen refused to meet their eyes. It was easy to do for she had practised the arts of introversion faithfully for years, that fey and enigmatic mien that armoured her against the hurts of the world.

Before she could descend the stairs to the main hall, though, the assembly bell began to ring and prefects were shouting and housemistresses appeared from the odd corners where they'd been lurking. Even the dog, Otto, who was sprawled in pride of place before the newly-lighted log fire, opened one eye, cocked an ear and then rolled laboriously over like a hibernating bear, while girls stepped over and around him as if he were an awkward piece of furniture.

"Colly, Colly, where have you been?" Daphne Gore smiled up at her from the bottom of the stairs. "I say, we wondered what you were up to."

221

Colleen side-stepped, brushed her hair back from her brow with her wrist and, to the accompaniment of murmurs and whispers, turned sharply right and headed along the passage against the flow of the tide.

Some of the afternoon's activities had already commenced. There was confusion in the music rooms and in the Harvey where the choir had just begun practice. A viola swamped the far end of the passage with floods of notes, not all of them quite in tune, and two of the younger girls, who were sneaking in some 'jumps' upon the domestics' stairs, stopped as if riven when Colleen sailed past them.

"I say, is that her?"

"Yes, I do believe it is."

"How awful!"

Goss and Frognall, in from the gardens, drew up short and stared at her but Colleen said nothing to them.

Only when she encountered Pauline at the door of the corridor from the house, did Colleen's resolve weaken. She put off her abstracted manner and hesitated.

"Are you all right?" Pauline asked anxiously.

"Never been better," Colleen answered.

"We thought – I thought . . ."

"Still here, aren't I?" Colleen said.

"Aren't you going to special assembly?"

"Not I."

"What's it about, I wonder?" Pauline said.

"Oh, I know what it's about," said Colleen and, with a wave, went on her solitary way.

She turned left into a passage that led to the deserted classrooms and a row of four lavatories.

She would be sorry to leave Teal. She hadn't realised before just what Teal had come to mean to her. She had associated the house with Stella for just too long, with a desperate striving to be accepted not by School or Teal or anything other than Stella Jackson and her clique. What a waste that had been, Colleen thought. If only she had been put in with Goss Johnstone at the start there would have been no squandered emotions and she might have made some genuine friends, like Pauline Verity. From her association with Stella she had gained nothing except, in the end, a kind of disdain for the pretty girl's heartless pranks.

Soon she would be an outcast again, exiled to Eggar or Ossian, wherever there was a spare bed. She was bound to be treated with suspicion, bullied a little perhaps by the prefects and monitors. She didn't mind.

It would have been so much worse to have lost her niche in the world, to have been sent away from St Austin's in disgrace. She had been lucky, very lucky. She had known what it was to be wanted and, however briefly, loved. And she had got away with it in spite of the fact that Miss Fergusson had seen right through her pretensions and pretences, had looked into her heart as if she'd been made of glass.

Colleen stepped into the last cubicle in the row. She closed the door and bolted it, seated herself on the pedestal, extracted the battered little gift box from her tunic pocket and carefully untied the ribbon. She leaned forward, propped her elbows on her knees and stared at the door for a moment or two, then she plucked a chocolate cream from the nest of crinkly paper and pushed the sweet into her mouth.

Who would play for *The Demon Drummer* now, she wondered, now that she was gone to another house? Would she be obliged to black her face and sing minstrel songs from out of the crowd, anonymous and indistinguishable? She would not be allowed to steal the limelight in Eggar House or Ossian and might even have to put her harp away until summer term. She dipped her fingers into the box and transferred four soft fruity creams to her mouth.

She sucked on sticky saliva. She munched and swallowed. She crammed four chocolates at once into her mouth and then another four. Her cheeks bulged with heavy saccharine sweetness. Angry at herself she stuffed in the last two creams with her forefinger and chewed the lot into a soft coagulated mass that threatened, suddenly, to choke her.

Doggedly she papped on the mess and then, with tears in her eyes and a sudden cold sweat on her brow, she slid from the seat and knelt, head hung over the toilet bowl, and waited for the last tangible evidence of her first love to be ejected and flushed away.

To Colleen's vast relief it did not take long.

# Twelve

*P*auline was nervous. She was not alone. Some principal performers had been so overcome with stagefright that they had thrown up their suppers and had had to be taken to the San and seated, heads between knees, until Old Flo and Mad Jamie had talked moral fibre back into them and sent them, shaky but resigned, to be dressed and painted for their performances. Pauline was not so overcome as Goss who had accoutred herself early in her Whaler Bill costume and had then had to endure the agony of a two-hour wait, hanging about Teal's common-room, mouthing her lines while staring bleakly at the clock on the wall as if it was execution and not recital that faced her at approximately a quarter past nine.

It had been the strangest month in Pauline's life. She was sorry that it was almost over. First there had been the business with Colleen O'Neal who had been whipped out of Teal House and resettled in Eggar where, so Frog said, she was treated like a pariah. Miss Milligan had been very upset by the implications of Colleen's transfer and had been less than her sunny self for a week or two. Then there had been evidence of a rift in relations in Room 13. Stella had become silent, almost reclusive, while Ronnie and Daphne had crept about together like – as Frog put it – a three-legged mouse. In fact in the corridors of Teal was a general mutedness as if each and every girl shared the shame that the Irish girl's escapade had engendered.

It was not that anyone had much time to mope. Class tests and external examinations were much in mind and 'study' in varying degrees interrupted the fun of concert rehearsals. Educational matters were put away by the 15th, however. Upon that night the school Christmas tree was brought in by Mr Guy Harvey and planted with due ceremony in an enormous half-barrel in the main hall and – this was also traditional, apparently – duly baptised by Otto in full view of all. In a great flurry of activity, main hall and dining-room were decorated with evergreen and paperchains, to the Calvinistic Miss Gaylord's chagrin and everybody else's delight. The following afternoon each of the houses attended to individual ornamentation and with that done the entire focus of St Austin's turned to final preparations for the concert.

If Goss's enthusiasm was tempered by nervous defensiveness, Elf had flung herself into the role of the Drummer with unalloyed delight. She had no words at all to speak but, without doubt, her appearances would be dramatic highpoints. To her surprise, Pauline had been chosen as one of a chorus of four narrators which included Bettina Grant. She had no difficulty in learning her lines but found the cues tricky and was glad that so much time had been allotted for practice. Frog was in charge of special acoustical effects. In taking over from Colleen, she had replaced the Irish harp with a xylophone and the shoeboxes with a variety of pans and trays borrowed from the kitchens. It was significant that Stella, Daphne and Ronnie were given no part to play in the presentation but were relegated to the status of humble stagehands.

The first dress rehearsal had been a fiasco. It had taken over five hours to stage, though Teal's contribution had gone fairly smoothly. The Harvey had not been constructed on the model of Drury Lane and entrances and exits had to be controlled with military precision. Consequently there was a great deal of hanging about in corridors and struggling against tides of choristers and minstrels and members of the orchestra as one group replaced another in the science laboratory which was set just below and behind the stage. Here teachers and nimble-fingered volunteers made final adjustments to costumes, refreshed stage make-up and did their best to calm the performers before they were ushered, hushed, into the wings.

It was all very exciting, yet sad at one and the same time. Ossian's classical actors were in tears minutes after they had taken their bows. Even the choir's leading soloist, beautifully steady and controlled, had had a fit of hysterics as soon as the choir had descended from the stage and had flung herself into Mademoiselle Jalabert's arms to be led, sobbing, away.

Pauline was scornful of such spinelessness and Elf and she had developed a supercilious attitude that angered Goss no end.

"It's only a show, one night in our lives," Elf would say. "It's not going to matter if your knickers fall down."

"It's not my knickers I'm worried about. What if I forget my lines?" Goss would say.

"That's called 'a dry'," Pauline would say. "The prompter will help you if you dry."

"What a knowall you are at times, Pauline," Goss would complain. "It's all very well for you. You don't have your father and mother hanging on your every word, all too ready to criticise if you make a mistake."

Later, after Goss had stalked off, Elf had put an arm about Pauline's shoulder and had said, "She didn't mean it, Polly. Don't take on."

"I'm not taking on," Pauline had answered. "I'm fine, really."

But she had been upset by Goss's reminder that Daddy would not be in the audience; would not be there to take her home to London the following morning where Mrs Dobbs and the cats would be waiting to greet her and Katy and Andrea would be round with little gifts, eager to hear her news and tell her all that had been happening in good old Glades Road while she'd been away. More than ever Pauline felt a well of loneliness within her, a strange sense of isolation that increased as term drew to a close. She did not doubt that she would be made welcome by her aunt and uncle at Flask Hall but it would not be the same as being at home, not the same at all.

Wednesday, the day of final dress rehearsal, was brilliantly clear, the evening breathtakingly cold. The sky seemed to shiver with the weight of stars upon it and town and village, glen and mountain were still and calm as far as the eye could see in contrast to the hot, fervid atmosphere within the Harvey.

Thursday brought more of the same weather and relief all round. By noon sundry relatives began to arrive to pay their respects to Miss Fergusson and to take lunch from a buffet laid out in the staff common-room. Morning classes went on as usual but concentration was at its lowest ebb as motor-cars and the school bus passed by the window.

Pauline did not demean herself by asking Stella when Uncle Lewis would arrive or where he would stay that night. Every inn and hotel between Pattullo and Crieff was booked solidly and the advent of the audience, in bits and pieces, served only to increase tension among the girls.

Supper was taken extra early. The dining room, for once, was muted. No calls for silence necessary when Miss Fergusson, already arrayed for the evening, appeared to wish everyone Good Luck and to issue last minute instructions to non-performers who would act as stewards and who would be required to be on duty at the doors by a quarter to seven. No girl, not even Colleen, was excluded from participation of some sort in the Gala event.

The reprobates from Room 13 had been assigned to cloak-room duty, under the command of Miss Shadbrook. Pauline saw nothing of her cousin in the hiatus after supper.

Costume baskets were lined around the common-room. Programmes, marked with times to the minute, were pinned to the wall and two 'runners' – sensible juniors – stood by to complete the line of communication between school and house. Choir and orchestra members were gone. By half past seven, when the strains of the overture drifted faintly along the corridors and across the lawns, the cast of *The Drummer of Dundee* was primed to face a long, long wait of ninety-seven minutes before it would be summoned to the lab for a last touch-up with powder and ushered finally up to the stage.

Unlike some of the girls Pauline had not put herself out to watch the arrival of parents and relatives and the flood of traffic, some of it horse-drawn, that came up from the village. She felt cut off from anyone not in costume as if she had been transformed by the dark-green ankle length tartan skirt and white blouse that she and the other narrators wore, as if her entry to that lighted stage would have no exit to round it off.

At eight o'clock Miss Milligan made tea. At twenty past

Morven Clark was sick and had to be taken to see Matron. At twenty to nine, Morven came back, pale as a ghost but steady. At ten minutes to nine, only seconds before a runner sent for them to come to the lab, Goss began to shake and shudder and mutter that she could not possibly go on with it. She looked quite ridiculous in gummed side-whiskers, baggy trousers and striped flannel shirt, hair arranged in a pump-handle pigtail. Sympathy was on the point of being offered by all and sundry when Frog took charge of the crisis. She stepped angrily up to her very best friend, thrust the painted broom 'harpoon' into her hands and told the tall, brown, shuddering girl to snap out of it.

Goss did. She gulped, gripped the prop as if it was a hockey stick and, just as the little runner flung open the door and shouted, "Time," managed to stagger to her feet and say unconvincingly, "Right, lads, let's give 'em socks."

Seconds later the Thespians of Teal trooped down the corridor in single file and, silent as nuns, entered the passage that led to the lab where they were immediately engulfed in waves of laughter that shook the stout walls of the Harvey.

Four flats of painted canvas mounted on castors waited in the wings. The scenes upon them seemed crude in the flood of light that slanted from the row of electrical bulbs along the base of the stage. Two thick ropes hung inconveniently against the columnar folds of the back-curtain and bounced in rhythm to the skipping steps of the reel that shook the stage. Pauline, waiting now, envied the highland dancers their poise and deportment, the fact that they were in motion. Mademoiselle Jalabert, the only teacher to take part in the concert, was set off to one side, her sturdy torso arched back against the weight of the accordion, fingers flying over its glistening keys. Out there everything seemed glamorous. Here in the wings was only shoddiness and pretence.

Perspiration dampened the grubby powder along Pauline's hair line. She was sure that it had stained the armpits of the borrowed blouse. Her mouth was dry and chalky. Gladly she accepted the glass of water that Miss Milligan offered and, holding her chin over the towel that Milly held to catch drips, sipped from it.

Across the angle of the stage Pauline could see a corner of the audience, dim and faded like an old painting. She stared hard, trying to identify features – but could not. Elf had already gone to her position back right. It was important that she hold an exact line when her cue came for the light would follow her, combine with face paint to turn her into a ghastly apparition. The drum was strapped about her neck but she had no sticks; a subtle touch that added to the spookiness and that old Milly hoped would draw an extra loud shriek from the audience. Head down and eyes closed, Goss was murmuring the first line of her speech over and over again. When she reached back blindly, Pauline took her hand and gave it a squeeze.

The reel finished on a sustained chord. The dancers bowed and curtsied and, as the curtains shook and rolled together, scampered past, all sweaty and real in white muslin and gaudy sashes and no longer ethereal as moths in twilight.

"Go," Miss Milligan hissed and covered by the thunder of applause from the mysterious side of the curtains the cast of *The Drummer of Dundee* ran quickly to their appointed places and, heads up, waited for the signal that the machinery was all in place. Pauline could hardly breathe. All the words had gone clean out of her mind. She was a blank – numb, dumb, frozen. Beside her Marion, a co-narrator, was saying "Oh, oh, oh, oh," over and over again and squirming her knees together. Applause diminished. A growling roar came from the nether world out there. And old Milly said, "Now."

Two out of three of the bulbs on the board of footlights flickered out and a great yellowish beam of light encompassed Pauline, dazzling her, as the curtains shuddered, parted and the show was on.

She had practised her projection. She had rounded her lips about vowels and smoothed away edgy London consonants. She had rehearsed the beckoning gesture that would accompany the introductory verse, a confiding tone, crisp delivery that would slow and become sinister before she stepped back out of the spotlight and made way for Marion – and now none of it meant anything. For an instant she gaped out at the packed rows of seats, blinked at the four little lights above the exit doors at the back of the hall. Then, seeing nothing, hearing nothing, she felt her features crease and relax into the required expression and the words that she had forgotten pop into her mouth and float into the rainbow void:

Oh, Magadalene Green is bleak and bare,
   At least so we've heard many people declare,
For I fairly confess we never was there;
   Not a shrub nor a tree,
   Nor a bush can you see;
Just seabirds and bleachworks and black rotting piles,
the tide of the Tay stretching eastward for miles;
   It's a very sad thing to be caught there at e'en,
When the dark's drifting down on Magadalene Green.

Pauline stepped back out of the light. Without hesitation, Marion slipped past her to take up the tale.

The worst of it was over. She had not dried. She had not fallen to her knees or dotted poor Marion on the nose with a flail of the arms as she had done in rehearsal. She had begun her performance well. Everything would be fine now.

Marion stepped back. The spotlight closed its glaring beam and opened again across the breadth of the stage on Morven, the third narrator. Out of the corner of her eye Pauline could see Goss poised to make her entrance.

Such were now the two men who appear'd beside the rill.
Tarry Waters was the short one, the tall one Whaler Bill . . .

Goss and a sixth former named Sheila reeled out on to the stage, pretending to be tipsy. It was all that Pauline could do to stop herself smiling. They looked so real and so comical. The audience laughed, laughed again at some bit of business from Goss. Pauline felt a warm, confident glow within her and, completely at home now, prepared herself to deliver her next line. And then she was looking at her mother.

She was seated in the third row, behind the Harveys. Pauline first recognised Mr Roddy, hunched and grinning, and then, as her eyes grew accustomed to the gloom, found herself staring at Grandpapa Haldane who was flanked on one side by Uncle Lewis Jackson and on the other by . . .

230

Marion nudged her. She realised that the spotlight had traversed to her again and she groped stupidly for the cue and the speech that would follow it.

Marion hissed, side of mouth, "Muttons."

Automatically Pauline intoned, "To return to our muttons – this mode of progression at length upon Whaler Bill made some impression . . ." Vaguely, she heard Goss utter the response: "Hillow, messmate, what cheer? How queer you do steer. Why, what's in the wind, Bo, What is it you fear?"

Mummy was sitting forward. She wore a dark dress and had a stole of some sort draped across her shoulders. She paid no attention whatsoever to the action on stage but fixed herself on Pauline. Perhaps it was that concentration, that undeviating stare that had magnetised her; Mummy looking up at her from a sea of shadowy faces.

For a moment Pauline felt exhilarated, claimed, and then she noticed the man beside Mummy and how casually he adjusted the stole and gave Mummy a familiar pat upon the shoulder. And Pauline was cold again, cold all through. She felt separated into two parts, one of which, thank heaven, projected the lines allotted to her, while the other shrank back in retreat from the realisation that the arrogant-looking stranger must be her new stepfather.

Thunder rattles dinned Pauline's ears. Lights flickered as lightning sheets were shaken in the wings. Goss and Marion were frozen in their tracks and to the accompaniment of a thudding beat upon a pot-lid, Elf, all ghastly, jerked down the wooden ramp between the flats and tapped a wooden rhythm with her phantom sticks.

The audience gasped, almost applauded. Everyone stared at the tiny figure, pale as ectoplasm, everyone except Mummy who gazed unremittingly at Pauline as if she and not Elf were the ghost.

The 1921 Gala Concert was over. What remained now was the informal supper, a meeting with parents and friends, a late dispersal and a short night of chatter and anticlimax that would dwindle into a breakfast of yawns and bad temper and, about half-past nine, a short service of thankfulness for the term that was over. Then there would be an exchange of presents and cards, kisses, hugs and handshakes before cars, dogcarts and omnibuses carried St Austin's girls off to enjoy other, less well-defined pleasures.

Pauline wanted none of it. As soon as she stepped from the stage of the Harvey she gave herself over not to tears or tantrums but to a stubborn refusal to have anything to do with celebration.

She ran back to the house, peeled off her blouse, skirt and shoes and left them neatly by the prop hamper. She was first into the cloakroom, first to the hot-water sink and, carrying her tunic over her arm, went directly upstairs to Room No. 11, changed into her nightgown, and clambered into bed.

The room was cold. Frost patterned the window panes. When Pauline switched off the light by the bed a haunting bluish glimmer outlined the empty bedsteads and tallboys. She put her head on the pillow and willed herself to sleep. No hope of that. She could not breathe properly, could not so much as blink her eyes. She felt gnarled by shock and, like a child, tried to hide from it in her own bed in the room that, in a mere four months, had become her home and her sanctuary. Frog was first to root her out.

"Where are you, Polly?"

"Here."

"What are you doing in bed? Don't you know that we're supposed to take supper with our guests? Did nobody tell you?"

"I don't want to," Pauline said. "I'm tired."

"Is it because you fluffed a line? Are you embarrassed? You needn't be. Everybody thought—"

"I don't much care what everybody thought."

"Won't you dress and come down with me?"

"No. Leave me alone. Please."

She lay now in a state of expectation. It was not that she wished to be coddled and coaxed; she simply could not surrender to the inevitability of having to confront her mother and the man who was not her father. She recalled with horror the sight of that casual touch, the intimate adjustment of the stole, so confidently possessive.

It wasn't Goss or Elf or even Miss Milligan who came

next but, ten minutes later, Stella – who did not even bother to knock.

She flashed on the ceiling light and snapped, "What the devil are you playing at, Pauline? The entire family's waiting for you."

"Go away. I'm not coming down. I'm far too tired."

"You conceited cow. After Grandpapa came all this way to see you—"

"He didn't come to see me. He came to see you."

"Your mother . . ."

"I'll meet them in the morning. That'll be time enough."

"Well, I ask you! What a cheek! I hope you're not going to sulk for a fortnight and spoil my Christmas as well as your own."

"Go away, Stella. Leave me alone."

"My pleasure, I'm sure."

Below, Pauline could hear the roar of motorcar engines, the laughter of departing guests. She felt silly but unrelentingly stubborn. Goss had been keen to introduce Pauline to her father. Elf had promised a meeting with her mother. Perhaps, Pauline thought vaguely, there would be time for those pleasantries in the morning. She tried to eliminate from her mind the reality of her situation, that Christmas would be spent in a strange place with people she either did not know or heartily disliked.

Almost to her surprise her eyelids had grown heavy and sleep was creeping upon her when the door opened once more. She suspected that it would be Miss Milligan and had already decided that if the housemistress insisted upon it she would capitulate, dress and accompany the woman downstairs. Better late than never. Pauline stirred and lifted herself a little.

"What's wrong, darling?"

"Mummy? Is that you?"

"May I put on the bedlight?"

"What are you doing here?"

"I came to see if you were all right."

Pauline wriggled and sat up. She could not see her mother who was stooped over, fiddling with the recalcitrant switch that hung from the twisted cable by the bedtable. The lamp

233

flickered and lit just as Barbara uncurled. For an instant mother and daughter were brought face to face, noses almost touching. Both were surprised and embarrassed by the proximity of the other. Pauline pressed herself back against the headboard while her mother, still on one knee and resting an elbow on the bed, sank back on to her heels.

It was very peculiar to look down on her mother. It was almost as if Mummy had become a small child again, too young, too small and unformed to be allowed to invade the domain of Middle School girls. For a split second Pauline felt haughty and superior, her own childishness forgotten.

Barbara scrambled to her feet. She seated herself upon the side of the bed. She wore the warm heavy dress without style and the stole was swathed shawl-like about her thin shoulders. Even in the soft glow of the lamplight she looked thinner and much older than Pauline remembered her to be, even before the baby.

Awkward now, Pauline could find nothing to say.

Mummy said, "You've grown, Pauline. In fact, you seem so very different from when I last saw you."

"That was only four months ago."

"May I – may I kiss you?"

"Of course," said Pauline stiffly.

How often had she dreamed of the moment when her mother would put an arm about her and draw her to her breast, kiss her cheek, her forehead, her lips as if she was still little Pauline Verity of Weymouth Street in London town; would touch her hair and straighten the seams of her nightgown, would sit by her and talk with her? But it did not seem right that it should happen here in St Austin's.

Pauline was ashamed of the equality that the situation conferred upon her; this was her place and she belonged here – and Mummy did not, not now.

She could not bring herself to respond when Mummy kissed her. She placed a hand lightly upon the stole, the other hovering, as if at any moment she might retract her favour and push the woman from her. Mummy's lips felt sticky and uneven, almost rough. There were lines about her eyes and creases, not dimples, by the sides of her mouth. She no longer appeared dainty, just small.

The woman sat back, forced a smile. "There now. That wasn't so awful, was it?"

Pauline said, "I'm sorry I didn't come down to supper. I didn't feel up to it. Did you enjoy the concert?"

"Very much. You were marvellous." Barbara glanced over her shoulder. "I wonder – do you mind if I smoke?"

"No, please do."

Mummy lifted her shoulders and tried to giggle, without success. "It seems naughty to be smoking in a dormitory." She took a thin tortoiseshell case from her reticule and extracted a cigarette from it, a box of miniature matches. "Would you like one?"

"No. Thank you."

"You don't have to pretend with me, darling."

"I'm not pretending."

Barbara lit the cigarette, looked around for an ashtray and, of course, found none. She seemed helpless for a moment and then with a shrug put the spent match, still trailing a wisp of smoke, into her reticule and shut the clasp of the bag upon it. She inhaled, angled her head away from Pauline and exhaled a frail plume of smoke into the room's cold, empty air.

"I wasn't here, of course," Mummy said. "This is all new to me. Much less austere than our dormitories. Quite comfortable, I'd say. Not much warmer, though. We had iron bedsteads, ten to a room, like a hospital ward, even in the Sixth . . ."

"Why did you have to bring him?" Pauline said.

"Because he's my husband," Barbara said.

"Couldn't you have waited until Christmas?"

"He – Mark is his name, by the way – he wanted to come."

"I can't think why." Pauline was struck once more by her mother's resemblance to Stella, though it was less acute than before, as if Stella had become more authentic and Mummy a faded memory of the original.

"To accompany Grandpapa, I think," Barbara said.

"Grandpapa?"

"He's old now and becoming frail. I suspect he won't have the strength to make the long journey another year. Mark offered to bring him in his motorcar."

"Why did Grandpapa want to come at all?"

"I expect he had some business with the Harveys. He put up at Kingsford last night and will do so again tonight."

"You too?"

"No, we're roughing it at the Hydro in Crieff."

"Am I going home with you?" said Pauline. "I mean to London."

"Of course not," Barbara said. "We're all of us going to Flask for the festive season. Haven't you been told?"

Pauline hesitated. "Will your husband be there too?"

"Naturally," Barbara said. "At least for part of the time. It'll be such fun to have the family all together. We'll have lots of opportunities to get to know each other again, you and I."

"Yes," said Pauline.

The woman looked around for someplace to put her cigarette. She seemed suddenly at a loss and confusion made her fleetingly petulant. She held the cigarette between finger and thumb, smoke scribbling the air, and said, almost snappishly, "Are you sorry to see me, Pauline?"

"No, it's not that. It was just such a surprise."

"Is that why you were so rude to us all?"

"I'm sorry," Pauline said. "I'll be all right tomorrow, I promise."

"I do hope so." Barbara paused, "It's so good to see you again, darling. You've no idea how much I've missed you." She held the burning cigarette at arm's length and with her free hand tenderly brushed Pauline's cheek. "Have you missed me? Even a little?"

"Yes, Mummy," said Pauline and, because she felt sorry for the woman, obediently returned her goodnight kiss.


"Old Milly isn't half fizzing," Goss said. "In fact if she hadn't been so jolly ecstatic at the way the *Drummer* went down, if her head had not been ringing with praise, she'd have been up here at the double to drag you downstairs in chains."

"I just didn't feel up to it," Pauline said.

"Well, best give her a sob story first thing," said Goss. "Tell her it was your time or something. She'll understand that. Sorry you didn't get to meet my father, though. I've told him all about you and he just can't believe that anyone so horrible could possibly be a pupil at St Austin's. Here, I brought you a little something to perk you up."

"What's that?"

"A sausage roll."

"And fruitcake," Frog put in. "Ignore the lint. It's been in my pocket for ages."

Elf said, "I'm cold. Aren't you lot cold?"

"No, old son, we have blood in our veins. Froggie, take the child under the wing of your dressing gown, there's a good chap," Goss said. "And you, Polly, try not to make crumbs."

Goss was still elevated by the success of her performance. She was most un-Gosslike in her garrulousness and bonhomie. Pauline was glad of the company. She had felt miserable in the minutes between her mother's departure and the girls' arrival.

Lights Out had sounded ages ago. To judge by the racket in the house there would be precious little sleep for anyone tonight but, with the holidays upon them, nobody seemed to care.

Wide awake now, seated up in bed with the quilt about her shoulders, Pauline munched the sausage roll. She said, "You wouldn't happen to have anything to drink, would you?"

"Ginger pop," said Elf. "One miserable bottle. I've been saving it for a special occasion."

"This is a special occasion." said Goss. "Out with it, Elfie, if you please."

It was one of the Toffee Shop's dumpy brown bottles and it did not go far among the four. For all that, the act of passing the bottle between them seemed, to Pauline at least, like a symbol of real friendship. She sipped her share of the ginger beer and passed the bottle on.

"If one of us has the measles," Frog said, "you realise that we're all done for."

"Nobody's got the measles," Goss said. "Drink up, me hearties." She paused. "Was that your mater we passed in the corridor, Polly?"

"Yes. Yes, it was."

"She's awfully pretty," Elf remarked.

"Didn't know she was coming, did you?" Goss said.

Pauline shook her head. She put the last of the sausage roll into her mouth and chewed vigorously. She found that she could contemplate the bleak prospect of Christmas vacation bravely enough now. She was consoled by the realisation that in three weeks time she would be back here, back with friends.

"Bit of a shock, what?" said Frog. "Enough to put anyone off their stroke."

"Change of plans for Christmas?" said Goss.

"No, I'm still spending the hols at Flask Hall."

"With Stella," Frog said.

"'Fraid so."

"Hard cheese!" said Goss.

Pauline shrugged. "Can't be helped. I suppose it'll be jolly enough once I get used to it."

"Will your mother be there too?" said Goss.

"So it would seem," said Pauline. "And her new husband."

There was silence from the others, an awkwardness. She wondered what they were thinking, if their sympathy was tinged with relief that they had in prospect a better time than she, with mothers and fathers, brothers, homes made cosy by familiarity.

"If I'd only thought," Goss said, "you could have spent Christmas with us in Edinburgh."

"Mummy would have had you, and welcome," Elf put in.

"Too late now," said Frog.

"It may not be so bad," said Pauline. "Fortitude, and all that. I expect I'll be glad to get back, though."

"Oh, yes," said Frog. "I expect, when the time comes, we all will."

"Meanwhile," Goss said, raising the bottle, "here's to us, to Teal, and to good old St Austin's."

"Merry Christmas, everyone," said Elf in her best Tim Cratchit voice and the others, Pauline included, drank to that greeting in turn.

238

# PART III
## Household Ghosts

# Thirteen

*H*owever mundane a residence Flask Hall might have appeared to members of the Upper Thousand, it held pride of place in the little wool town over whose streets and chimneypots it presided. The house was not at all as Pauline had remembered it. It seemed smaller and more comfortable, less baronial in scale and style. It had a façade of timber and brick, leaded windows and a general agglomeration of bits and pieces that disguised the fact that it had once been nothing better than a wool-merchant's domicile tarted up with touches of rococo Gothic to see it decently through the age of elegance.

Its position, though, was very grand indeed. The Hall, inside as well as out, seemed to partake of the loftiness of its surroundings, to become a part of the long, rugged outcropping of Scutt's Edge which reared romantically above the valley of the little river Fann. From the very highest room in the house – which once upon a time had been Aunt Bea's sewing room – you could look east and south and see the snaking coils of the Derwent flow down into Matlock. But that was not the view from the drawing-room and the salon or from the tiny, warm bedroom on the second floor that Aunt Bea had set aside for Pauline's use.

Behind the Hall, flanking a cobbled yard, were the old mews, converted now into servants' quarters and garages for Uncle Lewis's motorcars. The new stables, built just before the war, were some way down hill, for there was no safe riding in the immediate vicinity of the Hall where the ground sloped steeply in all directions. Even the driveway, running in a zig-zag up the diagonal of the Edge, seemed, to Pauline at least, quite perilously precipitous.

Pausing only to obtain petrol and water and to partake of

a light meal at some country hotel in the Lake District Uncle Lewis Jackson, Pauline learned, was wont to drive the entire distance between Pattullo and Flask in twelve or fourteen hours. Mr Straker had declared that he and the Ghost were more than up to it but that out of deference to the ladies and to Grandpapa Haldane an overnight stop say about Lancaster, would be a sensible and civilised requirement, particularly as motoring in the dark in winter could hardly be construed as safe.

Pauline was not sorry that the journey was broken. Motoring, she discovered, was exhilarating but uncomfortable and after the best part of seven hours in the padded brown-leather box that was the passenger compartment of Mr Straker's vehicle, she felt bruised in both body and mind and was relieved to step on to "dry land", as Mummy put it, in the yard of the Lancaster Arms.

Christmas began, really, at that moment. Dusk in an unknown township. The cold blue beauty of wide open countryside imprinted still on her eyelids. The hotel lit like a stage setting, all warm and welcoming. A decorated Christmas tree jingling and whispering in the yard, its branches reaching upward out of the glow into a dark, starry sky.

Dressed in a gargantuan overcoat, helmet and goggles hanging from his fist, Uncle Lewis had arrived only minutes before and while the others dived for the shelter of the hotel foyer he paused to breathe deeply of crystal clear air, tinged ever so faintly with the spicy odour of cooking. He seemed not in the least weary. His moustache, like a branch of fir, bristled. He came over to Pauline, put his arm about her shoulders and gave her a hug. There seemed to be no reason for it, except a kind of joyful affection which Pauline, at that moment, was pleased to share.

"Beautiful, ain't it?" Uncle Lewis said.

"Very."

"Cold?"

"No, not too bad, thank you."

"Hungry?"

"Very."

"Me too," said Uncle Lewis and still gazing up at the tree and the sky added, "Feeling a bit alien, are we?"

"A bit," Pauline admitted.

"I don't know these people very well either," said Uncle Lewis. "But I'm willin' to give 'em a chance. What-say, Polly-wolly, let's pretend we're just one big happy family?"

"I'll do my best."

"Atta gal," said Uncle Lewis and still with his arm about her steered her towards the hotel entrance.

Pauline felt better, much better, about the whole thing, about Christmas and its journeys and the prospect of spending time with Mummy, just the two of them, in the holiday that lay ahead. Though it was much on her mind, she did not mention the baby. There would be time enough to raise that grave and painful subject later, when all the jollity was past.

They left Lancaster early the following morning and, in spite of a thin fog around Manchester, reached Flask in perfect time for lunch.

"Hullo," he said. "I don't believe we've met. My name is Oliver and this object is my brother Too."

"Too?" Pauline shook the young man's hand.

"As in Lewis, Too," said the younger man, shaking his cousin's hand in turn. "I say, you do look a trifle skinned. Did Father have you riding up front with him, sans goggles?"

"No, I rode in the other car, with my mother."

"Ah, the Ghost. Jolly decent machine, what!" said Too, adding, with a faint blush, "Oh, sorry! Girls ain't interested in that sort of thing, are they?"

"Stella isn't," said Oliver. "Perhaps Pauline is, though?"

"Sorry; not particularly."

"Hosses?" said Too, optimistically.

"Well, I have been taking riding lessons at school."

"With the Silent Man?" said Oliver.

"Who?"

"The Harvey chap. The Silent Man. That's what Stella calls him," Oliver explained. "Won't you be seated?"

Pauline glanced round. She had changed quickly into her

party frock and, in response to a loud vibrating gong, had hurried from her second-floor room and found her way down the main staircase to the drawing-room.

She had been greeted on arrival by her Aunt Bea and had learned that her Grandmother was tucked away within the house and would be present for lunch. She was not entirely surprised to find her male cousins here. Flask was, after all, their home. But she had heard very little concerning Oliver and young Lewis Jackson for they were two and three years older than her and Stella seldom even mentioned them.

Pauline glanced at the sofa from which the brothers had unfolded themselves. It was very long, covered in grubby Morris-pattern chintz and scattered with newspapers. The enormous room was decorated with holly and ivy wreaths and at the nether end stood a Christmas tree in a wooden tub. A bay window admitted brilliant winter sunlight and gave a view of nothing but sky, as if the Hall, like a hot air balloon, floated on a tether above the earth.

Pauline said, "I thought I heard a luncheon bell."

"Oh, you did," Too answered. "But at this time of the year it's pretty meaningless."

"Not like school," said Oliver. "We don't run like clockwork here."

"Not a tight ship, you might say," Too added. "Good thing, my opinion. Chap wants a bit of rope in the hols."

"Unless you're hungry," Pauline said.

"Are you?" said Olly.

"Starving," said Pauline, unabashed.

"Actually," said Olly, "I am also. Too?"

"Famished. We've been waiting lunch for hours. What d'you say, Ol? Shall we set the last vestige of etiquette aside, lead our cousin to the groaning board and steal a march on the old Brown Windsor?"

"Shouldn't we wait for Stella?" Pauline enquired.

"Oh, devil take Stella."

Too added, "Which he probably will some day."

"*Mam'selle?*" Olly offered his arm. "*Est-ce que vous m'accorderez le plaisir de votre compagnie dans la salle à manger?*"

"*Je vous remercie, monsieur. Avec plaisir,*" Pauline replied and linking arms with her cousin let him spirit her through the hall in search of lunch.

In the days that followed Pauline found herself drawn into an unexpected rapport with the Jacksons. She was not used to the politics and strategies of large families and it came as a surprise to realise that, like it or not, she was a member of one. She could no longer delude herself that she was a Verity, an outsider – not with her mother there, an uncle and aunt, three cousins and grandparents shared in common.

It made her feel quite grown up to be taken in hand by Oliver and young Lewis Jackson. Olly was a boy no longer. He was reading Law at Cambridge. He certainly looked the part of a university man, not tall but very robust and with a certain refinement of features that made him infinitely more attractive than his father. Lewis Too was smaller still, hardly taller than Pauline, and wiry. He was entering the Upper Sixth at Harrow and, so Olly told her, was exceedingly nervous about his chances of gaining entry to Cambridge. He was, however, a first-class opening batsman and, in a better world, might have gone on to make a profession of cricket.

Though Pauline did not cold-bloodedly calculate it, she used her male cousins and her uncle as bulwarks against grandfather and against her mother's new husband. She sat between the boys at mealtimes and did not demur when they took her off to show her the estate. It was the Jacksons, father and sons, who drove her into Buxton early on the day of Christmas Eve to round up the last of the presents and it was Uncle Lewis, not Mr Mark Straker, who had the forethought to press a ten pound note into her hand and, pursing his lips and making his moustache bristle, insist absolutely that she take it.

"What shall I buy for you, Uncle Lewis?" said Pauline.

"Anything," said Uncle Lewis. "Anything that doesn't have a fox's head emblazoned upon it."

"But not a tasselled nightcap," said Olly.

"We have one of those for him already," Too explained.

"To cover his bald spot," Olly said.

"Get off with the three of you," said Uncle Lewis, gruffly.

"You have precisely two hours. I'm not happy in towns, I'll have you know, and I'll be driving off at half-past two o'clock – with or without you. Now, get ye hence."

Pauline had saved a little money of her own from the autumn term and, armed with her list and her cousin's sage advice, bought all her gifts in short order. She even managed to evade the young men long enough to purchase a book for each of them; nothing too solemn.

When they met again, bobbing about in the crowds by the shop doors, Pauline shouted, "That only leaves Stella."

"Gin," Too advised, at the top of his voice.

"Cigarettes?" said Pauline.

"Mother would not approve," said Olly. "Buy Stella a box of flowered handkerchiefs."

"Oh, yes, she'll hate that," said Too.

"Really? Shall I?"

"Why not?" said Oliver. "Whatever you give our sister she will only disapprove."

"Is she really so spoiled?" said Pauline.

"You tell us," said Oliver.

"Yes, she is," said Pauline. "Flowered handkerchiefs?"

"Far too good for her," said Olly.

It was only later, looking back on it, that Pauline realised that it was on Uncle Lewis's instruction that the boys had become her guardians. It suited them too, however, for there was no love lost between them and Stella. Stella had always been her father's little princess and, with the best will in the world, the boys, when young, had resented it. At the time, however, throughout the hectic preparations of Christmas Eve and the entertainments of the days that followed, Pauline was too relieved to have found allies to concern herself with subtle motives.

She was ambivalent in her attitude to her mother. She wanted to be close to her but still prickled with resentment at that long-ago desertion. She hated the way that her mother fawned on Mark Straker, hated even more the man's apparent authority, an arrogance unleavened by his occasional attempts at wit and humour. But she was also sorry for her mother who, when caught off guard, had a sad, neglected air about her, as if the jollity stirred up by Uncle Lewis was not enough to erase the memories of better Christmases in the past.

On Christmas Eve they all gathered in the great hall and there by a roaring fire sang carols and, at midnight, went out on to the apron of lawn that sloped away from the house and looked down into the vale of the Fann, at villages and hamlets and the lights of the little town and listened to the bells of the churches ring, then returned indoors to drink mulled wine and eat pies before bed.

On Christmas Day, hazy in the vale but clear above, they all went trooping down in Sunday best to Flask's sturdy little church for morning service. Pauline went on foot with the boys. Grandpapa, Grandmama and Stella came in Mark Straker's raffish motorcar, all wrapped up as if they were off on a rally. Uncle Lewis in the Alfa brought Bea and Babby on behind. The church was chilly in spite of being packed. Deference was shown to all Mr Jackson's relatives, bowing and hat-touching and silly curtsies from women older than Grandmother Haldane, greetings and chatter at the gate, and the stiff climb back up the hill to the Hall with Pauline and the boys trying, and failing, to outstrip the motorcars.

And lunch and dinner, presents – and then Boxing Day.

The five resident servants had been given the day off. Aunt Bea organised the kitchen and saw to the cooking. That too was fun, carrying trays and setting tables, washing up in the tubs at the back of the big warm kitchen. A party that night after dinner with all the Jacksons' friends from round about. Dancing and games, sweetmeats and chestnuts, streamers and paper hats and sparkling wines to drink. It was amazing that anyone heard the telephone. Pauline certainly did not. She was doing a sort of hopscotch with Too in the belief that it was the latest American rag, while a gentleman farmer from Matlock, with a fat cigar in his mouth, thumped away at the baby grand.

Somebody was close enough to the hallway to hear the telephone however, and a message was relayed to Aunt Bea who, in turn, conveyed it to Uncle Lewis who broke off his manoeuvres around the floor with Lady Emerald Pemberton-Stokes and came to Pauline and shouted in her ear, "A telephone call for you."

Pauline knew that it could not be her father. There was no communication of that kind that would stretch half way around the world. Intrigued and apprehensive, she trailed Uncle Lewis out of the drawing-room and let him point out the telephone on a Tudor table at the end of a long, unlit corridor. The main stairs curled away above the table and while the spot was as a rule hardly private at that hour of the night the little alcove was decently secluded.

Pauline lifted the receiver and timidly said her name into the mouthpiece.

"Hey, old son. How was the festive season?"

"Goss? What a surprise! Where are you?"

"Edinburgh. Dodging the most boring family gathering you can imagine. I don't think there's a spinster aunt on the family tree hasn't been shaken out for the occasion. I suggested charades and got a cumulative look that would have put snow on Arthur's Seat. Know what they're doing? They're playing 'The Minister's Cat.' Ye Gods, I gave up that nonsense when I was ten."

It seemed strange to hear Goss, her voice distorted by distance and the miracle of telephone wires. It was as if separate parts of Pauline's life had been roughly forced together like mismatched pieces in a jigsaw. She had been happy a moment ago, hopping about with her cousin. Goss Johnstone's Christmas, in the bosom of her family, was obviously not going so well, and Pauline, to her slight surprise, found herself resenting the intrusion. She struggled to feel sympathy, to utter commiserations. But all the while she wondered why Goss had not made a telephone call to Elf or to Frog who had known her for a much longer time. Perhaps – of course – Goss had called them too. Pauline had not yet adjusted to the uses that could be made of the telephone.

Goss said, "How is it with you? Awful?"

Cautiously Pauline said, "Oh, it could be worse."

"Well, at least Daddy knows I'm suffering. He's suffering too, I think, though he hides it very well. This is his way of cheering me up, letting me use the telephone."

"Have you heard from Elf?"

"No, I'm saving her for tomorrow," Goss admitted.

248

"Couldn't get our Froggie. I've the feeling this is pantomime night for Elfreda. What were you doing?"

"Nothing much," said Pauline. "Dancing."

"What – with a fellow?"

"My cousin, actually."

"Stella?"

"Her brother; one of them."

"I hope they're nicer than she is."

"Oh, they are," said Pauline just too quickly.

Goss was on to it like a shot. "Ah-hah! Come on, Polly, out with it. The truth now."

Pauline felt herself blushing. It was all she could do to prevent herself blurting out exaggerated confidences. She glanced round and looked down the passageway that led to the drawing-room and to her dismay saw her mother there. For an instant Pauline was deceived into thinking that it was Stella come to eavesdrop, for Barbara, in shadow, looked girlish again in a short-skirted evening dress of corded taffeta. Pauline turned her back, cupped the mouthpiece in both hands, the tulip-shaped receiver balanced on her shoulders, and whispered, "I can't talk now."

"Secrets?" said Goss, boredom gone out of her voice.

"It'll have to keep," said Pauline. "What I can tell you is that I got some lovely presents. Including a pair of riding boots from my uncle. Hunting is all the rage down here. There's a meet tomorrow, I believe, if it isn't too frosty."

"You're not going hunting?" said Goss, shocked.

"Oh, no. I'm not ready for that yet." Pauline glanced over her shoulder again. Her mother was still there. "What presents did you receive? Anything decent?"

The conversation continued for another two or three minutes and then with an exchange of kisses into mouthpieces, and promises of further communication perhaps, it was over.

Pauline hung up and, with a sudden little pirouette, swung round.

She almost collided with her mother.

"I'm sorry, darling. I didn't mean to seem so inquisitive. I thought it might be your father."

"Daddy? How could it have been Daddy? He's in Africa and telephone wires don't stretch that far."

"Don't they?" said Barbara, vaguely. "I just thought – oh, I don't know what I thought – that it would be nice to speak to him again."

"It's a little late for that, isn't it?" said Pauline. "In any case, it wasn't Daddy. So it doesn't matter." She hesitated. "If it had been, though, what would you have said to him? That you miss him? That can't be true – not when you have a new husband."

"Pauline, I don't think you understand."

"I'm sixteen years old, Mummy. I understand more than you give me credit for. Now, if you don't mind, I would really like to get back to dancing."

Barbara caught at her arm. "Why are you doing this to me, Pauline?"

"Doing what?"

"Cutting me off so."

"Am I? No, I'm not," said Pauline.

She did not meet her mother's eye but stared up the passageway to the lighted room, hazed with smoke and alive with the sounds of piano music, stamping feet, laughter. She glimpsed Olly dancing with a tall, solemn young woman, his face solemn too, his position copybook.

Pauline said, "Why didn't you tell me about the baby?"

"Oh!"

"Is that all you can say, Mother?"

"Grandpapa wrote to you, did he not?"

"Yes, but you didn't. Not a word."

"We – we didn't want you to be upset."

"I was upset," said Pauline. "More upset because I didn't know what was going on."

"I was unwell afterwards, quite unwell."

"And I suppose Mr Whatsisname was too busy to write a letter or make a telephone call?" said Pauline. "It was my sister that died, Mummy, in case you'd forgotten." Barbara was close to tears. She curled her fingers into small white fists, not in anger, but in anguish. A little more softly Pauline added, "Don't you think I had a right to be told?"

"Grandpapa—"

"That's right, blame Grandpapa. Everything that ever goes wrong in this family seems to be laid at Grandpapa's door."

"He – we thought we were doing it for the best."

"Well, you weren't. Now, if you don't mind, I believe cousin Lewis is waiting for me in the drawing-room."

"Pauline."

"What?"

"I'm sorry."

"So you should be," Pauline said and went off, not quite running, to find her dancing partner in the hope that Too might restore in her something of the gaiety that had prevailed before.

# Fourteen

*I*t was with some relief that Pauline saw that rain had fallen in the night and the weather had turned from cold to mizzling mild. For two days Uncle Lewis and the boys had been in a state of excitement that had eventually affected Stella and had even transferred itself to Pauline.

The immediate neighbourhood of Flask was not considered good hunting country but to the east, where the Fann swelled across the Shettle Vale, were rolling hills and open land enough to tempt fanatics and a hunt had existed there for over a hundred years.

Uncle Lewis would never be a Master of Foxhounds. He did not have the bloodline for it. Besides, that honour was handed down through the Pemberton family, father to son, and now to daughter. Lady Emerald Pemberton-Stokes was the current Queen of the Chase, Master of Foxhounds for the Flask and Shettle, and the only woman – apart from Bea – to whom Lewis Jackson had ever given his heart.

Lewis's admiration for the buxom widow had been constant for years. He had nurtured longings for her when he first rode out with the Flask and Shettle as a lad of ten and that combination of honourably-repressed sexual desire and recognition of her skill and courage had settled into an enduring friendship that, on Lewis's part, bordered this side of adulation. It was no secret. Everybody for miles around, Aunt Bea and the children included, knew perfectly well that Lewis and the Lady Emerald were thick as thieves, knew too that there was no harm in it. It was only thanks to Lewis's donations that the hunt had survived the blow of the war and the deaths in conflict of both Colonel Pemberton and Major John Stokes.

For a year or two, until the war was over, Lewis had felt guilty about his non-combatant status. He'd regretted the eagerness with which he had accepted a post as a civilian supplies officer, though the work was tedious and demanding in the extreme. Lady Emerald did not seem to hold it against him, however, and by November 1919 the Flask and Shettle pack had been reassembled, the horses run into a state of fitness and not a fox in twenty miles was safe.

Uncle Lewis had been careful to bring his horses to prime form. He had been riding out with the cub-hunters since the middle of September and both he and his mounts were fit as fleas by the start of the season proper. There had been some fine days in the field before hard weather had cancelled the meets but now, in holiday time, appetites were whetted to a keen edge and men and boys, women and girls, huntsmen and followers alike were hungry for sport.

They gathered early on the grassy sward behind the Priory Inn on the old Shettle Road. Pauline had been less than enthusiastic about joining the hunt but Stella, of all people, had talked her into it and Olly had promised not to abandon her, come what may. It was shyness, not principle, that held Pauline back. She was assured that she would be little more than a mounted follower and would not be permitted to upset the progress of the hunt proper.

Stella's enthusiasm was surprising. Even her brothers were puzzled by it. Stella was showing off, of course, flaunting herself as daring and courageous and, to use the country phrase, 'muscular' when in fact she was none of these things. She was merely a skilled rider who had learned young. Uncle Lewis seemed more than willing to let Stella go on making a fool of herself. He chuckled indulgently as her tales became wilder and more outrageous. Grandpapa Haldane too appeared to be amused by his pretty little pet and, from time to time, would give Mr Straker a nudge with the head of his walking cane as if to say, "Ain't she swell?"

Only Aunt Bea, who rode not at all, was moved to admonish her daughter. She would tut, shake her head and say, "Oh, come now, darling. It wasn't really like that, was it?" And Stella, not breaking stride, would dismiss her mother's protests with a wave of her hand, "'Course it was, 'course it was," and would continue unabashed, slyly catching Mark's eye to see if he believed her, if he was impressed.

253

They had been up early, long before dawn. They break-
fasted in the dining room in boots and habits. There was a
blazing fire in the grate and the curtains had been thrown
back from the tall windows so that they could peer out into
soft moist misty darkness while they ate their ham and eggs
and sausages. Uncle Lewis was transformed by his hunting
rig. His moustache, vigorously brushed and waxed, stood up
perkily at the ends. Stella, even Pauline had to admit, had
never seemed more vivacious or prettier, and Olly and Too
had not the heart to be scathing.

By then it was obvious what Stella was up to. For some
reason she had taken it into her head to lord it over Mark
Straker who, poor devil, had never sat astride a horse in his
life let alone strump over hedges and ditches on one. There
was a teasing quality in Stella's sallies with the man which he
took in good enough part. He had declared himself fit enough
to follow the hunt on foot all day long, before lunch and after,
and had told Stella that he would be there to walk her in again
after she fell.

He wore a strange conglomeration of clothes, a sort of
battledress jacket over a holey old brown pullover and a
khaki shirt, coarse tweed plus-fours wrapped tightly to his
calves with webbing. He had strong, nailed boots upon his
feet, though, and a flapping thorn-proof coat with many
pockets and many patches, and a stalker's cap. Within the
Hall he looked fairly comical but once outside, he took on
a determined and deliberate manner as if he knew what
he was doing and, without a horse to control, might make
more ground than anybody and have, after all, the best view
of affairs.

The Jackson groom and stableboy had the horses out and
a high heavy pony ready for Pauline. She had been taught to
ride on a man's saddle but was quite prepared, in the long
black skirt that Uncle Lewis had found for her, to perch upon
the side. It was more comfortable than she had supposed it
would be and the posture made her feel not only ladylike but
somehow decently removed from any need to keep up with
the pack.

Nothing, thank heavens, was expected of her.

They walked the horses down hill and across a broad

254

iron bridge that spanned the river to join a procession of black-coated, bowler-hatted gentlemen and gallant ladies that clopped through the cobbled back streets of the little town and out into the country lane that led to the inn. Uncle Lewis and Too were on tall black horses, magnificently groomed. Another pair would be brought down for the afternoon, for father and son expected to ride hard. Not so Oliver. He rode a quiet little chestnut mare that set him hardly higher than his cousin. He kept close to her even in the mêlée on the grass in front of the inn.

While they waited for the hounds to arrive Olly told Pauline that Lady Emerald was a very efficient master. She had built up the Shettle pack by purchase as well as breeding, not for looks but for stamina. She was also a considerate landlord and had obtained from her tenants permission to ride their fields, as well as land adjacent. She would ensure too that any damage done to hedges, walls and fences would be repaired at the hunt's expense. She also had in her possession letters from three farmers who had spotted foxes in the vale and had marked the coppices from which a quarry might be drawn.

At length the pack was brought, clabbering down the little hill between stripped oak trees, with the red-coated whips and Lady Emerald behind. Pauline had supposed that the meet would welcome only gentlemen like her uncle but this was not the case. Among the riders were a number of humble farmers and artisans mounted on what even Pauline recognised were nags.

She could feel excitement stir in her. Even her pony seemed to have been charged with a fresh vigour by the muster. Above the chimneys of the old inn the sky had broken a little. It showed buttermilk streaks that gave colour to the scene and delineated the contours and textures of the land over which the hunt would pass and the great rim of Scutt's Edge which marked like a saw-blade the distant horizon. At that moment Pauline understood the unrestricted passion of the hunt, the animal nature of it. She saw too why Stella did not ride at St Austin's, why gentle trots and cautious gallops through the woods around Fourstones held no appeal for her cousin. There was appetite here, discipline, manners but no petty restraints.

Mounted, booted, with her hands on the reins Pauline felt infinitely superior to the drab spectators who lined the route north-west of the inn and even to the followers, Mark Straker among them, who legged it out in the wake of hounds and horses. She had no thought of morality, of balancing this huge superior elation against its ultimate aim. It was too physical, too corporeal for that. She accepted without question the tradition that a hunt should end in a little death.

It was all Pauline could do to control herself as the assembly followed the pack along a lane and around the back of an old brick granary and at last through a wide-open gate that led to grassy fields. She could feel frost still in the ground, little shudders of cold fibrous earth passing up through the pony's hoofs into her body. She waited for stimulation to dwindle into discomfort, into boredom. It did not happen. And when she caught sight of the pack and the red-coated huntsmen as they climbed the easy diagonal into fleeting silhouette against the sky she felt as if she might explode from the impatience that consumed her like an unfulfilled desire.

"Are you enjoying it?" Olly called to her.

"Yes, yes!"

"It hasn't even begun yet," he said, laughing.

She saw how the sport had changed him. He was not so boyish now, not so suave. He could not hide his pleasure in being out behind the hounds. She wondered only that he could check himself from riding up closer to the pack, up with his father and brother, ready to drive hard the moment the fox was sprung.

"I must learn to ride properly."

"Of course you must," said Oliver. "But not today."

They came at last over the slope, were themselves part of the silhouette against the skyline. Pauline saw the hounds tracking across moor towards a ruined building that clung to rocks in an isolated stand of thorn, driven wide from the lee side so that the fox would not get wind of their approach.

She could hear no belling yet on the wind that strayed along the roll of the ridge. Below was the old Matlock Road, gritstone walls, closed gates, a broad ditch, mole-like hillocks, a long trench where a field drain was being laid. Followers of the hunt who knew a thing or two were arranged along the wall waiting for the fox to come darting down with pack and riders in hot pursuit, flying through and around and over every obstacle.

It was uncannily quiet. You could hear the snuffling of horses, clink of stirrups, the thud of hoofs on hard ground. And then, out of it, the sudden tongue of the hounds and, squeaky and out of tune, the toot of the horn. Pauline stared at the ruin so hard that her eyes watered. She saw the first three hounds wriggle out of the thorns and Lady Emerald and two red-coated men come round at the gallop. Then she heard somebody cry, "There, there goes the little blighter."

The fox was off like a dart, a flash of russet low to the ground at first then breaking clear and running fast.

Pauline stifled a cry.

She felt a shocking elation at the sight of the fox, a wild sort of sympathy for it but most of all a sense of completion, as if the last piece of a complicated puzzle had been found and fitted into place.

All around her horses were dragged and hauled, some rearing. There was a check, a queer unexpected pause, while Lady Emerald and the leaders of the hunt came pouring down the hillside after the hounds. Pauline could no longer take it all in. The scene had become too gaudy, too mobile. She glimpsed a hound struggling under a bough of thorn then racing to catch the rest, the abrupt charge of the members of the hunt, who had minded their manners long enough. They went streaming away, coat-tails flying, skirts flapping. She saw a bowler hat pop off, tumble and roll like a black billiard ball across the grass and, an instant before Olly caught up with her, noticed in amazement the tiny red dart of the fox already down on the flat by the Matlock Road, racing due north along the base of the gritstone wall.

They were almost alone now, Olly and she, except for a few children on ponies and one long-necked old woman in a faded black habit, who had risen up to bellow, "Tally Ho! Tally Ho!" but seemed content to hold her mount on the rein and view proceedings from a distance.

Olly clapped Pauline's shoulder. He was grinning. He shouted, "Yes, he's a cunning 'un, that. He's headed for the Fann. He'll double the hounds there and cut back over the walls for Copplestone wood."

"How do you know?"

"Seen it done before."

"Surely they'll catch him?"

"Not this side of the wood, I doubt," Oliver cried. "Come on, Polly, follow me."

A half hour later they were back within sight of Flask. Olly, along with several of the followers, was of the opinion that the hounds had drawn a blank in trashy country in the loop of the Fann and that the fox had not been, after all, inclined to do what was expected of it but had found some novel manoeuvre to cast away the scent.

There was a certain air of anticlimax, the hunt far off, the horns plaintive. Pauline could not interpret the calls but Olly could and so, it seemed, could all the folk who had come out on foot to watch. Pauline had time to look about her. The ride down the slope had sweated her, had shaken her excitement into a froth that had rather too quickly settled. She had trusted Oliver to know what he was doing but suspected, darkly, that he had deliberately led her away from the hounds. She was cold now. The milky gleams had gone from the sky which was clouding and lowering by the minute, threatening more rain.

She looked about for Stella or Mark Straker, saw no sign of either.

A number of aimless riders were strung out across the field that lifted gently from the back doors of the brick granary towards a skullcap of trees in the distance. Now and then there was a glimpse of hounds quartering ground between the woods and the Matlock Road. Bottles and silver flasks were going the rounds. Olly drank from one but Pauline did not, though her mouth was dry and the very smell of the whisky was sharp and warming.

After ten minutes or so Olly said, "Come along, we'll ride along the wall and see what's what."

Pauline was becoming sore from the unfamiliar position but the pony seemed unbothered and took her where she directed him at a half-trot.

Turning, Olly said, "We must be careful."

"Why?"

"If the blighter comes out we might inadvertently head him off. That's considered awfully infra dig."

"I wonder where Stella is?" Pauline said.

Olly turned again, "With Straker, I expect."

"What?"

The young man shrugged and pulled a face, rueful and at the same time apologetic.

"Haven't you noticed how she's setting her cap at him?"

"No, I can't say I have. Are you sure?"

"Sure enough."

"But she's – I mean, Mark Straker's married to my mother."

"Oh, I shouldn't worry," Oliver said. "My little sister has been making sheep's eyes at men, married and otherwise, since she came out of napkins. Haven't you seen her in action at school?"

Too embarrassed to elaborate, Pauline said, "There aren't any boys at school."

"That's never stopped her yet," said Oliver. "Don't worry, Straker's no fool. He'll shake her off without denting her pride." He laughed. "I'm glad I won't be around when Stella grows up."

"Is that how you think of us?" said Pauline. "As children?"

"Well, aren't you?"

"Certainly not."

"What are you then?"

"I'm . . ." Pauline could not answer.

"You see!" Oliver grinned. Dropping back, he brought the horse into line with Pauline's pony, reached over and patted her shoulder again. It made her think of Roderick Harvey, though her cousin's touch was patronising not soothing. "You see, you don't know what you are. I'll tell you, shall I? You're in no-man's-land."

"That sounds rather indecent."

"What? God, yes, I suppose it does. Right, let me rephrase it. You're—"

The sentence was never completed. At that moment the fox appeared, scratching and clambering on to the top of the

259

gritstone wall some eighty yards in front of them. It looked exceedingly small, but not at all vulnerable. Its tongue lolled and it appeared to be smiling as it daintily picked its way along the wall top.

"Good God!" Oliver exclaimed under his breath, reining his horse to a standstill and drawing Pauline's pony to a halt too.

As the fox tripped on towards them, Pauline whispered, "Has he seen us?"

"Oh, yes. Now be quiet. Watch him, see what he does."

The animal looked too alert to wring pity from Pauline. Its russet coat was sleek, the brush full and that false smile made it seem as if the fox was enjoying the thrill of the chase. It had its head up and observed them with the same sort of interest as they watched it, aware but not wary. It picked its paws up carefully, poised in perfect balance, then stopped. It was close enough for Pauline to see it blink, hear its panting breaths, watch its tongue coil and lick and loll out again. From far off uphill towards the woods came the flat mournful cry of a huntsman's horn.

"They've lost the scent," Olly whispered. "The little devil's shaken them off. He'll be heading for the town. If he gets among the gardens we'll never catch him."

As if he'd heard and agreed, the fox nodded. He bunched and, swerving in the air, jumped neatly down from the gritstone and made to dart past the riders in a beeline for the granary and the town.

"Oh no, you don't," Oliver cried. "Pauline, wait here, don't move."

The pony reared at the abrupt motion of Oliver's horse. Pauline was almost thrown. She clung on, eased then tightened the reins and pressed her heels down upon the stirrups. In spite of Olly's warning she let the pony break into a trot. Oliver, meanwhile, had cut across the fox's line. He rode superbly well, dashing as a Cossack, leaning out and down from the saddle to flap at the darting fox with his silk hat as if he hoped to scoop the creature up like a minnow from a pool. He yelled fiercely, turned the fox from him and with his horse prancing, diverted it back across the grassland towards the Copplestone woods.

Pauline's pony followed the galloping horse at a pace that was no longer rolling and sedate. It was as if it too had been roused by Oliver's cries and longed to be in at the kill. She clung on, not tensely, bouncing and rocking in the awkward saddle, and watched with an inseparable mingling of horror and triumph as the hounds swarmed over the hill.

Lady Emerald Pemberton-Stokes came after the hounds, riding almost on their tails. She was flanked by red-coated huntsmen and followed, not far behind, by a bunch of bowler hats, all riding hard.

Pauline urged the pony on. She could not see the fox now, only Oliver, silk hat stuck on the back of his head, one arm raised high. And the sudden wheel of the pack. And in profile her cousin Too, crouched like a jockey to the mane. And Uncle Lewis, elbows out, pumping up and down on the big black gelding, fair flying like the rest of them.

When Pauline reached the crest of the hill she saw what the alarm was about. The fox had changed course again, had shot away from the direction of the woods. The animal was clearly visible. Leading the whole baying pack by thirty yards or less it ran arrow-straight for the line of the enclosure. Pauline had somehow imagined that the empty pasture was limitless, that it would fold untrammelled down to the bottom of the dale. But there was a thorn hedge scrawled across it, bushy black and taller than a man. Scribbles of wire were stretched between the roots and, here and there, were a rusty sheet of iron or a bedstead, dribbling piles of stones and one leaning wooden gate. Beyond the hedge, scampering away in all directions, were sheep.

Pauline did not check the pony at the summit. She let it gallop down towards the hedge. She could see everything very clearly. Huntsmen in a line, hounds rushing at the wiry hedge and, just ahead of them, the fox flattening itself even as it ran. It vanished into the dense thorns. She glimpsed it again as it emerged from behind the bushes and, with an almost impudent bobbing motion, headed away downhill amid the panic-stricken sheep. Then the hounds were into the hedge and swarming through it, yelping. Some peeled off to leap the leaning gate instead. The first horsemen flew the obstacle – Lady Emerald, a red-coat, cousin Oliver –

then three or four more gentlemen, all hoofs and hats and coat-tails, crashed through the thorns, then Uncle Lewis on the black gelding.

The gelding took off too soon, too fast. It kneed the boughs in the gap, baulked and wallowed and, momentum carrying it on, stamped and hoofed and surged until it seemed to be perched on top of the hedge like a weird piece of debris stranded there by a flood. Separated from saddle, stirrups and reins, Uncle Lewis was seated in mid air above it. The man went over first. The gelding followed, hoofs flying. And Too, who had reined in as best he could, seemed to force his horse back into a crouch so that it took off vertically and soared over the tangle with white space between its belly and the thorns. More farmers poured into the gap while others, less daring, trailed the hounds and leapt the fence instead.

Pauline gripped the reins tightly. She knew what the pony intended to do and allowed it head. Cleanly it took off over the fence. Pauline was drawn with it. Dark boughs and branches whisked away on each side of her. She was punched up into the air. For a split second she saw nothing but acres of empty sky, the colour of pipe clay. Then she came down again on to the sliding saddle, jarred. Pitched forward, her spine twisted, she fought desperately to hold balance. The pony, however, did not stumble but found stride immediately and sucked Pauline breathlessly on towards the rabble of hounds in the middle of the pasture.

Oliver caught her. Guiding his horse across the pony's nose, he checked its gallop and helped Pauline bring her mount to a halt.

"Are you all right?"

"Yes, I'm fine."

"I thought you'd never jumped before?"

"I haven't."

"Well, you have now. You took that gate wonderfully."

"What's happening?"

"The kill," Oliver explained. "The hounds caught the fox on the open ground. Do you want to see what's left?"

Pauline shook her head. Her heart was beating like mad, her legs trembled and her body felt bruised, yet she was filled with great surges of physical pleasure of almost unbearable

262

intensity. She glanced back at the gate, astonished at her feat and enormously gratified by it.

"I thought," said Olly, "that you'd lost control."

"Almost," Pauline admitted, "but not quite."

One of the huntsmen was down off his horse now and blowing his horn victoriously. Pauline saw wagging tails, snuffling muzzles and then a sodden remnant of fur flung into the air. The huntsman ducked, snatched away the bloody foxbrush, held it up and shook it in Pauline's direction, grinning.

"Do you want to be blooded, Polly?" Oliver asked.

"Oh, no!"

"It would certainly be something to tell your friends at school."

"No," Pauline said again, emphatically.

Afraid of losing the wild unsentimental sensations that still galloped inside her, she shied away from the final barbaric submission to ritual.

"It's your entitlement, your honour," said Oliver, cagily. "I mean, it isn't many who are up with the hunt on their first time out. Females – not at all."

"Next time. Not today."

Oliver made a signal to the huntsman who shrugged and tucked the sad trophy under his armpit before he set about mustering the pack.

More members of the hunt had gathered by now. Twenty or thirty of them clustered around the guzzling hounds or stood off, watching. It had been a fine morning so far. And it wasn't over yet, not by a long chalk. There was laughter, a trading of flasks, remarks both rude and complimentary. Pauline had a sudden urge to join them, to swank to that rural congregation. Olly was right; it would be something to tell the girls back at St Austin's.

She lifted herself confidently in the saddle just as Oliver exclaimed, "Good God! It's Papa. He's come off again."

"No," said Uncle Lewis angrily. "It isn't my collarbone. It's my arm, damn it. I think it's broken."

"Are you in pain, Lewis?" asked Lady Emerald.

"Of course I'm in pain."

"I'll take you back to the Priory. We'll find a motorcar and have you driven to the cottage hospital in Shettle. They'll soon put you right."

"No need for you to accompany me," said Uncle Lewis. "The boys will do it. Off you go, Emerald. It's far too fine a day to abandon hunting just because a silly old codger came at a fence from the wrong quarter."

He spoke through his teeth. He was as white as chalk under the raffishly tilted bowler hat which Too had retrieved from the hedge. The left side of his body was caked with mud, his jacket and trousers smeared with it. A hunt servant had retrieved the gelding and waited nearby, holding it and Lady Emerald's horse.

The woman had been first to reach her fallen comrade. She had swung herself majestically from her stallion and had shown, just for a moment, how much she cared for Lewis by her concern for him. Only Too had been close enough to see the solicitude with which the lady had lifted the man into her arms and had cradled his dazed head against her bosom. Now that Lewis was on his feet and clearly not mortally wounded, the lady of the hunt had replaced tender concern with cool efficiency. Other members of the hunt trooped past, heading towards the Priory where the hounds would be taken for a second assembly.

"Naughty horse, Lewis, old chap?"

"Naughty rider," Uncle Lewis answered through gritted teeth.

"Much damage, old boy?"

"Arm. Broken, I reckon."

"I say, tough luck."

"Be out for the rest of the season?"

"Shouldn't be surprised."

Disconsolately, Uncle Lewis put one foot in front of the other and, unsteadily at first, headed for the bottom corner of the pasture from which point a sheeptrack cut round the hill to the Priory. Lady Emerald Pemberton-Stokes walked with him but did not, Pauline noticed, attempt to render physical support. Too had ridden on ahead to arrange transport to the hospital and Oliver and Pauline were left to flank the sad little party which trailed the hounds and red-coated huntsmen through thickening drizzle.

"What shall we do?" Pauline said to her cousin. "Do we go on hunting – or what?"

Oliver gave a grunt of wry amusement. "If it was me hobbling in with a damaged flipper I expect that's what Father would do. Go on hunting, I mean."

"No, he wouldn't," said Uncle Lewis, who had obviously overheard the exchange between the youngsters. "Father would simply have you shot."

"I take it," said Oliver, "that you're going to live?"

"Probably," said Uncle Lewis. "Though at this very moment I cannot think of a good reason why I should bother."

"How bad is it?" said Oliver.

"I can feel the bone scraping."

"If it's a multiple break they'll probably keep you in hospital overnight. Perhaps even for a day or two."

"Yes, they might." Uncle Lewis squinted up at Pauline and squeezed out an apologetic grimace. "Sorry to have ruined your day, Pol. Were you enjoying it?"

"Very much," said Pauline.

"In at the kill, eh? Quite an achievement."

"Stop jabbering, Lewis," Lady Emerald commanded. "Conserve your strength."

Pauline noticed that her uncle was shivering. Her own shoulders were pearled with falling rain and cloud had all but obscured the rim of the hills and had already consumed the fretted edge of the ridge beyond the wood.

Defiantly Uncle Lewis asked, "How's my nag?"

Oliver answered, "A few minor scratches. Perkins will see to him, never fear."

"Well," Uncle Lewis said, "in case the sawbones does tuck me up for the night your mother had better be informed. Oliver, will you be good enough to come with me to Shettle?"

"Of course."

"The horses can be left in the livery at the Priory for Perkins to collect," Uncle Lewis went on. "Too can trot back to the Hall with Pauline as bearer of the sad tidings."

"Lewis, can't you stop?" said Lady Emerald.

"I'm fine. I'm fine. Straker can drive my grievin' spouse

over to Shettle to hold my one remaining paw and . . . Where is Straker, by the way?"

Pauline caught Oliver's peculiar look and warning frown. She was still too charged up with the ride and its aftermath to interpret it properly.

Uncle Lewis turned his head, winced, and said, "And where's Stella? Just where the hell is Stella?"

To which Oliver unblinkingly replied, "I really have no idea."

Much to Pauline's relief her mother went off to Shettle with Aunt Bea and Too and left her more or less alone in the rambling mansion for the best part of the day.

Aunt Bea had been much less phlegmatic about her husband's accident than everybody else, though it was, Pauline gathered, the third or fourth injury that Uncle Lewis had sustained in the course of the years. Aunt Bea was very upset indeed. She went into an unaccustomed flutter, particularly when it was discovered that there was nobody in the household who could drive any of the cars that nestled in the garages by the stables and that neither Mark Straker nor Stella had thought fit to return from the hunting field.

To calm his mother, Too had finally confessed that he had sufficient knowledge of motorcars to attempt to fill the role of chauffeur and, when pressed, admitted that he had sometimes taken the wheel from his brother on those rare occasions when Oliver had been permitted to drive one of the precious vehicles. A bag had been packed with Uncle Lewis's overnight things while Too had gone off to change and to fetch the Alfa up from the garage and, Pauline suspected, to experiment in peace and quiet with its mechanical mysteries before risking the public highway.

With the house emptying about her, Pauline had supposed that she would be condemned to lunch in the dining room with her grandparents. The prospect dismayed her considerably. Grandpapa Haldane had not been feeling at his best, however, and had elected to spend the day in bed while his wife read to him or nodded in a comfortable chair by the fire in his room.

Pauline ate alone in the long, gloomy dining room. It was

very odd to have the services of a butler all to oneself and she did not dare engage the man in conversation. She did have sufficient confidence, though, to order a second lambchop and an extra helping of the cook's excellent Charlotte Russe. She was absolutely famished and, now that she had leisure to consider it, somewhat miffed at missing out on a communal lunch at the Priory and the rest of the day's hunting.

She had bathed, and changed into a warm pleated skirt and a blouse that did not show the lines of her heavy lambswool underwear. And, after lunch, feeling not in the least tired, she had put on her overcoat and outdoor shoes and had gone out into the drizzle, protected by a large black umbrella from the hallstand.

Dusk had come down early. Veils of light rain eased over the valley, shrouded the peaks and drowned the town, gathered into it a weird diminishing light that made Flask's stately trees appear like negatives on a photographic plate. From the edge of the lawn, the umbrella tipped back a little, Pauline could feel the rain upon her face and taste the flavours of the countryside, broken grasses, rotting leaves, ploughed earth and horse-dung, subtle and disturbing. She thought she heard the toy-trumpet toot of huntsmen's horns, distorted and vague, the tonguing of hounds in full flight, but the sounds were far off and faint, like a dream or an imagining. She had just begun to feel rather abandoned and was on the point of returning to the house when off in the trees to her right she glimpsed movement and heard, quite distinctly, laughter.

She knew at once who it was. She had heard that laugh often enough in the past months for it to be unmistakable. She waited motionless and watched Stella and Mark Straker emerge from the pearly gloom and, following some path of which Pauline had no knowledge, vanish again behind the house.

Pauline hesitated. Stella was in riding togs and walked her horse behind her on a long rein. Quite oblivious to Pauline's presence she had one arm looped about Mark Straker's waist as if helping him to climb the hill. Her little heart-shaped face had been upturned. She had laughed in that gay and charming manner which so entranced certain susceptible teachers back at St Austin's, women who should have recognised affectation but somehow did not. Pauline watched from under the rim of the brolly until the man, the girl, the horse all disappeared behind the bulk of the Hall. Then she swung round and, almost running, took herself to the gravel forecourt in front of the house into which the woodland track debouched from behind the south wing and out of which the road curved downhill to the stables. She ran on down the road, brolly clenched in both hands, its stem bouncing on her shoulder, then she stopped, swung about and casually began to saunter back towards the Hall as if she had just emerged from the stables.

Stella and Mark Straker had separated. They were no longer touching. At a distance the man looked as drab and shabby as a fieldhand or factory labourer. His cap was crushed down upon his head, the wisps of hair that escaped from it were beaded with moisture and his jacket was black with rain. The horse looked hangy and to Pauline's inexpert eye appeared to be limping very slightly. Only Stella had a shine to her, an elliptical sort of radiance that ducked the elements in spite of the mud that smeared her skirts and bodice and clung to her boots like tar.

"Why, it's Pauline." Mark Straker showed neither surprise nor any trace of guilt. "Looking very solemn."

"Only Pauline," Stella said. "I say, are we too late for lunch? I'm so hungry I could eat an ox."

Pauline said, "I'm afraid you've missed lunch."

"Never mind. Cookie will fix us something," Stella said. "I say, where is everyone?"

Pauline did not answer Stella's question. Instead she asked, "How was the hunting?"

"Gave up, did you?" Stella said. "The sport was excellent, quite excellent. You missed a treat."

"Did you take another fox?"

"Pauline," Mark Straker put in, "what's wrong? Something's wrong? Perhaps you should tell us what it is?"

"Everyone," Pauline said, "is at the cottage hospital in Shettle. They've been there most of the afternoon, in fact. I'm surprised nobody saw fit to tell you what's happened."

"Well, they didn't," Stella snapped. "So perhaps you'd better."

"Your father had a riding accident. His arm is broken."

"Good God!" Mark Straker exclaimed and, in pique, struck out with his stick at a withered tassle of fern by the roadside. "When did it happen?"

"Mid-morning," Pauline answered.

"Were – were they looking for us?" Stella said.

"I think they wanted someone to drive the motorcar."

"Damn, damn!" said Stella. "Poor Daddy. Mark, what should we do, d'you think?"

"Has your mother gone there, Pauline?"

"Yes, with Aunt Bea and the boys."

"Mark?" said Stella, anxiously.

"We'll telephone." The man nodded. "We'll telephone. See what's what, how the land lies."

Behind them the horse, shivering slightly, lost patience and flung up its head, neighing. Stella started and angrily snapped the rein to force it to be still and submissive.

Mark Straker said, "Best lead him in first then get yourself out of those wet clothes. Meanwhile I'll go and make that telephone call. Pauline, where's your grandfather?"

"Upstairs. Resting."

Mark Straker nodded and frowning turned on his heel and strode away towards the Hall. Stella hesitated. She looked directly at Pauline, her blue eyes honest and innocent. "I got lost, horribly lost. It's so humiliating. You won't tell anyone, will you?"

"Tell them what, Stella?"

"I'd have been out there still, riding in circles, if Mark hadn't found me. He walked me in from miles out."

Pauline said, "What's that on your face?"

There were three smears upon Stella, like tribal marks, moist but distinct, one dabbed on each cheek and a third upon her brow.

"It isn't blood, is it?" Pauline said.

"Of course not, silly," Stella answered and wiped them away with her cuff.

"I thought you'd been blooded?"

"I have," said Stella and, snapping the rein in her fist, hastily led the weary horse towards shelter in the stables behind the trees.

# Fifteen

"You shouldn't really be here, you know," Stella said softly.

"I don't need you to tell me that," Mark Straker said.

"A lady's bedroom is—"

"Sacrosanct, yes."

"Now you're here, however, you may perform a small service, if you will."

"By all means. First let me close the door."

She watched him in the mirror over her dressing-table. He was dressed in a dinner suit with a pert little bow tie in the collar of his shirt, links gleaming in his shirt cuffs.

Stella held up the pendant on its fine gold chain.

"There's a catch," she said, "which is rather awkward."

She kept her back turned, felt him slip the chain from her fingers and slide it around her throat. She had not lied to him; the catch was awkward. It took him a moment or two to fit the thing. When it was done, he did not move away but stood behind her, hands resting lightly on her shoulders. In the mirror's reflection, man and girl regarded each other solemnly.

"A penny for them, Mr Straker, sir."

"My thoughts? Worth a deal more than a penny, Stella," the man said. "I was thinking how pretty you are in that dress."

"I think you're thinking that you would like to kiss me." She turned upon him suddenly, skirts brushing his trousers. He seemed very tall; her chin came up only to the middle of his chest. She might have rested her head on his breastbone. "Am I not right, Mark?"

"Do you know what you are, Stella Jackson? You are a tease and if I were not a gentleman I might be tempted to test your mettle, to see exactly what you're made of in that respect."

270

"Sugar and spice?" said Stella.

"Spice, perhaps – but not the other."

"Oh, how unkind. Don't you think I'm sweet?"

"I think you're dangerous, if you must know."

Stella smiled, and inched her dainty shoes towards him so that the pretty dress was crushed against his legs. Still he did not retreat. He put his hands about her tiny waist and held her, poised on a knife-edge of uncertainty. She could not be sure if he intended to tug her into his arms or if he would lift her from her feet and just as suddenly set her back from him. In the tiny fragile voice that she could put on when it suited her, she said, "I think I like being called dangerous."

He dipped his knees until his face was on a level with hers and peered into her blue eyes. He looked more craggy, older too, in the shaded light from the dressing-table lamp. He had no parallel in Stella's experience and for a split second she was afraid of him.

"You have no idea, do you, what's going on?" Mark Straker said.

"I don't know what you mean. I know you want to kiss me."

"Of course I do. That isn't all I want to do. That would not be the end of it, Stella. I'm not one of the spotty boys that trail you about with their tongues hanging out."

"That didn't seem to stop you the other day."

"I was testing you, that's all."

"Huh!"

"Oh, I don't mind risk, little miss. If you must know, I think you'd be worth it. But I'm not quite prepared to be ruined by you."

"Ruined?" said Stella, with interest.

"I have far too much to lose."

"And what about me?"

"You're not ready yet."

"Isn't that for me to decide?"

"No, it is not." He lifted her away from him now just as Stella became certain that he would do the other thing. "You're too young to realise what you're about."

"I won't be young for ever."

"In that case, you'll keep."

"I think that's rather insulting."

"Think what you like." Mark stepped past her and adjusted his tie with the aid of the mirror. "I'm not much concerned what you think, Stella. You're careless and indiscreet. Headstrong. Yes, that's the word – headstrong." He tapped the bow with his fingertip and turned to face her again. "At your age you have every right to be. But I can't afford to be impulsive. I have to be patient instead."

"Silly? Do you think I'm silly?"

"Stop it." He placed his hands lightly upon her shoulders again but only to hold her at a safe distance. "You know perfectly well what I mean."

"Aunt Barbara?"

"Her too."

"My father?"

"I haven't been accepted yet. Once I'm accepted – and once you have learned discretion – things will be different, I promise."

"That sounds very definite."

"Very," he said. "Now, straighten your stockings and your dress, let us go and collect Pauline and sally down to supper, shall we?"

"Yes," Stella said. "Wait."

She appeared to be obeying him. She seated herself on the side of the bed – the bed she had slept in since she was a child, patchwork quilt and carved wooden footboard so familiar, so unchanged – stretched out one slender leg, tugged up her frock and petticoat, smoothed her stockings, adjusted her garters. She did not so much as glance up at him, was so quick and insouciant that it might have been naivety, not calculation that fleetingly exposed her thighs to his gaze. She leapt up and, with a little twisting gesture settled her undergarments smoothly into place. She held out her arms, like a doll.

"Better?"

"You'll do," the man said, and moved towards the door.

She skipped to him, stopped him, fingers curled about his wrist. "Mark, do you think they believed our story?"

"Some of them did," Mark Straker said.

"Only some of them?"

"Pauline didn't."

"Oh, Pauline! What does she matter?"

"I don't know that just yet," Mark Straker answered and, disengaging Stella's hand, tugged open the bedroom door and stepped cautiously into the safety of the corridor.

Pauline did not go hunting again. It was not that she did not long to do so but the weather had turned foul and, with Uncle Lewis stuck at home with his left arm encased in plaster from shoulder to wrist, it was only the boys, Olly and Too, who ventured out to the morning meets and came back, drenched but satisfied, in the dusk.

Uncle Lewis's accident had put a damper on the festive season's second act. Though he did his best to keep spirits up and made light of his injury, it was no secret that he was in constant pain and found the weighty grey cast infuriatingly cumbersome. He was not sleeping well at night and would spend most of the afternoon sprawled, dozing, on an old chaise in front of the fire in the library that he used as an office, the wrapped arm hanging limp, knuckles resting on a cushion on the floor. The black Labradors, which had been put out to stay with Perkins, the groom, for the duration of the holidays were fetched back to offer some comfort to the master. Old though they were, they scrabbled excitedly up and down the corridors and made general nuisances of themselves, except when they lay with Lewis in the library, quiet and loyal and watchful or when Lady Emerald came to call and barked back at them and caused them to scuttle off with their tails between their legs.

Grandpapa Haldane had also been under the weather, though Mr McGeoghan, a 'Scotch' doctor brought in from Buxton, could find nothing obviously wrong with him, except the myriad minor complaints that age and winter weather brought to the surface. Grandpapa would not hear of a nurse being employed to tend his demands and voluntarily confined himself to the sickroom on the Hall's second floor where, by means of an electrical bell, he kept the servants on the hop, morning, noon and night, and Grandmama too. He seemed to have lost interest in the lesser members of the household. He did not require his grandchildren to pay homage to him, did not give audiences to them. He was content to lie in the huge Jacobean bed, propped up by pillows, and scowl out at the changing shades of light through the long mullioned windows and keep his thoughts to himself.

Mark Straker was the only visitor who was made any way welcome. This newcomer, this stranger, craggy and handsome and sly, seemed to have established some sort of rapport with the dour old man. He would spend two or three hours of the afternoon or a long period after dinner closeted away with Grandfather, the pair of them murmuring and, now and then, laughing as if they'd been comrades in youth or perhaps in some previous incarnation entirely.

New Year was celebrated with a sullen sort of pessimism that stemmed entirely from the older generation. For one hour, stretched across the cusp of the year, Grandpapa and Grandmama Haldane graced the drawing-room with their presence. She, as always, was clad in rusty black and he in a heavy plaid smoking-jacket worn over a cardigan and flannel trousers. To Pauline her grandfather seemed in no way changed. He was neither more nor less wispy than he had been in the summer of the year that had passed as he clacked his stick upon the chair leg and ordered the setting up of the ritual of toasts and greetings by which he set so much store. There was whisky in a decanter, ruby wine, four great cartwheels of shortbread, sent down from Edinburgh, broken into chunks and piled on silver plates. A man was elected to be Flask Hall's 'first foot'. He was dispatched at a minute to midnight to shiver on the gravel drive, gifts of a coal lump and a fresh-caught fish clutched one in each hand to bestow a pagan blessing of plenty on Uncle Lewis's household in the year that lay ahead.

Oliver and Too were unimpressed by this traditional nonsense. They muttered caustically under their breaths even as they trooped solemnly to the door and watched their father fling it open just as the last of midnight's twelve strokes sprang from the grandfather clock in the hall.

Pauline could not share her cousins' cynicism. Perhaps it was a masculine trait or had to do with the fact that they were older than she was and had seen more of the world. She tried to think of Oliver and young Lewis as she thought of her father, to bring them into some kind of apposition, but she could not. On that New Year's Eve she stood quite apart, lonely and aloof, struggling to understand to whom she belonged and how the parts of her had come together in this pattern, like the scraps in a kaleidoscope; and why she could not shake off the thin tormenting rags of sentiment that her cousins, all three, seemed to have discarded years ago.

Mark Straker was Grandpapa Haldane's appointed agent. Though he was not dark he was tall and assured and sporting enough to play to the hilt his role as a harbinger of good fortune. He grinned as he dumped the coal into Lewis's good hand, did not wince when Lewis thumped him heartily upon the back with the heavy cast; laughed when he kissed Bea and everyone by the hand, dispersing scales and black dust willy-nilly. He kissed Stella's cheek with a perfunctoriness that did not please her. He drew Barbara into a prolonged and dramatic embrace that had Uncle Lewis calling out, "Now, now. None of that there 'ere, if you please," and made the boys squirm with embarrassment.

Pauline watched with a strange reserve, affected less by the Scottish customs than by the realisation that these were her relatives and that kinship bore deep. She watched Mark Straker solemnly shake hands with her grandfather who stood at the junction of the hall and dining-room corridors out of the cold draught, his little black-garbed wife by his side. She watched Mark Straker kiss Grandmama's lace-mittened knuckles and heard him wish the couple a long life, health and happiness. It was all so hollow, so insincere that she wanted to cry out a warning. But what would she warn them against? She had no idea.

She was being kissed now, tickled by Uncle Lewis's moustache, bussed on the cheek by her cousins, hugged first by her aunt and then by her mother who, in that tender and sentimental moment, clung on to her arm so tightly that Pauline had not the heart to break her hold and slip away from her.

"I do hope you'll be happy, darling," Mummy said.

"I am happy," Pauline said.

They were moving towards the drawing-room now, out of the cold hall, away from the zone of cold air that still hung about the doorway even though it had been closed for several minutes.

"Why won't you talk to me, Pauline?"

"I do talk to you."

"Not properly, not as you should."

"Perhaps I don't have anything to say."

Mother sighed, blinked. Ahead of them Uncle Lewis had already begun to dispense drinks, amber whisky, ruby wine, sweet blackcurrant cordial in stemmed glasses for the girls.

"You resent him, don't you?" Mummy said.

"Yes, I suppose I do."

To Pauline's surprise her mother nodded, said, "I don't blame you," and let her go.

Ten minutes later, after toasts to 1922 and benedictions to the year that was gone, the family arranged itself around the fire. Still feeling strangely detached, Pauline seated herself on the carpet at her mother's feet. Stella was similarly positioned by Mark Straker, her thin arm draped along the arm of his chair. The room was large enough to put space between the Haldanes and the Jacksons, with Grandpapa and Grandmama sharing the sofa closest to the blazing fire and the boys, holding themselves separate, on chairs towards the window bay. It was all very well for Oliver and young Lewis. They would be gone on Monday, chasing off to stay with friends for the remainder of the holiday.

It was quiet, the conversation lulled. Pauline could tell that Uncle Lewis's arm was hurting for now and then he would massage the plaster as if it were flesh, tug at the gauntlet that covered his wrist and scratch the back of his hand. He had a half full tumbler of whisky and water balanced precariously on the chair arm and Aunt Bea had her eye on it, nervously twirling her cordial glass round and round in her fingers. Nobody, at that moment, seemed to know quite what to say or what to do, what Grandpapa Haldane expected of them.

Pauline felt her mother's fingers brush her hair but did not flinch or shift away. She was oddly undisturbed by the gesture. She felt vaguely charitable and superior, but also indrawn, thinking not of Daddy sweltering in the African sun but of her friends from St Austin's. She was wondering what they were up to, how jovial the parties they might attend would be; if there was more sadness than laughter in Elf's house, if Elf's mother wept; if Frog's father, now that she was sixteen, let her stay up late to celebrate.

To break the awkward silence Uncle Lewis had just begun to crack a feeble joke, his mouth hardly open, the whisky glass picked up and poised, when from outside the drawing-room came a mysterious noise.

Head cocked, Uncle Lewis paused. The noise was slight, a faint peevish whining that seemed to take its strength from the echo in the corridor, the quietness of the empty rooms. Everyone looked towards the panelled door and Uncle Lewis grunted. "Dogs. The daft brutes have obviously got out of the kitchens. Oliver, let them in."

Olly rose at once, walked to the door, opened it and stepped aside to admit the Labradors. He waited, grinning and for some reason slightly embarrassed – then he peeked out into the corridor. "Pev? Pev, come on, good boy. Lakey? Lakey, heel."

Pauline was watching the doorway. She did not see her grandfather's sudden movement. Only her mother's hand closing over her arm alerted her. She glanced away from the dark vertical, from Oliver. Grandpapa had risen to his feet. He had done so without the aid of the stick which lay along the carpet at his heels. He had a glass of whisky-soda in his hands. His old gnarled fingers curled around it as if to crush the crystal. His face had turned deathly white. His eyes were no longer faded but popped from his head like beads of pale blue glass. The old woman tried to clutch at him but he staggered away from her, trotting jerkily towards the open door.

Barbara and Bea got simultaneously to their feet. Pauline heard her mother say, "Papa, Papa, what is it?" But neither of the women were quick enough. Grandpapa was across the floor and at the door before anyone, even Mark Straker, could prevent it. Oliver put out his hand to steady his grandfather but the old man, shuffling, brushed straight past it and went out into the corridor.

Uncle Lewis struggled to his feet. Bea turned to him, "What is it? What's wrong with Papa?" she enquired.

"How the hell do I know."

They converged upon the drawing-room door, all except the old woman who with a stoicism that seemed to border on the callous remained exactly where she was. Her head was cranked towards the fireplace. The glimmer of the flames reflected dully in her tired eyes as if she could not bear to watch her husband make a fool of himself – or perhaps had no need to do so.

"Papa, come back," Barbara said, beseechingly.

Pauline and Stella were side by side. Her cousin's arm brushed her own and Too, curious and frowning, crowded behind them, leaning upon them as they craned to see what phenomenon had so animated the old man and brought life to his aged limbs.

"Where's he going?"

"I don't know."

"Shouldn't we fetch him back?"

"No," Mark Straker said. "Leave him be."

"But . . ."

"He sees something there. Like sleep walking."

"Oh, God! Oh, God!" said Barbara.

They were all out in the corridor now, looking towards the hallway and the house's main door. Two or three steps would have taken all or any one of them to Donald Haldane's side but none dared make that move. Disciplined and drilled to accept as correct this outbreak of plain dementia they were all too much in awe of Donald Haldane's authority to suppose that it would dissipate so suddenly, stripped suddenly away like leaves caught by an unseen wind. The old man stopped before the closed main door. Cold air hung like a vapour and they could see his breath cloud in it, blow like ectoplasm from his lips.

"Margaret?" he said quizzically. "Margaret, is that you?"

"Papa, there's nobody there," Barbara told him.

"You're having a dream, that's all," said Bea.

The old man would have none of it. "Margaret, Margaret, Margaret," he shouted.

Endeavouring to reach out to the apparition that only he could see, he spilled whisky from the crystal glass down his breast and trousers. He stood back a pace, arms akimbo in horror and stared down at the wet stain that spread across his thighs. When he looked up into thin air again his face was dark with rage. "Now see what you've done. You – you idiot." He swung his fist violently, scything at nothing, and roared, "Mama, Mama, will you take this child away."

"Do something, do something," Bea moaned but Barbara had already put a comforting hand on her father's shoulder.

He swung again, caught the woman unprepared and, weak and flailing though the blow was, struck her across the mouth with sufficient force to send her staggering. Oliver caught her, supported her. She dabbed her mouth with her wrist and Pauline saw blood freckle her sleeve.

"Damn it all, that's enough." Lewis plunged forward and snatched at the old man with his good hand while Mark Straker, more composed and stronger because of it, caught the fists that thrashed at empty air.

Donald Haldane struggled. He roared, "Why have you come here? Who invited you here? I don't want to see you ever again. You hear, Margaret, you hear?" And then abruptly he swooned backward into his son-in-law's arms.

With the house servants given time off, the kitchen, with its stone-flagged floor and monstrous black-iron cooking range, was deserted save for the dogs. The animals had been delighted to have company and had waddled from their baskets, tails wagging, to be petted by Oliver and Too and, when the larder was unlocked and cold meats brought out, were fed tidbits to keep them quiet. Pauline had gone willingly with her cousins. She had no desire to be left in the drawing-room with her near-hysterical aunt, to have to watch her grandmother's flickering little smiles as the old woman was fed brandy and needlessly pampered.

Grandpapa, quite unconscious, had been lowered on to the hall rug and, after discussion, lugged upstairs on it by Mark Straker and the boys while the women, all except Grandmama, fluttered and fussed and wrung their hands about the litter and trailed it upstairs to the bedroom. Pauline and Stella had been left behind. Neither of them had known quite what to do. They had gravitated into the drawing-room again where they had found their grandmother at the long table carefully pouring herself brandy.

"Grandpapa's been taken poorly," Stella had said.

"So I gathered," the old woman had said.

The girls had watched as she had carried the brandy glass back to the sofa and had seated herself once more by the fire.

"Should you – I mean, wouldn't you like to go up? He may need you." Stella had suggested.

"He doesn't need me," the old woman had stated. "It's only another of his turns. He'll be cold for a good hour before he starts again."

"Has he had these fits before?" Stella had said.

"Often."

"I don't think we – any of us knew that."

The old woman had sipped the liquor and had raised her shoulders, like two little bat's wings, in a shrug. Stella had glanced over her shoulder and then helped herself to brandy in a cordial glass before she had approached the old woman. She'd stood before her grandmother without fear or reticence and had asked, "Who's Margaret?"

The old woman had refrained from answering. She had sipped from her glass and, to Pauline's astonishment, had hummed contentedly to herself as she let the liquor lie in her mouth.

"Granny, who is Margaret?"

"His other daughter."

"Dead?"

"I have no idea."

"Did you ever meet her?"

"Not I."

"Granny, you're being very naughty. You really should be by his side, you know. Come on, I'll give you my arm."

"Take your hands off me, young woman. I'm perfectly content to remain here."

The woman had scowled ferociously. She'd looked so pug-like, so fierce and unpredictable that it would not have surprised Pauline if she had shown her teeth and snapped at Stella's hand.

"There are times when I think you are all imbeciles," the old woman had said.

Holding the glass delicately in one mittened hand, she'd swept her black shawl about her shoulders and had sunk down, humming faintly, into a posture that was thoroughly hostile to intrusion.

No amount of telephoning had been able to trace the whereabouts of the Scotch doctor from Buxton. An appeal to Lady Emerald had separated not one but two reputable physicians from the whirl of the hunt ball and Mark Straker had been dispatched in the Ghost to fetch them from Pemberton House. Lewis and Barbara had remained with the patient who, according to Too, was stretched out on top of the Jacobean bed like something tumbled down from a cathedral roof. The sight of the mighty fallen had proved too much for Aunt Bea, however. She had been sent downstairs again to console her mother who, on her second brandy and smoking a cigarette from the box on the table, had been gracious enough to console Bea instead.

In due course the doctors arrived. Oliver had been delegated to greet them and escort them directly upstairs. They were both quite youthful men. Flushed by drink and dancing they had looked somehow too good to be true in cloaks and dinner suits and fine silk hats. Only one of them had carried a bag, however. They had been upstairs for no more than ten minutes in all before Olly had accompanied them downstairs again, had given them each a glass of spirits, had shaken their hands and solemnly walked them out to the Ghost for the return trip to Pemberton House. Bea had been hovering anxiously in the hall. Pauline found it strange that the women – wife, daughters and granddaughters – had been excluded from the medical palaver, like some parody of a birthing in reverse.

"How is he, dear?" Aunt Bea had asked.

"Oh, on the mend, I'd say. He's conscious and alert. But he remembers nothing of what happened."

"What did the doctors say?"

"Something about a passage of blood across the brain. Awfully common in old chaps, apparently."

From the drawing-room had come the crackling question, "But is he going to die?"

And Stella had gone hastening in to her grandmother and, stooping, had shouted an answer into that pugnacious old face: "Sorry, Granny, not this time."

A half hour later, packed off with her brothers to cut sandwiches and make coffee to sustain the family in its vigil, Stella had been even more outspoken: "If you ask me the old boy's going quietly off his rocker."

"Not so quietly," Too had put in.

"I wouldn't voice that opinion in front of Mother, Stella," Oliver said, carving through the crust of a cottage loaf. "She's upset enough as it is."

"I don't see why she should be upset," Stella said. "I mean, he's ancient, simply ancient. His mental powers are bound to be in decline."

Stella was seated cross-legged upon the table, elbows on knees, a cigarette wisping smoke in her fingers.

Oliver wagged the bread knife at her, warningly. "Just don't."

"Oh, come now," Stella said. "Mother's not really upset. If she is she must be the only one. God, none of us like him. None of us have ever been able to stand the sight of him. Don't you remember how . . ."

"I remember a good deal more than you do, Stella."

Oliver applied himself to sawing off neat, thick slices from the loaf. He seemed very domesticated, Pauline thought. It was Oliver, not Stella, who had known where the bread-bins were, the cold box where the butter was kept, who had directed Too to the coffee percolator and the grinder, who, with the masterful efficiency of a butler, had taken charge. He had draped his jacket over a chair and rolled up his shirt sleeves. His arms were slender but corded with muscle. Cricket and rowing had done that for him, Pauline supposed. She had a sudden desire to rub her hand upon her cousin's arm, to nuzzle against him like one of the Labradors, in the sure knowledge that Oliver was too gentle to rebuff her.

"Oh, yes, jolly good," said Stella sarcastically. "All right, look down from the pinnacle of your wisdom and experience, Ol, and tell me the name of one person, one single person, who can stand the old devil."

"Mr Straker seems to like him well enough."

Stella waved her cigarette, drawing patterns in the air with smoke. "Mr Straker is just the same as the rest of us – after a share of Grandpaw's dough."

Too, who had been stripping the butter pat with a metal curler, looked up quickly. "Did Straker tell you that?"

"He didn't have to," said Stella. "It's patently obvious. Why on earth would a chap like Mark waste his time with bumpkins like us, let alone a doddering old goat like Grandfather, if not for profit?"

Oliver clicked his tongue in disgust at his sister's cynicism and dealt the slices of cut bread on to an oval plate as if they were playing cards.

Stella leaned forward, one leg kicking in impatience. She sucked on the cigarette, seemed to wrestle with herself for a second and then blurted out, "Mark knows exactly what Grandfather is worth – and it's a lot, believe me."

"What do you call 'a lot', Stella?" Too enquired.

"A quarter of a million."

Too whistled and raised his brows. "You don't say?"

"I do say – over a quarter of a million pounds."

"Pauline?"

"Yes, Oliver."

"Do you mind buttering? Warm the knife first."

Stella hopped down from the table. "Is that all you can say, Olly? There are times when you are quite insufferable."

Oliver wetted his finger, dabbed a fragment of black crust from the tabletop and put it in his mouth. "What other secrets has Mr Straker imparted?"

"Well, we're all in to receive legacies."

"Are we indeed!" said Too.

Nibbling on the piece of crust, Oliver turned and walked the length of the kitchen and entered the larder. He reappeared a moment later with a huge platter of cooked meats; a roast, a gammon and an ox-tongue in jelly. He carried the platter in both hands to the long board where the slicer was and set it down. He removed the cover from the slicer and dexterously set the gauge of the circular blade, gave the handle an experimental crank.

"Haven't you anything to say?" Stella demanded.

"I'm just wondering why you're so thick with Mr Straker," Oliver said. "Why would he take the likes of you into his confidence?"

"Why shouldn't he?"

"Because you're only a child."

"Damn you, Oliver!"

"Cigarettes and silk stockings don't fool me," Oliver said, "and I doubt if they fool Mark Straker."

"Oh, don't they?" Stella cried. "Well, I'll have you know that he . . ."

"Go on," said Oliver quietly when Stella, one hand clenched into a fist, bit off the conclusion of her statement. "Go on, Stella. I'm sure we're all intrigued."

". . . that he considers me very mature."

"He's only being nice."

"He means it, every word," said Stella. "What's happening to the coffee?"

"Nothing's happening to the coffee." Oliver patiently carved the cold roast into thin slices. "When the water boils in the percolator then something will happen to the coffee. Don't change the subject, Stella."

"No," said Too, who was rather clumsily decorating a serving plate with lace-edge napkins. "Tell us more about dear ol' Grandfather's famous fortune."

"Why should I?" Stella said. "According to Oliver it's just childish prattle."

Pauline said, "I don't see what it has to do with us. I mean, he isn't going to die, is he?"

"Of course he is," said Stella.

"What?" said Pauline. "Soon?"

"Oh, not tonight or anything," Stella leaned on the table, the last inch of her cigarette pinched between finger and thumb. "But he is on the way out, make no mistake. And after he pops then we – the meek – shall inherit the earth."

"Surely," said Pauline, "whatever there is will be passed on to Grandmother or to his children, not directly to us. Oliver?"

"I'm sure I have no idea how Grandpapa Haldane has arranged his will and dispositions. Perhaps there will be something left for us. I doubt if it will arrive as cash in hand, however. More likely it'll be put into trust for us."

"What does that mean?" said Stella.

Too answered, "Means you won't get your claws on any of it until you're too old to enjoy it, Stell. Sorry."

"Nonsense."

"Marriage might secure it for you," said Oliver. "That's common when it comes to females. Trustees are left specific instructions, you see."

Too said, "Is there really a quarter of a million in the inheritance kitty, d'you think, Olly?"

Oliver paused. The blade of the meat slicer grated edgily and he peeled away a crescent of lean brown beef before he answered. "I'd be inclined to take Mr Straker's word on it. He seems well versed in financial matters and interested enough in Haldane affairs to have made it his business to find out. Dad has informed me that Grandfather still owns a great many properties. If all the assets were capitalised, I suppose . . ." Oliver shrugged.

Pauline said, "But aren't there others besides us who might be entitled to a share?"

"What others?" said Stella.

"His first family."

"Oh, them! I doubt if they even care whether Grandpa Haldane is alive or dead."

"I wouldn't bank on it, Stella," said Oliver.

He came to the table with cold cuts piled on a plate and, with a gesture, indicated to his brother that he should begin manufacturing the sandwiches. In an alcove under a burnished copper canopy the tall metal coffee urn gurgled and chugged and suddenly swamped the kitchen with the luxurious aroma of Old Java.

"Right you are, Olly," Too said. "When there's free money in the offing all sorts of folk are liable to appear caps-in-hands out of the wainscot."

"How many other children did Grandfather have?" Pauline asked.

"Not quite certain," Oliver answered. "I've only ever heard of one."

"They must be quite old now," Pauline said. "Perhaps they're all dead."

"One of them certainly is," said Too.

"Are you sure?" said Oliver.

"Of course. The one called Margaret. The one whose spectre stalked our hallway."

"That wasn't a spectre," said Oliver. "That was hallucination. Something Grandfather imagined. For all we know Margaret is still alive and kicking."

Stella gave an unexpected chuckle. She dropped the shreds of her cigarette on to the stone floor and ground them out with her toe. She glanced up and winked mischievously.

"I know how we could find out," she said.

"Check through the registers, I suppose," said Too.

"Simpler than that," said Stella. "We could use the board."

And Oliver, his head jerking up, cried, "No."

Stella skipped and rubbed her breast against her brother's back, skipped away again, purring: "Ooo! Is he scared of the board then? Is he still scared of the board?"

Pauline, mystified, asked, "What board?"

But nobody answered, not even Oliver who, hard-eyed and scowling, had gone back to trimming beef.

# Sixteen

$B$y the third day of the New Year the holiday was well and truly over and Pauline had nothing much to look forward to except getting back to St Austin's. With the boys gone, Mark Straker returned to London and Uncle Lewis as busy as his plastered arm would allow, she was pushed into the company of her cousin and her mother whether she liked it or not and was obliged to share with them, and Aunt Bea too, a certain ill-expressed anxiety about the future.

On the advice of the local doctors Grandpapa Haldane had been wrapped in a swaddle of rugs and blankets, placed in Mark's motorcar and, with Grandmama tucked beside him, had been driven back to Hampstead to receive expert medical attention. Pauline could understand that. She could also understand that Mark Straker had his living to earn and that with the exchanges back in operation he needed to be in London. What she could not understand was why her mother had been left behind. She had a vague feeling that there had been a row about it. There was certainly a good deal of tension between the adults on the morning of Grandfather's departure. Tears from Aunt Bea were to be expected but tears from Mummy seemed somehow anomalous and Pauline could not fathom out whether her mother was weeping out of sorrow or out of anger, weeping for Grandpapa or for herself.

Pauline had not spoken to her grandfather since his illness. She was reluctant to approach him, so frail and husk-like had he become. Both she and Stella stood well back as Mark and two male servants half-carried the invalid from the house to the motorcar. Grandpapa was quite conscious of his surroundings and aware of what was happening to him. He tried to issue orders to the servants in a voice as whispery as wind in thatch, a thin, dry, peevish rustle too faint to sustain authority. It was only at the very last moment when Mark was already in the driving seat and had the engine fired that Pauline and Stella were summoned to the car. The daughters, Bea and Barbara, had taken their farewells and it came as a horrid shock to Pauline to be nudged towards the open door of the passenger compartment and beckoned in by her grandmother's tiny claw-like hand.

The motorcar's interior smelled of leather and oil but those pleasant smells were overlaid now by a strange astringent odour that grew stronger as she leaned across her grandmother's lap and, as bidden, kissed her grandfather's cheek. He was propped up by pillows, clean-cased and lace-edged. He had still about him that scraped, scrubbed, ethereal quality, though pinkness had been replaced by grey and his cheek, when Pauline brushed it with her lips, felt coarse as sackcloth and the odour was strong enough to make her want to gag. It was as if the rugs and blankets, the alpaca overcoat, velvet jacket, cardigan and pretty silk cravat were wrapped over something unclean, something neglected and corrupt. It was all Pauline could do not to pull away. He stirred, though, moved his right hand slowly and rested it on her shoulder, holding her while he laboured upright, two or three inches, and whispered into her ear, "You're a good girl, Pauline, a good girl," before he subsided against the soft supporting pillows once more and, with a grunt, let her go.

"What did he say to you?" Stella asked as they walked back to the Hall from the drive.

"He told me I was a good girl."

"Hmmm! That's what he told me too. I thought the old skinflint was going to slip me a fiver. No such luck."

Stella paused and stared up at the frontage of the house, at the high eaves dripping with foggy moisture and the brickwork chimneyheads which, from this vertiginous angle, seemed about to topple and crash down.

Half to herself, Stella said, "It's going to be awfully boring without him."

"What? Grandpapa?"

"No, you idiot. I mean Mark. He's just what this family needs. Someone young, someone alive and go-ahead. I wish he was my stepfather."

"You're welcome to him," Pauline said.

Stella glanced at her speculatively for a moment, blue eyes quite wide with surprise, then she laughed, reached for Pauline's hand and, as if they were both children, dragged her eagerly towards the open door.

"Come upstairs with me," Stella said.

"Why?"

"I'm dying for a ciggie if you must know."

"Can't you smoke on your own?"

"Can but don't want to," Stella said. "Besides we're cousins and we're supposed to act like chums. Come on, Polly-wolly. Cover for me."

"Oh, all right," said Pauline reluctantly, and followed the girl indoors.

In the days that followed Pauline and Stella spent a good deal of time together. Pauline, however, was under no illusions that her cousin was using her as anything other than a stay against boredom and that if Mark Straker, or any other personable male, had been around then Stella would hardly have spared her a second glance.

Pauline was not jejune enough to ignore the value in having Stella as a companion. She was desperately afraid of being drawn into a confidential or sentimental relationship with her mother, of being touched or softened by that strain of pity that she had experienced early in the holiday. At least with Stella she knew where she stood. School gossip was permitted but certain areas of conversation tactfully remained taboo. Colleen, Goss, Daphne were mentioned only in passing and the feud between one set and another was carefully skirted and neither confidences nor secrets were sought or exchanged. Even so Stella seemed to find dialogue with her younger cousin effortless and the pair spent hours together prattling away in the library or in one or other of the bedrooms, while Stella smoked and Pauline gorged herself on what remained of the Christmas candies.

Two long letters from Daddy reached her at Flask. She was much excited by their tone of ebullience. Daddy was going 'away' for Christmas, to spend a week as the guest of an English mining engineer and his American wife on their farm in the bush some forty miles out of Durban. Ostermann's was doing good business and he had made several reliable friends and was not, after all, chained to a desk in town as he'd feared he might be. He wrote interestingly about the Africans and their tribal differences and entertainingly about his visits to the Durban picture house. He asked Pauline for news about what new pictures were showing in London and went on at some length about how he missed the theatre, sentences that brought Pauline up short with the realisation that she had lost connection with and interest in that former passion.

She managed to evade Stella long enough to write back at length. She recounted for her father the circumstances of Uncle Lewis's accident and, in a second letter, imparted news of Grandpapa Haldane's illness. She was very careful to censor all but passing references to her mother and made no mention of Mark Straker at all. She gave the letters to Uncle Lewis to post in Derby.

"Still miss him, do you, Polly?" Uncle Lewis had asked.

"Yes, of course I do."

"Natural, natural," Uncle Lewis had said, scratching away at the ring of bruised skin around his plastered wrist. "I do hope, though, that when your Papa comes home again you won't abandon us completely."

"It's ages until Daddy comes back," Pauline had said and then had thought better of it and added, "But, no, of course I won't abandon you. I'll come up for the huntin', if you'll have me."

Uncle Lewis had raised his arm, clublike. "After one of these, are you?"

"Rather not." On impulse Pauline had lifted herself on tiptoe and had kissed her uncle's cheek affectionately. "I'm grateful to you, Uncle Lewis. You've been very kind. Much kinder to me than I deserve."

"Nonsense, nonsense!" the man had protested but had made a little trumpeting sound that had told Pauline that he was more pleased than embarrassed.

It was not until the following weekend that Pauline learned what plans had been made to return Stella and her to

St Austin's. She had somehow expected Mark Straker to arrive from London for the weekend and when he did not, had been curious enough to broach the subject with her cousin.

"He's coming up next Friday and on Saturday he'll drive us north," Stella had said.

"Why don't we just take the train?"

"The train? It's horrid. Don't you like motoring?"

"Well, yes, but isn't it dreadfully inconvenient for Mr Straker?"

"You really should call him Mark, you know," Stella had said. "No, it isn't in the least inconvenient. Mark's like Papa in that respect. He just adores motoring and will seize on any excuse for making an epic journey. Besides, he'll just love having two young ladies all to himself."

"How long will the journey take?"

"That rather depends on the weather. Mark says that if the roads are clear we'll do it in a day. If we encounter ice or fog, or snow perhaps, then we may have to stop over. We'll be back in plenty of time for the start of term. Mark will make sure of that."

Pauline had listened with growing alarm to her cousin's outlining of travel arrangements. For a moment or two she'd been tempted to plead with Uncle Lewis to send her back to Scotland by train. But she had no reason at all to be churlish. The fact that she disliked Mark Straker had nothing at all to do with it. She was, she supposed, predisposed to dislike any man who had married her mother. She wondered sometimes about the other men her mother had known over the years. Were they all as cold and arrogant as Mark Straker? What really dismayed her, though, was the news that she would be alone with her stepfather and Stella for the best part of a day. She had a feeling that she would be regarded, by Stella certainly, as a sort of wallflower and prayed that the weather would be decent enough for the trip to be made without an overnight halt.

Stella had said, "I suppose you'll be glad to get back?"

Pauline had answered, "Oh, yes."

"You like it there, don't you?"

"I must admit I do."

Stella had shaken her head, but without ridicule or mockery. She'd said, "The only reason I'll be glad to get back is that it's one step closer to leaving prison for good."

"Do you really hate it so much?"

"Like poison," Stella had said.

Stella's restlessness became more palpable as the days passed. She took Pauline riding over woodland tracks that wound about Flask Hall and the back end of the town. She rode with an effortless ease that Pauline knew she would never be able to match but Stella was not inclined to be proud of her talent or to show off her skill and the rides were pleasant without being exciting. They went down to Flask on two afternoons, browsed about the shops, bought ribbon and elastic and hairpins, had tea in a stuffy little cave of a teashop and met three girls of about Stella's age who would have been friendly if Stella had chosen to encourage them.

The days were shaped by prolonged breakfasts and lunches and, with Uncle Lewis presiding, dinners every evening at exactly half-past seven. Cards sometimes followed, communal games played for peppermints or halfpennies, or board games played with dice, not much by way of conversation. News from London was encouraging. Grandpapa Haldane had been examined by specialists. Apart from high blood pressure, he had been pronounced 'very fit' for a man of his age. The incident in the hallway at Flask, his swoon, had been put down to a mild fever and apparently there was no lasting damage to the brain or nervous system. He was, Mark Straker reported by telephone, "practically his old self again," whatever that meant.

Now that the holidays were almost over Pauline believed that she was going to escape without having to confront her mother face-to-face and that her disconcerting anxieties about there being 'scenes' had been, after all, just childish imaginings. She had not been pounced upon, had not been smothered, had not been obliged to feign affection where little existed.

There was no sign of snow. The newspapers did not predict it. Uncle Lewis claimed to be green with envy and was tempted to come along with Straker and the girls just for the excursion but did not, in the end, relish the idea of being a mere passenger. He had marked off a suitable route on his road maps and had put these into an oilskin pouch along with his copy of the RAC guidebooks and had handed this treasure over into Stella's care for it had already been agreed that she would sit in front with Mark and "keep him on the right road for Scotland".

Pauline was keen for the holiday to end. She spent a long, dreary rain-lashed afternoon in her bedroom repairing her school clothes and trying on various garments to make sure that she could still get into them. She promised herself that she would attend Mad Jamie's Highland Dancing class regularly and stretch herself upon the wallbars until her tummy regained its graceful proportions. Just thinking about St Austin's made her long for the company of her friends, for a session of chat with Goss, Elf and the Frog, bookish talk with Miss Milligan, instruction from Mr Roddy and, when the weather warmed, tennis on the quiet maroon-coloured courts under the tall privet hedges; nothing to worry her until the end of spring term.

She did not hear the Ghost's arrival. Dusk had swept down on the wind and Pauline, packing complete, had not felt in the least inclined to go in search of Stella. She had poked up the little coal fire in her bedroom and added a few lumps from the brass bucket to cheer it into a blaze and had lain on her bed and reread her father's last two letters. From below she caught faint sounds – Stella's laughter, the slamming of a door. She thought that Mark Straker might be once more upon the premises but, languid and comfortable, she had no desire to go downstairs to join the welcoming committee. A short time later she heard footsteps in the passage outside her room but she did not so much as sit up. She had no curiosity about what was going on in the house or what news Mark had brought from Hampstead. In due course she fell asleep.

She did not waken until after seven which meant that she had to scramble to bathe and dress for dinner. There was nobody in the corridors, nobody on the stairs. She could hear a murmur of voices in the dining room and, making her way there, discovered that Mark Straker had indeed arrived and that he and the others were already seated at the dining table waiting to begin the meal.

As usual, Uncle Lewis wore his dinner suit. But Mark Straker was casually dressed in sports jacket and flannel trousers. He looked so at ease at the table, however, that he made the others seem quite stiff and portentous in their finery. Pauline greeted her stepfather with a nod. She apologised for her tardiness and slipped on to her chair, opposite Stella.

Her cousin was aglow. There was no other word for it. Stella had risked parental disapproval by applying lipstick, a touch of rouge and by thickening her eyelashes with Coloura. She had done something too to the bodice of her frock and displayed what there was of a figure – feminine yet boyish – to best advantage. Pauline had the impression that words had already been crossed between Stella and her mother and that Aunt Bea had lost the exchange. The woman was tight-lipped and uncommonly sulky. Pauline's mother too had a hurt, defensive air about her that suggested a row about something.

"All present and correct?" Uncle Lewis enquired.

"Fire on all guns, Papa," said Stella.

Uncle Lewis reached beneath the table and pressed the pearl button that rang an electrical bell in the kitchen. Two minutes later, the maid and butler entered bearing soup. While serving was going on, Pauline arranged her napkin on her lap and addressed herself to Mark Straker. "Is my grandfather in better health?"

"Yes, he appears to be recovering."

Stella fixed Pauline with a wide-eyed stare and mouthed the word, "Pity!"

"What did you say?" Aunt Bea asked.

"Nothing, Mother. I was asking Pauline to pass the pepper, that's all."

Pauline passed the pepper.

"Begin," said Uncle Lewis by way of blessing.

Pauline dipped her spoon into leek-and-potato.

Stella said, "Now, Mark, do tell us what you got up to in London?"

The man did not answer and Pauline caught the glance that he exchanged with her mother.

"Stella," said Uncle Lewis, "don't be rude."

"I'm not being rude."

"Inquisitive then."

"Oh, Mark doesn't mind. Do you?"

"I don't imagine that you would find it at all interesting," Mark Straker said.

"Tell us the good bits then."

"Stella!" Aunt Bea warned.

"Yes, dearest, why don't you tell us the good bits," said Pauline's mother.

"All pretty humdrum, actually," Mark Straker said. "Work, visiting Hampstead, that sort of thing."

"Didn't you dine out?" Barbara asked.

"Once or twice."

"With whom?"

"I told you – with Sydney."

"And Silvia?" Barbara asked.

"No, not with Silvia. I didn't see Silvia at all."

"Oh-hoh!" said Stella. "Who is Silvia?"

"What is she?" said Uncle Lewis then, hastily clearing his throat, added, "Sorry."

"Silvia is the girlfriend of my partner. That's all."

"That's all," said Barbara, not quite mockingly.

"Is she very lovely?" said Stella.

"Not very, no."

"I thought she was," said Barbara. "I thought you thought she was."

Uncle Lewis rattled his spoon on his plate and proclaimed loudly, "Jolly good soup, what!"

"Is Silvia Mr Sydney's 'constant companion'?" said Stella.

"Can't beat a dollop of the old leek-and-potato on a cold winter night," said Uncle Lewis.

"She's engaged to be married to him, if that's what you mean," said Mark Straker tactfully.

"No, that isn't quite what I meant," said Stella. "Actually, what I meant was . . ."

"Stella, stop," said Uncle Lewis.

"I'm only making conversation."

"Then make conversation about something else."

"But why?"

Uncle Lewis brought his plastered arm from under the table. The material had turned shiny and grey as gunmetal. He raised it like a weapon, fingers clenched. "This is why," Uncle Lewis told his daughter. "In case you've forgotten what exactly this is – it's an iron hand," he tapped the plaster with his knuckles, "in a velvet glove."

"Bully!" said Stella without a trace of animosity.

Mark Straker laughed and, leaning slightly, touched Stella's forearm. "Since you're so keen on making conversation, Stella, why don't you tell us what you've been up to?"

"Oh, we've had a wonderful time," said Stella. "Been riding in the woods, shopping in the village. We've finished two whole jigsaws." She flung her wrist against her brow. "Madly, madly gay."

"Have you been enjoying yourself, Pauline?" Mark Straker asked.

"Yes. It's been very relaxing," Pauline said and to her consternation heard Mark Straker laugh again as if she had said something funny.

There was an air of lassitude, almost of exhaustion, about everyone that evening after dinner. Even Uncle Lewis could not whip up enthusiasm and his suggestion that a game of Charades might restore a final flicker of festive spirit was met with blank silence.

"We must do something," Uncle Lewis said. "We can't just let the girls go off without doing something, not on their last night of freedom."

Stella hesitated then, as if the idea had just occurred to her, said brightly, "Well, if you're really keen on a little *divertissement* for half an hour or so, I know what we could do."

"Nothing too strenuous," said Uncle Lewis. "I only have one sound hand, remember."

"One hand is all you'll need," said Stella. "Wait."

She went skipping out of the drawing room, leaving the door ajar.

Uncle Lewis sipped cognac and puffed on his pipe. Mark

Straker lit another cigarette, sat back in the sofa and jogged one shoe contemplatively.

"What is she up to, dear?" said Aunt Bea.

"Some silly game we've all forgotten about, I expect."

Rain beat against the tall windows and a moaning wind bellied the drapes like a lugger's sails. Stella returned, hiding some object behind her back.

Uncle Lewis put down his glass. "Well now, what've you got there?"

"*Voilà!*" Stella exclaimed.

She waved in the air a plain but peculiar looking wooden object the like of which Pauline had never seen before. The indulgent little smile died on Uncle Lewis's lips.

Aunt Bea sat bolt upright, coffee cup chattering on its saucer on her knee. "Oh, no, no, Stella. Not that board. You know how Oliver hates that board."

"But Olly isn't here, is he?" Stella said. She leaned on the back of her father's chair and rubbed her chin against his hair. "Go on, Papa, let's all have a little thrill. You used to enjoy it."

"Where did you find it, Stella?" Uncle Lewis said. "I thought the damned thing had been thrown out when Nanny Godolphin left."

"Nanny Godolphin wouldn't let me throw it out. She said it was bad luck to try to get rid of one of these. You remember how superstitious she was."

"Only too well," said Uncle Lewis.

"It's been stuck away in the back of the nursery cupboard for ages," Stella said. "Quite by chance I just happened to stumble across it the other morning."

"Well, I think you should put it away again," said Aunt Bea. "It's not a suitable sort of game for present company."

"Oh, Mummy, don't be so stuffy."

Mark Straker beckoned to Stella who went to him willingly. He took the wooden object from her and examined it. A plane of varnished wood a quarter inch thick and slightly smaller than a dinner plate, it had two little brass legs on the underside to each of which was attached a tiny buttonlike wheel made, Pauline thought, of ivory.

Drawn by curiosity she inched her chair closer to Mark

Straker's to see the object more clearly. It was almost heart-shaped. The brass holder formed the apex of the triangle made up by the miniature wheels. Into the brass holder was screwed the stump of a pencil with a blunt point.

"What is it?" Pauline asked.

"God, I haven't seen one of these for years." Mark Straker turned the object over and over in his hands. "It's a planchette, rather a nice one too. How long have you had it?"

"Years," Lewis said. "Far too long, in fact."

"The children's nanny brought it with her," Aunt Bea explained. "Long ago, before the war. She would bring it out from time to time to communicate with her sister. I thought it was just a harmless toy until I discovered not only that Nanny Godolphin's sister was deceased but that she had the children playing with it too. On one occasion, Oliver got badly frightened by it."

"Oliver was a cry-baby," said Stella. "There's nothing wrong with the thing. They're all the rage now. Ouija boards, they call them."

"They're dangerous," said Aunt Bea.

"Oh, Mother, what nonsense. It's only a bit of harmless fun."

"What does it do?" said Pauline.

In a high wavering voice Stella informed her, "Contacts the spirits."

Pauline had a vague notion that she had known the answer to her own question, that she should not have asked. She reached for the board and took it from Mark's hands. It didn't feel as smooth as it looked, as if the varnish had not quite filled the grain of the wood. She spun one of the little wheels with the ball of her thumb while Mark, leaning on his elbow, observed her closely.

Stella said, "Tell them, Mark."

"Fun, certainly," Mark Straker said.

"You seem to know a lot about it," Barbara said. "You never told me that you'd dabbled in the occult."

"My grandmother did. She was a believer, you see; a spiritualist. She had all sorts of strange objects in her house – including a planchette, of course. That's how I know about it."

298

"How does it actually work?" said Pauline.

"Come along then," Mark Straker said. "We'll have a brief demonstration, shall we? Just to round out Pauline's education."

"Hmmm! Well—" Uncle Lewis hesitated. "Bea isn't awfully keen on this sort of thing."

"We only need four participants." Mark Straker retrieved the board from Pauline and held it flat on his palms, wheel-castors and pencil projecting downward. "Eight fingers should do it."

"I don't want to touch it," Aunt Bea said.

"Tell you what, dear," Lewis got to his feet. "You and I will watch. Let the youngsters get on with it." He crossed the carpet to the armchair where his wife was seated, relieved her of cup and saucer and then seated himself on the arm by her side. "It is only a bit of innocent entertainment, after all."

"Promise you'll get rid of it after tonight, Lewis."

"If it'll make you happy, dear – I promise."

Mark Straker had drawn an oval sided table closer to the centre of the room and was in process of arranging four chairs about it. "We need paper, Stella."

"Shelf-paper," Stella said, "which, oh master, I happen to have secreted in advance in this very drawer."

She drew a roll of cheap paper from a drawer in the table and unspooled it across the rosewood surface. Mark adjusted the paper and laid the planchette upon it, balanced castors and pencil point.

"Shall I put the lights out?" Stella said.

"No, dear, no," murmured Aunt Bea.

"Leave on the standard lamp." Uncle Lewis squeezed his wife's hand reassuringly. "Otherwise we won't be able to see a thing. Fair enough, Stella?"

"Fair enough," Stella agreed.

She switched off the cluster of bulbs in the electrical chandelier and the big soft-shaded lamp by the window then returned to the table.

The tremor of apprehension that had been in Pauline from the moment she had taken the planchette into her hands increased as shadows crowded the corners of the room.

Logs in the fireplace crackled but seemed to grow darker too as Pauline was ushered to a chair. Stella seated herself, placed her fingertips upon the table top and drummed lightly as if practising a scale upon a keyboard.

Mark turned and held out his hand. "Barbara?"

Barbara shook her head. "No."

She had said not a word in protest until that moment, had remained silently in the armchair opposite her sister. Mark Straker gave a soft little snap of his fingers and repeated her name. Pauline watched her mother climb meekly out of the armchair, be led submissively to the table and slip tamely on to the fourth chair. She glanced at Pauline and managed a faint, brave smile.

Stella patted her arm. "There, there, Auntie. Have no fear. It's only a game."

"No, it's not," Mark Straker said. "It's deadly serious. Much hush, please."

He adjusted the planchette so that it sat on the middle of the paper scroll then rested the tips of his index and middle fingers, spread into a vee, upon the heart-shaped surface.

"Ladies, do likewise, if you please," he said. "Do not press downward, simply allow your fingers to contact the board."

Tentatively Pauline obeyed.

She had developed an extraordinary sensitivity all of a sudden. She imagined that she could feel the stickiness of the varnish, even the grain of the wood beneath. She wondered if the board quivered at her touch or if tension in the tendons of hand and wrist imparted that sensation of vibrancy. Logically she suspected that it was a trick, that any motion of the pencil would be created by subtle muscular forces and not spirits in the atmosphere.

Stella set her fingers confidently in place and, throwing back her head and adopting a quavering tone, asked, "Is there anybody there?"

"Ssshh!" Mark told her. "We are not yet complete. Barbara. Join us."

Pauline watched her mother uncurl her hands from her lap and stretch out her fingers, middle and index spread. She held them poised an inch above the varnished surface and glanced at her husband, frowning.

"Mark, what if—"

"No danger, Babby."

"But—"

"Not dead," Mark Straker told her.

"Are we ready?" said Stella impatiently. "All set? Good! Then let us begin."

Pauline stared at the pencil. She tried hard not to press down upon the board. They had been at the table for two or three minutes, all gawking down at a silly inanimate lump of wood. She was annoyed at herself for taking it seriously. And yet there was still a feeling in her, a bizarre sensation, as if a current was passing through her. She noticed that the fine dark hairs on her forearms had become erect, that the smoke from her uncle's pipe seemed to hang motionless in the air unaffected by the draughts that stirred the curtains. The bulb in the standard lamp flickered.

Her mouth went dry, as it had while she'd waited in the wings of the Harvey to spout her lines from *The Demon Drummer*. It was a different kind of nervousness now, though, much more real and without promise of deliverance.

"Move, damn you," Stella whispered. "Why is it being so stubborn tonight?"

The pencil stirred, jerked, fashioned a long curving arc, heavily impressed upon the paper, the board chasing away under fingertip touch, little ivory castors squeaking faintly.

Pauline gasped.

Stella said, "You did that."

Pauline said, "I did not."

"Anyway," Stella said, "we're not doing it properly. We have to ask it something and let it reply."

"Ask it something then," Mark said.

In an unaffected voice, Stella said, "Is there anybody there?"

In a huge rolling loop of letters the planchette instantly wrote out the word "YES."

"Oh, good. It's working at last," Stella said. "Now, let me see. Do you have a message for someone?"

301

"YES," appeared swiftly on the shelf-paper.

"Someone at this table?"

Again – "YES."

"Is it a man?"

"NO."

"Well, that's you off the hook, Mark," Stella said.

Mark ignored the girl's remark and put the next question, "Is it a female?"

"YES."

The letters were intertwined in a lacy sort of pattern that as far as Pauline could make out was entirely random that had no meaning of its own. Her heart was beating loudly. She seemed to have become separated from her fingers which had taken on a volition of their own and followed the board willingly as it skated out its answers.

She started when a shadow fell across the surface of the paper and darted a glance to her right. Uncle Lewis, pipe clenched in his teeth, had stolen up to the chairs. He stood a pace or two behind Stella, watching intently. By the fire, Aunt Bea had covered her eyes with her hands. The wind billowed the curtains and Pauline imagined that she could hear the soft surging roar of the sea.

She could bear it no longer. Loudly, she said, "Do you have a message for me?"

The board remained motionless.

Pauline tried not to lean into it, to coax it with her fingertips. She watched Stella – for she suspected Stella – but saw that her cousin for all her bravado was puzzled too.

With considerable effort, a limping uncertainty that broke the letters into a series of scratchy strokes, the pencil printed, "NO."

Pauline let her breath out and, for a split second, closed her eyes.

"Your turn, Stella," Uncle Lewis murmured.

His voice sounded remarkably deep but quite matter-of-fact. Pauline did not take her eyes from the board.

"Is it me?" Stella enquired. "Do you have a message for me, please?"

Instantly – "NO."

"Oh, my God!" said Pauline's mother.

"You're doing this, Mark, aren't you?" Stella said.

"No, I'm not. I swear."

"You are. You must be," Barbara said.

"Ask it something else, Babby," Mark Straker suggested.

"No. I can't. I won't," said Barbara.

Pauline did not dare to intervene. She had no saliva in her mouth and her tongue was stuck to her palate. Outside – or in her head – the foaming rush of an ocean had become almost deafening, thrusting and pushing the question from her throat to her lips.

She heard herself ask, "Who is it that you want?"

Before the words were properly uttered the board was in motion.

No great whorled loop of letters or even stabs of lead, it moved almost like the platen of a typewriting machine, inching in a narrow line across the paper from left to right and left behind it a crabbed, humpbacked script. Letter after tiny letter appeared with astonishing rapidity, a flying skein of m's and a's, all linked.

"What the devil—" Uncle Lewis caught Stella by the shoulders and snatched her back from the table, tilting the chair's hind legs. Mark Straker too reared away. For an instant only Pauline and her mother were in contact with the board, fingers darting after it as if they could trap it, silence it and make it cease its chatter.

Barbara screamed, rose. Her chair toppled. Her hands were held in that position by which prisoners surrendered to an enemy. Pauline, alone, was left in contact with whatever moved the board.

She could feel the resistance of the pencil point, the drag of lead upon paper. She tried to make it stop, balling her fist and squeezing down. But the force was too great. It absorbed her resistance and forged on with its wild repetitive message.

When Uncle Lewis pushed Pauline away from the table and her hand slid from the surface of the device, the planchette, untouched, still went on writing, "mamamamamamamamama mamamamamamamamamamamamamamamamamamamamamama-mamamamamamamamamamamamamamamamamamamamamama-

mamamamamamamamamamamamamamamamamama," until the
pencil stump broke and the board spun off the edge of the
table and fell with an almighty clatter to the floor.

"My sister, it was my sister, wasn't it?" Pauline cried.

"Don't be ridiculous," Mark Straker said.

"It was certainly something odd," said Stella. "I mean, it
wasn't any of us. Did you see it? Did you see how it went
on and on even when we'd let it go?"

"I told you, I told you," Aunt Bea moaned.

They were all badly shaken, even Mark Straker. He
had helped his wife to an armchair by the fire and had
supplied her with brandy which she held in a trembling
hand.

Recollections of Old Flo's classes in basic first aid told
Pauline that her mother was in shock but she was too
distressed to care. She had asked the question and the
board – or whatever motivated the board – had answered
loud and clear: Mama Mama Mama. It couldn't be a trick.
Neither Stella nor Mark Straker could possibly have been
that clever or that cruel.

Hands on hips and trembling, Pauline confronted her
mother. "You know who it was, don't you, Mummy?"

"N . . . no . . . I . . . I don't."

"Stop lying. Why are you all lying?"

Mark Straker endeavoured to put an arm around her,
saying, "Come on, Pauline, you've had a shake too. Calm
yourself."

"Take your hands off me."

She pushed the man away and once more confronted her
mother directly. "Why did it call out for Mama?"

Barbara leaned forward, glass tucked into her hands, hands
almost hidden in her lap. She had stopped shaking but her
eyes were glazed and she appeared to be having difficulty in
drawing breath. Stella came up behind her and craning over
the back of the armchair offered her aunt a lighted cigarette
which Barbara accepted. She put the cigarette to her lips and
drew in a lungful of tobacco smoke, sipped brandy and, in an
involuntary gesture of gratitude, patted Stella's arm. The girl
continued to lean over the chairback, smoking too, intimate

and consoling, as if she was Mummy's ally and could keep the raging child at bay.

"Leave her alone, Polly," Stella said.

"Who wrote those words?" Pauline demanded.

"It was just a damned joke that misfired," Stella said. "Let it go, Pauline, for heaven's sake."

"Mother, I want you to tell me."

Barbara shook her head.

Mercilessly Pauline said, "It was her, wasn't it?"

Barbara whispered, "Yes."

Hands clamped on Pauline's shoulders, Mark Straker swung her round. Her stepfather's expression was fouled by rage. He looked dark and dangerous now with all his arrogant, affable charm stripped away. He did not shout, though. He spoke in a sneering sort of tone, tainted by disgust at Pauline's stupid persistence. "For God's sake, what do you think it was – a ghost?"

Pauline hadn't had the courage yet to put a name to the power that had moved the planchette.

She opened her mouth to answer but found herself rendered dumb by the pressure of his hands. His thumbs dug into the flesh of her shoulders. His teeth were small and very white, something she had not noticed before, and his lips, which were sensuous in anger, peeled back as if he intended to bite her and suck the silliness out of her like a poison.

Pauline heard her mother say, "Mark, don't hurt her."

At the same time, voices twined and overlaid, Mark Straker was saying, "How can it be a ghost when she isn't dead? That's right: she isn't damned-well dead."

A wave of relief passed through Pauline like an enormous sigh. She had linked in her mind those autumn dreams with death, had shrunk from inexplicable visions of seascapes and merbabes, from the piping voice that had found expression at last in the pencil stump of a parlour toy.

"Oh!" Pauline said. "I see." She stepped back from her stepfather. He did not try to prevent it. She slipped back and back and felt Aunt Bea's armchair bump against her thighs and rested herself on the arm, her legs stretched out before her, hands placed light and flat on her knees. "I see, I see."

She looked up. "Where is she then?" she said. "What have you done with my sister?"

Nobody spoke for a moment then Uncle Lewis said, "I think the time has come to tell Pauline the truth."

Mummy was by her side, kneeling, seeking out her hand. "Oh, darling, darling!"

"Tell her," Mark Straker said.

"I didn't want to — " Mummy began then broke down in tears.

"If you won't, I will." Mark Straker snatched at one of the straight-backed chairs, spun it round and straddled it. He thrust the chair between the woman and the girl and stuck his chin forward, showing Pauline once more white teeth and curled lips. "She's been put away, your sister, if you must know. She was born an imbecile and she won't live long anyway. So we put her out to be cared for – for her own good."

"She's a baby, an infant," said Pauline. "How can you be sure she's—"

"You silly little cow," Mark Straker said. "You don't know anything about real life, do you. Well, it's time you found out."

"Steady on," said Uncle Lewis.

He stood behind Mark Straker, behind Mummy. He held the planchette in his good hand, down by his side, half hidden. He looked solid and grave and dependable and Pauline was glad of his presence. Somehow a nod from Uncle Lewis stamped Mark Straker's statements as true, gave them an incorruptible veracity.

"Your sister – your mother's child – was deformed," Mark Straker said. "Physically and mentally deformed."

"I don't believe you," Pauline said. "I think you didn't want her – either of you – and that you just got rid of her."

Uncle Lewis shook his head. But Pauline did not relent even though she could see her mother doubled over and weeping sorely; see the top of her head and the skirts of her dress spilled about her like a puddle of silk.

"You still haven't answered my question," Pauline said. "Where have you put my sister?"

"None of your damned business," Mark Straker told her.

Aunt Bea helped Mummy to her feet. Pauline did not change position. She remained perched on the arm of the chintz-covered chair with Mark Straker directly before her and Uncle Lewis behind him.

Pauline said, "Did you know about this, Uncle Lewis?"

He nodded. "'Fraid so, Polly-wolly."

"Why didn't you tell me the truth?"

"Asked not to," Uncle Lewis said. "In fact, told not to."

"Told—"

"By your dear grandfather."

"So that's it," Pauline said. "He had the baby put away. Why didn't you just get rid of it properly, all of you? Chuck it off a cliff or drown it in the bath? Think of all the inconvenience, all the money you'd have saved yourselves."

"Polly, the child's in the best place," said Uncle Lewis, crimson-cheeked with embarrassment.

"Do you really believe that?" said Pauline.

Mark Straker gave the elder man no opportunity to reply. He leapt in with, "It's got nothing to do with your uncle, Pauline. Leave him out of it. It was my decision, our decision. If you're so all-fired keen on the truth, girl, it was precisely because we knew that you'd carry on about it that we decided not to tell you."

Mummy tried to put her hands about Pauline's waist but Pauline shook her off. "You say she's deformed – what does that mean? Two heads, three legs – what?"

"Do you know what a mongol is?"

"Yes," Pauline spat out, though she had no more than a handful of images in mind of the strange, big-headed children that she had seen shuffling about in the parks or on the streets back home in London; children who had clung to an adult's hand, who had gazed vacantly past her. And when she had asked Daddy or Mrs Dobbs about them she had been told that they were "poor souls" and had harboured along with her sympathy a certain resentment that they should be allowed out in public. Now she had a sister like that, a sister put away out of sight, out of mind. Shame burned in her like a beacon, not shame that she was kin to such a creature but shame that she had not bothered to enquire further from Daddy or from Mrs Dobbs, to challenge their embarrassment at the time.

"The infant needs special attention," Mark Straker was saying. "How can you possibly expect your mother to cope with – with that? There's nothing we can do for it, Pauline. It's an Act of God. We're fortunate we can afford—"

"He's paying for it, isn't he? Grandpapa, I mean?"

"What if he is?" Mark Straker said. "It won't be for long. They never last long."

"Where is she?"

"In a special place, a nice place. In Sussex."

"By the sea. Sussex by the sea," said Pauline. "An asylum in Sussex, by the sea."

"Stop it, Polly, please," said Aunt Bea from somewhere behind her.

Pauline said, "You don't even go to see her, do you? Grandpapa won't allow it. He'll pay the bills and you'll all just try to forget that she exists. Well, I shan't forget." She got to her feet. "I don't care what she looks like or how – how tainted you think she is, she's still my half-sister, and I intend to—"

"Don't interfere, Pauline." Mark Straker wagged a finger. "It's best left as it is. There's nothing you can do that hasn't already been done."

"I could love her," Pauline said.

Still holding back her tears, she moved with something approaching dignity to the door. She paused there, turned. "By the way, what's my sister's name?"

Barbara sobbed, face down in Bea's lap, and Uncle Lewis gave a sigh and tapped the edge of his plastered wrist upon the tabletop.

"Well?" Pauline demanded.

Avoiding the girl's eye, Mark Straker looked down at his shoes and shook his head.

Pauline said, "She hasn't got one. You didn't even give her a name. God, what a family!"

Head up, she walked out into the passageway and made it – just – to her bedroom before she broke down in tears.

"For Christ's sake, stop it, Babby. She had to find out sooner or later," Mark Straker said. "As for that other thing, that bloody Ouija board, that was me. I fixed it. I manipulated it, just for a bit of harmless fun."

"I must go to her," Barbara scrambled to her feet. "She'll need me."

Mark snagged the sleeve of her dress, ravelled it until he could grip her thin wrist.

"No," he said. "Leave her. She wanted the truth. Now she's got it she must learn to live with it."

"She's only a child, Straker, for God's sake," said Uncle Lewis.

"Leave her. Let her be. She doesn't need you, Barbara. She doesn't want you. It's time you admitted that Pauline wants nothing to do with you."

"She does, she does."

"Not after tonight, she doesn't," Mark said. "Tonight put the lid on any fond hopes you may have had about winning her round."

Stella had remained motionless and silent during her cousin's outburst. Leaning across the back of the empty armchair, hands folded under her breasts, she said, "Doesn't it really have a name?"

"No," Mark told her. "You don't give something like that a name. You don't try to pretend that it's just an ordinary human baby gone skew-whiff. It's a mongolian, an idiot. Quite hideous. I didn't want this to happen, you know. I wanted a real child. Oh, yes, I know you all think I didn't but I did. What I didn't want – and won't accept – is something dragged out of the Haldane family closet."

"What's that supposed to mean?"

"Bad blood," said Mark.

"Pardon?" Stella glanced towards her father but he did not communicate with her as he had done with Pauline.

Mark drew Barbara to him and held her shoulders as not so long ago he had held on to Pauline. "Kept that little secret dark, didn't you, Babby? You and your father between you."

"Secret?" said Stella. "What secret?"

"I don't know, I didn't know, darling, I didn't know anything about it," Barbara said.

"None of us did," Bea said. "Not until you told us, Mark."

"Told you what?" Stella persisted in exactly the same sort of tone as she might have used to wheedle a schoolgirl confidence from Daphne or Colleen. "What on earth are you talking about, Mark?"

"Margaret Haldane."

"Who?" said Stella. "Oh, you mean Grandpapa's first family. The daughter who died. What's she got to – you don't mean to say she was a mongolian?"

"It was in the blood all the time, wasn't it, Lewis?" Mark said. "And not one of you had the guts to warn me."

"Bea's right, old chap. We none of us knew anything about it. I certainly didn't – not until it was too late." Lewis shrugged. "Would it have made any difference?"

"A mongolian strain – Christ, of course it would."

"I thought you were bent on marrying Barbara at any price. Marrying into the Haldane clan is what I really mean," Lewis said.

"With one of those things hanging on the family tree? What the devil do you take me for, Lewis?"

Lewis did not give an answer. He inched closer to Bea and said softly, "It wouldn't have made any difference to me, dear. I want you to know that. I'd have married you no matter what. No ogres or skeletons would have put me off."

Bea dabbed her nose into a handkerchief, her gaze proudly fixed on her husband as, with a little grunt, he stepped past her and tossed the planchette on to the fire.

The varnish blistered and gave off an odour that reminded Lewis Jackson of sheep-pens and sailing ships. Hunkering down he took the iron poker and stirred the logs beneath the board and watched the flames nibble into and blacken its wooden heart. Stella was suddenly kneeling beside him.

"Daddy" – she hardly ever called him that – "was Aunt Margaret a mongolian too? It's important that you tell me, you know, because I might have children of my own one day."

"Yes, dear, she was."

"How do you know this?"

"Your grandfather made a point of telling me – but only recently, when he realised that his days might be growing short."

"Does mongolianism run in families?"

"I really couldn't answer that," Lewis said.

"What happened to Aunt Margaret?"

310

"She was put away, put out to be cared for when she was very, very young."

"I think I've been lucky," Stella said, sitting back on her heels.

"In what way?"

"Not to be born one of those," Stella said. "What happened to Aunt Margaret in the long run?"

"She died," Lewis said.

"Young?"

"I really couldn't say."

Using her father's shoulder for support Stella pushed herself to her feet. She brushed her hands down the front of her dress and touched her hair with her fingertips. She felt oddly stimulated by what she had learned, as if there were now reason and justification for her own heartlessness, something bred in the bone of her character. For a moment or two she had experienced pity for the poor mongolian child, sympathy for Pauline. But that phase had passed swiftly leaving in its wake a residue of pride that she, not Pauline, was the true inheritor of valuable Haldane traits.

"I suppose that's how Grandfather knew exactly what to do?" Stella said, thoughtfully. "Because he'd done it before. Everything's so much easier the second time." She looked down with faint disdain at her Aunt Barbara. "Just as well, Auntie, don't you think? Best thing, really, for all concerned."

Barbara did not answer. Mark was still holding his wife but there was no affection, no sympathy in it. He was, in fact, restraining her while he fed her little sips of brandy from a glass.

"Mark, oh Mark," Barbara said. "I must go to her."

"No."

"Please."

It was very humiliating to watch a grown woman beg and Stella told herself that she would never put herself into such a position, no matter what.

"Drink it up, Babby," Mark said, "and then I'll take you to bed."

Stella watched her aunt capitulate and, with a sob, lean her head weakly on Mark's shoulder. She envied her aunt the right to that intimacy, that promise, and was envious too of the experience that she had not yet acquired but to which she was drawn as to a mystery.

She caught Mark's eye and held his enquiring gaze fear-lessly for a moment. Then, because the fun was over, she bade everyone a brusque goodnight and left the drawing-room quickly just as her father, leaning forward, brought the poker down upon the heart-shaped board, broke it into fragments and let the flames consume it, piece by piece.

# Seventeen

*A*nger had kept Pauline awake into the wee small hours and had wakened her early. The wind that had beat and battered about the old Hall's gables, that had shaken the chintz curtains and sucked the coals in the iron grate into a fierce hot glow seemed to have become not a mere accompaniment to her mood but a creation of it, as if she had discovered the power to bend the weather to her will.

She was up before anyone else in the household, bathed, dressed and ready for the road long before daylight. She was not in the least tired by the sleepless night or drained by the emotional upheavals of the evening that had preceded it. She kept within her a sense of righteous outrage that did not diminish with the new day but grew even stronger, transformed itself into a competence that was almost frightening in its energy. It was as if the knowledge that she had a half-sister had charged her with responsibility and that all the things she did now were done not to satisfy her own ends but for the sake of the little nameless creature who shared her blood.

Nothing that she did that morning seemed tedious or mundane. She packed the wicker hamper with a care that would have astonished Mrs Dobbs, put on her school best uniform with an attention to neatness that would have brought jeers from her room-mates. She went the whole hog, down to the belted green raincoat and the round jade green winter hat, the polished shoes. She checked the drawers of the little dressing-table, the wardrobe and the space beneath the bed, stowed small items she might need for the journey into her brown leather satchel and with the satchel slung over her shoulder stalked out into Flask's echoing corridors.

Politeness, the silly scheme of 'manners' that had been

313

erected around her seemed just then like another manifestation of hypocrisy, part and parcel of the whole adult conspiracy that hid the world's cruelties and callous indifferences behind trifling dicta. Pauline did not care who was wakened by the clack of her shoe-heels on the wooden floor, who heard her call out for the butler or what, indeed, the servant thought of her when she ordered him to fetch her hamper down into the hall at once and then, as soon as possible, to serve her breakfast in the dining room.

When, still fastening on his starched collar, the butler had gone off to attend to her bidding, Pauline felt a certain deflation that it took her a moment to shake off. She stood by the tall clock in the cold, dark hallway and listened to the sounds from upstairs; the creak of a door, the flush of the first-floor lavatory, coughing, something that may have been a yawn, the intimate sounds of her uncle's household roused by her brusqueness.

From the kitchen quarters she caught the complaining growl of the butler's voice, the clatter of a pot, the yelp of one of the Labradors, made scapegoat for an irritation that she had caused. It did not make her feel guilty or in the least regretful but somehow restored her steeliness. Still dressed for the road but with her hat removed she was seated in the big clammy dining room some five minutes later when her uncle wandered in.

He was partly dressed for the day but wore a thick corded dressing robe over his waistcoat in lieu of his suit jacket and had not yet wrestled with shirt studs or collar or, it seemed, with shaving brush and razor. He looked, Pauline thought, like death warmed up.

"Polly! What on earth are you doing up?"

"I'm waiting for my breakfast."

"At this hour?"

"I thought we were starting early."

"Yes, but not quite this early." Uncle Lewis reached out and pulled a chair back from the table. He seated himself upon it, laid his plastered arm across his knee and leaned into it, brow almost touching the tablecloth. "I'm sorry, Polly, truly I am."

"Sorry for what? It's not your fault."

314

"I should have insisted."

"On what?"

"Well – on the child being given a name for a start."

Pauline, prim and upright, nodded. "Yes, I think that's the worst thing of all. I can accept the fact that Grandpapa and Mark Straker would be that awful but I thought Mummy would have been more responsible."

"You mustn't blame her too much, Poll. She's had a bad time these past few years."

"Has she?" Pauline said. "It seems to me, Uncle Lewis, that Mummy's 'bad time' is mostly of her own making."

"You still can't forgive her for leaving you, can you?"

"No, I can't. What's more, I realise now that I probably never will," Pauline said. "Do you know where my sister's been put?"

The man pushed himself from the table wearily and scratched at his wrist. The flesh seemed mottled now, as if it was gradually decaying, not healing.

He said, "I don't, Pauline." She said nothing, obliging him to add emphasis to his denial. "Honestly, I don't. I may have been slack about this, Pauline, but I hope you know me well enough to realise that I wouldn't lie to you."

Tacitly she conceded that point then asked, "Who would be able to tell me where my sister's being kept?"

"Why do you want to know?"

"Because, at the very least I'd like to be sure that she's given a name. I'd also like to visit her."

"It's a long way down to Sussex, you know." Uncle Lewis huddled the robe about him, shivering slightly.

"Can you find out the name of the place?"

"I can try."

"It occurs to me," said Pauline, "that even Mummy doesn't know. Wouldn't it be typical of Grandfather and Mark Straker not to tell her, just in case she caused trouble and upset their little applecarts?"

Uncle Lewis was leaning on the table again but some of his weariness had gone. He was looking at her with guarded interest. "You really do mean to do something about it, don't you, Polly?"

"Of course I do."

315

"But you're only a—"

"Only a child?"

"Well . . ."

"When do I stop being a child, Uncle Lewis? Tell me that? Do I have to wait until Grandpapa gives me permission?" Pauline said, and added, "I'm not going to do anything silly, you know."

"Silly?"

"Like running away from St Austin's."

"I say, I hadn't thought of that."

"Well, I'm not," Pauline said. "But I do intend to find out where my sister is and to make sure that she's blessed with a name, whatever else."

"Pauline – now don't fly off the handle – I think Straker may be right about one thing; the poor little thing may not survive very long."

"But what if she does?"

"I wonder," said Uncle Lewis, "just how – how . . ."

"'Bad' isn't quite the right word," Pauline said.

"No," her uncle said. "I'm not sure what the right word should be. Unwell? Damaged? Imperfect?" He shrugged.

Pauline said, "Unfinished?"

"Yes, that'll do." He gave himself a little shake. "You know, I'll have to find out something about this dreadful condition. It's ridiculous that I know nothing about it. Something Stella said last night really brought my ignorance home to me."

"That it runs in families?"

"Oh, you thought of that too?"

"Grandfather's daughter, then his daughter's daughter. It could have been me, you know."

"Uh-huh! That's what Stella said too. Her children."

"And mine."

A clatter at the door of the dining room diverted both the man and the girl from conversation. The butler nudged his way into the room, bearing a tray.

"Sideboard or table, sir?"

"Here, put it here," said Uncle Lewis.

"Will the others be down soon, sir?"

"Yes, bring the lot, John, but leave the covers on."

The butler unloaded the tray on to the table and went

316

off again to be replaced almost at once by a maid with more dishes. Uncle Lewis told her that he would serve and, as if to demonstrate capability, poured Pauline coffee hot from the silver pot and scooped scrambled eggs on to two plates. Pauline began to eat at once, watching her uncle's dexterous manoeuvres as he steadied his plate with the rim of the cast and worked his fork with his good hand.

"God!" said Uncle Lewis, apologetically. "I'm actually hungry. Didn't think I would be, but I am. Must be all this conspiracy stuff that's brought back my appetite."

Pauline said, "Do you think they'll try to stop us?"

Uncle Lewis wiped his moustache with his knuckle. "Old Donald will – if he has the strength."

"What about my stepfather?" said Pauline.

"You don't much like him, do you, Polly?"

"No. Do you?"

"Can't honestly say that I do."

Pauline opened another dish and helped herself to a grilled kidney, put one on her uncle's plate. Outside the day had grown lighter in spite of the rain that blew wildly about on the wind. She glanced towards the door and listened, heard nothing yet but the rattle of a bucket as one of the maids tackled the cleaning and setting of the drawing-room fire. There was a faint smell of toasting bread in the air and the aroma of roasting coffee.

She said, "Perhaps we shouldn't tell anyone what we intend to do, Uncle Lewis?"

He pursed his lips. "I'll have to tell Bea."

"But not Stella."

"Why not?"

Pauline could not answer him honestly. She longed to warn her uncle that Stella was untrustworthy, that Stella would run straight to Mark Straker with the information.

Instead of the truth, she said, "I'd rather nobody at St Austin's knew about it just yet. There's a chance that Stella might let it slip. Unintentionally, of course."

"Point taken, Polly-wolly." He put down his fork and leaned across the dining table, patted her hand. "What if she tells anyway?"

"I think she'll be too ashamed of having a defective cousin to want to blab about it."

"Never thought of that," said Uncle Lewis. "Aren't you afraid of ridicule?"

"I've done nothing wrong," Pauline said then, frowning, asked her uncle, "Have I?"

"Not a sausage, Pauline," Uncle Lewis said and, just as the door opened and Mark Straker entered the dining room, patted her hand again. "Leave it to me, though, will you?"

"Can I, honestly?"

"Honestly," said Uncle Lewis.

The bitterest disappointment that Pauline suffered came at the last; her mother did not come down to see them off. Some muttered, off-handed excuse was offered by Mark Straker for Barbara's absence from the breakfast table and from the farewell party in the hall some twenty minutes later. Last week, last night even, Pauline might have been inclined to blame herself for Mummy's selfishness. Mark Straker said only that Barbara was feeling poorly and, whether that was true or not, Pauline had no inclination to challenge the feeble excuse, to plead to be allowed to go upstairs to say goodbye.

Pauline's coolness contrasted with Stella's ebullience. Her cousin seemed almost tipsy with enthusiasm for the long journey and could hardly sit still long enough to eat breakfast so great was her eagerness to be on the road. Not for Stella the formality of school uniform. She had put on a new swagger coat with a brushed fur collar and a tight little scarlet hat that she wore tugged down on her brow. Her hamper, together with Pauline's, had been strapped on to the Silver Ghost's boot but Pauline noticed that Stella carried with her a soft kidskin weekend bag which she clutched close to her breast, as if fearful that someone might insist on inspecting the contents. The bag was a little too large to be the repository of the spring term's supply of filched gin and smuggled cigarettes and, Pauline suspected, contained items for more immediate use.

When she intercepted a glance between her cousin and her stepfather, Pauline realised that the pair had no intention of reaching St Austin's that same evening and that whatever the weather and regardless of her feelings on the matter she was destined to spend the night in an hotel somewhere along the way. She said nothing, though, kissed her aunt, hugged her uncle, walked quickly to the waiting car and put herself straight into the passenger seat without being told.

It was very, very cold in the motorcar. She took one of the plaid rugs that were laid on the seat and wrapped it around her. Through the window she could see her aunt in the doorway, Uncle Lewis and Mark Straker in conversation under the portico that sheltered the step. She glanced up at the vertical windows that looked gloomily down from the stairwell but saw no sign at all of her mother.

Her confidence waned again, fluttered like a candle-flame now that she was out of the protection of her uncle's house and had so far to go before she reached the sanctuary of St Austin's. She longed to be back, to be among real friends. She had already decided to heed the advice that Miss Fergusson had given her on her very first night at St Austin's and to make no secret of her half-sister's existence or of her desire to visit the baby as soon as she could. It would not be easy. She was under no illusions on that score. She would have Goss, the Frog and Elf on her side, but she had no notion of what the attitude of the other girls might be or just how much practical support she might expect from, say, Miss Milligan.

She trusted Uncle Lewis to do what he could. But it might not be enough. She wished that Daddy was not so far away and out of touch. But he was. And that was that. She would have to be independent, adult in her approach to the matter, and try, for her half-sister's sake, not to behave foolishly.

Rain whirred across the windshield of the motorcar and pattered on the roof. Pauline watched Stella rush to the vehicle and hurl herself into the front seat. Spots of rain from the open window freckled Pauline's cheeks. Mark Straker did not shake Uncle Lewis's hand. He swung away quickly from the elder man and strode towards the Silver Ghost, his expression set and grim. He wore a heavy rainproof motoring coat, all flaps and straps and pockets, which emitted an angry slashing sound as he pulled open the driver's door and thrust himself behind the steering wheel.

319

"What did Papa say to you?" Stella asked.

"Nothing." Mark Straker answered.

"Last minute instructions?"

"Something like that, yes."

The motorcar's powerful engine roared and roared, drowning out all possibility of conversation. The vehicle reversed, tyres shooting gravel in all directions, then ploughed forward, heading downhill between the trees and away from the Hall. Pauline was content to watch her uncle's house disappear through the oval port in the roof's curved back. But Stella leaned out of the passenger window and waved a little flowered lace handkerchief in a frantic parody of farewell.

"Goodbye, Mama," she cried in her shrill little-girl voice. "Goodbye, Papa." And then, as the motorcar pulled down into the tree-lined drive and out of sight of the house, she wriggled quickly round in the leather seat and said in quite a different voice altogether, "Hello, Mark."

"Hello, Stella," the man answered and returned, though not in kind, her flirtatious and adoring smile.

It came as no great surprise to Pauline when, not long after nightfall, her stepfather began to talk of tiredness and the dangers of fatigue.

The Rolls Royce had covered the many miles of roadway swiftly, arrowing, it seemed, from one garage to the next to take on petrol like a thirsty elephant. Big-headed pumps, like fantastical dolls, and spindly pumps slimy with oil that reminded Pauline of creatures out of an H.G. Wells novel, marked the Ghost's progress north from Derbyshire.

Pauline, of course, had no clear notion of the geography of the shires and Stella did not offer to relinquish the maps that she pored over or the guide books to which she now and then referred. Mark did not seem in the least unsure of the route, though it was not the same one, Pauline guessed, by which they had come down from Perthshire almost three weeks ago.

They lunched, late, in an inn in the middle of nowhere, with nothing but the prospect of a cobbled yard and a flock of miserable-looking sheep peering over a drystone wall to make it memorable.

"Where are we?" Pauline asked.

"Lawton Bridge," Stella answered.

"Is that in Scotland?"

"Of course not, silly."

"How far do we have to go?"

"A long way yet," Mark Straker told her.

The lunch cost half-a-crown and was substantial enough to lull Pauline to sleep again almost as soon as the journey recommenced. She drifted off, smelling cold smoke from cigarettes, seeing only the grey mist of moorland heights, the back of her cousin's collar, the metronomic flicker of the windscreen wiper beyond her stepfather's ear. When she wakened it was almost dark and the Ghost's headlamps cut a strange swathe through the oncoming night and Mark began his little song-and-dance about fatigue.

Memories of conversations she'd had with Goss Johnstone suggested to Pauline that they were nearing Edinburgh. She recognised names on signposts and identified the outlying villages that clung to the city's suburbs. A clock above the door of a public house told her that it was just after six o'clock. She knew then, for sure, that Mark had no intention of delivering them to St Austin's that evening and she was not in the slightest surprised when, a half hour later, he steered the motorcar off Edinburgh's main thoroughfare and into a large underground garage where he brought the Ghost to a halt.

Clutching her kidskin bag Stella was out of the passenger seat almost before the car had braked.

"We're only about seventy miles from home, you know," Pauline said.

Fiddling with some mechanism on the dashboard, her stepfather did not so much as look round. "I know."

"Why can't we go on?"

Stella thrust her head and shoulders back into the car and answered tartly, "Because Mark is very tired, that's why."

Pauline climbed stiffly out of the vehicle and stretched. The electrical lighting was dim and there were not many motorcars in the parking garage. She could hear the metallic shriek of railway trains close by and her nostrils were assailed by the acrid reek of coal-smoke.

Mark Straker said, "Do you have night-things handy?"

"In my hamper."

"In that case the porter will bring the luggage to your room."

The porter, a uniformed boy, was found within the confines of an elevator and hopped to do Mark's bidding as soon as he was tipped a shilling. Another porter, older and with a crippled leg, operated the mechanism of the elevator which carried them up into the heart of the hotel.

Elegant but somehow gloomy, the North British Station Hotel was not in the least like the Savoy. Pauline reminded herself that she had dined in the same room as London's most famous folk and had not made a fool of herself. She was dressed like a schoolgirl now but that did not seem to matter for the hotel foyer was not glittering and glamorous and it was, perhaps, Stella in the scarlet swagger who looked just a little out of place. Nonetheless, Pauline kept very close to her stepfather as he strode from the mouth of the elevator to the reception desk.

He turned on her, "Wait over there."

"Why?"

"Until I secure rooms."

"Oh! Aren't our rooms already reserved?"

Hands on hips, the driving coat unbuckled and thrown open, he stared down at her for ten or fifteen seconds, saying nothing, then he swung round and headed once more for the reception desk.

Pauline followed close on his heels.

The clerk resembled a character from a Walter Scott novel; polished forehead, high, stiff collar, a braided black vest and jacket. Pauline would not have been surprised to discover that he wore knee breeches. He spoke in clipped sentences, without a smile, and she noticed how his pale, experienced eyes sized up Mark Straker and how they slid speculatively to Stella. He had her, Pauline's, ticket straight away but he could not card index Stella quite so easily. Pauline could feel the unpleasant breath of moral disapproval emanate from the clerk, like the smell of peppermints in church. The anger in her had not gone away after all. She was not intimidated by the pompous little clerk and it was not she but Mark who was, for a moment, disconcerted by the unspoken question that hung over the desk.

She did not feel at all detached, though the confidence with which she spoke out took her briefly by surprise. From somewhere in the past, from some drama or naughty comedy, she gathered images that clarified the situation perfectly.

"I do hope they've reserved a nice room with a bath for Stella and me, Papa?" She even managed to pronounce Papa in the French way, and to tilt her chin haughtily. "You know how much we hate sharing a bathroom with others."

She was directly against the counter now, close by Mark Straker's elbow. He glanced down at her, one eyebrow raised very slightly and, to her annoyance, the faintest hint of a smile upon the corner of his mouth.

Pauline said, "You did remember to book in advance, didn't you, Papa?"

"Of course," Mark Straker said.

The clerk was abruptly efficient and as close as he would ever come to deferential. He flipped open a blue-bound register and ran his finger swiftly down the columns.

"Mr Straker?"

"Yes."

"One twin with bath. And a single, likewise?"

"Yes."

"Dining with us tonight, sir?"

"Yes."

"Eight o'clock, Mr Straker."

"Eight o'clock will be fine."

The clerk raised a hand in the air and snapped his fingers, a gesture which seemed to Pauline to add a touch of theatrical unreality to the whole awkward little charade.

The bellboy in brown uniform and pillbox hat, the keys, hand-luggage, the desk clerk bowing now, Mark striding away towards the lifts with Stella beside him, hobbling just a little on the loft-heeled shoes that she had 'borrowed' for the occasion from her aunt: Pauline, resentment undiminished, followed sedately on behind.

"You really are a cow sometimes, Pauline," Stella said as she emerged from the bathroom in a haze of steam.

A towel was wrapped about her hair to keep it dry, a dressing-gown fastened tightly over her pyjamas. It was her second bathe of the evening and she looked, for Stella, uncommonly pink, like, Pauline thought, a half-boiled shrimp.

"You spoil everything, don't you?" Stella went on. "I mean, a perfectly charming evening – ruined."

"You only wanted a chance to flirt with him," Pauline said. "That's the only reason we're stuck here in Edinburgh at all, to give you an opportunity to sharpen your claws on my stepfather."

"Oh, don't be ridiculous."

"I'm not the one who's being ridiculous," Pauline said.

"'Course you are. Refusing to put on something nice for dinner. Sitting there in the dining room in school uniform."

"Better than sitting there looking like a Piccadilly tart." Pauline put the G.K. Chesterton novel that she had been half-heartedly reading down on the quilt and propped herself a little higher against the pillows. "Are those new pyjamas?"

"What if they are?"

"You won't get away with wearing those at school."

"I've no intention of wearing them at school."

"Why did you bring them then?"

"Some of us," said Stella, "have some sense of style."

Pauline said, "You should have worn those at dinner. Perhaps then you'd have got more attention."

"I got attention," Stella said. "At least I showed some gratitude for what was being given me. Instead of sulking and muttering like a spoiled child."

The bedroom was large and exceedingly comfortable in a plain sort of way. The walls were panelled and the furnishings, including the beds, were heavy and old-fashioned. One enormous window looked out from the fifth floor across the gardens, the roof of the railway station and down the length of Princes Street. There was nothing to be seen of the classical view, however, except a moist blur of lights and vague brown shapes, for a dank January fog had swirled up from the Forth to cloak the city.

"I really do not understand why you are so down on poor Mark." Stella drew the dressing-gown even tighter to hide sight of the revealing pyjamas from her cousin for as long

324

as possible. "He's doing his best to be nice to us. I mean, he didn't have to make this long journey. I'm sure he could have found better things to do."

"Perhaps he likes small girls."

Stella had been standing at the dressing-table, her back to Pauline and the beds. The cousins could see each other in partial reflection in the oblong mirror that backed the table. But Pauline's last sentence caused Stella to whirl round.

"I am not a small girl, Pauline."

"All that breathless hanging on his every word, all that batting of the eyelashes." Pauline sat forward and hugged her knees under the covers. "You amuse him, Stella, that's all. He's laughing at you most of the time."

"He damned-well is not."

Pauline sat back. "In any case you've had it now. I assume not even you would dare to arrive in that red swagger coat and those lofted heels. The Dragon would have a fit and might even bawl you out in front of Mark. Think how humiliating that would be."

Stella opened her mouth to protest. But there was too much sense in what Pauline said and, pinker than ever, she turned back to the dressing-table and plumped herself down on the long horsehair bench before it and toyed with the silver cosmetic box that she had unpacked from her kidskin bag. The hampers were on a floor rack by the door, virtually untouched, yet the hotel bedroom had the look of long occupancy, a litter of Stella's possessions strewn carelessly about it.

In a curious way, Pauline was enjoying herself. She had been afraid of Stella until now or, more accurately, afraid that she would detect in her stepfather some unpleasant response to Stella's flirtatiousness. Pauline did not believe that Mark Straker could possibly take her cousin seriously, could be other than tolerantly amused by the sort of antics that might do very well to impress Daphne Gore, Ronnie and a legion of silly juniors but that must seem incredibly juvenile to a grown man.

The anger in her had settled down now to a kind of superiority, a missionary zeal that elevated her above her cousin. She had not yet acquired the concentration needed to hold to her purpose with deadly seriousness at all times, and found herself slipping into and out of one vain mood after another, without consistency.

She was relieved, though, that the trip would soon be over, that she – and Stella – would soon be safe back at school; a night's sleep, a breakfast, a couple of hours in the back seat of the Rolls Royce and then – good old St Austin's. The worst was over. No harm could come to her – or to Stella – now.

She said, "Don't tell me you're going to paint your face again?"

"Why not?"

"Before bed? That's awful!"

"What's awful about it?"

"It's . . . mucky."

It was Stella's turn to be supercilious. She swung round on the bench, a fat sable brush charged with powder poised in her hand, and stared at Pauline without speaking.

"What?" Pauline said, after a while.

"I'm just wondering when you're going to grow up," Stella said.

"I'm as grown up as—"

Stella put the brush down carefully in an amber pot and leaned one elbow on her knee. Pauline had a disconcerting recollection; her mother in precisely the same pose, eight or nine years ago. Half a short lifetime.

Stella said, "Don't you realise, Pauline, that in two years, two-and-a-half, say, we'll be put on the marriage market, you and I?"

"Speak for yourself."

"No, it's true. Daphne is already half-promised to the son of a landowner whom she's only met about twice. He's twenty-three or four and he's ready for her now. Just waiting."

"I don't see what—"

"She'll go from a desk in St Austin's into bed with a grown man."

"No, surely, she'll—"

"In thirty months, Pauline."

"Well, I shan't."

"Thirty months," Stella repeated and, as if she had scored a winning point, turned again to the powder brush and began to apply the substance to her cheeks. "It can happen to any of us. Even you."

"I have other things to do with myself."

"It's not what you'll do but what might be done to you," Stella said. "Sometimes you just can't help these things."

"Well," said Pauline, disconcerted in spite of herself, "I doubt if I shall marry at all."

"Of course you will. We all will," Stella said. "It's what we're put here for. If you don't, you'll wind up like the Gaiety Girl and I wouldn't wish that even on you."

She traced a lipstick about her lips, lightly defining them. Her mouth was not full, not sensual. It had, Pauline noticed for the first time, a lack of firmness that the cosmetic did little to disguise.

Stella went on, "I know why you're sulking. It's because your Mama didn't tell you about the baby."

"That's none of your business, Stella."

"I suppose not. Except that idiots seem to run in the Haldane family and I certainly wouldn't want to be burdened with one. I'd do the same as your Mama did. Put it away safely out of sight and – well, just get on with my life."

"Do you know where she is?"

"Who? The baby?" Stella lifted away the lipstick and shook her head. "No. Haven't a clue."

"You could find out from Mark Straker."

"Why don't you ask him yourself – nicely."

"He won't tell me."

"Perhaps because he thinks you'll cause havoc with his, and Grandfather's, best-laid plans."

"She's my flesh and blood, Stella. I want to see her at least once."

"More fool you," Stella said. "It won't do anyone, least of all the infant, any good at all. Take my advice, Polly, don't interfere." Stella put away the lipstick and powder pot, snapped the catch on the box and then unwrapped the towel from about her head. "Tell you this, dearest, Mark won't stand for it." She tossed the towel on to the carpet and switched out the electrical light that illuminated the dressing-table. "He'll fight you."

327

Pauline said, "I'm not afraid of him. There's nothing he can do to me."

"Is there not?"

Stella untied the dressing-gown, let it fall to the floor. The pyjamas revealed what figure she possessed, clung shimmering to her limbs like a second skin. Pauline averted her eyes as Stella climbed into the bed next to hers and settled herself cautiously down under the clothes.

Stella said, "Hasn't it occurred to you that if you rile Grandfather he might haul you out of St Austin's?"

"I don't think he'd do that."

"I wouldn't be too sure," Stella said. "I mean, we all know he isn't quite right in the head. If I were you," she inclined her head just a little, "I'd keep my nose clean, Polly, and be a very, very good little girl."

"But you're not me."

"Thank God!" said Stella. "Now are you going to read that book or not?"

"I'm not," said Pauline, and promptly switched out the light.

Pauline did not deliberately keep herself from sleep. It simply did not occur to her that Stella had not yet played all the cards in her hand and that there had been a point to the last, late-night applications of paint and powder. She lay awake for what seemed like ages, however, troubled by the things that Stella had said, not least the suggestion that Grandpapa Haldane might withdraw his financial assistance and she would find herself thrown on to the charity of other members of the family.

In the unfamiliar hotel bedroom, propped above misty Princes Street with only the sounds of shunters and goods waggons and the occasional bellow of an express train to give dimension, Pauline lay and fretted about the paradox that Stella had unwittingly defined. She longed to remain true to her purpose, to assume, if she could, responsibility for the poor castaway infant and to develop in consequence a sense of independence. But to do so she needed the support of other people, of men. At the back of that realisation was the underlying fear that she would be sucked into an early marriage, drawn into it not out of love but out of necessity.

She tried not to think of what that might mean or to relate it to those things that Stella seemed to know that she did not. Almost for the first time, however, as she lay in the warm sheets with the tip of her thumb against her lips, she experimented in matching herself with men that she knew; Lewis and Oliver, Mr Roddy Harvey and, because she could not keep him out of her thoughts, no matter how hard she tried, Mark Straker.

Drifting and unanchored, Pauline found herself thinking of Colleen O'Neal and the scandal that had titillated the school in the autumn term. At the time she'd had no real understanding of what the fuss was all about, why the gossip had such spice to it. Now, though, she had a glimmering of the relationship between need and consequence and felt a suffusion of pity for Colleen and a certain vague envy of the experiences that the Irish girl had had that she had yet to face.

Why was it, she wondered, that she felt so different from other girls, so inhibited and wrought with little fears and anxieties? And why had the din of life's passing become like that of trains in the night, an echo of empty platforms, solitary journeys, passengers glimpsed only as shadows in the dark?

At some point, she must have dropped off, for she did not hear the intruder just at first, heard nothing in fact until a narrow shaft of light from the door to the corridor printed itself for a second upon the wall.

Pauline stirred and sat up. "Stella?"

There was no answer from the bed next to hers.

"Stella, somebody's in the room." Still no answer: Pauline called out, "Mark, is that you?"

The shaft of light had gone now. The room was in darkness once more and Pauline, in a little panic, slid from her bed and knelt by Stella's, groping for her cousin's shoulder to shake her into consciousness; then, trembling, she found the switch of the bedside lamp, depressed it and flooded the room with electrical light.

"Stella?" she hissed, blinking.

Stella's bed was empty. Stella had gone.

Pauline rose and ran to the bathroom. She flung open the door and switched on the light there. She was praying, praying that her cousin would be there, but was not in the slightest surprised to discover that she was not. She knew perfectly well where Stella had gone, and the reason for it, acknowledged at last the evidence of scheming and betrayal that had been growing around her during the past few days and which she had been too naive to recognise.

For two or three minutes she did nothing positive. Leaving on the bathroom light, she leaned against the washhand basin and regarded herself in the square mirror that was panelled above it. Her nightgown was crumpled and the cotton material, caught about her hips, accentuated her breasts, showed, like two halfpennies, the contours of her nipples. Her hair was tousled and she had a drugged and dopey look, as if she had been awakened not from light, early sleep but from a long, deep slumber.

She felt absolutely alone and isolated; yet the feeling was not so numbing as she might have expected it to be. She had a faint receding reluctance to accept that the image she saw before her was herself, was Pauline Verity, her mother's daughter, Daddy's little sweetheart. The reflection that the mirror gave back was of something else, someone new and original, not even Pauline's Pauline but a person she could not immediately identify.

Stella's dressing gown was gone from the floor. Gone too were Stella's cigarette case and ivory holder.

Pauline seated herself before the dressing-table and brushed her hair carefully. She could not decide what to do, what was to be gained from any one particular course of action. She was half hoping that Stella would crash back into the room again, smarting with rejection, full of venom and excuses. But that was not why she, Pauline, delayed. She was afraid of what she might find not only in her stepfather's bedroom but in herself.

At length she fished out the green school overcoat and put it on over her nightgown. She hesitated about shoes but decided to go barefoot, to pretend that she had just wakened from sleep and had stumbled unwittingly into her stepfather's room, into knowledge of the affair. But as she

330

crossed the empty corridor, even as she put out her hand to grasp the knob of the door of Mark Straker's room the need for pretence left her. She had done nothing wrong. She had no obligation to share his guilt or Stella's, to be tormented by shame on their behalf.

She closed her fingers on the handle, twisted it and to her astonishment found that it yielded, that the door was unlocked.

She pushed it open and stepped quickly over the threshold before she could change her mind.

Pauline had never seen a man in that state before for her father had always been modest about the house while she was growing up.

Mark Straker was clad only in a knee-length robe of damasked material that, by accident or design, exposed chest, thighs and legs, all downed with crisp dark hair. He was not upon the room's single bed but lolled some four or five feet from it on a heavy wooden chair that was tilted on its hind legs and braced against the wall. His feet, which in the flood of light from the bedside lamp seemed monstrously large and pale, were propped casually on the rim of the dressing-table, and crossed at the ankles. He was smoking a thin, dark-brown cheroot and had in his lap a solid glass ashtray into which, even as Pauline entered, he dabbed the silver grey tip of the cigar.

He glanced at Pauline, then at Stella on the bed. He shook his head and said in a tone that was more resigned than angry, "God, Stella, I told you to lock the damned door."

Pauline leaned her weight against the door, heard the click of the lock behind her. She did not move, though, and came no further into the room. She saw Mark only out of the corner of her eye as he lowered the chair's front legs to the floor and, holding the glass ashtray in his left hand, uncrossed his legs, leaned forward and tucked the folds of the robe down between his thighs. He put the cheroot into his mouth and tugged on it, looking at neither of the girls but straight down at the pattern of the carpet between his outspread feet.

"Jesus!" he said, softly.

Stella had moved, though not swiftly enough. She had been

upon the bed, sprawled back against the bolster and white pillows, slender legs stretched out, shimmery silk pyjamas clinging to her body, cigarette holder spewing smoke cocked in the fingers of her left hand. With her right hand she fumbled with the tiny buttons that held the top of her pyjamas together, trying in vain to fasten them again and cover her breasts from Pauline's sight.

She rolled from the bed and shot to her feet, twisting away from Pauline and almost knocking over the lamp on the bedside table in her frantic haste.

She shouted, "Damn it, Pauline, don't you know enough to knock? What's wrong with you? Have you no manners?" She placed the cigarette holder on the table, worked furiously – all thumbs – on the buttons. "What do you want here, what do you want? You shouldn't be here, damn it. I thought you were asleep."

Pauline said nothing. She had to resist the temptation to stare at the little glimpses of her cousin's breasts, to gape at Mark Straker's long, naked legs. An instinct told her that she had interrupted the couple in the process of love-making, in the course of some sort of play that would lead to touching, to . . . she did not quite know what. She shook her head slightly as if to shrug off Stella's chattering, the shrill almost-hysterical gush of accusation that came from her cousin's lips and that seemed to float in the air like the coils of tobacco smoke.

Mark Straker took the cigar from his mouth and dropped it into the ashtray. He placed the ashtray on the carpet between his feet. Stooped over he turned from the waist and looked up at Pauline. "What are you going to do?"

If her stepfather had not asked that particular question at that particular moment Pauline would have done nothing. She would have been reduced to tears of embarrassment, would have begged forgiveness for her rudeness, would have fled in shame. But something in Mark Straker's manner, a deference that was more adult than she deserved, steadied her and brought home not only the enormity of what she had discovered but also the power that went with it.

Frowning, Mark Straker said, "Are you going to tell anyone about this, Pauline?"

Pauline answered, "I haven't decided yet," and, turning on her bare heel, promptly left the room.

She folded the school coat and put it neatly over the back of a chair then climbed back into bed. She tucked the bedclothes around her waist and adjusted the pillow behind her and, arms folded, waited for Stella to burst in upon her. It did not take long.

Only seconds after Pauline had settled herself, the bedroom door was flung open and kicked shut and Stella, without Mark, confronted her.

"Nothing happened," Stella began. "I swear to God, Polly, nothing happened. I only went to talk to him because – because I couldn't sleep. I went there to – to smoke a cigarette, that's all. If you think – I mean – if you imagine that anything happened." She tried to laugh, and failed, "I mean anything like that then – he didn't touch me, didn't even kiss me. I swear, Pauline. Nothing happened."

"You were in his room, Stella," Pauline said, evenly. "In the middle of the night. In your night-clothes."

"I didn't feel well. I . . ."

"I'm tired, Stella. I want to go to sleep. We'll discuss the matter again in the morning. All right?"

"If you tell anyone, Polly, anyone, it could have serious consequences. For Mark as well as for me." Stella did not lean across the bed. She seemed reluctant to come too close to her cousin as if she, Pauline, had suddenly become contagious. She stood by the bed-end, fists pressed against her breastbone, tears running down her powdered cheeks. "I'm not – I'm not old enough, you see."

"I know that," Pauline said, though she hadn't really considered the issue before.

"And – and we didn't do anything."

"Because I stopped you."

"NO."

"Well, it doesn't matter," Pauline said.

"What?"

"I'm going to sleep."

"What doesn't matter?"

"Whether you did or didn't. You were there and I suppose that's enough to count against you."

Pauline tweaked the ears of the pillow and pushed it down. She eased herself beneath the sheet and drew blanket and quilt up over her head until only her face peeped out. She turned her back on Stella, closed her eyes, and sighed.

"Pauline . . ."

"Shut up."

Moments later she heard the stealthy sound of Stella creeping into bed, a faint snivelling, the blowing of a nose, and then the light went out.

Pauline, strangely warm, sighed once more and tried to think of nothing until sleep came, to put what she had seen clean out of her mind until morning.

# Eighteen

Stella and all her belongings were gone before Pauline rose next morning. She had no concern about that for she was certain that she had not been abandoned in Edinburgh. Cosmetic box, cigarettes, the kidskin bag had all been whisked away, yet Stella's presence remained tangible in bedroom and bathroom; a dusting of powder on the dressing-table, a trace of lipstick on the pillowslip, a single long blonde hair curled in the porcelain of the sink. The assurance that she had felt yesterday morning at Flask had not diminished and Pauline kept herself busy just in case she was undermined by panic at what her stepfather might do to her in the remaining hours of their journey together.

She left for the dining room at a quarter past eight, clad in her school uniform, her nightwear packed away into the hamper in her room, coat over her arm and hat in hand. Stella's hamper, she'd noticed, had already been taken away and, presumably, strapped on to the boot of the Rolls Royce in the garage underground. She locked the room but kept the key in her hand and, in the foyer, sought out a porter and instructed him what to do with the wicker hamper and to return the key directly to the clerk at the reception desk. She was not at all sure if this was the proper procedure but she acted as if it was and even found a shilling with which to tip the boy.

That done, she went directly into the dining room and straight to the corner table where Stella and Mark Straker were already eating breakfast.

Stella too was clad in St Austin's uniform, the red swagger coat and Parisian hat put away. She looked, Pauline thought, even younger than her years, and rather unwell.

The dining room was much more crowded than it had been last night. There were a surprising number of pupils from other schools breakfasting there, prominent in their colours; more boys than girls. Pauline looked around in the hope that she might find a friend or acquaintance from St Austin's to buffer her against an inevitable confrontation with her relations, but among the students and parents found, to her disappointment, no familiar face.

She nodded a wordless greeting to her cousin and stepfather, pulled out a chair and seated herself. She plucked a menu from the silver clip that nestled between a flower vase and the cruet and scanned it as if it meant something. On Mark's plate were a pair of plump kippers, hardly touched. He was smoking a cigarette. Stella, eyes cast down, was listlessly paddling a fork in a dish of scrambled eggs, not eating.

Pauline gave her order to the waiter and looked out of one of the great plate-glass windows, which showed nothing more interesting than a spectral building lurking in the mist on the other side of the street.

"Fog," she said.

"Yes," Mark Straker said.

"Slow going."

"Until we clear the city, certainly," said Mark Straker. He asked her what she had done with her luggage. She told him. He nodded. Stella said not a word.

Pauline ate porridge. Mark Straker lit another cigarette. He sipped coffee. Stella drank tea. Pauline ate two poached eggs, a slice of toast and marmalade. Mark watched her every mouthful, as if he was concerned about her appetite, or the cost of it, perhaps.

Pauline finished a second cup of tea and put the cup down. Mark said, "Wait for us in the car, Stella."

"Oh, are we leaving?" Pauline reached down by her chair for her overcoat and hat.

"Not you," Mark Straker said. "Stella. Go."

Pauline had seldom seen her cousin behave with such meekness. It did not become her in the least. She watched Stella trail away through the tables and vanish out of the room's open door. She looked across at the man, not boldly but without apparent fear.

She was thinking of yesterday morning, how long ago it

seemed now. Mark Straker was not like Uncle Lewis Jackson, though, and the North British, in spite of the mist outside, was not so bleak and gloomy as Flask Hall. She could feel the eggs, which she had eaten a shade too quickly, lie in a little lump in the base of her throat. She poured a dash of tea, very brown, into her cup and drank it to wash the lump away.

Mark wore a heavy chequered shirt and a regimental tie. His jacket was of fine tweed but well-worn and rather shabby. He put his hand into the lining pocket and brought out a sheet of hotel stationery, folded neatly in half. He offered it to Pauline, extended between finger and thumb. His hand, Pauline noticed, was trembling very, very slightly.

"What is it?" she asked.

"It's what you say you want."

Puzzled, Pauline took the paper, opened it, read a name and a long address printed there in blue ink. Still puzzled, she frowned at the man across the table.

"Who's Sarah Haldane Straker?" she said.

"Your sister."

"I thought she didn't have a name?"

"Of course she has a name. I had to register the birth, didn't I?" Mark said.

"Why didn't you tell us that you'd given her a name?"

"It wasn't anyone's concern."

"Does my mother know that you've given her a name?" Mark shook his head.

"Why didn't you tell her?"

"She isn't interested."

"I don't believe that," Pauline said.

"I didn't want it to become a person. Giving it a name . . ." He shrugged again. "It would only have made things more difficult."

Pauline looked down at the paper once more.

She said, "Why did you call her Sarah?"

He hesitated. He had a matchbox in his hand now and he turned it over and over between his fingers.

"Why Sarah?" Pauline insisted.

"It's my mother's name."

"Oh!" Pauline, taken aback, paused before asking, "Does your mother know about the child?"

"Yes."

"And what you called her?"

"It was my mother's idea."

"Aren't your parents ashamed of it too?"

"They aren't Haldanes," Mark Straker said.

"Neither am I," said Pauline.

She folded the sheet of stationery carefully and put it into the breast pocket of her blazer.

She said, "Why are you being so obliging all of a sudden?"

"You know why."

"You're bribing me to keep my mouth shut about what I saw last night."

"You didn't see anything last night." Mark Straker leaned across the table and lowered his voice to a harsh whisper. "Do you honestly think I'd have done anything to her, anything harmful?"

"She was on your bed. In her pyjamas. And you – you didn't have any clothes on except your robe." Try as she might Pauline could not help but flush as she spoke the words. "And she – Stella had her buttons . . ."

"She came to me, damn it!"

"You could have sent her away."

"I tried, but you know what she's like."

"You were – looking at her."

"God!" He sat back suddenly, then just as suddenly shot forward again. "Listen, I know you hate me . . ."

"I don't, not hate . . ."

". . . and I know the reason for it. I'm sorry you blame me for marrying your mother but, for Christ's sake, Pauline, surely you don't want to ruin me? I should have thrown Stella out by the scruff of her neck, yes, but I damned well didn't. I don't know why."

"Because you like her."

"This isn't a schoolgirl crush, Pauline. Don't you realise I could go to prison? And even if it didn't come to that, consider what it would do to your mother if she ever found out."

"I've thought of that," Pauline lied.

"What do you want from me?"

"I want to see my sister."

"Is that all? That's easily arranged. I'll take you there myself."

"When?"

"At Easter."

"All right."

"I warn you, Pauline, you won't like it. She isn't what you suppose her to be. She isn't all smiles and dimples."

"Perhaps she'll change."

"Oh, she'll change," Mark said. "She'll get worse. If, that is, she doesn't die in the interim."

The instant that the words were out Pauline saw that he regretted them. She knew, deep within her, that he had lied to her or, at best, had distorted the truth. She also realised that he had credited her with more maturity than she possessed, had equated her too closely, perhaps, with her knowing cousin. The baby, even if she did have a name, made no claim on Mark's feelings. Everything that he had told her was intended only to soften her up by appealing not to her understanding but to sugary sentimentalism.

Pauline could not put words to it. She could not explain even to herself what it was that came over her or why she found the confidence that she had experienced yesterday suddenly, almost miraculously, strengthened. It was as if she could hear in her head the mewling of her half-sister, lost in a cot or crib a thousand miles away, the puny merbabe voice crying out to her, not this time in a dream or in the inexplicable scribble of a pencil on paper but as a part of her own consciousness.

Pauline heard herself say, "She'd better not."

"What do you mean?"

"I mean that my sister had better not die, not before Easter at any rate," Pauline said. "'Cause if she does, I'll tell."

"Tell who?"

"Mummy, Uncle Lewis – anyone who'll listen."

"Are you serious?" Mark Straker said.

"Absolutely."

She watched his fist ball about the matchbox, heard the crackle of wood and pasteboard as he crushed it. He dropped the wreckage to the tablecloth and eyed Pauline with cold hostility. She felt a little surge of triumph, scary in its implications, but, because she knew she'd been right, did not back down.

"Are you mad too?" Mark Straker demanded. "How the hell can I keep her alive?"

"You'd better try," Pauline said.

"And if I don't?" he said. "If I can't?"

"I'll tell somebody in the family, or perhaps at school, what I saw last night."

"Stella will deny it."

"No," Pauline said. "Stella will just blame you."

She had never seen anyone, man or woman, with such anger bottled up in them. If they had not been in a public place he would have struck her for sure. It was all she could do not to buckle, not to apologise, to keep her eyes upon him and suffer the cold, egotistical hatred that she saw there. At length, after a half minute, he got himself under control.

He grunted and said, "You're right. She will."

Pauline had had enough. "I want to go now. Straight to St Austin's, if you don't mind."

She stooped and lifted her school hat and overcoat from the spar of the chair and was on the point of getting to her feet when he stopped her, gripping her arm.

"Why are you doing this to me, Pauline?"

"Perhaps . . ." She hesitated. "Perhaps because I'm more of a Haldane than I thought."

She stepped back from him, slipped into her coat, put on her jade green hat and followed him out to the hotel foyer to wait while he paid the bill.

By the time the Silver Ghost reached the borders of Perthshire the last traces of fog had been left behind, the sky was brilliant blue and the high hills, folding and fading off into the distance, were dusted with snow. In the glens cattle herds and farms stood out sharp as etchings and the great plantations of pine and fir that spilled down the mountainsides were black and glossy as pitch-blende.

Pauline sat up perkily in the back seat of the motorcar. She could see nothing of Stella save the crown of her hat and little of Mark except a quarter profile now and then when he swung the vehicle into a bend. Neither the man nor the girl addressed a word to her during the drive north, a silence that suited Pauline to a tee, left her free to enjoy the scenery and revel in the anticipation of being back again, home again in good old St Austin's.

Farm waggons, most of them horse-drawn, and huge loads of timber began to appear upon the road, checking motor traffic and rendering Mark impatient. He seemed, Pauline thought, to be spluttering like a fuse with the need to be shot of her, and possibly of Stella too. He parped the big rubber horn frequently, drove round lumbering obstacles at a speed that was more dangerous than daring, roared arrogantly past other motorcars and slung the long bonnet of the Ghost wildly through the twists and turns of the rural byway that led westward into the Pattullo hills.

Then there was the little town, Burnham's Brae, the Toffee Shop, the gates. Still Mark did not brake the Ghost or check its speed. He shot around the school bus on the long bend that enclosed Big Field and got a sharp toot on the horn from young Tom MacAdam for his temerity, cheers and waves from the Haley's occupants as he flew past. Pauline glimpsed faces in the windows, hats, scarves, gloved hands pressed against the panes, the Kaiser staring haughtily down her snoot. And then the bus was left behind and there were the tennis courts, the little pavilion, house and school, and the Dragon waiting on the steps.

Pauline had her hand upon the door handle. She felt an impulse to fling it open and throw herself out even before the motorcar finally braked and slowed. Mark did not halt before the steps, however. He drove on along the gravel, stopped and reversed, bucked the motorcar forward so that when he finally brought it to a halt the bonnet was facing toward the gates, his escape route clear and easy.

Pauline threw open the door. The past two or three days had been draining, as a bad dream is draining, but she showed no sign of weariness as she scrambled from the car and waved to Miss Fergusson and, beyond her, to Miss Milligan who was already engaged in consoling a tearful junior who, most likely, was bereft at parting from a pet dog or cat and not seriously homesick at all.

"Pau-leeen!"

"Elfie! How are you? Good to see you! Is Goss back yet? Be with you in five minutes, when I've unloaded the goodies. All right?"

"Leave your hamper in the hall. We'll round up the gang for haulage directly after lunch," Elf shouted.

"What's on the menu?"

Elf, at the top of the steps, sniffed theatrically. "Boiled Otto, I reckon. The poor doggie must have died,"

"That's quite enough, Elfreda," said Miss Fergusson. "Go inside at once, please."

The Dragon had on her fixed and somewhat rigid smile, the one that she used to greet parents, not pupils. She wore a brand new black woollen cloak and floppy black cap that made her look, Pauline thought, like an old Dutch navigator. She had restyled her hair, though, loosened it so that the grey did not show so much. Her cheeks were weather-roughened and her eyes crinkled at the corners as if she had been out-of-doors for much of the holiday, skiing perhaps, or motoring madly about the countryside with the windscreen down. She did not descend from her lofty perch on the seventh step but waited, fluffing herself up a little like a quail or a partridge, to meet the man who owned the powerful new Rolls, a machine unique enough to distract her from the imminent arrival of young Tom MacAdam and the school bus.

Mark Straker, however, had not the slightest intention of tarrying at St Austin's, of indulging in small talk with teachers. He had the luggage unstrapped and dumped upon the gravel in seconds and, almost before Stella dragged herself from the passenger seat, was back behind the steering wheel.

The Haley loomed, horn honking. It squealed to a halt some yards short of the Rolls, the vehicles bonnet to bonnet like two metallic beasts spoiling for a fight, young Tom and Mr Straker glowering at each other through the windshields. Pauline, unaided, dragged her own hamper then Stella's from gravel to verge just as the bus disgorged its passengers and then driveway and steps were suddenly swarming with green uniforms, Stella, seemingly dazed, lost among them.

The Ghost rolled backward and Pauline saw Mark beckon to her from the motorcar's open window. She stepped closer, inclined her head. She could hardly hear what he said above the babble of new arrivals.

"Be careful," he told her.

His chin and upper lip were bristled with stubble and in the worn old driving coat he looked, she thought, more like a prisoner of war than a wealthy London stockbroker. She had a memory flash of naked chest and thighs all matted with hair, coarse over lean muscles.

She blinked and waited for him to say more, for a threat, a promise, an apology, perhaps, but Mark Straker had had enough. He withdrew his arm, snapped down the brim of his cap, and, even as he reached for the gear lever, gave her one last cold-eyed stare.

Pauline stepped hastily back. The engine roared. The Ghost rolled backward another five or six yards then leapt forward, tyres spraying gravel, as Mark Straker fisted the steering wheel and bounced the motorcar away across the grass, wide of the bus and the gaggle of girls around it, a plume of blue exhaust smoke trailing in its wake.

It was only then that Pauline caught sight of Stella. Her cousin was running, running like the wind. Her hat was off, caught around her throat by its strap, blonde hair almost white in the winter sunlight, unbuttoned overcoat flapping clumsily about her as she sprinted after the car.

"Mark, Mark, Maaa-ark."

If he heard her, if he noticed Stella's desperate pursuit, he paid not the slightest heed. He fisted the steering wheel savagely, swerved the Ghost back on to the driveway and accelerated away through the trees, leaving Stella, outstripped, behind.

Pauline was not alone in watching the strange, almost pathetic chase. All the girls were silent, staring at Stella Jackson, sharing not her passionate disregard for modesty and decorum but, in advance, her embarrassment. Only when the Ghost was out of sight and Stella, shoulders slumped and chest heaving, had begun her lonely trek across the lawns did the buzz begin. The new term, it seemed, had got off to a fine, firecracker start.

Pauline whirled round at the touch of a hand on her shoulder.

Frowning, Janis Fergusson said, "Who is that man?"

"My stepfather, Miss Fergusson. I believe you met him at the Christmas concert. Don't you remember?"

"I can't say that I do," the Dragon answered, "but I'll certainly remember him next time. What's wrong with your cousin? Why is she so distraught?"

"I really couldn't say, Miss Fergusson," Pauline said and, before she could be drawn into yet another lie, excused herself and ran indoors to find Elf.

The hall was the same. Otto, unbutchered, lay snoozing on the rug in pride of place before the fire. Boxes and baggage were strewn about and the hot, heavy aroma of cooking already filled the air. Pauline inhaled it like a breath of spring, let it filter down into her, purifying the taint of all the lies and deceptions that had marked and marred her Christmas with the family.

She was no longer a new girl, no longer a suspicious stranger. She had begun to take on an individual identity, one that could not be disguised by a gym slip and a green blazer, that refused to be lost in the crowd. Had she carried it with her always, she wondered, or had she found it in the world outside St Austin's, coupled to her new-found sense of responsibility for the sister she had never seen, the poor, dumb, ugly infant who, for better or worse, would never really know what made her what she was?

She felt a welling of confidence, an assurance in herself that did not depend on blue eyes and bright blonde hair, on knowingness and the easy art of pleasing unworthy men.

Stella, not she, was the stranger here.

"Pauline?"

She found herself looking up into Miss Milligan's soft grey eyes and, on the spur of the moment, threw herself into the housemistress's arms and, for a brief moment only, hugged Irené to her and felt safe, safer than she had ever been now that a new term had begun.

**HILARY NORMAN**

FASCINATION

Maddy Gabriel, a passionate and headstrong woman. Zurich, Davos, Paris, New York. Eternal love. Dark secrets. Vicious treachery. And a work of art priceless enough to kill for.

'An engrossing novel about the effect that a priceless treasure can have on three generations of one family'
*Glasgow Evening Times*

'A grand yarn, touchingly told'

*She*

'Elegantly written tale'

*Daily Telegraph*

**HODDER AND STOUGHTON PAPERBACKS**

## MORE NOVELS AVAILABLE FROM
## HODDER AND STOUGHTON PAPERBACKS

**HILARY NORMAN**

| | | | |
|---|---|---|---|
| ☐ | 49351 8 | Chateau Ella | £4.99 |
| ☐ | 41117 1 | In Love and Friendship | £4.99 |
| ☐ | 56635 3 | Shattered Stars | £4.99 |
| ☐ | 58088 7 | Fascination | £4.99 |

**AUDREY HOWARD**

| | | | |
|---|---|---|---|
| ☐ | 57397 X | A Day Will Come | £4.99 |
| ☐ | 54294 2 | The Mallow Years | £4.99 |
| ☐ | 56236 6 | Shining Threads | £4.99 |
| ☐ | 58627 3 | All The Dear Faces | £4.99 |

*All these books are available at your local bookshop or newsagent or can be ordered direct from the publisher. Just tick the titles you want and fill in the form below.*

Prices and availability subject to change without notice.

HODDER AND STOUGHTON PAPERBACKS, P O Box 11, Falmouth, Cornwall.

Please send cheque or postal order for the value of the book, and add the following for postage and packing:

UK including BFPO – £1.00 for one book, plus 50p for the second book, and 30p for each additional book ordered up to a £3.00 maximum.

OVERSEAS INCLUDING EIRE – £2.00 for the first book, plus £1.00 for the second book, and 50p for each additional book ordered. OR Please debit this amount from my Access/Visa Card (delete as appropriate).

Card Number ☐☐☐☐☐☐☐☐☐☐☐☐☐☐☐☐☐☐

AMOUNT £ .................................................................................

EXPIRY DATE .............................................................................

SIGNED .......................................................................................

NAME ..........................................................................................

ADDRESS ...................................................................................

..................................................................................................